SOME WHERE

Matthew Reed Williams

BROTHER
MOCKINGBIRD

Library of Congress Number: 2024946913

Cover Design by: Alexios Saskalidis
www.facebook.com/187designz

No part of this book may be reproduced or transmitted in any form or by any means without written permission from the publisher.

For information please contact:
Brother Mockingbird, LLC
www.brothermockingbird.org
ISBN: 978-1-960226-17-4 Paperback
ISBN: 978-1-960226-21-1 EBook

To Elena
para siempre

CHAPTER ONE

Easing my car to a stop in front of the white, iron gate, I stared up at the old antebellum structure, its face unwavering, a dumb, relentless attention, no less sinister for its vacuity. The house was obscured from below by a wall of maple trees but situated on a prominent hill in such a way as to peer out over the center of the town below. It was imposing, but I felt a shiver of excitement. This would be my home for the foreseeable future. Well, part of the home would be.

A woman named Mrs. Mindy Copeland agreed to rent out the attic as an apartment, which I readily agreed to despite never stepping inside. When I was visiting the town a few months back, I saw a community board advertisement in The Book and Bean, a Main Street coffee shop, but I was already on my way out of town, so I jotted down the phone number and called her later. She couldn't send me any pictures of the apartment–landline only–but I recognized the house in the ad. It was one of dozens of late Victorian and Federal-style houses dotted around the small town, resting upon the many hills that surrounded Main Street: watching, silent guardians.

Mrs. Copeland's probably out, I thought, as I parked my old manual transmission Ford Aspire in the empty wrap-around driveway, the car a discontinued hatchback and relic of the early '90s. Turning off the car, I sat reflectively for a couple of minutes, halfway registering the town sprawled out in front of me: descending the Missouri hills like those coastal Italian towns I'd seen in travel magazines, colorful buildings stacked on top of each other to form a rich, geometrical tapestry. Except these houses were not nearly so colorful nor built quite so closely together as those Mediterranean paradises. Still, there was a feeling of expanse, like the sea, as the edifices slowly petered out and gave way to a mixture of wild grass, farmland, and forests, the glimmer of beauty that Missouri offers in an otherwise sweltering, humid August heat.

The last several months had been a whirlwind. I graduated from college, a proud moment, I guess, but it was just a small, Midwest university in the Ozarks of southern Missouri, a bit of a culture shock from St. Louis (even if St. Louis wasn't exactly Chicago or New York). I got my degree in art history, a program that was *not* one of the few areas of middling notoriety offered by the university.

For one semester, I studied abroad in London where I smoked my first cigarette. I don't know why that's important, but I guess it kind of was. I had always grown up being taught to *Just Say No*, so that was my weak-ass version of rebellion. When I came back and began smoking a pipe, I was at the height of pretension and douch-ery. It's funny because while I was abroad, I was secretly miserable, but the moment I stepped back on campus, I was the guy who had traveled and come back, misunderstood and underappreciated, too good for those Midwestern rednecks.

But that didn't fully capture how I felt, something I was unable to put into words. I was restless and didn't have an outlet for my agitation. Plus, I had an art history degree and didn't know what to do with it. Earlier that spring I had finished, wrapping up a capstone research project on the spirituality of British painter Stanley Spencer. It was alright, I think. I managed to feel proud of my work when it was done, and my capstone supervisor said it might be publishable. But what did she know? MFA from who-cares-university, some super obscure place like Northwestern Southern Indiana State College Extension School at Insert-Town-Name-I've-Never-Heard-Of. With two published articles in magazines read only by the authors and editors that publish the articles. So here I was in Somewhere, Missouri.

No, seriously: Somewhere, Missouri.

Missouri has all kinds of crazy-ass town names: Peculiar, Halfway, Devil's Elbow, Goodnight. And then there's the towns named after other places: Cuba, Mexico, Lebanon, El Dorado Springs. But that last one's pronounced el doh-RAY-doh. As if our state wasn't already hillbilly enough.

I heard a tapping on my window.

"Ope! Sorry to startle you," an older woman said after I'd twitched away from the window.

"Hi, Mrs. Copeland," I said, offering my hand as I stepped out of the car. "Nice to see you in person."

"Here's the kitchen," Mrs. Copeland gestured with a sweep of her hand. I had climbed up the back stoop and into the kitchen from the rear of the house. Despite the gravitas of the house from outside, the kitchen itself was outdated and a little cramped. The floors were black and white tile, the counters a forest green Formica, the stove an old Jenn-Air range, and the refrigerator had a dingy, mustard yellow tint. On the wall over the door was a cat clock with eyes and tail that swayed like a pendulum. It seemed to laugh at me, like that crazy cat from *Alice in Wonderland*: "We're all mad in here." Still, the kitchen was cozy enough. A small table with four chairs sat in a corner, and I imagined many quiet mornings ahead, sitting at that table hunched over a bowl of cereal and a mug of coffee while reading.

"Help yourself to whatever you need to cook. I ask that you keep your own stuff on the top shelf of the fridge and on the right side in the freezer. You can use any condiments you might need, but please don't eat my food." She grinned as a forced gesture of kindness, but I got the hint–don't mess with her shit.

I never did see a car which meant that Mrs. Copeland must walk a good deal, down that steep driveway to wherever she was going and then all the way back up. I felt winded just thinking about it. Many older Missourians, including my parents, had ample waistlines after a lifetime of Midwestern eating habits: from Kansas City barbecue on the western side of the state to Italian food on The Hill in St. Louis and all sorts of local favorites in between, not to mention tailgating, ballpark hot dogs, funnel cakes and deep fried Oreos from the state fair. Mrs. Copeland, however, seemed to avoid the extreme consequences of that Missouri diet. Or maybe just compensated for it by staying active?

"Finally," Mrs. Copeland said, eyes boring into me and face taking a very severe expression for a moment, "though I am leasing that studio to you and giving you access to the kitchen, please remember that the rest of the house is mine. I'll be happy to see you from time to time here in the kitchen or around the yard, but I like my privacy. Do *not* go into any other part of the house. Understood?"

Don't mess with her shit. For a second time. Got it.

"Yes, ma'am." I felt like I was being reprimanded by my own mother. It reminded me of the rules I received when we would visit my grandparents; everything was fragile there, and my parents wanted to avoid the embarrassment caused by one of my cousins who broke an antique ceramic angel and received the brief wrath of my grandma.

Mrs. Copeland relaxed her serious tone and pulled up the curtain of her mouth again, like smiling was a grueling sport. She even chuckled. It didn't suit her.

"The Lord knows I can be rather particular about my things, but I do appreciate your understanding. Now, since it's your first day here, could I treat you to dinner? The Black Bird Diner has a world-famous casserole."

"Oh...um..." I hesitated. "Uh, sure, yeah, I'd like that."

"What, already have plans in a place you've been staying for less than thirty minutes?"

"Well, sort of. I saw a poster for a fair in town tonight. I thought I'd check it out." I'd already seen the fair set up just past Main Street, and I thought it'd be a great way to spend my first night in Somewhere.

"You're very right, and you *should* go. It's too much for me these days, though. I'm an old woman and need my quiet."

"Can we take a raincheck?" I asked.

"Certainly. Glad to have you here. Have fun this evening."

"Thanks."

I exited and walked down that back stoop. Despite the early August heat, a watery thickness that stuck to my skin even now that the sun had gone down, I was happy and felt light. For now, I wasn't a directionless college grad; I wasn't known. I was just me, Lee Thompson. I felt free, and more adult in a way, like I was carving out a place that was my own. I couldn't be claimed on my parents' taxes; I had found a job and an apartment by stumbling somehow into this backcountry paradise, a place I would have never believed existed in Missouri. But there I was, like I was meant to be there.

I *was* meant to be there.

CHAPTER TWO

Wanting to get to the fair before it got too late, I decided to leave my things in my car and unpack later. From Mrs. Copeland's, I could have taken a straight line south to Main Street and entered in the center of downtown, about halfway into the street's descent which began among a cluster of houses above. Instead, I opted for the longer route: winding my way through the venerable grandeur of historic, Federal-style houses or the eccentric, old Victorians with all their mismatched parts and angles–belvederes and turrets and elaborate trimming–still disbelieving this step through time. This was my place–for now–and in the noise of the fair's anticipation and the people filling the shops and sidewalks around me, I had one of those not-so-uncommon premature ramblings of the mind, envisioning myself settled there in Somewhere until *I* was an old-timer with my own peculiar house.

In fact, the vision was strong. I had just passed Buddy's Boutique, a dog groomer, and I glanced at a bench where I saw myself.

Another version of me–but older–was perched there like it was the most common thing in the world. I should have felt shock at this, but I didn't.

In this vision of me, I had aged considerably but not poorly. I appeared to be in my fifties or something, younger than what Mrs. Copeland must have been now but not so much younger. That version of me wore the physiognomy of someone happy, someone content, like I had been living a good life. A gorgeous lady walked out of Buddy's Boutique with a Scottish terrier in tow, fitted with a new, gingham-print bowtie. Older Lee stood up and walked over to the lady and surreptitiously

Matthew Reed Wiliams

pinched her ass.

I, the present me, gawked. I would never do something like that. But I saw the look of playful acceptance on the lady's face. Her eyes darted around, and then she whispered into Older Lee's ear and... had she copped a feel of Older Lee's junk? Embarrassingly, I was turned on watching this older version of myself getting touched in all the right places. What had she whispered? Whatever it was, Older Lee quickly escorted her away and out of sight as if he was in a hurry for something... pleasurable?

I thought of that woman: tall and youthful despite appearing roughly the same age as older me, with light brown hair laced with flecks of silver, an august beauty.

Okay, not bad, I grinned to myself.

I found myself accepting this conjuring of my mind as something more than daydream, more than fantasy, something solid like fact.

I glanced up, finally disengaging myself from the vision. I was standing still on the sidewalk, facing the shop just past Buddy's Boutique. The glass was opaque in this spot. I saw my reflection as a blur, the glow of the street lamps providing just enough light to see my image in the glass. Over my shoulder, though, a woman stood. The woman from a moment ago? I turned to greet her, but only spun in circles. There was no one standing within fifty yards of me.

I continued ambling down Main Street.

Everything about the vista rolled out before me was perfect, a sublime moment of pure contentedness. Shadows grew longer, the sun was just a splash of fiery honey on the milky sea horizon. Though it had been in the mid-nineties during the day, it felt cooler now with the strong breeze, a rarity in Missouri's summer dog days.

The fair greeted me below sprawled out across a wide open space just beyond a covered bridge and before a train depot way out in the distance: tents mushroomed up, zig-zagging lights striping their sides—first one way, next another—as carnival lights whirled and jigged ludicrously out of step with the calliope music of "Ragtime Cowboy Joe" or "Dixie." Bubblegum-popping colors of booths dotted here and there. *Tck-tck-tck-tck-tck* and slow, heavy chains pulling carts of giggling children to the pinnacle of the roller coaster's peak before an explosion of screams, cheers, and, of course, the silence of the death-white knuckle grip who lost all voice in the rushing descent.

Despite the fair's tractor beam-like pull, though, I detoured to grab some coffee at The Book and Bean: part coffee house, part bookstore. Being somewhat of an addict, I had already visited before and felt proud to return, marking my territory or something like that.

"Well, well, look who's here," the lady behind the counter said. I smiled, glad to be recognized, and surveyed the small cafe, everything as I remembered it: eclectic art hung over exposed brick, fireplace with couches arranged whopper-jawed by the latest group of customers, other mismatched seating pinning mismatched rugs to the scratched, wooden floors. Tables, no two alike, sometimes covered in tablecloths—purples, oranges, yellows, reds, emerald greens—sometimes not. A bohemian fixture, a hippy paradise. For me, it was a sanctuary where the coffee gods had kept me going since tenth grade when I was first introduced to the bitter elixir.

"Hi," I responded, walking up to the woman. "I didn't expect anyone to remember me."

"Yes, well, Mindy is in my Sunday School class and told me that a gentleman from out of town was gonna rent a room from her. I didn't know it was you, but when you walked in here, I realized that of course it must be you. Didn't you tell me the last time you were here that you'd love to live in a place like Somewhere?"

"Yes, ma'am." I blushed with gratitude at this warm reception.

"And you're gonna be workin' with Tom at the art gallery?"

"I am. How'd you know?"

"You're in smalltown Missouri. Here news travels faster than a jackrabbit under gunfire."

"I guess so," I laughed. "Though I didn't really expect it to be news. Probably not the most exciting."

"Maybe not for you. But we get excited about new people. We're tight-knit folk. We don't get very many outsiders settlin' down here, but when we do, it means *a lot* to us."

I chuckled.

"Well, happy to be a source of news, I guess. But maybe I'll try to stay under the radar going forward."

"We'll see, we'll see," she said, almost to herself as she brought her attention back to the pallet of mugs she was toweling.

"Anyway," I added, "I'm sure there are plenty of people who would want to live here. It's so... so... cute?"

She laughed.

"Feel weird callin' a place cute?"

"A little bit, yeah."

"Well, you know, to go back to what you said, we really don't get as many as you'd think. It's like they pass right through us." She stuffed a towel into the mug's bowels. "People are in such a damn hurry, and so many young people are movin' to Kansas City or St. Louis or just leaving Missouri and the Midwest altogether. No one has a sense of place anymore." She was sermonizing now. "My family has been on this land for generations. We understand what it means to belong to the land. We can't escape it.

"That's why I like you," she continued. "You're a young person, but you see us. You see there's somethin' special here. I'm just, well, I've seen a lot over the years; my family's seen a lot, and this town has persevered through every trial. I'm proud of this place. And I thank you for wantin' to share a piece of it with us."

I hadn't really known what to say as she seemed to be speaking more to herself than to me, but now I smiled.

"I'm happy to be here."

"Stupid me," she said, setting down the towel and giving me her full attention. "I'm just blubberin' away. Are ya wantin' to order something?"

"No worries," I assured her. "I'm glad to have a friend. Just a coffee, please."

"You got it. And Mindy told me your name, but I've forgotten."

"Lee. And yours?"

"Barb," she said, pointing to the name tag I hadn't noticed before. "Barb Hamilton. Like the Founding Father but no relation as far as I know."

She filled up a paper cup with coffee and handed it to me along with a wax paper bag, the shadow of a cookie peering at me, chocolate already staining the inside. My stomach gurgled.

"On the house," Barb insisted when I got ready to pay. "This is my friendship offerin' to entice you to come visit me."

"Oh, I will," I promised.

Fair lights overwhelmed my vision. Smells of funnel cake mixed with hot dogs, popcorn, and a general fog of cholesterol. Sounds, sounds, sounds pummeled the air.

"Step right up, step right up!"

"Enter here if you dare!"

"Three tries to get the prize!"

Large, bearded, bellowing men, dressed in top hats and coats with tails. One guarded the entrance to a house of mirrors. The other two stood before a large area of carnival games: ring toss, plate breaking, basketball, darts and balloons, the high striker with hammer and bell, and at least a dozen others.

Matthew Reed Wiliams

I smiled to myself, remembering all the allowance money I had lost playing carnival games at the state fair growing up. Continuing along the midway (and stopping for a funnel cake, something to wash down my cookie with!) I soaked up the moment, imbibing it through my skin. The Somewhere Fair was somehow both nostalgic and new.

The "carnies" didn't look like a bunch of vagrant drunks but were all dressed brilliantly with exotic colors and costumes, flitting about like fairies, a wondrous intersection of human and otherworld. Most interestingly, the extravagant workers wore on their faces a real expression of earnestness, a performance more than a job, while families traversed the grounds from one amusement to the next, laughing, eating, conversing, playing.

Rather than a typical state fair that drew in crowds of well-to-do strangers from towns miles away, the Somewhere Fair was more of an elaborate, local ritual, a celebration among close and intimate friends, a dance of satyrs among fairy rings in some secret and forgotten grove. I had the same feeling when I first visited over a year before, like I had stumbled onto something, and they hadn't had enough time to scatter before I saw them, so they allowed me to stay (or, in my case, return). There was a magic here, a gut-sensation of elation and wonder, a moment of mystical ecstasy, if you will, as if I'd gotten a chance to peek behind the curtain.

After roaming around for an hour or two—and adding cotton candy to my meal of cookie and funnel cake—I decided to leave. I still needed to unpack.

I sauntered towards the exit, a.k.a. the covered bridge, and noticed a group of people about my age hovering around the high striker nearby, amused by one poor guy's inability to strike the puck up above "Nice Girl," not exactly the most "PC" game in history.

I glanced over at them, smiled in that weird Midwestern greeting, and continued on. But then I spun back.

There were four of them, two girls and two guys. One of the guys with his hand on the back of his buddy who was emptying his pockets for more chances at a less humiliating result on the high striker.

One of the girls stopped laughing and looked over at me, like she sensed my presence. She was beautiful: tight jeans, a loose-fitting t-shirt, chestnut brown hair. Her head turned slowly, and our eyes locked. She was younger than before, but there was no mistaking the woman from my vision.

"Lee?"

I spun around. A man approached me with a look of bewilderment.

"Lee, is that you?" he said again.

"Um, yes."

"Oh my God! I can't believe it!" he shouted. He began laughing and crying simultaneously.

Uncomfortable and embarrassed, I wanted to move, aware of everyone staring at me. The stranger's arms were open as if to embrace me, but when he was about five feet away, my expression changed. I recognized him. But from where?

"Okay, bud," I heard from my left. Two men had swooped in, taken the man by the shoulders, one on each side, and began escorting him away.

"Wait," the man cried. "Wait, wait, wait. Wait!" He struggled weakly. "I know him! I know him!" But they were quickly lost in the crowd.

"Hey, don't mind him," another man near me said. I turned to him, still bewildered.

"That's, uh, Carl, the town, uh, you know... well, the town crazy person. His mom takes care of him, but he must've wandered away to visit the fair."

"How did he know my name?" asked.

"Oh, well, it's a small town, Lee."

CHAPTER THREE

I woke up the next morning feeling refreshed. Shortly after my awkward encounter with "Carl," I departed, trudging the couple miles back to Mrs. Copeland's residence.

I climbed up the stairs with a load of stuff from my car, leading up to my attic-turned-bonus room studio on the back side of the old Victorian. An attic sounds a bit cold and inhospitable, but the space was finished and cozy. I had never lived in a house with a finished attic, but I dated a girl in college who made me watch HGTV home renovation shows, and I'd seen it done several times. The walls were slanted inward, contouring to the shape of the roof, and the room itself was long, running *almost* the entire length of the house. There was a door on the far end which opened to an unfinished storage area where some flat boards were laid down on top of ceiling beams, a precarious passageway to boxes and other assorted items piled here and there.

Aside from that, my room was furnished sparsely but comfortably. A small sitting area, a loveseat and an oversized chair around a circular area rug and a coffee table. Beyond that, a dresser on one side and my bed on the other, small area rugs both along the edge of my bed and in front of the dresser, anticipating a little extra needed warmth for my toes in the cold months, I suppose. Past the bed, a section of wall jutted out where the bathroom was built in, a small but usable space consisting of a tiled floor, a pedestal sink and mirror, toilet, and shower.

The only windows were at the entryway, but they were large enough to let in a decent amount of light. There was no overhead lighting; a floor lamp and table lamps would have to suffice. As for decoration, well, that was a curious thing.

Apart from two small vases of silk flowers on the coffee table and on the dresser, there was one framed image on the wall behind the sitting area, on the right wall as you walk in. It was the print of a painting titled at the bottom, *"The Census at Bethlehem," Pieter Bruegel the Elder, 1566.* In spite of the title, the scenery of the facsimile was obviously European, a small 16th century village blanketed in snow with people in the middle of various activities including several who were trudging over a frozen river, laden down with large sacks. The eye was drawn, though, to a crowd gathered around what I presumed to be an inn standing next to a bare tree that ran almost the entire height of the painting. A Christmas wreath hung over the inn's window where a man was engaging with the crowd while writing in his registry. Just on the outside of the crowd was Mary draped in blue, sitting on a donkey, Joseph nowhere in sight. There was nothing particularly meaningful to me about the painting, but even in August, the scene appeared chilly and somber, a vastness and solitude, Mary just on the edge of things.

There was also a small TV and DVD player on a table where the dresser was set up against the wall. It seemed to be almost an afterthought. I saw a few DVD cases of old sitcoms: two seasons of *Everybody Loves Raymond* and a season of *Friends*. Nothing was plugged in. But hey, it was there. It didn't matter, though. I didn't move to Somewhere to spend all my time watching movies or TV. Mrs. Copeland had warned me that she didn't have any WIFI, and, as part of my grand experiment to sort of get away from everything, I had actually chosen to get rid of my cell phone. It was part of my Thoreauvian version of "living deliberately." Mrs. Copeland had assured me I could use the house phone in the kitchen below.

All in all, I was very satisfied with my room and foresaw many a cozy morning or evening there reading or lounging in the sitting area. After getting the tour from my landlady, I had headed straight for the fair, so I was left to unpack the Aspire when I returned: a suitcase, backpack, bag of shoes, some camping gear, a milk crate filled with books, and a typewriter. Despite my Spartan insistence on no cell phone, I brought an old iPod Mini with me stored with about 250 songs, including a jogging playlist for the rare occasion that I might be able to motivate myself to do so.

My books were a smattering of random literature, a testament to my trying to live out this whole angsty young adult thing: *The Stranger* by Camus, Rumi, *Catcher in the Rye*, a collection of Emerson's essays, *On the Road*, poetry by Allen Ginsberg, and a Bible. The crate also had a handful of unused journals. The typewriter was old, something I found at a thrift store, but it still worked, and though I didn't consider myself a writer, I brought it along with me since I wouldn't have an actual computer to write with.

So that was my room and that was my stuff. I rolled out of bed the next morning, content. So content, in fact, that I did something I had told myself I certainly wouldn't do.

I decided to go to church.

It was Sunday after all, and church is sort of what you do if you live in the Midwest. *What the hell?* I thought to myself. *When in Rome, right?* pretending like I hadn't grown up in church. Truth be told, church was hardly foreign territory for me even if it had missed my presence the last couple of years. Besides, church was probably the best place to get to know the people of Somewhere. I even had my own Bible with me—for academic purposes only, I told myself—so I was prepared, more or less. I actually had no intention of bringing it with me to the Sunday service. Instead, I grabbed the collection of Ginsberg's poetry, clearly trying too hard *not* to be the church guy.

I did dress up, however. Nothing too fancy but nice enough to avoid any stares. It's funny; in college, if you want to blend in, you dress down. In church, if you want to blend in, dress up. Church attire expectations are a bit different in the city—more cool, more casual—but in college I quickly learned that in rural Missouri, we do things differently. "Sunday's best" was not an archaic phrase, and if you wanted to change the system, you drew the ire of the preacher and most of the parishioners. And don't try to prove anything from the Bible about how Jesus or John the Baptist may or may not have dressed, oh no, just know your body's a temple and when your earthly temple goes to worship at God's temple, you better damn well make sure it's maintained and adorned properly. Of course, a "well-maintained" bodily temple in Midwest Christendom applies to cleanliness and wardrobe, not to anything like a reasonable diet or exercise regimen. There are too many church potlucks for that.

Dressing up wasn't easy for me, though, since I had intentionally packed somewhat minimally, a commitment not to stuff but to experience. "Simplicity, simplicity, simplicity!" Thoreau had said. I would need to do laundry a little more regularly. Which reminded me, I needed to ask Mrs. Copeland if she had a washing machine.

I finished buttoning my shirt. I thought about tucking it into my brown chinos and grabbing a tie, but A, I didn't have a tie, and B, that was too much. A shirt with a collar on me was a win for any stodgy preacher in this town.

I grabbed my book and headed down the stairs outside and to the kitchen, but as soon as I stepped inside, I realized that I had not yet stocked up on groceries and had nothing to eat. No matter; I headed straight to Main Street, this time taking the more direct route downtown. En route I passed by the Baptist church and saw the service times:

Sunday School, 9:00 am
Morning Worship, 10:30 am.

I still had almost an hour to spare before the service, so I walked over to The Book and Bean where I grabbed coffee and a muffin, though Barb wasn't there this morning. I passed the time sitting by the window and perusing a copy of the *Kansas City Star*, Ginsberg remaining an accessory rather than actual reading material.

I learned that the Royals were wrapping up another disappointing season, but as a devout Cardinals fan, I didn't really care. The Chiefs were playing today, the second game of the season. Besides the random decent season from the Royals—like the 2015 World Series champion team—the Chiefs were the team everyone cared about anyway. I had enough friends in college from the Kansas City area to halfway follow their sports, but I think the Ozarkians–technically closer to KC than St. Louis–felt that they were far enough away from Kansas City to pledge their baseball allegiance to the more historically successful Cardinals team. Also, the Springfield Cardinals, the AA minor league affiliate of the major league team, was not far from me, another reason to follow "the Birds on the Bat."

Guilt was a flimsy afghan lying on my shoulders that morning as I walked into church. I grew up in church: Dad was an elder, and Mom was a children's Sunday School teacher. Even through my freshman year of college, I continued attending church faithfully.

I was less faithful by my sophomore year. By junior year, I was only going with Mom and Dad when I was home visiting. I wasn't a burnt out, cynical, ex-Christian. No, it was less sexy than that. I was just bored. So, after a while, I just stopped going.

First Baptist Church of Somewhere had a funny ring to it (as did a lot of places in a town called Somewhere), but the red brick building had an aesthetic quality that a lot of the Baptist churches I'd seen or attended had lacked, theirs a theological (and perhaps fiscal) decision to present an unadorned, straightforward Gospel. But the First Baptist of Somewhere building actually looked like they were trying a bit harder when they designed it.

Walking inside felt familiar: a lobby area that served stale coffee, people milling about drinking from Styrofoam cups. Everyone was dressed up nicer than I was, but not so much that I stood out: the sweet spot.

Taking advantage of a solitary pew *near* the back, I managed to avoid the "back row Baptist" moniker. After settling in, I glanced around at the sanctuary: baptismal font elevated over the stage with a cross hanging on the wall behind it, the American flag on one side of the stage, the Christian flag on the other, and a small sign plastered to a wall with the numbers from the previous week's attendance and offering. Very typical Baptist sanctuary, though the wood-paneled and vaulted ceiling along with the stained-glass windows were a nice touch.

We began by singing Hymn #107, "I was sinking deep in sin," turned to Hymn #83, "Be Thou my Vision," and ended with the classic "Amazing Grace." I didn't even have to look at the hymnal, recalling the words from memory.

The service was moving along at its normal slow pace, but there was a nostalgia in that steadiness; I grew comfortable, happy even. Stepping into the healing waters, I let it take me. Music hushed, the effect an after-image exposure that continued to pluck harmoniously at the chords of my soothing spirit. And the preacher rose to the pulpit.

The name Amos Whitaker had a biblical ring to it, prophetic. His appearance seemed to both capture and defy my expectations of someone with the name Amos Whitaker, a man whose presence immediately commanded attention—he struck me as someone accustomed to getting what he wanted—but whose charisma and behavior was disarming, winning.

"Good morning," he bellowed deeply and richly with a great big smile on his face.

"Good morning," the congregation responded.

Pastor Amos, as he was simply called among the parishioners, was large. He had to be about 6'4, but it was a solid, stocky 6'4. Early fifties maybe. Full head of hair. Not fat by any means; he wore his weight well, like he knew exactly how he meant to carry himself, and his thick legs and arms and slightly protruding gut added to the persona of immensity. He wore deep brown pleated slacks, a cream-colored button-down shirt with the sleeves rolled up, and suspenders. He had no tie, but instead left the top two buttons undone. He looked like he had just finished doing some work on the farm in his Sunday best and then ambled over for church. Virile, he gave no impression of a man slowing down with age. Pastor Amos was not nimble on his feet but rather moved about the stage with great, slow strides, a mighty oak with roots wading through the earth.

"It's good to be in the house of the Lord." He surveyed the room. As his eyes scanned past me, he did a double-take and looked at me again. I felt very seen. His smile grew larger, warm and inviting, as he continued surveilling the sanctuary, connecting in that manner with his flock.

Pastor Amos stood behind a pulpit, but he moved from behind it and started pacing, a deliberate act of bringing himself before the audience, the pulpit a symbol of elevating God's word and the office of pastor, a Mt. Sinai of sorts whereby the holy man convenes with God before delivering his message from the heights. Leaving the barrier of the pulpit for a moment, he makes himself available to the poor, wandering Israelites. That's what I thought about, anyway. About how Moses would have to wear a veil in front of his face after meeting with God because the glory of God on his visage was too strong for the mortals around him.

"Turn with me to 1 Kings 17," he said, and we did. I grabbed a Bible from the back of the pew, but the majority of the parishioners grabbed their own. My hand strayed to the copy of Ginsberg that I pushed even deeper below my left thigh, now regretting my decision to bring it.

We read of the widow that the prophet Elijah met after the Lord commanded him, "Get thee to Zarephath." Pastor Amos's message was that this lesser-known biblical character, who even questioned the request of food from the prophet, ended up being used by God in a scope far greater than her simple act of faith could comprehend, that those in the congregation have a similar role of offering their small sacrifices and trusting God to use them beyond what they can understand, that God will bless and care for them beyond what they can fathom, just like the widow whose "barrel of meal" miraculously never ran out again.

"But..." and the preacher went quiet even as he continued pacing across the platform, now wagging a finger above his head "... the woman's son dies.

"Even after all that, the story doesn't end. The woman's son dies. At times we see the hand of God in our lives, we are touched by the hand of God in our lives, we believe in His divine action. We have climbed the heights!" Pastor Amos' voice reached a crescendo. "But lo, we topple down the other side and land right in the valley of the shadow of death.

"God, how could you? I've been faithful. I've been faithful." Emotion clearly etched itself onto Pastor Amos' face as his voice, summiting at the top of the mountain, now descended with the congregation into mere whisper.

"Did you know," he eventually resumed, planted now back behind the pulpit and speaking in a matter-of-fact voice, "that Elijah, who raised the boy to life through the power of God, *that* Elijah was the proto-resurrectionist? He is the first person recorded in the Bible raising someone from the dead.

"The scriptures are *filled* with this miracle. Eli*sha*–Elijah's protege–raising the Shunammite woman's son, a near copy of Elijah's earlier miracle, a validation that a transfer of power had occurred from prophet to prophet. Of course, there's Jesus who raised several people from death to life during his public ministry. The widow of Nain's son, first of all. In fact, the details are uncanny, the young boy of a widow, just like Elijah in

Zarephath. Jesus was establishing himself as a new Elijah. Progressively revealing that he was prophet, but also more than prophet, that he would repeat and then surpass the ancient prophets of Israel, those giants among men, they who had walked with God.

"Jesus also raised the daughter of Jairus, he raised Lazarus, and most peculiarly, on the day Jesus was crucified, the dead came alive *en masse*." From memory he quoted:

"Jesus, when he had cried again with a loud voice, yielded up the ghost. And, behold, the veil of the temple was rent in twain from the top to the bottom; and the earth did quake, and the rocks rent; And the graves were opened; and many bodies of the saints which slept arose, And came out of the graves after his resurrection, and went into the holy city, and appeared unto many."

Pastor Amos once again paused, allowing his words to hang in the air like invisible seraphim and cherubim.

"And the miracle of resurrection continued in the life of the early church. Peter raises Tabitha. And like the transfer of power from Elijah to Elisha, Paul raises Eutychus."

Pastor Amos made several more points, encouraging the congregation when they felt useless. He summarized his ideas and then finished with a flourish, letting each word march out of his mouth like little toy soldiers, each subsequent one larger than the previous:

"YOU   WILL   KNOW   RESURRECTION."

After the sermon there was an altar call–two people went up for prayer–and a final hymn. I was beginning to think of lunch. I'm pretty sure that's a Pavlovian response I picked up from childhood. Every time I reach the end of a church service I start salivating, thinking of all the Sunday afternoon feasts I've eaten over the years. But halfway through "A Mighty Fortress Is Our God" my attention was diverted and my hunger forgotten.

About the three pews in front of me and to my right was the girl. Like before, as though she could read my thoughts, she turned and looked at me with "though this world, with devils filled should threaten to undo us" growing fainter and fainter on her lips until she fell silent completely, beautiful mouth closed, her eyes communing with mine in a wordless greeting. They were an intense brown, ancestral, flecked with shades of earth, filled, I thought, with depth and meaning.

CHAPTER FOUR

Heat spread through my body, and for a moment I struggled to bring my attention back to my present surroundings. In truth, I wasn't in a dark room where only this girl and I existed under halos of light.

Rather, I was in a church service and the pastor was giving the final benediction, one hand outstretched over the audience. After the final farewell, soft music played in the background as congregants shifted towards the exits, half moving, half socializing.

I remained rooted in place contemplating what I should do, still aware of the girl who had now turned to speak to an older couple. I had no real charisma in the female department. I wasn't the *most* awkward person, but that was mainly because I had simply eschewed any manner of potential embarrassment by avoiding such situations altogether. I had dated from time to time, but I basically had never initiated. Mutual friends, blind dates, a note passed to me from a girl's friend when I was in fifth grade, that sort of thing. But this felt different. I just wanted to be near her. Like I was supposed to. I was attracted to her but in that more literal sense, like she had me in the pull of her tractor beams but in a good way, not in that Death Star sort of way. I stepped towards her.

A hand fell on my shoulder.

"Hello there," I heard, turning. It was the preacher, towering over me, smiling. Okay, so I had thought that he exuded a commanding presence before, but standing only a few feet from him was something else altogether.

Shit, you're huge! my mind announced, and for half a second, I was afraid I'd said that out loud.

"Hi," was all I really said.

"This must be your first time here." He extended his hand. "Amos."

"Lee," I replied, taking it, consciously telling myself to give a *firm* handshake as though that'd be something this giant would appreciate. Was that a slight nod of approval?

"So, I hear you're staying with Mindy Copeland."

"Yes, sir. It seems like word has gotten around."

"Very accurate. Welcome to rural Missouri where everyone knows everyone and over half the town is related either by blood or by marriage. We're pretty well connected here. You might even say we're a bit nosy, but everyone means well for the most part."

"Yeah," I smiled, "that's okay. I mean, I'm from the St. Louis area, so not exactly small town, but I just graduated from Ozark College which is basically rural Missouri with a college stuck in the middle of it."

"Very true!" he said. "We love our community, though. Hey, I gotta go and greet some other folks, but I'd like to invite you to lunch with me and my family."

I would have been suspicious and hesitant to accept a random stranger's invitation to lunch, but this was the rural Midwest. If anything, it might be considered rude if Pastor Amos *hadn't* invited me over. In college, I had been the guest of many church families, always eager to feed a college student. Or introduce him to their daughter. Of course, I was never so lucky as to enjoy the latter.

"I'd like that," I confirmed.

"Great! Meet me in the lobby in fifteen minutes." He clapped me on the shoulder with an accidental hurricane force that caused me to take a step to maintain balance. I was just thinking about where I should hang out for the next fifteen minutes and suddenly realized that I had lost track of the girl. I glanced around the sanctuary but didn't see her. I made my way to the lobby. Nothing. Outside the church, still nothing. I was disappointed, but my one consolation was that, as Pastor Amos noted, Somewhere was a small town; I was sure I'd see her again soon enough. Hopefully.

I waited on a bench in the lobby until Pastor Amos found me, a good deal more than fifteen minutes later, but that's the life of a pastor. "Someone needed me to pray with them," he explained. I assured him it was no problem, and we made our way to the parking lot. I assumed we'd just walk, that we'd be grabbing a bite from one of the Main Street restaurants, but, anticipating my thoughts, perhaps, he declared that the best diner this side of the Mississippi was on the edge of town by Highway 3. I trusted him at his word as I had very little sense of direction besides Main Street and the few streets I couldn't name between it and Mrs. Copeland's house.

He had an old Chevy pickup, and we drove for about ten minutes, winding through streets south of Main Street, the side of town opposite where I was staying. He drove slowly, with the windows down, and waved at nearly half the town, it seemed. Besides feeling like a stranger, I was enjoying myself, the breeze tickling the hairs on my arm. Pastor Amos noted a few points of interest along the way.

"That's the Lutheran church up on that hill. As a Baptist minister I'm not supposed to like them, but they're good people. Plus, me and Clem 've been meeting up once a month to discuss church affairs." He had paused, giving me a quizzical eye like he was determining if he could trust me. He must have felt safe because he grinned before finishing. "We usually meet at *his* church because the Lutherans can drink, and so I say, when in Rome!" I grinned.

"And that's Clive and Angela's house. They're members of the church. They've got *eleven* kids. Now, I'm pretty much an advocate of letting the Lord do what the Lord wants to do, but damn! That's a lot of kids." Pastor Amos gave me a sheepish look, an unspoken apology for his language I guess. Yep, I liked him.

We pulled up to a diner aptly named Route 3 Diner. It didn't have a parking lot so much as a strip of about ten parking spots, but every single one of them was occupied, and vehicles were parked up and down the road in both directions. We joined the diaspora and hiked back to the restaurant where Pastor Amos introduced me to his wife and two daughters.

Tracy was of normal stature which wouldn't be noteworthy except for her husband's massive size; she looked more like a reserved elf in his shadow. Anna, reading a book–*Wuthering Heights*, a mature read that elicited a raised eyebrow from me–was eight and Charlotte, coloring, was five. They gave me a friendly greeting, seemed to pause an extra second, maybe deciding if they wanted to interact with me more, but then returned to their activities. I sensed that going out to lunch with random parishioners was something they were accustomed to.

"So, how do you like it here, Lee?" Tracy asked me once we got settled with our orders.

It was one of those establishments where you order and grab your food first and then sit down. What do you call that? Fast casual or something like that? It was certainly no Michelin star restaurant, but it definitely could have been showcased in Guy Fieri's *Diners, Drive-Ins and Dives*. I was doing all that was in my power not to savagely tear into my food like some wild thing. I had ordered the Route 3 burger, a messy combination of tender seasoned beef, cheddar cheese, caramelized onions, some pickled something or other which I believe included jalapenos, mayo, and "Jo's sauce"—whatever that was—served on a toasted, buttered bun. Seriously, it might have been the best burger I'd ever tasted. It was actually a force of will to respond to Tracy and take my attention momentarily away from my taste buds.

"It's great," I replied, "but I've been here less than 24 hours so far."

"I hear you've visited before," she continued. Her face displayed a keen interest in this point.

"I did." And, as the Whitakers were looking at me as if to finish explaining, I set my Route 3 burger down—not yet halfway eaten—with an eye of longing and began explaining what had brought me to Somewhere.

"I grew up in St. Louis," I began, "or a little outside of it, one of the suburbs just south, and got my degree in art history at Ozark College in southern Missouri. During the fall semester of my junior year, I studied abroad in London—"

"—Did you see the queen?" Charlotte interrupted, suddenly putting her crayons down.

"Charlotte, honey, don't interrupt," Pastor Amos chided.

"No, it's okay. Actually, yes, I kind of did see her. I was visiting Buckingham Palace and got lucky because the queen was arriving, but I could only see her waving inside her car."

"That's so cool!" and "No way!" declared both girls at once.

"It *was* pretty cool," I agreed.

"So yeah," I continued. "I got back to St. Louis just before Christmas. I guess that would have been two Christmases ago. It was nice to be back with my parents—"

"—any siblings?" Tracy interrupted this time with a stern glance from Pastor Amos *and* the girls, and she blushed.

"No, I'm an only child. My mom miscarried when I was two or three, and they never tried again." I didn't know why I shared that last part. "Anyway, it was nice to be back that Christmas because London was great and all, but to be honest, I had gotten kinda lonely after a while.

"It was weird, though, because once I got back to the States, I sort of felt different. I know I wasn't in England too long, but I guess after living in a Midwest bubble all my life, spending a few months abroad was... I don't know... *opening* or something. I'm not sure how to describe it. Sorry, I feel like I'm rambling, but it connects, I think, to what brought me here."

"No, go on," Pastor Amos assured me. "We don't get too many stories of the wide, wide world, at least not face-to-face."

"Okay, well, I went back to school after Christmas break ended, and I kept feeling off. If I'm being honest, I was a bit of a pretentious di—" I stopped myself, seeing the girls sitting there with full attention. "—demon. I was a bit of a pretentious demon, acting superior to others back at school. But I did really have this sense of having an experience outside of the norm of my life, and unless I was with the handful of students who had also studied overseas, I began to have difficulty connecting.

"That spring break, I was back in St. Louis for a few days, and then I went to see a friend of mine in Kansas City the weekend before school started up again, but that's when I came here for the first time."

"But," Tracy pointed out, "we're pretty far from Kansas City."

"Just let him finish, hon," Pastor Amos reminded.

"Yeah, I actually hadn't ever driven to Kansas City before, but I decided to give myself some extra time. My buddy was expecting me in the evening, but I left early in the day even though it's only about a four-hour drive usually. I wanted to stop and explore some, maybe find some hiking at a state park or something. Anyway, I ended up detouring and heading up to Hannibal for a bit—it was my first time there. It was nice. I like all the Mark Twain stuff—Then I just drove west through the northern part of Missouri and eventually wound my way to here."

I paused because Tracy looked stupefied, Pastor Amos looked amused, and the girls did not understand why I was pausing.

"But, Somewhere isn't—"

"—interesting!" Pastor Amos butted in.

"Yeah, I know, Somewhere still isn't exactly on a direct route from Hannibal to Kansas City, but I just wanted to get lost and had time to kill, so I took some random roads until eventually I stumbled my way into Somewhere."

The story I told them was almost true, and I think Tracy was skeptical. The reality is that I *hadn't* planned on taking a detour, I *had* planned on being at my friend's in the early afternoon and ended up arriving very late, but I *didn't* drive up to Hannibal before wandering around northern Missouri. I had visited Hannibal on a field trip in ninth grade and just made that part up.

Actually, I had been driving a straight shot on I-70. That four-hour drive is uneventful if pleasant, so I found myself in a pensive mood. I liked driving for that reason. And I wasn't lying about being in a weird state of mind ever since studying abroad. So, there I was cruising along, no music on, just giving my mind free space to roam.

I was thinking about college and what I was doing and what was next and what I really wanted and the American Dream, which felt like an enigma to me, especially after spending time away from the USA and what I felt like were its talons.

I remember in my head repeating that I want to get away, I want to get away, I want to get away. But I didn't know what that meant. I was just so angsty, and I didn't know why because that had never been me before.

And so, just past Columbia, about halfway to Kansas City, almost without thinking I exited. It was by a winery, I remember that. But beyond that, everything was kind of a haze, like a pleasant dream. I had been in a cloud of my thoughts, and exiting there never felt like a conscious decision. It's just the thing that I did. And the cloud didn't lift really, but I felt a peace, and I felt assured that this *was* getting away, like even though I was in Missouri, it was still somehow *away*. I was in new territory. In many ways it was very similar to the terrain around my university in southern Missouri, still the rural Midwest. Yet it was new somehow.

For one, I wasn't on a noisy interstate. I was winding around country roads. It was March, so the trees were still bare, but grass and undergrowth were springing back: a deep, vibrant green. I passed rivers and woods and old farmhouses, pastures with sheep and cows, wide open spaces and enclosed spaces of forested lanes. I don't know why, but I was viewing my world with radically different eyes. I might as well have been trekking through a fairy grove back in England, yet this was distinctly Missouri with its own unique and magical flourishes.

And somehow, suddenly, I was in a misshapen grid of all these old houses. A left here and a right there, and eventually I turned onto Main Street in Somewhere, Missouri.

At that point, the dreamlike state I felt while driving had lifted, like I had never actually driven but had instead been plucked out of my parents' home and plopped down in this unfamiliar town.

I definitely caught the small-town vibes immediately because people kept glancing at me, an obvious out-of-towner, but still, they were friendly.

"Hey, you're new around here," I remember Barb saying when I entered The Book and Bean for the first time. However, though I may have caught the eyes of some folks upon arrival–or "landing"–the town immediately won me over with the enchantment of its historic downtown, the quirkiness of all those old Victorian homes dotted here and there. The gothic architecture would have seemed sinister, perhaps, if it hadn't been spring and green filled with the *tweet-tweet* of freshly arrived migratory birds.

And then the people themselves! As I made one giant loop down Main Street's hill and then back up, people were smiling at me and several made small talk about the weather, the Chiefs, and where I was from. They genuinely wanted to know me.

I can't fully describe it, the switch inside me, the flip of my perspective, but I felt at once like I was in another country, like I was in a charming English village in the Cotswolds (somewhere I had visited one weekend while studying abroad) and, simultaneously, like I was home. And

I was all the more pleased in the end because I wasn't abroad, but I was in my own beloved Missouri, mundane somehow transformed with this fresh vision.

I remember reading about some thinker or moral philosopher once, and while I can't remember the overall message, they gave an illustration about an English explorer trying to claim a new exotic land for king and country but who had miscalculated his voyage and managed to land back in England. The point was not the explorer's foolishness or embarrassment but rather the immense delight of both the adventurousness and terror of going abroad combined with the immediate security of coming home again. It was that living paradox of desiring both the exotic and the recognizable.

I remember the fairy tales my parents read to me when I was just a kid, that strange tingling sensation, the mixture of wildness and domesticity: sitting in a room where I was cozy and comfortable while on a dangerous and brave journey of the imagination. That's sort of how I felt the magical day I stumbled into Somewhere, Missouri.

"—so that's how I discovered Somewhere," I said, finishing my account to the Whitakers. "After spending a really pleasant afternoon here, I finished the drive to Kansas City to see my friend and then went back to school. This sounds terrible, but for a little while there, I had almost forgotten about this place. You know, senior year, staying busy. But then last fall, one night when I was stressed out studying for an exam, it just popped into my head again—" *like literally just popped into my head out of nowhere*, I thought "—and so I skipped class that Friday and came up here again. I didn't even have any plans, but one thing led to another, and like providence or something, I found a place to stay, and the next thing I knew, it was settled: I was moving to Somewhere after I graduated. And here I am."

"Here you are," Pastor Amos beamed at me after exchanging a look with his wife. "Well, we're mighty glad that you're here and that you didn't forget about us after visiting the first time. We love our little out-of-the-way place. We don't get a lot of visitors, but we're awfully glad when we do and try to make them feel welcome."

"Tell us more about England," Anna jumped in.

"Were there princesses?" Charlotte prodded.

"Now, girls, let's let Lee finish his meal," their father chided, saving me. "I know he loves that Route 3 burger."

I nodded in agreement, already tearing back into the juicy meat.

CHAPTER FIVE

"Hello, Lee."

Mrs. Copeland greeted me as she entered the kitchen from *her* side of the house. As she closed the door, I could see into a long hall that ran all the way to the front door.

On the one hand, I was perfectly content with her asking for privacy and only allowing me access to the kitchen and my rented space, but on the other hand, the rest of the house was clearly a beautiful space. I noticed the dark wood floors and trim, the Victorian wallpaper, the antique furniture. I had always been impressed with older homes: the history, the craftsmanship, the aura of age and beauty. It seemed a little unfair that she wouldn't at least give me a small tour.

Still, she was kind enough to offer me a place to stay. I was a stranger. She was making a bit of side money by renting out this space, but she was also taking a bit of a risk. I figured she'd warm up to me–I'm a likable guy–and maybe relax more as time went on.

"Hi, Mrs. Copeland."

"I see you've gotten some groceries." I was sitting at the small table with a ham and cheese sandwich, a bunch of grapes, and a newspaper.

"Yes, ma'am. Getting settled in. Uh, I hope it's okay that I grabbed the newspaper off the counter." I wasn't sure. If she was so protective of the rest of her house, might she not be protective of all her things?

"Of course," Mrs. Copeland replied, putting my mind at ease. "So, tomorrow is your first day at the art gallery?"

"It is. I'm excited to get started. Tom seems like a nice guy." Tom Burley was the store manager. He was nice enough to interview me over the phone after verifying with Barb at The Book and Bean and with Mrs. Copeland that I was at least somewhat normal and then checking the references in my application. It was a little unconventional, but it worked, and it saved me a trip from home over the summer. I'd meet him face-to-face the next day.

"Tom is a good man. You will like him."

"Um, Mrs. Copeland," I asked, changing the subject, "I forgot to ask earlier, but do you happen to have a washer and dryer?"

"What?" The tone of her voice cooled suddenly.

"A washer and dryer? I just realized earlier that I'm not sure where to clean my clothes."

"Oh, um…"

"Or how did your previous tenants do their laundry? Is there a laundromat in town?" *Please don't make me go to the laundromat*, I was thinking. Surely she wasn't *that* protective of her space that I couldn't at least clean some clothes from time to time.

"I will do your laundry for you," she declared.

"What? No, I wasn't trying to suggest that I expected *you* to do my laundry."

"No, no, no," she tut-tutted me. "I apologize. I thought I had said that when we discussed the rental agreement. Laundry services are free. Just, uh, put any laundry in a basket I will have over here," she pointed, "by Saturday mornings before 9:00, and they will be ready by Sunday morning."

"Um, okay," I half-agreed. "I feel bad, though. Are you sure? I mean…" I trailed off. I mean she *did* know that dirty clothes include underwear and such, right?

"Young man, I have three grown children. I am accustomed to dirty laundry. If you prefer, there is a laundromat, but it is on the *other* side of Main Street and would be quite inconvenient." She threw on a face of disapproval, so I relented.

"Alright, alright," I declared, putting my hands up in surrender. "Well, thanks."

"My pleasure. Now," she spoke matter-of-factly with no hint of invitation or amicable feelings, "I have been meaning to sit you down and teach you how to play bridge. Or do you already know?"

I laughed and admitted my ignorance. She sat down across from me and taught me a two-person version of the card game, and this would become our thing for quite some time.

Closing the door to my apartment behind me, I let out a deep sigh after an hour of learning, failing, and kind of, sort of getting the hang of bridge. I enjoyed it, but I was happy to spend some time alone in my room. Only a few days had elapsed, but with each passing moment, each new experience, new place, new person, I perceived more of that double sense of adventure and home, the idea that had gripped me when I was at lunch with the Whitakers. I was shocked by this lingering notion because I had felt so intensely the opposite when I returned from studying abroad: Missouri had become gray, drab, boring. It was unbearably hot in the humid summer, bone-chillingly cold in the winter with no persistent snow to assuage the low temperatures. Filled with cultureless, backwards-thinking rednecks and hillbillies. The locals' idea of a good time was engineering the latest contraption for getting cold beer to one's mouth while buoyed by a bunch of Styrofoam noodles on the Lake of the Ozarks or Table Rock Lake or some meandering river. For someone who loved the arts, I had become sick of the Midwest, mollified only slightly when I was in the city. Maybe there was a rich history of the arts here in Missouri, but to my mind, it wasn't cultured enough. As far as I was concerned, Thomas Hart Benton , Missouri's most famous artist, might as well have been coloring with crayons.

Somewhere, though, was reforming my feelings about Missouri, my heritage. Not only had *this* spot captivated me, but it reframed my earlier experiences: the dumb fun of country summers, float trips on the rivers, the cultural contributions of blues and jazz music both in St. Louis and Kansas City, the literary legacy of Mark Twain, Oktoberfest in Hermann, the kitschy festivals of Silver Dollar City. Not to mention all the unique state parks: Elephant Rock, Johnson's Shut-Ins, Ha-Ha Tonka, Meramec Caverns. Perhaps familiarity breeds discontent, and all we need is a new place to rekindle the enchanting vision of our own roots.

Growing up with the stories my parents would read to me, I've often bemoaned the lack of fairy tales associated with America, especially the Midwest. That feeling has only intensified over the years; the more I grew in my understanding of art history, fairy tales became distinctly European. Somewhere, however, gave me a funny inkling that somehow in our modernism, our youthful pride, our desire to be so keenly distinct from our European ancestry, we'd dug the graves of all the mythical creatures, we'd stolidly done away with that nursery nonsense, that Catholic superstition (the Puritans play a more central role in our values and ethics than we'd like to admit). Sure, we had Tom Walker, we had the Headless Horseman, the products of British influences that managed to filter through our tightly knitted sieve of unbelief, born into a New England that was geographically closest to its overseas namesake. Why is everyone so infatuated by legends of Salem? Because there's something innate, a foothold of mystery in the human spirit, that causes us to want those old ghost stories after all.

In Somewhere, I felt the light dance slant just enough to make me think of the fairies again, not transmigrated from Europe but spawning up out of our own Missouri mud. That's what I felt in my spirit. That's what was caught up in my sigh of contentment. A place where all the old stories are possible and are not bound regionally, but descend on the back of every mote of dust, a glinting gold of magic.

Even so, Somewhere would test me, tempt me, warn me: maybe, after all, it's better to let the old stories lie. Maybe digging up what lies beneath is a practice in madness. Who knows what other monsters might stir?

I plunked myself down into the overstuffed chair and cozied up with a book. I had half a mind to watch an episode of *Everybody Loves Raymond* but disciplined myself to use my time better. My crate of books sat next to the dresser, a monument to the image I tried crafting of myself instead of a true reflection of my reading interests. Rather than grab one of those, I picked up a Stephen King novel, a recent purchase from The Book and Bean. I'd already begun reading the book, easing into the story effortlessly, a strength of King's master story-telling abilities.

Darkness pressed against my windows. Only the lamp shone beside me, swallowed up quickly by the brown hardwood floors running the length of the attic space. I read and read, hooked into the book's plot. In the back of my mind, I knew I had my first day of work the next day. *I don't start until 9:00 anyways,* I reasoned whenever the thought creeped into my head.

On the wall in front of me, the faces of medieval villagers, the imagination of Pieter Bruegel the Elder, surveyed me. Watched, watched, watched. Eventually, convinced that I *had* to get some sleep, I changed into pajamas–an old t-shirt and my high school gym shorts–brushed my teeth, and turned off the light before climbing into bed. I was asleep in seconds.

But sometime in that indefinable space between *middle of the night* and *very early morning*, I was awakened momentarily by a sound. Deep in the house.

CHAPTER SIX

I heard the door chime, and I looked up to see a pair of familiar faces: Bill and Lacy, two of our more frequent visitors. They seemed to always have some house project that needed the touch of local art, but after nearly a dozen visits in the past month, they'd only bought a small print which was essentially worthless aside from a tiny flourish around their nightstand. I suspect, though, that the small purchase was probably a way of paying for the services of my attention.

At that point, I'd been working at Main Street Art Gallery and living in Somewhere for over a month, as satisfied as when I'd just arrived. Tom had greeted me the first day with enthusiasm. Not only was he the manager, he had been the sole employee, but he confessed that the job was a bit lonely all by himself. He was probably in his early forties, skinny, long hair pulled back in a ponytail, and sporting a goatee. He looked a bit like a hippie without the "far out" ultra-relaxed vibe—he was a pretty energetic guy.

The first week I had worked the register and familiarized myself with the shop. The gallery itself represented about ten different artists, all from Somewhere, but only four of those artists had more than two pieces displayed and, in regards to talent, were clearly a cut above the rest. The "Four," that is what Tom and I called the four most talented and prolific artists showcased in the store which, incidentally, included him, a pretty quality artist himself. I liked to teasingly refer to the Four as the Ninja Turtles in honor of their Italian Renaissance namesakes: Raphael, Michelangelo, Donatello, Leonardo.

We took a somewhat low commission, 30%, because we wanted to promote Somewhere's artists while still staying afloat. I was pleasantly surprised in my first month, though, to discover that business was relatively steady. We had sold six pieces, ranging from $350 to $1,200. It wasn't a ton, and ironically, as an art history major, I knew very little about the world of art galleries, but I sensed that in a small town, we were doing well.

Tom was a pretty smart guy, though, so there were a few other revenue streams to keep the shop's bottom line healthy: In addition to the local art, we sold prints of famous works. We also had a section devoted to little art-related tchotchkes—figurines of artists and coffee mugs, shirts, pens and of famous artwork—art supplies, and a surprisingly popular selection of local, handmade jewelry. And since not everyone was adorning their walls with art, we also sold custom frames built by a local woodworker. Those also sold pretty well; people were always adding new photos of their families, and if they weren't spending extravagantly on art, they didn't mind shelling out some cash for a beautiful, handmade frame.

Next, we offered a myriad of art classes–mostly aimed at kids–including a summer art camp, but we also featured a monthly Friday night art and wine combination for adults–always a sellout. Finally, the shop hosted various exhibitions in tandem with downtown festivals. In fact, we were launching right into that busy season: Halloween, Thanksgiving, Christmas. Really, any reason to host a parade or market, entertain the kids, or put a beer in the hands of the adults.

And if all that wasn't enough, next to us was an ice cream shop with some outdoor seating. Most of our foot traffic was actually the collateral of the ice cream shop's success, but it worked.

So even though I had initially questioned how I'd be able to fill my time there, I stayed pretty busy.

"Alright. What about the color palette?" I asked Bill and Lacy. "A

Bohemian style usually has layers of colors." My tone was a bit proud. I'd actually been looking through some design books we had in the gallery to better educate myself.

"Umm, well, we got a dark green wallpaper with a flowery design thing. I don't know how to describe it. Honey?"

"Yeah, he's right," Lacy laughed. "But I don't know how to describe it either. Some of the other things in that room are colorful. The sitting chair is yellow, we have some ornamental pieces on a little table that are yellow and red. The pillows are turquoise. Lots of different colors. But we can change those."

"It's fine, it's fine," I assured them. "That just helps me get an idea on maybe something I could recommend. Come on, you guys know the drill. You've been in here once or twice." That elicited a shrill laugh.

I walked them around the gallery like I had several times before. This time, though, I actually had the perfect piece in mind. One of the Four had brought in a piece just this last week, and I'd completed the display the day before. Maggie DeJong was the only artist of the Ninja Turtles with a more experimental and abstract style. She was also the only one who had a more Bohemian vibe herself, a Professor Trelawney type: long flowy dresses, shawls, headbands, necklaces, bracelets and rings, and wire-rimmed glasses. She didn't really fit the Somewhere aesthetic, but as I had only lived there a month, she made me feel less like an outsider.

"Here," I said and parked myself in front of a painting that Maggie had titled "Blue - Red - Yellow," and I thought it fit perfectly for the style of sitting room Bill and Lacy had just described to me. The artwork presented a mess of geometric shapes of varying shades of–unsurprisingly–blue, red, and yellow. These overlaid a cerulean background that spread out on the canvas with an undulating, navy border. Like all the forms were fitting inside a storm cloud. One section of the shapes gave the appearance of a head's profile which added a dimension of intelligence and humanity to the array of chaotic, colorful components.

Bill and Lacy stood for a minute, studying Maggie's piece. The painting measured 39.4 by 27.6 inches with a mahogany frame, so it was sizable. I wasn't sure what they'd think, but they put my mind at ease.

"Well, that just about fits perfectly," Bill finally stated.

"Maggie did this, huh?" Lacy queried.

"She did."

"She may be a strange one," Lacy noted, "but she *does* make some great art."

"Lee, do you mind if me and my wife take a quick walk around ourselves?"

"Certainly."

I walked back to the counter and flipped through the design book I'd been perusing. About five minutes later, they walked back up.

"We'll take it," Lacy declared, all smiles.

I was taken by surprise. They'd been in and out the whole month I'd been working in the gallery and had yet to buy anything except a Picasso coffee mug for Bill's aunt.

"Really?"

"Really," Bill affirmed. "Don't look so surprised. We weren't stringin' you along these past few weeks. Just takin' our time."

"Of course, of course. Well, that's great," I was the one doing most of the smiling now, feeling like I'd really played a key role in this sale. After ringing them up for $1,500, I looked forward to calling Maggie and letting her know that she'd just made over a thousand bucks. From the little I knew of her, she'd probably give me some nonchalant response, bordering on dismissive, but she'd be happy. Hey, an artist's gotta eat!

I spent the next fifteen minutes or so dismounting the artwork, packaging it delicately in paper and bubble wrap.

"Thanks, Lee," Lacy called as they slipped out the door.

I walked to the back of the shop, now needing to find a new piece to present in place of the other. We had about half a dozen come in the past week but only one from the Ninja Turtles. I heard the door chime, checking my watch and realizing it must be Tom coming in. He'd be better at deciding which composition should be displayed in place of Maggie's.

I returned to the front of the shop, expecting Tom's wiry frame, but I was mistaken. Immediately my mouth went dry, and a weird movement circulated my gut.

It was *her.*

Apparently I had returned to the front stealthily because the girl was quietly browsing the artwork and had not turned to me. I was suddenly conscious of every little sensation: the way my hands felt, the shape of the inside of my mouth, each blink of my eyes, the sway of my body upon my legs, the way the light fell through the window, and, most notably, how everything had gone silent. I heard nothing outside, nothing inside, besides the slightest resonance of her footfall and the more prominent beating of my heart.

Then I just felt awkward. How long had I been standing there without moving? Thirty seconds? Thirty minutes? I might accidentally startle her. How should I make my presence known? This had been going on too long. I felt like a creep, a voyeur. But I *could* just stand and stare; I'd be content.

Come on, Lee. Get a grip!

"Hi there," I said in the most cheerful, natural voice I could muster. I imagined that it came out like the croaking of a pubescent boy, and I was ready for her to jump in fright, but she simply turned to me and smiled.

"I heard you worked here," was all she said. But wait, what did that mean? Had she been inquiring about me?

"I do," I replied, shifting on my feet. I let the silence hang long enough to become awkward before adding, "I've seen you around town."

"Same. I've been meaning to come in here and say hi."

"Really?"

"Yeah. It's nice to get new people to Somewhere, especially someone closer to my age." She resumed looking at one of the paintings. It wasn't completed by one of the Ninja Turtles, but it was still pretty good: a wide open stretch of brown land with leafless trees along the edges, with its emptiness contrasted by a bright red barn and a brilliantly created blue—almost surreal—sky.

Unlike most of the painting, a post-it had been affixed to the upper right corner, presumably stuck there by the author. In deep purple ink was written *The Curse*.

"Edith Sutter," Rose said.

"I'm sorry?"

"Edith Sutter. She's the one who painted this. She's friends with my mom and used to babysit me and my brother when we were younger."

"She's talented. She's not one of the Four—"

"—the Four?"

"One of the four most frequently displayed artists in our gallery and, typically, considered the most talented. I also call them the Ninja Turtles."

"Ninja Turtles?"

"Yeah, you know. Raphael, Donatello, Leonardo, Michelangelo. They were all named after famous Italian Renaissance artists."

"Oh, yeah," she chuckled softly. She didn't seem to be tracking. I got embarrassed, so I quickly jumped back in.

"But Edith's painting is still one of my favorites. There's something captivating about the juxtaposition of desolation with bright colors and open sky. The sort of yin and yang that a lot of artists try to capture."

"Hmm..." she contemplated. "I hadn't seen it that way." She glanced at me and then blushed a little. "But you're the expert," she added.

"No, no," I assured her. "How do you see it?"

"Well, you can see a pattern to the brown land. It's soil that's been plowed. The trees are bare which means this would be sometime between late fall and early spring. The only reason a field would be plowed but with no remnants of harvest during that time of the year would be in a fallow season."

"A fallow season?" I queried.

"Yeah, every few seasons a farmer will plow a field but not sow any seeds. It's a method of recovery. To me this painting doesn't represent desolation but something like punishment, recovery, and potential."

I was a little embarrassed by the depth of her answer and my own obvious ignorance. She was probably right. A bit self-consciously, I ambled up to the painting, standing only a few inches from her. At first, I glanced at her, almost frozen once again, but I told my brain to tell my eyes and neck to swivel back to the painting.

Sure enough. There were subtle striations over the land, obvious furrows in the soil.

"Well, I guess you're—" I was about to admit defeat, but something caught my eye, something I hadn't noticed before. "What the…"

The red barn was located on the right of the painting, but at the edge of ground and sky and just a little left of the barn was another small object. I stepped closer to the painting, my eyes scrutinizing the image from mere inches away.

I was astonished and stood there a moment, verifying that my brain was receiving the correct image signifier from my eyes. I stayed, steady, ready for the image to unblur and transform into something normal or into nothing, realizing that it was only a trick of the eye. But it wasn't. The image remained.

A gallows, with a woman hanging by the neck. How had I not seen this before? The figure was small enough to demand this close attention, and I guess it could be almost imperceptible when swallowed up by the rest of the painting's landscape. And she was dark. A shadow. From afar, the eye certainly wasn't drawn to the hanging woman.

I studied her more carefully. Her face was painted only a little lighter than the rest of her body, capturing the pallid expression of asphyxiation. And she had one eye open.

I was lost in the revelation but comforted by the soft touch on my shoulder. Despite staring at this painting, warmth spread over my body.

"What is it?" she asked. I turned to her and let out a gasp.

For the slightest fraction of a moment, I saw not the beautiful girl but a wraithlike deformation of her, like a body rotted and leathery from the decay of death. It was only a moment before my sight re-formed the image into reality, the same attractive girl as before.

"What is it?" she asked again, alarmed.

"No, nothing," I breathed out, forcing a smile. "Just nerves I guess. Did you see this other part of the painting?" I turned back to it, to show her. She inched closer, her arm brushing up against my arm. Okay, now I was completely focused back on her, the hanged woman in the painting nothing more than acrylics and the over-imagination of some random townsperson who wasn't even one of the Ninja Turtles.

She leaned in. I was in another world. Gazing at her hair which fell just below her shoulders, her arms, her contoured back, her...

She yelped.

"Oh my God!" she exclaimed. "What the hell? That wasn't there before."

"What do you mean?"

"I mean..." she stammered. "How could I have not seen that before? That's... that's messed up."

She must have bumped the painting when she yelped because when I looked, the post-it was gone. I glanced at the floor to grab it but was whisked away as Rose grabbed me by the wrist and brought me to the other side of the shop. Okay, I was back under her spell again.

"You should tell Tom about that painting. That needs to be taken down."

"Why? I mean, it's a little creepy. But it's not even that weird compared to a lot of other artwork I've seen."

"I know. It's just... not appropriate. I appreciate all art, but this is a small town. Kids come in here. If they were to—"

"—okay, okay," I interrupted. "I see your point. I'll take it down."

"Just let Tom do it." I looked at her quizzically. But she seemed earnest.

"Okay, I'll tell Tom to do it."

"Thanks."

We stood there in silence, I, once again, at a loss for words.

"So..." she grinned at me. There was that sensation again, moving through my body, to *all* parts of my body. I grinned back at her. "...Lee Thompson."

"Hey, how do you know my name?"

"Small town—"

"—small town, yeah, yeah," I butted in. "Everyone really *does* seem to know everyone here," I laughed. "Okay, so you know my name. What's yours?

"Rose. Rose Weaver"

"Nice to meet you, Rose, Rose Weaver." I teased. I hesitated then stuck out my hand. Do you shake hands in this situation? I immediately regretted my decision, but she shook my hand.

"Nice to meet you, Lee. So, I have to get going, but I also wanted to see if you'd like to hang out with me and some friends Friday. We're going bowling."

"Yeah, definitely. Sure," I blurted out.

"Great. We'll be there at 6:30."

"Okay, thanks for inviting me."

Rose turned and walked out, sending one last smile my way before leaving. I wasn't able to concentrate well for the rest of my shift. I forgot to tell Tom about the painting, nor did I remove it myself.

The next morning, however, it was gone.

CHAPTER SEVEN

I awoke with a gasp. What little light illuminated my room sifted in through the windows or glowed at me from the digital clock on my nightstand. Otherwise, darkness enveloped me. I glanced at the time.

3:00.

I sat up slowly. What had woken me? A dream?

I peered about, seeing only unclear forms of shadow. After a minute or two of this, I sank back into bed, clutching the covers more tightly about me, trying to ward off the unusually cold draft that had filtered in. My eyes shut.

I heard the subtlest of movements, a sound coming from the direction of the art frame, the scratching of object on object, like the art frame had shifted a millimeter. I heard nothing else though I strained in anticipation for minute after slithering minute. With some effort, I managed to fall back to sleep, but the next morning, I walked immediately over to the painting and examined it, the villagers of Pieter the Elder's landscape frozen in space and time like before. I adjusted the frame and got ready for work.

"Hey, Mom." I propped the phone up to my ear as I ate dinner later that evening, a ham and cheese sandwich and applesauce. One of the several drawbacks to not having a cell phone: no speaker phone option in times like these.

"May I ask who's calling?"

"Mom, it's me. Lee."

Silence.

For a moment, I wondered if she'd hung up, but I heard breathing and movement on the other end. Finally, she responded.

"I'm sorry. Who's calling?"

"Lee," I spoke louder. "Your son."

Another brief pause.

"Lee!" she exclaimed. "How are you?"

I hesitated for a moment, waiting for her to acknowledge whatever had just happened, but I got nothing. It bothered me and scared me a little. Was she losing her memory? The next time I visited them, I'd need to take her to the doctor.

"Ray," my mom called for my dad. "Ray, Lee's on the phone."

"Who?" I heard my dad yell. Him too?

"Lee, your son!"

"Oh, Lee! Be right there!" Okay, maybe he just misheard. Hearing loss is better than memory loss in my opinion.

"How are you, Son?" my dad asked a moment later.

"I'm good. How are you guys?"

Despite everything, despite the sense of needing to get away, I did miss my parents. Not a lot of time had yet elapsed since finishing college, but leaving a place has a way of clarifying relationships. I only had a handful of friends back home that I stayed in touch with during college. I had a few more friends from college that I anticipated keeping in touch with (although that hadn't happened yet since moving to Somewhere), but those few friends were a lot less than the wide community I had my freshman year. There's just something about starting a new chapter that causes you to unconsciously begin filtering through your relationships. You feel that inevitability and draw closer to the ones you want to keep and slowly start letting go of the ones you don't. The funny thing is, you often don't know who that is until that very moment arrives, maybe not until afterwards. From this vantage point, several months removed from graduation, I had a keen sense of who would be in my life for the foreseeable future and who wouldn't. It was a strange sadness, an acknowledgment that that unique season of life was over, would not return.

"Anyway," Mom responded, "What are you up to in... you're in Kansas City, right?"

"No, Mom. I'm in a little town called Somewhere."

"Really? Funny name."

"Well, I'm here working at an art gallery. It's not *exactly* art history, but at least it's related. A lot of my friends are already working jobs that they didn't even study for." I always felt like I had to justify my degree choice even though I paid for about 75% of my tuition. It's probably the defensiveness of anyone who majored in a humanities field.

"Oh," Mom said. "I thought you worked at a coffee shop in Kansas City."

Might as well be, I thought.

"Nope. But yeah, things are good here. The house I'm staying in is nice, the art gallery's nice, I've gotten to know the pastor's family more. Remember, I told you about them the last time I called you?" Again, I could almost see through the phone, see the look of confusion that was plastered across the silence between us. I ignored it.

"Anyway, I, uh, well... there's a girl that's kind of nice."

"There you go, Son," Dad responded.

"Have you asked her out yet?" Mom followed up, her go-to follow up question to any statement of interest in girls.

"No, Mom," I groaned. "I've hung out with her and a few other people, and I'm actually meeting them for a Halloween parade in just a little bit."

"Is she Christian?" Dad's go-to follow-up.

"She is." *Well, she goes to church anyway.*

It was late October, and the day of the Halloween parade had finally arrived. Nearly two months had passed since I went bowling with Rose and her friends. I was sure that I acted awkwardly the whole time and that they would never invite me to spend time with them again, but apparently I hadn't embarrassed myself too much. Since then, I'd been out with them a few other times—bowling again, a movie once, and a few times with no real aim besides hanging out—and I was feeling more at home.

Mattie, Kenny, and David were the ones who were with Rose when I saw them at the fair. Not Dave. David. He had made that very clear. But he was a likable guy. They were all together each time we hung out, and a girl named Eleanor also showed up the second time we went bowling. I was becoming one of them, I hoped, so it was with a mild sense of ownership that I traipsed my way into the Halloween crowd to find my friends.

Navigating a sea of little vampires, ghosts, fairies, a menagerie of various animals, and all other kinds of exotic costumes, I met up with Rose and everyone in front of The Little Flower Shop. Eleanor was there again, and also a guy I hadn't met before, Mike. Otherwise, it was Mattie, Kenny, and David as usual. And, of course, Rose.

When the parade began, I thought of that scene in *The Lion King* when Simba looks up the walls of the gorge and sees a stampede of wildebeests sprinting down. At one moment the streets were cleared, and at the next, the first giant float crested over the upper end of Main Street.

I was impressed. Like the fair, the town really got into the Halloween parade. The soft glow of the street lamps on Main Street was just the right mixture of small-town cozy and Halloween eerie fun. Fake spider webs were strung everywhere, but the more extreme decor—blood, body parts, gruesome corpses, and terrifying monsters—were not displayed in this family-friendly event.

The floats, though, were certainly the main attraction. Trucks pulled flatbed trailers with a wooden pirate ship, a haunted castle, a fairy grove, a dungeon, and more. Each float was sponsored by some local business ("Main Street Art Gallery" was painted in dripping, red letters on the skirt of the dungeon float). Elaborately clad townsfolk flitted about, jumping onto and off of the various floats, and tossing candy to the kids squealing and racing for the sweets.

I laughed at Kenny who would join the kids in chasing after the candy (I'm pretty sure I saw him knock one little ninja boy over), but the rest of us would occasionally stoop down and grab a neglected piece here and there, usually the leftovers no one wanted–Tootsie Rolls, Necco Wafers, Smarties. Kenny would surreptitiously pass me the good stuff, though, the spoils of his conquest: Twix, M&Ms, and, my favorite, Butterfingers. At all times, I was keenly aware of Rose's location, though Kenny's antics were the closest thing to distracting me.

At one point, though, when we were all reaching for the unwanted candy left over after the other kids (and Kenny) had picked it over, Rose was beside me, brushing up against me as we crouched down together. We inadvertently reached for the same piece, and our skin touched, an electric current shooting up my arm. She turned to me and smiled. Cheesy. The classic meet-cute, but I was water when she looked at me like that.

I think I smiled. I can't be sure. I froze.

"I'll take that, thank you," she announced, snatching a fun size M&M's bag, somehow missed in the frenzy before.

"I can't believe Kenny missed that," I managed to say.

The parade only lasted about ten more minutes after that not-so-innocuous arm graze, but she remained beside me for the rest of it. Every bump, every slight touch was my drug. My insides were in a state of suspension, my body a lightning rod of sensation. I'm pretty sure I managed not to give myself away as some kind of pervy zombie, but if I pulled it off, I did so barely.

Finally, the last float crawled past us, an insane asylum—one of the more frightening displays. It was about 7:30, and I was disappointed, coming down from my high, ready to wander back home.

Rose grabbed my arm.

"We're going out for drinks. You're coming." She demanded. There was zero fight in me. Or, rather, the only impulse I had to fight was not appearing *too* eager. *Damn, play it cool*, I lectured myself.

"Sure," I replied with a forced calm. "Wait, are you even old enough?" I teased but seriously wondered, suddenly realizing I didn't know how old she was.

"Hey, I just turned twenty-one this summer. Are *you* twenty-one, Old Man?"

"Eighteen," I joked. "I graduated college early. I'm such a fucking genius." I got quiet, realizing I had said that a little loud with kids nearby. Rose just laughed. Kenny, who had heard me, also laughed and swung his arm around me.

"Hey, don't be so fuckin' shy. It's just a bunch of damn, son-of-a-bitch kids in all their shit costumes crying to Mommy that I kicked their asses in getting candy." He cracked up after continuing through his dictionary of swear words.

All of us strolled down Main Street, passing a couple of bars as we continued, but apparently David was serious about his beer. "Bud Light is shit in a can," he mentioned—several times—and pulled us all to Amendment 21 Brewery, a craft microbrewery a few blocks from downtown and overlooking the river.

We landed at a large table on the outside patio under the dull glow of hanging lights, live music drifting from inside. We were huddled near one of those tall heater things that look like a street lamp, beers in hand. I had an Imperial Lager.

"You know, David," Kenny observed, "I don't know why you make such a big deal about this place. All beer tastes like piss to me."

David, with a note of irritation, responded, "Yeah, well then why are you drinking it?"

Kenny, putting his hands up in mock defense, answered, "Who says I don't like piss?" and laughed raucously.

"You guys are so gross," Mattie shook her head.

"Excuse me. *Kenny* is so gross," David clarified.

"Kenny *is* so gross," Eleanor chimed in with a wry smile.

"Not what you said last night," he retorted, winking at her.

"To Kenny!" Kenny declared himself and offered his dewy glass towards the middle of the table. We all followed suit, laughing and clinking glasses.

"So, Lee, tell us more about yourself," Mike requested once we all got settled down again. "It looks like I'm the only one who hasn't met you yet." Mike said this kindly, smiling, but did I detect a hint of malice?

"Well, I first visited Somewhere about a year and a half ago," I began, sharing with them essentially the same story that I had shared with Pastor Amos and his family months before. Though I had spent time with all of them besides Mike, I really hadn't shared a lot about myself, nor had I learned much about them. They listened tentatively–that or the alcohol was putting them into an amicable stupor–and Mattie especially seemed to relate to my feelings of restlessness back at college.

"I would like to leave Somewhere so bad," she said. Everyone responded with uncomfortable but knowing glances at each other. I surmised that there was maybe some history to Mattie's statement, but I obviously shared her sentiment. In fact, I felt a fondness towards Mattie–not the pure attraction that transformed me into a befuddled teenager around Rose–but she reminded me of a close family friend, Miriam, who was like a mixture between an aunt and big sister to me.

For one thing, I noticed Mattie was wearing a Beatles shirt. Miriam was always wearing band t-shirts. Beyond that, though, there was just this vibe that Mattie exuded, a self-confidence and a toughness. A quiet intelligence. I learned that she was a high school science teacher though she didn't strike me as one, but then again, it also strangely fit this persona: reserved intellectual, bookish but layered and cultured with her band t-shirt, dark hair pulled back in a ponytail, round glasses. Maybe it was the beers, but I felt this sort of brotherly affection towards Mattie.

"Yeah," I encouraged her, "you should. I mean, just get away, see things. It doesn't have to be forever." I said the latter to pacify the not-too-positive glances I noticed from the others. Even Rose looked at me like she was trying to transmit some unspoken message. Thankfully, David broke up the awkwardness to ask me several questions about London, mostly about the beer and pub scene.

I enjoyed myself that night. David and Mike, I learned, both worked for Mike's dad on their farm, though David was not hesitant to share his own ambitions of owning a microbrewery; he'd already started experimenting with a number of different beers. Kenny was the heir-apparent of the largest grocery store in Somewhere, Fresh Foods, and supposedly he was pretty good at what he did. *I hope none of those kids he knocked around earlier recognize him at the grocery store,* I mused. Eleanor was a nurse in the small clinic, and I already knew that Mattie was a teacher. Rose I also knew, but I was ashamed to realize that I hadn't spent much time talking to her about her baking job. In my defense, bowling and sitting in a movie theater are not the most conducive to deep conversation. So I learned that, while she loved baking, she was a little self-conscious due to her parents' lack of approval.

"You're talking to an art history major," I reminded her. "Not only is it not a lucrative career path; I had to pay tens of thousands of dollars for a piece of paper declaring me competent in a field I probably could have studied on my own!"

She smiled, and that was that.

We hung around Amendment 21 Brewery until about midnight. At one point it was just me and Rose and Mike as the others went inside to dance, and I wished Mike would have gone in too, but I had no such luck. I got the sense that he was a reluctant chaperone.

We all disbanded, though, when Rose declared that she needed to get going. I was learning that Rose was very much the glue of the group.

"Yeah, I should get some decent sleep after picking up an extra shift this week," Eleanor decided.

"Bleh, I've got to grade labs," Mattie wretched.

Kenny, though, ambled over to me, threw his arm around me and declared, "I'm not going anywhere!" This he shouted but then whispered not so subtly in my ear, "Unless I can find some more of those damn kids and take more of their candy."

I ordered one final beer out of politeness, gulped about half of it down in a few minutes, and then excused myself.

I made my way back to Main Street. When I left the brewery, I was drowsy, thinking longingly of my bed, of the cool room and the thick, heavy blankets I would cozy up in. I imagined Rose beside me there, her body contoured with mine, the delicate touch of her skin against me, wearing nothing but a t-shirt and underwear. But the exercise and the cool temperatures woke me up. There was an occasional light on in the houses I passed, but mostly I was guided by streetlight. The brewery's music continued to drift on the air, lingering faintly, until it had dissipated entirely as I arrived once again to Main Street.

Vestiges of the parade could still be seen: candy and candy wrappers littered about, trash bins filled to overflowing, street barriers that were now pushed to the side, and the floats parked down by the farm supply store. Spider webs and gory decor still hung about (only now do I remember that the more violent decorations had not been there during the parade), a chilling sight in the quiet of midnight, the faint illumination of these antique street lamps. I looked to my left beyond the farm supply store: the covered bridge, the river, the small train depot.

When I think back on all the events that would later transpire, I imagine that was the turning point. It was a literal left or right, a diverging of paths: right up Main Street and back to Mrs. Copeland's in about ten minutes, or turn left and wander around the edges of Somewhere.

I hung there suspended on the precipice for an incalculable amount of time. At that moment, there was no real reason for my pause; I presume that my unconscious or some other force recognized the monumental significance of that small choice between two routes home. Looking back, I still don't know what the *town* wanted for me at that moment, left or right. But I went left, and as Robert Frost wrote, "that has made all the difference."

My feet fell—up, down, up, down—on the cobblestone. Milky clouds ribboned across the night sky. While I walked under the yellow-orange of the street light, the moon's absence didn't matter, but the final lamp stood watch at the feed store. Everything beyond was visible only through shadow.

The floats were scattered about in various stages of dismantlement. If I hadn't known the context, I could almost imagine them having been picked over by a group of delinquents hoping to sell parts for cash, the scene of some rundown city neighborhood. They appeared gutted and flayed, like a careless mortician suddenly deciding his day was done and leaving guts and mess discarded about the corpse.

After walking another fifty yards or so, nearer to the covered bridge, I turned around and looked at the town. No car moved now, nothing. Simply stillness. Straight ahead was Main Street, bathed in dim light, and bodies hung listlessly like the scene of a massacre. Were these props for the parade that I hadn't noticed before? Street lights projected their faint illumination up through the puzzles of houses abutting downtown, like flashlight beams with fingers covering the lens. As Main Street climbed up the hill opposite me, the old houses appeared as ominous sentinels, sentient almost.

My mind, though, was over-imagining, turning the mundane into the fantastical. I was simply going for a walk, a scenic route that would end with me back in bed, sleeping in on a Saturday in which I had nothing planned. If I had felt any differently, I would have retraced my steps and headed straight back to the house. I pivoted and continued towards the river, towards the bridge and the field on the other side.

As I left Main Street, I breathed easier. Not that I'd been tense before, but I'd simply forgotten the beauty of a private walk, the thrill of independence even in such close proximity to civilization: the mind free, the body free, the refreshment of movement, alone. Someone once told me that *loneliness* and *aloneness* were two very different experiences, and I felt that truth then.

The faintest sound of running water reached me from below as I crossed the covered bridge, containing an even inkier blackness despite the windows. The field that had hosted the fair months ago was completely empty; not a trace of it remained. I remembered that it was the first time I had seen Rose. *Well, present-day Rose*, I reminded myself, remembering the vision I'd had of her outside the pet store. A warmth spread over me just thinking about her, and she dominated my mind as I continued forward in the dark.

I reached the train depot, something I'd only seen from a distance previously, and strolled around the perimeter of the building and to the train tracks. No platform, just tracks running right past the building, maybe fifteen yards away. The whole structure was red brick with a simple, gable roof. Large doors were built on the two larger sides (one looking east towards the tracks, one facing the town to the west) and small windows circled the building. Abutting one wall was a large, metal granary. And past the tracks, gentle hills rose above the horizon.

Having nothing else to see, I followed the train tracks further away from Somewhere, hands in my pockets, content. The moon peeked out occasionally, a brief silvery revelation of the landscape, but mostly I walked in darkness. Being in the perfect place to see stars without light pollution, I was hopeful, but nothing peered out of that thick blanket of night.

I don't know how long I went on like that. I had no way to tell time. Eventually the tracks, which had been running parallel to Somewhere, veered away. I finally changed course, aiming to my right, more or less a 45-degree angle back towards what seemed like an island of houses clustered around Main Street. I guessed that I was probably a mile or two away from the closest house. The landscape was no longer so wide open; trees were dotted about here and there. I had to cross back over the river, but from this location it was basically a stream, no problem for me to scramble over even in the dark.

I was sleepy by this point, halfway cursing myself for my midnight stroll as I longed for bed, but the other half of me boasted a somnolent pride at my own little adventure. I trudged onward but was startled back to complete wakefulness and lucidity when I heard a noise.

Not a squirrel-through-the-leaves noise. Something bigger. Someone was here, and they weren't trying to make their presence a secret. I looked first at Somewhere, far away in the distance while I stood in the dark, my pulse quickening, my gut filling with the juices of fight-or-flight adrenaline. Then I saw it.

About fifty yards from me, a figure was trudging through the grass, weaving its way around the occasional tree trunk. I shrank back for a moment but quickly realized the figure was not moving towards me but away from me. Then it collapsed.

Hesitancy crept over me. Now I was kicking myself for my stupidity, the weight of midnight pressing in heavily, negatively. My joyful jaunt was revealed for what it was: foolishness. I turned towards home.

I heard a groan. Sighing, I walked slowly towards the direction of the sound. But...

It was singing.

"Twisted by the heat
A thousand miles to wait
And I ain't gettin' no sleep
I see her there
At the edge of somewhere
And I ain't gettin' no sleep..."

The voice whispered that final *sleep* and quieted as I approached. The scent of sour beer hung in the air as I got nearer, a warning to be even more on my guard. People do crazy shit when they're drunk. When I could see the person lying on their back, they tensed suddenly.

"Who's there!" a voice yelled, and a young guy–had to be about my age, maybe a few years older–scrambled to his feet, his head on a swivel, scanning his surroundings wild-eyed.

The guy standing before me, however, exhibited signs of inebriation that I'd never seen before, a level of panicked, paranoid fear in his face that struck me as more than standard drunkenness.

"Hey," I said reassuringly. "You seem lost. Thought I could help." I actually glanced over my shoulder, alarmed by his reaction. Was he seeing something I wasn't? But there was nothing.

"What! Hey, what!" He turned in place, a ball of frenetic energy and craze. He was shaking as he held his hands out midair as if he was walking in the dark, afraid he might bump into something. Most unsettling, though, he would never look directly at me. His stare would sweep past me.

"Are you from Somewhere?" I asked.

"WHO IS THERE!"

To my amazement, the man fell to his knees and began sobbing in fear. "It's true, it's true, it's true, it's true," he repeated through gasps.

"What's true?" I asked. He grew stiff, alert, moving only his head, jerking it about from side to side, searching. Instinctively, I crossed over to him and put a hand on his shoulder to calm him.

He screamed and returned to his feet.

I jumped back.

The man continued to look about himself wildly, shaking and chattering in abject terror. I saw that he'd wet himself. I was absolutely bewildered.

His left arm remained suspended in the air while his right, trembling, began groping around his leg, patting his thigh, reaching for...

"Shit, man! Chill!" I yelled as he raised a gun and swung it around convulsively.

"FUCK YOU!" he screamed. He was now finally staring directly into my face, but no sign of awareness was visible in his eyes.

I hit the ground immediately as he shot wildly all around me. I crawled away; he seemed to be too busy firing to hear my movement through the grass. When I got to a safe distance, I ran for cover behind some trees and eventually slunk away back towards Somewhere, leaving the man alone in the darkness.

CHAPTER EIGHT

I didn't tell anyone about that night. I don't exactly know why either. I didn't plan *not* to. But whenever a chance arose, I'd think, *No, not you* or *No, not now.* I'd wonder, *Is that really even what happened?* It was late. I had been drinking. I was tired. In fact, the memory only existed as a dream: foggy, fragmented, surreal.

What's more, that night marked the beginning of my dreams in Somewhere. Nearly every night I started replaying some version of that scene over and over again in my sleep.

I wanted to talk to Rose about it. But to be fair, I wanted to talk to Rose about everything. What I wouldn't give to be cozied up beside her, to look into her eyes, see the expression of concern, have her grab my hand sympathetically, place my head upon her shoulder before gently lifting up my face again, bringing my mouth to hers.

"Hello."

I snapped out of my trance, my face flushing red.

"Oh, uh, sorry."

Pastor Amos sat across from me. We were at The Book and Bean near the windows looking out at Main Street. I had been attending First Baptist pretty much every Sunday, and this was now the second time that Pastor Amos had invited me for coffee before church. Barb opened her shop from 7:00-2:00 on Sundays, pretty uncommon in a small Midwest town. Most stores remained closed until the afternoon on Sundays since so many were attending church, or they were pretending to. When Pastor Amos and I had first gotten coffee a few weeks before, he had told me that The Book and Bean used to be closed on Sundays altogether, and when Barb had decided to open it, there was quite a scandal.

"The Assemblies of God church organized a boycott and tried to get it shut down," he had said. "We Baptists know a thing or two about boycotting, but," he lowered his voice, "I didn't really give a damn."

The boycott was effective for a couple of weeks apparently, but right when Barb was about to throw in the towel, things got better and not for any change of heart on the part of the town. Somewhere simply moved on from the drama of the moment, and soon enough, most of the people were secretly grateful. And most churches—the Assemblies of God church not included—actually started serving Book and Bean coffee on Sunday mornings for their parishioners.

"This *is* my sanctuary!" Barb had declared when she overheard us.

"Now Barbera," Pastor Amos said, swiveling in his seat towards her, "you know that I'm obligated to disagree with you. The church is a *gathering* of believers around the liturgy of the Word."

"Liturgy of the Word? You sound kinda fancy, Amos. You sure Clem's not rubbing off on you? That sounds like somethin' they'd be sayin' up at Good Shepherd."

Pastor Amos laughed.

"Besides, this is a gatherin' if I'm not mistaken." She gestured to us having coffee. "And there's the Word over there," she nodded towards the shelves of books.

"Well, how can I dispute that logic?"

That conversation was weeks before, and here we were again. I was ruminating on how much had changed even in such a short amount of time. On the one hand, it seemed that after two months of living in Somewhere, I was really beginning to feel at home. Not that I hadn't felt welcome before, but of course there's always a period of adapting to a new environment. I sensed that I was making genuine progress, that I was finding a rhythm, and my community was growing. On the other hand, whatever had happened the night of the Halloween parade—only two nights prior—sat inside my gut like an uninvited guest.

Pastor Amos lounged in the seat beside me, one leg crossed over the knee of the other, holding his coffee with one hand. He always seemed to carry himself in sort of a wide-open, lordly posture, carefree and in control of his environment. I, on the other hand, had a tendency to hunch over, closed off, timid even. At that moment, I was leaning forward with both hands cradling my mug.

"So how are you feeling these days, Lee?"

"Good, good," I replied, my standard response to such questions. But he didn't continue the conversation immediately. Peering out the window a moment before, I now looked over at him in the hanging silence. He was staring at me with eyebrows raised, inviting more.

"Lee," he continued when he saw that he had my attention, "how are you *really* doing?"

"Um... I guess things are *mostly* good."

"Yeah? Why do you say *mostly* good? What's going on these days? I see you spending time with a certain young woman," Pastor Amos prodded, smiling.

I blushed some and admitted that I had been spending time with Rose but also listed Kenny and Eleanor and some of the others.

"And what about that is only mostly good?"

"No, that's all good," I replied. "It's just..." I hesitated but decided to open up a little. "It's just that...okay, this is going to sound weird," I said, re-situating myself in the chair, "but I've been having...uh...weird dreams lately."

The truth was that my persistent string of dreams hadn't really even started yet, so my comment was somewhat prophetic. But I *had* dreamed the previous two nights, replaying the scene with the stranger. I wasn't ready to share what actually happened; it was easier just to label it a dream. Anyway, I still wasn't convinced that it had not been a dream.

Pastor Amos, rather than being inquisitive or inquiring more, sat down his coffee, folded his hands, and looked up at the ceiling. Twice I thought I saw his mouth twitch as if he was about to tell me something but then resumed his silence.

"To sleep, perchance to dream," he finally muttered. At first he said this to himself, but then he looked at me with a faint smile. "There's the rub. For in this sleep of death what dreams may come."

"The Bard!" Barb yelled from across the room, spoiling any moment of gravity that Pastor Amos was attempting to create. He leaned into Barb's vision and grinned.

"Hmm... So what about those dreams?" Pastor Amos asked.

"I don't know. I don't know how to describe it. But it's sort of put me in a weird state of mind." Pastor Amos leaned in, forgoing his easygoing, open posture.

"Lee, do you know what *thin places* are?" He resumed in a serious tone, free from Barb's interruptions.

It seemed as though I had heard the term maybe, but I couldn't recall the meaning.

"No, not really."

"Thin places are points in the world in which the natural realm and the supernatural realm overlap."

"What are you saying?" I asked, an unexplainable clamminess coating my skin. Pastor Amos leaned back in his chair, smiled, and returned to his normal demeanor.

"Nothing much. Just that dreams can be more than simple manifestations of our subconscious and all that Freudian bullshit."

"I guess as a pastor you kind of *have* to believe in that stuff, huh?" I chuckled lightheartedly, but he did not laugh in response.

"On the contrary, very few religious people do. Their religion is antiseptic, clean, tidy. I'm not saying they're unbelievers, just that they don't want their spirituality spilling out of their nice little boxes; they don't need the lid coming off. They perpetuate a very rigid system out of fear. That's what I believe. Their *calling*, if you will, is not to present the truth but rather to make the truth more palatable to modern minds. They tell themselves that they're protecting their flocks from what lies beneath, but they're actually scared as hell and don't want to see for themselves.

"But you know what's funny? I once read that around 80% of Muslims practice some manner of folk religion. Amulets, charms, the evil eye, all that shit. That's not part of the formal religion. The Imams don't teach that. The people just do it. The people. So, try as they might, the religious leaders can't stop the people. Which makes you wonder, who's really running the freak show?" I shrank back a little as Pastor Amos's eyes flashed, a side of him I hadn't seen before. I could tell he was just getting started.

"And if you think," he continued, "that the blending of folk religion with the culture's dominant religion only happens in the Middle East, or maybe even in Asia, you're a fool. It happens everywhere. Look at druidism in England. Or go read *The Scarlet Letter*. Seriously. The genius of that book isn't its story of sin, penance, and divine justice. That's all been overdone, and it had been overdone by Hawthorne's lifetime. No, the genius of the book lies in its amalgamation of Puritan Christianity and the wildness of folk religion embodied in the character of Pearl. Whether or not Hawthorne believed in it himself, he tapped into the *true* New England consciousness. Puritanism was all about white-washing the faith, erasing the superstition of Catholicism, boarding up its icons. But it doesn't work. The magic always creeps back in.

"Jesus talked about this in a way: 'When the unclean spirit is gone out of a man, he walketh through dry places, seeking rest, and findeth none. Then he saith, I will return into my house from whence I came out; and when he is come, he findeth it empty, swept, and garnished. Then goeth he, and taketh with himself seven other spirits more wicked than himself, and they enter in and dwell there: and the last state of that man is worse than the first.'

"Puritanism was all about emptying, sweeping clean, and garnishing the house of the Lord after kicking out the demon of Catholicism. But what Hawthorne showed us is that the spirits always come back, and when they do, it's almost always in greater force than before. That's what I'm telling you. Folk religion, magic, it's everywhere.

"It's all over Latin America. It's in the voodoo of the Deep South. It's in Catholicism with all its relics and talismans: crucifixes, holy water, medallions from saints. Any time you imbue a natural object with supernatural abilities, you're practicing folk religion.

"Our ancient mothers and fathers saw spirituality everywhere; it's in the evolution of our blood to do the same. And don't just blame Catholic superstition. It's in Protestant religion, too. Guardian angels are just the other side of the coin shared by the evil eye. Hell, we even turn the Bible into some sort of literal, magical object. I see it all the time."

My head was spinning. I inquired about a drop of water, and he was teaching me the ocean.

"So, the thin places that you mentioned, these are in the Bible?" I asked.

"No and yes," he said. "Thin places are not called by that name in the Bible. The idea can be traced to the Pre-Christian Celts, and there are similar concepts in other religions as well, but medieval Christians soon adopted the concept. But the Bible is filled with transfigurative *places*— not just moments—where people walked with God, where heaven and earth embraced. The Garden of Eden. Mount Sinai. The temple.

"Like I've been saying, this is all only fractionally related to religion. Religion is, in many ways, antithetical to true spirituality. I'm one of the weird ones, though. I'm a believer." He paused. I was staring out the window again, my mind focused on everything that Pastor Amos had said. And, to be honest, I was a bit amused by this string of ideas I never would have expected from a Baptist preacher in rural Missouri.

"It's true," he finished. My head snapped back, recognizing those words.

In the service that day, Pastor Amos preached from 1 Samuel 28. I assumed that it was a coincidence that he had chosen that text, although I guess he could have quickly changed his sermon based on our conversation at The Book and Bean before. He seemed to have that kind of ability to adapt on the fly. Or perhaps his sermon preparation influenced his lengthy response earlier.

"Many of us don't know what to do with a passage like this," he was saying. "It doesn't fit into our categories of biblical orthodoxy. Hebrews 9:27 says, 'And as it is unto men once to die, and after this the judgment.' And yet, here we read that Saul visits a witch and calls up the ghost of Samuel. Though scholars argue how this could be, Samuel answers as though he is the real Samuel, the famous prophet who was already dead. There is no indication that the Samuel of this scene is anyone other than the true Samuel. 'Why hast thou disquieted me, to bring me up?' Samuel asks of Saul. Other biblical translations use the word *disturb* instead.

"So why would I choose this passage for today's sermon? We *have* just celebrated Halloween, but that's not the reason. Is it to convince you that ghosts are real? Maybe." He chuckled and looked at me from behind the pulpit. The rest of the congregation gave a chuckle in response; I couldn't discern if the congregational laughter had an edge of discomfort or if this topic was nothing out of the ordinary.

I was sitting next to Rose, Eleanor, and a girl named Jane. David wasn't at church that morning, and everyone else from my growing circle of acquaintances attended other churches or didn't go to church at all. Jane always sat with us on Sundays but was a very conservative girl who never went out with us on the weekends; she was nice, though.

"I think the real reason, however," Pastor Amos continued, "is that I want to teach the whole scope of the Scriptures, not just the easy parts. And truth be told, this passage has always fascinated me, haunted me even. On the one hand, this section indicates one more manner in which King Saul has been disobedient, calling upon the aid of a sorceress, a medium, to perform necromancy for his own convenience despite the fact that necromancy and the magical arts had been outlawed in Israel. The passage also demonstrates just how much Israel depended on the prophetic gifts of Samuel. Even in death he was sought out as a more reliable source of truth than the living prophets. However, while this may not be the specific purpose of this section of the Bible, I want to focus on a secondary lesson from these verses.

"There is a spiritual realm beyond what most people can see. I *know* you believe me in this." He paused dramatically for effect. "And as I was saying to my friend Lee when we were down at Barb's grabbing coffee..." All eyes turned to me. Rose elbowed me and whispered, "Wow, you're so famous." I reddened, but I actually didn't mind the attention.

"I was telling him that while many people will give an intellectual assent to the spiritual realm, very few truly embrace the mystery of the supernatural. And friends," he lowered his voice and scanned his audience slowly, "it... is... a mystery."

Our small group of four was chatting about the service afterwards while we stood in the lobby of the church, other congregants milling about and conversing as well. Rose and Eleanor were joking about how we'd just sat through another one of Pastor Amos's strange sermons. Apparently, he *did* have a bit of a reputation for using unusual Bible passages and preaching unusual messages. Jane, on the other hand, was quiet, but I noted that, in this case, it didn't appear to be a timid quietness. Rather, she seemed to be deep in thought about something.

In the middle of our conversation, Pastor Amos walked over and pulled me aside. He invited me over to the house sometime and said the girls wanted to hang out with the British man again.

"Well, I don't know about a British man," I laughed, "bu' I guess I c'n wo'k on my accent mor'," I added, butchering my attempt at sounding British.

I rejoined the group, and Eleanor gave a loud, fake cough that sounded a lot like "teacher's pet."

CHAPTER NINE

Tom walked into the store as I finished helping a customer.

"Hey, Lee. Has the order come in?"

It was Friday, almost a week after "The Incident" (as it had come to be known in my mind). Fridays were the days we received new stock or shop supplies.

"Yep, it arrived just before that lady came in. I haven't had a chance to put it away."

"No worries. I'll do it," he said as he nodded towards another person coming in and meandered to the back. A woman, tall and commanding, entered. She wore tan, baggy pants, an oddly patterned sweater, large glasses, and her wildly curly hair contained some kind of beaded braid. Flecks of paint speckled her arms.

"Hi, Maggie," I beamed. She smiled back.

"Hello, Lee Thompson."

"It's good to see you. It's been a few weeks. How can I help you?"

"I have another finished piece, friend. How have you been?"

We chatted for a few minutes before she walked back outside to grab her painting. I held the door open for her as she brought it in and set it on the counter.

I inhaled sharply and dropped the coffee mug I had been holding. Both hot coffee and splinters of ceramic painted the counter, and I quickly scrambled to clean it up while Maggie jumped in to assist.

"What is it, Lee Thompson?"

"Oh, nothing," I responded, brushing everything into the small wastebasket behind the counter. "It's, uh, it's enchanting. Does it have a title?"

"I'm calling it 'Self-Portrait, Somewhere at Night.'" She eyed me, but her look of concern now transformed as she furrowed her eyebrows. "Friend," she said with an edge in her voice, "you do not strike me as someone who is so easily affected carnally by female anatomy."

It's true, the painting presented Maggie nude, and say what she will, if that's how she looked undressed, it was hard not to notice.

But that's not why I had gasped.

"Um, it's not that," I mumbled. "It's just, you have presented Somewhere in a way... the way you've painted Somewhere speaks to me."

She seemed unconvinced.

"Where is this?" I asked.

"What? What do you mean?"

"I mean, where were you for this painting? Like, what's the vantage point?" I was fumbling.

"Well, this view of the town would be a little south of here. I don't know, maybe a couple of miles. I took a walk over there and sketched out the perspective before returning to my studio. Why?"

I continued staring at the painting, unnerved. Maggie's naked form appeared in the lower left corner, but, besides the shading, she used only one color to paint herself: white. It was a translucent white, though; the landscape could be seen through her. Above Maggie, in the distance, was Somewhere. Her painting employed Impressionist techniques—layered colors and short strokes, an effect of movement throughout the piece—but the perspective was clear: through the eyes of the stranger last Saturday, this is exactly how I would have been seen (naked, translucent features aside).

"It's just coincidence," I finally responded, "but I was literally walking in this same spot the other day. I was just surprised to see Somewhere from this angle. It was a nice walk and a great view of the town." *Also, I had this weird altercation,* I wanted to say, *and it seems that you've painted*

this through the eyes of some stranger you've never met, and the naked fig-
ure's not you; it's me.

Maggie continued to look at me; I couldn't decipher her thoughts or expressions. In the end, though, my answer seemed to satisfy her. She smiled again, and her warmth towards me returned.

"You know what, Mr. Lee Thompson? I would like to invite you for dinner." As Maggie left–after I gratefully accepted her invitation–I reflected, not for the last time, on my immediate affection for Somewhere.

"It's true."

I stared into the stranger's face. Rather than fear, rather than blabbering, the face was almost completely expressionless, vacant.

"What's true?" I asked.

"It's true."

I looked down at myself: my hands, my arms. Translucent. I was standing there naked. But I only knew it like a fact. There was no embarrassment even though I was staring at this stranger who was fully clothed himself. Over my shoulder I saw Somewhere. Just like the other night. Just like in Maggie's painting.

"It's true," he repeated, unprompted.

"What is? Did something happen? Is there something I need to know?"

"It's true."

My querying was futile. I tried to stir from my place, but though I could turn my head to look around me, I was unable to detach my feet from where they were rooted. I strained as anxiety swept over me. I needed to run away. I needed to escape this man...

"It's true."

"Dammit! What, man? What's true?"

"It's true."

"Let me leave!" I cried.

I heard a rustling and jerked my head around. I had a moment of confusion. When I was in this place the other night, the rustling indicated this stranger's movement, but he was still in front of me.

"It's true."

I gazed through the trees. Maggie. She approached—fully clothed—until she stood next to the stranger.

"It *is* true, Lee Thompson." Her face exhibited more lucidity than the stranger's, and she didn't keep repeating the same phrase over and over again. She wore a look of kindness, maybe condescension even. Like she cared about me, was babying my ignorance but could do nothing more about it.

"Maggie? Why are you here?"

She simply smiled faintly.

Another movement.

Rose.

I felt a brief electrical charge as she walked nearer; I was standing there naked after all, and she was seeing all of me. The *fact* of my nakedness was now more than just something I was aware of offhand. I forgot about everything else, aroused by Rose's presence, self-conscience of my inability to hide my arousal. I followed her movement, the shape of her legs in the denim jeans, the way her shirt rustled and fit over her body, her chest, the shape of her.

But she planted herself on the other side of the stranger, opposite Maggie, and the momentary passion was gone.

From the corner of my eye, I noticed my skin changing. It was solidifying, losing its translucence. I glanced up. The opposite was happening to the others. Flesh and blood before, now dimming, fading.

Rose, who hadn't yet spoken, said, "Look closely," before disappearing altogether along with the others. My feet unstuck. In fact, I felt like

I wasn't moving myself but simply walking along unconsciously, like a scene was floating by me, but when I looked down, I saw my feet and legs performing the act of walking.

I passed by gravestones, not the clean-cut, squared markers of newer plots but rows and rows of strange angles and stunning figures: dramatic angels with wings spread wide and melancholy angels sitting pensively, crosses of varying shapes and sizes, mausoleums, obelisks, and other monuments. Gray and worn, lichen crawling over the bodies of stone.

As I glided by the tombs, I peered at the inscriptions but couldn't see. *Look, Look*, kept playing in my head, but I couldn't. I strained my eyes. I tried to slow down. I was desperate.

And then I was awake, alerted by the same sound I had been hearing most every night. I glanced at the clock beside my bed.

3:00.

The loud creaking of a door and the thud of feet descending stairs somewhere in the house.

In the beginning, I thought nothing of this. Mrs. Copeland was, after all, living in the rest of the house. She was older. Old people pee frequently at night, right? But there were things that left me uneasy: the absolute precision of this occurrence when it happened—3:00—and the fact that, though I heard footsteps descending stairs, I never heard them ascend.

There was more, though: an energy in the house, a force, a movement, a buzz. I normally heard the door and steps below whenever I was already half-awake or lightly sleeping. At other times, though, I heard stirring right around me, jolting me awake when I was sleeping more soundly. Was it the furniture in my room scraping along the floor, only a fraction of a second, a millimeter of movement perhaps? Or the frame tapping on the wall like the other night. Once, the shower started, the cascading water ending abruptly, leaving me only with my doubts—*Is this all in my head?*

When I asked Mrs. Copeland about it—casually one day, embarrassed by childish fears—she shrugged and mentioned the New Madrid Fault Line running through the southeastern portion of the state. The shower, she said, is just one of those things that happen in an old house. *Let me know*, she had told me, *if it happens again, and we'll get a plumber out to take a look at it.*

I was aware of the fault line; it ran closer to where I grew up in St. Louis than it did to Somewhere. Still, that wouldn't account for the clockwork precision of the tremors' occurrences. What began to take shape in my head, though, were the ramblings of Pastor Amos: *thin places.*

I was happy to visit Maggie and Lenora, her housemate. After knocking on their door, I waited and surveyed my surroundings: a wide veranda that wrapped around the side of the house, trees now almost all entirely disrobed of their colorful leaves, leaves now lying in heaps of varying shades of brown. I remembered that Thanksgiving was only weeks away.

Concerned by mom's strange memory lapses, I had decided to go home and see my parents. Besides, I loved Thanksgiving and have always enjoyed spending it with my family (and our friend Miriam). And the day after, the beginning of the Christmas season. I had always said that Thanksgiving was extra special because it was a great holiday in its own right, but it was also the gateway to Christmas and all its festivities and traditions. While on Black Friday everyone else was out mauling each other or glued to their computer monitors shopping online, we would put up the Christmas tree, drink hot chocolate, and watch *National Lampoon's Christmas Vacation.*

I was absorbed in this reverie when Maggie and Lenora opened the door. I hadn't yet met Lenora. She was a noticeably stark contrast to Maggie. Whereas Maggie always appeared to me as some sort of woodland nymph with her wild hair and her free-flowing style, Lenora looked as though she could be going to work in the city. She wore a simple, burgundy dress that went down just past her knees and a white cardigan along with white flats, a white belt, and a pendant necklace. Her hair was a dark brown, tastefully cropped and carefully maintained.

"Lee Thompson!" Maggie greeted me with warmth. "This is Lenora."

"Hi, Lee, it's nice to meet you," Lenora said, offering a firm handshake. *Did* she work in the city?

"Did you find your way over here okay?" Maggie asked.

"Yeah, no problem. I live just a few blocks away."

"You live with Mindy, right?" Lenora asked.

"Mindy?"

"Mindy Copeland. Or am I mistaken?"

"Oh, yes, yes. Mrs. Copeland. I keep forgetting her first name is Mindy."

"Sorry, yes, Mrs. Copeland. For some reason I've always been a bit informal." Which, I noted, was ironic considering the aesthetically disheveled of the two was the one who only referred to me by both my first and last name.

"Come in," Maggie said, gesturing. "Let us show you our space."

I stepped into the entryway. The walls were lined with lavender wallpaper spotted with eggshell-white lilies. The hardwood floors and trim—baseboards and intricate crown molding—were all a deep brown. Stepping in a few feet more, Maggie and Lenora pointed me to a library sitting room on the left. A leather loveseat and oversized chair set rested on top of a Persian rug and made an *L* shape, connected by a small end table. Shelves of books lined each wall, and two great windows let in ample light. I was dazzled by the sight and a bit disappointed that this was my first time getting to see the inside of one of these great houses (and, to be honest, a bit annoyed that Mrs. Copeland was so rigid).

"This is *my* space," Lenora smiled.

"Yes, and over here is *my* space," Maggie said, dragging me across the hall. "The parlor." Maggie gestured to the room with a sweep of her hand. The parlor was about twice the size of the library but clearly the territory of an artist. It wasn't difficult to imagine what it could be if decorated in a more traditional fashion, but there was nothing traditional about how Maggie had taken over and claimed it as her studio.

What appeared to be a great chandelier hung down the middle of the room, but it was covered with a black sheet. ("I can't paint with a million refractions of light dancing all over my canvases," she had pointed out.) The trim was the same around the room, but the wallpaper was a Toile de Jouy design: a white background with the classic French sketches peppering the walls from floor to ceiling. The rest of the room was a menagerie of shapes: trunks of varying sizes, end tables not sitting at the end of anything, dressers, oversized chairs, sofas, loveseats, rocking chairs, stools, ottomans, and a hundred random and uncategorizable objects placed throughout. All of these were visible amidst a patchwork of canvas drop cloths of dried, splattered paint. And finally, easels stood up through it all like little Eiffel Towers. Several large windows also let in sufficient light, and Maggie stood back proudly.

"It may look like a mess," she noted, "but this is my paradise. Here I can do real work."

"As long as I'm *really* quiet," Lenora added, rolling her eyes.

The whole environment only added to the persona of Maggie's eccentric genius. I smiled to myself, thinking again of the association I had made between Maggie and Professor Trelawney. There was a similar aesthetic, sure, but there was something about Maggie and the work she produced that clearly demonstrated a keen vision, the eye of a true prophet rather than the mouthpiece of an accidental mystic (no offense, Trelawney!).

After finishing the tour on the second floor, the three of us made our way back to the kitchen where a breakfast nook table was already prepared, the aromas of French cooking inviting me like a siren song: "boeuf bourguignon and a Niçoise salad" Lenora told me. "Maggie said you were an art history student; it's not every day we get someone who has a little more taste for culture than our neighbors." She said this not in derision but playfully. As we re-entered the kitchen, though, I noticed a door on the far end was ajar.

Coldness emanated from that door and enveloped me.

I stood staring while Maggie and Lenora continued with some side conversation about what they needed to pick up at the store for the following week. I don't know how I arrived, but the next thing I knew, my hand was grasping the edge of the door, pulling it further open. The cold was unsettling but curiously inviting. Steps descended into the dark, an ice cave. It begged to be explored. I imagined a faint hum, like a living thing.

Slam!

I jumped back, startled, a spell broken.

"Sorry, Lee Thompson," Maggie said kindly but firmly. "Just the cellar, but dinner's ready so let's have a seat."

"Yes, I'm very sorry. I don't know what I was doing."

"No harm," Lenora stated sweetly, coming over to usher me to my seat.

We spent the whole evening talking, aided in part by the bottle and a half of red wine we managed to get through together. Lenora didn't work in the city, but she was a small-town lawyer with urban sensibilities (that's how she described it to me anyway). She noted the difficulties of being stuck in a place like Somewhere and the ways in which a small Midwest town bristles at unconventional female figures, but she admitted to still being in love with Somewhere and that she got along well with *nearly* everyone.

Maggie discussed her art some, which was really intriguing to me, but like a true artist, she was content with surface level discussion about her process, unable, she said, to articulate everything that goes on in her mind when she's working. However, she seemed fascinated by my stay in Europe and would ask for some of the most minute details. I had to really strain in order to remember "exactly what you saw, every nook and cranny" of Bourton-on-the-Water in the Cotswolds. Though I've spent plenty of time describing art, I didn't have the adequate vocabulary or memory to do justice to the quaint village whose rustic charm had been fanatically maintained over the years.

Eventually I said goodnight, stepping down from the veranda and into the brisk, cool night. After winding around a few street corners, I realized that navigating between Maggie and Lenora's house and my apartment was easier in the daytime, but at just that moment I glimpsed a prominent street that I could follow all the way to Mrs. Copeland's driveway. Only I was wrong.

Somehow I had strayed down unfamiliar streets and found myself staring through black, wrought-iron bars to the gravestones beyond. *Laurel Hill Cemetery* read the sign hanging from the gate, and I thought back to my dream. *Look*, Rose had told me in my dream.

I pulled gingerly at the gate but realized that a chain and padlock kept it fastened shut. I turned to resume my search for the way back to the apartment.

Look, echoed in my head, a scene from my dream. Suddenly, I was filled with an unquenchable desire to look at the headstones, at the inscriptions.

The fence was not too formidable; I could easily climb over. I had just placed my foot on a lower crossbar when I heard the crunching of steps. Spinning around, I saw a friendly-looking man walking a panting collie in my direction. I quickly returned to the road and smiled sheepishly.

"Good evening!" he remarked.

"Hello."

"Out for a bit of a stroll?" His tone was chipper, but he seemed intent on understanding what I was up to. He was slightly built, long skinny legs, matted down dark hair and a pallid face. I couldn't get the image out of my mind of Pee-wee Herman standing in front of me. With an effort I caught the chuckle before it frog-leaped out of my throat.

"On my way home from some friends' house," I responded.

"Ah, I see," he said, stupidly wagging his head up and down in sync with his dog's swishing tail. "Laurel Hill Cemetery is very old, you know."

"Yeah, it looks pretty fascinating."

"Sure, sure. That it does. You know, no one really visits the cemetery much anymore."

"No?"

"No. It's become a bit of a landmark for us, you know. Best way to maintain something, look but don't touch." He laughed like it was a hilarious joke.

"Lee, right?"

"Yep, it seems everyone knows my name around here."

"Of course, of course. You know, it's not every day we get a new friend in Somewhere. I'm Charles by the way." He offered a handshake like it was a broken arm, and I accepted it gingerly and awkwardly.

"Nice to meet you," I said, inadvertently wiping my hand on my pant leg. "Well, I'm headed back to my place. Have a good night."

"Good night!"

After another missed turn or two, I found a familiar street and made my way back home.

CHAPTER TEN

For the second night in a row, I ascended the porch steps as the invited guest to someone's home. Unlike most of the other houses in Somewhere, the Whitakers lived in a very modest church parish, a white, one-story house with wood siding. The Whitaker girls, Anna and Charlotte, answered the door, screamed "It's the British man! It's the British man!" and ran away *eek*ing and *aah*ing. Pastor Amos sauntered over to the door, chuckling.

"See what you've done. I told you. If I hadn't invited you myself, my girls would have found a way to. Come on in."

I stepped inside, and Pastor Amos ushered me over to a love seat while he took a seat in a La-Z-Boy recliner. Barely had I sat down, though, when the girls were back, no longer squealing. In fact, they had assumed a regal air, with pursed lips, noses up, and standing up straight and proper.

"This way if you please," Anna stated with an affected British accent.

"Yeah, this way please," Charlotte added, garnering a glance of annoyance from her older sister. Smiling, I looked over at Pastor Amos who merely shrugged. I followed the girls down the hallway and into Charlotte's room. On a small table they had prepared a tea party.

In one chair sat a teddy bear with a plastic crown worn like a necklace since it was too large for the bear's head. The other three chairs were empty for us though I had to set mine aside and just sit on the ground.

"Welcome to high tea," declared Anna as she scooped up the plastic tea pot and began pouring the invisible brew into play cups. Charlotte didn't wait for Anna and just grabbed hers before pressing the cup's rim to the teddy bear's lips.

"Here, Prince Bear," she said, clipping all the *r*s when she spoke, a small reminder that she was only five years old.

"Not now," Anna hissed. "I haven't even served you tea. You're not even giving Prince Bear anything to drink." Charlotte's eyes drooped as she whispered "Sorry" and returned her cup to the table.

At first the tea party began somewhat formally. Anna would ask in mock elegance for more accounts of my time in England. I told them about taking trains everywhere which fascinated Anna especially.

"We have a train stop here," she noted, "but Daddy says it's not for people."

"Tell us about princesses!" Charlotte shouted after a few minutes of such proper manners, unable to contain her own enthusiasm.

"Charlotte, stop interrupting," Anna scolded.

"But I want to know about princesses," she pouted.

"If you keep interrupting, I'm going to tell Mr. Lee about the woman." Charlotte's eyes immediately bolted first to me and then to her sister with a look of pleading and apprehension.

"What woman?" I asked, intrigued by this sisterly secret.

"Oh, sometimes Charlotte draws bad things," Anna stated, looking down at the teddy bear that she now had in her hands. "One of them is the dead woman."

The temperature in the room seemed to drop about ten degrees. Both girls were quiet now, fidgeting awkwardly at the miniature table.

"We're not supposed to talk about her," Charlotte whispered in a mousy voice. I swung my head back and forth, a metronome of confusion.

"You...uh...draw a dead woman?" I finally said, feeling my thoughts smooshed around in my head like oversized furniture in a warehouse. Charlotte appeared to be on the edge of tears.

"She visits me," Charlotte whispered, and she grabbed a stuffed animal that hadn't been invited to the tea party. I sat puzzled.

"Maybe you could get rid of those bad drawings," I suggested.

"She's not supposed to," Anna replied, trying to appear disinterested. I was confused. Not supposed to draw bad things or not supposed to get rid of the drawings? I didn't ask.

"Anyway," I said, "you know, there's more to England than just princesses."

"Like what?" Both girls straightened up and their demeanor communicated that they were ready to change subjects. Anna even handed Prince Bear to Charlotte who received him gratefully. Not being a father myself and, therefore, not privy to the bizarre world of young kids' imaginations, I was only happy to oblige.

"Like Arthur and the round table and Merlin?" Anna asked.

"Wow," I said, impressed. "How do you know about them?"

"Books," Charlotte responded and rolled her eyes at her sister. At that moment, Pastor Amos poked his head in.

"Okay, little fairy princesses, dinner's ready."

"I'm not a fairy," Anna responded adamantly.

"I am!" Charlotte shouted as she sprinted over to him and jumped straight into his arms without even waiting for him to open them. But Pastor Amos deftly caught Charlotte and twirled her around before marching towards the kitchen. Anna darted after them, and I, too, got up to go, but something caught my eye.

All over Charlotte's room, crayon drawings were hanging up, mostly different animals. I noticed some of Charlotte and Anna and one with the whole family. But one was visible hanging on the wall in the back of the half-opened closet and was different from the others. I inched over, holding my breath. Rather than the bright colors of all her other drawings, this one was done in black crayon. When I got close enough, my suspicions were confirmed.

There was drawn a woman, lightly shaded, with what appeared to be a rope pulled up above her head though not attached to anything. No face visible.

My heartbeat thumped inside my chest, echoed in my head. Unconsciously I reached my hand out and slid the tips of my fingers over the drawing. As I did so, a shriek pierced through my head. I jumped to my feet, crashing my skull against the hanging bar inside the closet. Gingerly rubbing the growing bump, I spun around and poked my head into the hallway.

Glancing momentarily back at the closet, an image formed in my mind: a closed door gently opening. As if the latch hadn't completely set in place, the door slid out an inch or two–a sigh rather than a heaving breath.

Despite having only seen the living room and Charlotte's room, I knew this door was in the Whitaker's house, though I didn't know where. I grew colder. I willed the door to swing open just a little more, enough for me to slip beyond it.

I jumped as I felt a presence beside me. It was only Charlotte standing in the door frame, holding her teddy bear limply by her side.

"It's time for dinner," she uttered mechanically, with zero show of emotion, before leaving.

Dinner was great, and Charlotte had returned almost immediately to her chipper self. After dessert—brownie sundaes with an assortment of colored sprinkle options–was story time, and after that, Tracy took the girls to get ready for bed.

"Good night Mr. Lee!" Charlotte and Anna both said before being ushered down the hall.

"Story time before bed," I mused when they were gone and I was alone with Pastor Amos. "No TV. I'm impressed."

"Yeah, well, we rarely have guests over, so I think they were on their best behavior. Tracy and I too, I guess, because we usually let them watch their favorite TV show before story time, but we agreed that the brownie sundaes would be the compromise for no Bugs Bunny."

"Bugs Bunny? Classic. I didn't know kids were still watching that these days."

"DVD," Pastor Amos admitted, picking up the case. "I don't really know what's on TV these days; we don't watch it much, and the kids don't know any difference, so Looney Tunes it is. Hey, do you have to get going? If not, I thought I'd show you the private den."

"Private den?" I asked, grinning and raising my eyebrows, bemused

"Well, I've always hated the term 'man cave,' and if anyone in this house has a cave, it's my wife. She's basically commandeered the guest bedroom and turned it into her own luxury island of house plants. Besides, my private den is really just my office."

He guided me through the kitchen to the back door. As we were exiting into the frigid November night, I glanced over my shoulder and saw the door from my earlier vision. I gasped inaudibly.

Pastor Amos directed me to a large shed on the back corner of their property. I nearly laughed at this "private den." From the outside it looked like a den alright, something fit for animals perhaps but nothing akin to an office or man cave. I imagined a folding chair and ugly end table sitting near a dilapidated bookshelf and surrounded by garden tools. However, as I walked inside, I was clearly mistaken by this perfect example of not judging a book by its cover. Isn't this what mafia hideouts are like?

"Oh, wow!" I exclaimed when Pastor Amos had flipped on the light and closed the door behind us.

The room's layout was simple enough, just a square space. It *was*, after all, a shed. But that was the only thing simple about it. Rather, I felt like I had stepped back in time to a miniature Old World library or maybe a sitting room in Oxford. Besides gaps where the two windows were and where we had just entered, shelves lined each of the walls and were filled completely with books. A Persian rug was spread out on the floor so that only the thinnest lines of concrete were visible. A small desk and wooden rolling chair were situated in the space under one of the windows. Two high backed, leather chairs with ottomans sat slightly back from the middle of the room beside an end table and lamp. There was also a space heater hidden nearby that was already warming the place.

Pastor Amos, smiling at my expression of disbelief, gestured towards one of the chairs. We both sat, and he pulled out two whiskey glasses and a bottle of expensive-looking scotch from a cabinet in the end table.

"A little nightcap," he said, winking and pouring a shot—or two— into each of the glasses.

CHAPTER ELEVEN

"Hey, Tom," I said, getting his attention as he leaned over some book-keeping ledgers in the back of the shop.

"What's up?"

"I was planning on visiting my parents for Thanksgiving next week."

He sat up straight, giving me his full attention.

"I, uh, thought I'd take advantage of the time off and go see them," I continued. Something in Tom's face expressed displeasure. I had been meaning to make a bold request and ask off through Christmas in order to try and figure out more of what was going on with my mom, but that request stuck in my throat.

"And?" Tom said with a slight edge in his voice.

"And, uh, umm, I don't know. I was just saying. So, what do you usually do for Thanksgiving?" Something felt off about this exchange. I wanted to go back to the counter.

"I'll go to the parade—"

"—there's a Thanksgiving parade?"

"We're a small community. We like to celebrate whenever we can."

"Really? Wow." I was impressed and maybe even a tad disappointed to be leaving. Tom's demeanor changed slightly. He smiled.

"Yes, it's a lot of fun. It's no Macy's Day parade, but it's every bit as big as our Halloween parade."

"And let me guess, Christmas too?"

"Nah. We have lots of different events, though. The tree lighting, Christmas markets. The candlelight Christmas walk."

"How do more people not know about this place? Somewhere should be in every Missouri guidebook and tourism webpage."

"Well, we may like our festivals and gatherings, but we're still private. It's a small community." *Small community. Yeah, that's a theme around here*, I thought.

"Anyway," Tom resumed, "all my extended family will be getting together and eating until we can't fit into our pants. Eating is like a sport for us Burleys. Well, except for the actual sport–the Turkey Bowl."

"Turkey Bowl?"

"A little backyard football game. It's a Thanksgiving tradition. In fact, we'll probably get some other families to come over and play too. You know, Lee," he paused somewhat dramatically, "we'd sure love to have you over. What do you say? Come on, you just moved here. You've spent, what, *every* Thanksgiving with your family?"

He wasn't wrong.

"What's *one* Thanksgiving spent with new friends in a new community? I guarantee you'll love it. Besides, you'll probably be wanting to go home for Christmas too, and that's only a little over a month away."

Though something told me that Tom would have this same conversation with me as Christmas drew nearer, he did have me thinking. It really *would* be fun to be here at Thanksgiving, especially if it's as big as he was making it out to be. And of course, well, Rose.

Always Rose. I never stopped thinking of her. She was constantly in the back of my mind. And maybe I'd get to see her for Thanksgiving. Maybe her family had a similar day-after Thanksgiving tradition like my family. Maybe I'd sit beside her, the two of us in our pajamas sipping hot chocolate and watching Clark Griswold figure out how to connect his monstrous Christmas light display.

I was in full daydreaming mode but forced myself back to reality, back to Tom.

"Yeah, okay, I'll think about it."

He looked like he wanted to say more, but then shrugged, acting like it was no big deal either way.

"Whatever you decide is fine," he said, turning back to his ledger.

I had always wanted to become such a regular at a coffee shop that the workers knew my name, like that line from *Cheers*. There was a Starbucks down the road from where I grew up, and I remember an old guy named Jerry was always there when I was, and all the workers knew Jerry and joked with him. It helped that he was retired and *literally* there every day, but still, that had stuck with me. At The Book and Bean, Barb had known my name from day one, but the satisfaction of that turned to a fear that if I didn't maintain my frequent visits, I'd lose my hallowed position. *Not like I'm really in danger of people forgetting my name* here, I mused.

"Well, hello, young man," Barb greeted me from behind the counter. "What's on the menu?"

"I'll have a mocha, please." She raised her eyebrows.

"Mixin' it up today, I see. Not your usual black coffee." The corner of my mouth twitched upward, suppressing an involuntary grin. She said *usual*. Like, *I'll have the usual, please.* Yeah, I was in.

"Yeah, something different," I admitted.

"Whatcha reading now?" Since finishing my King novel, I had continued to use the bookstore to resource my reading material, only occasionally leafing through one of the other books I'd brought with me.

"Um, *Pride and Prejudice* actually." I tried to avoid the *actually*, as if guys aren't typically allowed to enjoy works of romance by female writers. Besides, from what I'd read so far, characterizing Austen's work as simply romantic literature would be a gross generalization. But the *actually* slipped out. To make up for it, I stood up a little taller, a bold and dignified embrace (in my mind at least) of my reading selection.

"Good choice, good choice." Barb smiled. "I always say, the best guy is one that can read Austen or Bronte. They're just more in touch with their feelins." I wasn't sure if she wasn't making my point about who's expected to read what, but I nodded, grabbed my mocha, and found my *usual* seat by the window.

After about thirty minutes and no one in the shop but me, Barb strolled over.

"So, how things been goin', sweetheart?"

"Wonderfully," I replied, slipping in my bookmark just as Elizabeth was defending her choice of reading over playing cards while caring for her sister at the Bingley house.

"I hear good things about your work over at the art gallery. People been sayin' that you're a mighty helpful young man."

"I guess. I mean, it's not too demanding. I enjoy helping customers bring meaningful art into their homes, and Somewhere has an unusually artistic community."

"Yeah, well, summa them's been honing their craft for a very long time.

"So what're ya doin' for Thanksgiving'?" Barb asked, changing the subject. "Lotsa big gatherings, plus there's the parade."

"Yeah, I was talking to Tom about that some. I didn't realize there's a parade for Thanksgiving, too."

"Yep, the last few months of the year are always a lotta fun. Halloween, Thanksgiving, Christmas. We like to celebrate."

"Um, well, I'm not sure what I'm doing, to be honest," I said. "I was thinking about going to see my family back in St. Louis, but I'm kind of reconsidering it."

"Oh." Barb looked a little taken aback. "I was just askin' 'bout where you'd be here. I hadn't thought about you leavin' us."

"I mean, I'm not *leaving*, leaving. Just wanted to go see my folks since it's not too far a drive and I have a few days off work."

Barb's eyebrows were furrowed, appearing to process quickly.

"Are - are you sure you don't have to work?" she asked. *Odd.*

"Um, yeah, we're closed Wednesday through Friday which gives me several days, especially if I leave Tuesday night."

"Yeah, yeah, of course. Silly me," she answered, trying to shrug off her nosy question. "Well, anyway, I wanted to invite you over if you don't have plans." She forced a smile and then scrambled away awkwardly.

Weird.

I turned back to my book, spending about five minutes staring at the same page, processing my conversation with Barb, and finally got up and left, unable to focus.

I nearly slammed into the pavement outside, bumping hard into Pastor Amos. He actually grabbed my jacket to steady me though I managed to slosh a good amount of the remaining mocha onto me.

"Woah, bud," he hollered with a smile. "Funny coincidence seeing you here."

"Oh yeah?"

"Yeah, Tracy and I were *just* talkin' about you. Your ears must have been tickling."

I chuckled consciously, still shaken up by my near wipeout.

"We wanted to invite you to spend Thanksgiving with us."

Oh my God! What is going on with these people today?

"Uh…" I was now in a hurry to get away, tired of this same conversation. "Wow, yeah, that's really nice of you. Let me get back with you. I'm kind of in a hurry to meet up with some friends, so I need to go get ready."

"Oh yeah?" Pastor Amos continued. "That's nice. Who are you hanging out with?"

I shot him a look. *What did he care? Mind your damn business,* I wanted to say.

"Mike and David," I lied. "Okay, gotta go."

When I stepped inside Mrs. Copeland's kitchen several minutes later, I wasn't even surprised to find her there waiting to ask me something. But I gave her the same line about meeting up with friends. She frowned, but I just ignored her, grabbing a banana and then dashing back out and up to my room. There I threw myself down onto my bed in a huff, trying to sort out what just happened.

I sighed and closed my eyes.

Sometime later I woke up... a *long* time later. The room was completely dark save for the sliver of moonlight visible in the window. It must have been the middle of the night.

Was it the time? Was the house about to tremble, to move, to come alive?

I heard murmuring. At first, I couldn't tell where it was coming from. The sound was muffled.

I sat up in bed, uneasily turning my head, trying to determine the source of the noise, but it seemed to emanate from the room itself. As the volume rose, the murmuring became more discernible.

"It's true, it's true, it's true, it's true..." I heard, cadenced and unceasing, continuing to grow louder. Where was it coming from?

A cold sweat broke out across my body.

Then I understood.

Mechanically, I rose out of bed, stepping onto the hardwood, and walked over to the wintry landscape, *The Census at Bethlehem.* The chant was coming from there.

I stared at the painting, rubbing my eyes, disbelieving. What had once been a scene of villagers scattered about in various acts of labor—along with a sizable crowd gathered around the window of an inn—was now transformed. Every single villager was now crowded around the tall tree beside the inn, though Mary and her donkey were nowhere in sight. Through the upper branches of the tree a blood-red sun was visible on the horizon.

"It's true, it's true, it's true..." continued to pound in my ears.

I looked and saw the heads of every villager tilted upwards towards the tree. A woman was hanging dangling by a rope in the branches.

Then everything hushed—total silence. Such deep silence that I wondered if I had really heard anything before, or had it simply been my imagination? Such deep silence that I began to wonder if I had lost my hearing.

I straightened up, shuddering as I cast one final glance at the hanging woman.

I peered around the room, everything was in its proper place. I tapped on the wall and nearly jumped out of my skin, frightening myself with the sharp sound splitting the unusually heavy quiet. *At least I'm not deaf,* I thought.

I waited.

And then I heard another sound.

A creaking of boards. Someone else was in the attic. Just on the other side of the wall closing off the unfinished section. I fixed my eyes on the door at the end of my room.

"Hello?" I managed, feebly. My call dissipated like a puff of smoke. I couldn't bring myself to say anything again. The movement had stopped on the other side of the door.

I crept over to it, unable to stop myself, unsure if I was dreaming or awake, and I twisted the handle. At my feet, in that minute space between the bottom of the door and the floor, I could make out the slightest hints of movements, shadows swaying as whatever it was, whoever it was, shifted noiselessly on their feet.

I opened the door.

And sharply inhaled at what I saw. I had opened the door onto the fields surrounding Somewhere. Stepping through, I walked toward the stranger.

A quick glance over my shoulder. Where I expected to see houses, there was only the open door to my bedroom.

I halted in front of the man.

He said nothing to me, but his eyes locked onto mine. Gradually, I began to notice a change. He was changing, aging.

I had no concept of time while standing there, but I could see him grow older.

When I first saw him that night several weeks ago, I would have put his age a little more than mine, maybe mid-twenties. But I watched as his smooth skin became rougher, as his hairline receded, thinned, began to gray. Wrinkles formed around his eyes and mouth, his skin started to sag. Soon he was hunching, unable to stand up straight. His nose, his ears were elongated, the skin below his chin hung looser. He was now a wraith, on the final throes before death.

Then, in horror I watched as his eyes rolled into the back of his head. His skin started to decompose, and that's when I began to scream.

His flesh split open, and I saw bones and intestines beneath, like white chopsticks poking out of a bowl of red-soaked, oozing noodles.

With sickly, rotted flesh, a decaying hand grabbed my wrist. He leaned into me, staring at me with empty sockets, where his eyes had completely rotted away.

"It's true."

My screams grew louder as I tried to wrench away. My sight grew dim. I was losing consciousness.

CHAPTER TWELVE

I glanced at my clock and realized that less than an hour had elapsed. Still, the memory of it shook me. I changed quickly and blundered out of my room into the icy blast, my senses suddenly pulled back from their lethargy like the curtains pulled back from a dark room. I needed fresh air. I needed what little remained of the day's fading sunlight. Pulling on a hoodie, I bounded outside.

Walking aimlessly and thinking, mostly I processed whether or not I wanted to go home for Thanksgiving. This led me to consider my mom's health and the concerning memory loss I'd been noticing. But as far as urgency, there probably wasn't much difference between visiting next week versus visiting at Christmas time—*As long as I don't get a thousand pressing invitations for Christmas as well,* I thought. Well, regardless, I would definitely be seeing them at Christmas. The question was whether or not I also wanted to visit for Thanksgiving.

I felt someone approaching me, the pitter-patter of quickening feet. *Could be a jogger.* But Somewhere wasn't exactly the most exercise-conscious place. Come to think of it, the only joggers I'd ever seen were high schoolers, presumably on the cross country or track teams. I kept my head down and continued walking.

The person pulled up beside me and slowed down, not saying a word. After about thirty seconds of awkwardness I glanced over.

Rose.

She was grinning at me, and when I had finally looked at her, she laughed.

"Took you long enough," she said. "What's the matter, Mr. Loner?"

Everything changed: my demeanor, the weight I had been carrying in my shoulders, the cold. Her cheeks—and lips—were pink from the frosty air, and I had the urge to hold her in my arms, to pull her close to my body. The added body heat was also an enticing bonus.

"Who are you calling a loner, Miss Let's-Talk-To-Strange-Men-In-Hoodies?"

"*You're* the strange man in this scenario!" she retorted, giving me a playful push. "Besides, there aren't strange men in Somewhere. Well, I should rephrase that. There aren't *unknown* strangers in Somewhere. Small town, remember?"

For a moment my smile faded, thinking that I'd seen at least one strange man that she probably hadn't, unless she recalled being in my dream the other night. I blushed.

"So, what's going on?"

I tested the waters, paranoid that Rose would be my next Thanksgiving invitation.

"Nothing," I replied, "just getting some fresh air."

"Okay. Mind if I join you?"

"Actually, my mom told me not to talk to strangers," I said, turning it back on her. "And if you have candy, I'm calling the cops."

"No candy, just a rusted out van over there, but I'd love to give you a ride." Then Rose dropped her voice in what I can only assume was her attempt at a creepy kidnapper voice. "You can trust me."

I snorted, breaking character.

"Why do you want to take me to your van, Mister?" I resumed.

"Oh, no reason. I just want to do all kinds of things to you."

We were both awkwardly quiet for a long moment, the innuendo plastered between us, and then began laughing. Why was everything so easy with her?

Did she feel the same about me?

"Hey, Rose..." I stammered, unsure. "I actually do have something on my mind, but I feel kind of weird saying it."

"Yeah?"

When it came to it, I felt stuck. How do I condense down into mere words my experiences at Mrs. Copeland's and expect Rose to be able to help me? But if this was someone I liked and cared about, shouldn't I invite her into this weird thing in my life, embarrassing or not?

"So, I don't really know how to say this, but...um...something keeps happening at Mrs. Copeland's house where I'm staying."

"What do you mean?" she asked, stopping. I could tell that she was caught off guard, probably expecting the conversation to go in a different direction. I paused as well and found myself staring at my feet regretting bringing anything up.

"I know it sounds crazy," I managed, "but every night at the same time the house sort of comes alive. Some nights more than others. I mean, the shower has come on in the middle of the night, there are noises all over the house, furniture moves slightly."

Rose looked at me quizzically, wordlessly, and her lack of response sent me over the edge, overcome by my immature fears.

"I mean, I know it's nothing," I jumped back in, rushing my words. "I even brought it up to Mrs. Copeland who said maybe it had something to do with New Madrid's Fault or something. Plus, when I was chatting with Pastor Amos the other day–" I stopped all the sudden, wondering how well his little *thin places* monologue would go over with Rose. I had to remember that she was still, after all, a member at a Baptist church. I wasn't sure how she might take the news that her revered pastor had such offbeat–hardly orthodox–ideas about religion.

"Uh huh?" she nudged after my extended quiet.

I felt the need to protect Pastor Amos, so I quickly changed directions: "Um, Pastor Amos said that unresolved spiritual anxiety can manifest itself in strange ways," I lied on the spot. "Uh...visions of sorts, I guess."

"Do you have unresolved spiritual anxiety?" This took a bewildering turn.

"I don't know. I'm just being weird." I tried laughing it off and forced a grin, now furiously attempting to backpedal out of this mess of a conversation. "I also just woke up from a weird dream before coming here, so I think it's put me in a weird headspace. I'm sure I've just been dreaming a bunch of strange things, or it's probably just normal groans in an old house."

Rose's facial expression softened pityingly.

"You know, you have to give yourself a break," she spoke tenderly. "You're in a new place. I mean, *I'm* not going to tell you that you're just hearing things. Sometimes I wonder if there are such things as ghosts or, like, unexplained supernatural phenomena, but yeah, it could just be strange dreams."

I nodded in agreement, just wanting to put this whole thing behind me.

"Yeah, thanks. Sorry, it was definitely the dream I had before coming here; it just put me in a weird funk. Want to keep walking?" I offered in a forcefully cheerful tone. Of course, I knew there was more to these events than just dreams or "unresolved spiritual anxieties"–*Where the hell had that come from?*–but I sheepishly admitted to myself that I probably *was* exaggerating those things.

Rose and I continued walking through the dusk, silently at first but soon chatting naturally about whatever came to mind. The sun finally dipped below the horizon, the world lit by a glow of diminishing light, street lamps now popping on. The longer we walked, the more that a tightness developed in my chest, a pretty common symptom of spending time with Rose. As we continued our stroll, I inched closer to her.

My arm brushed against hers. It wasn't exactly a shock of ecstasy; we were both outfitted in several layers of clothes, dulling any significant sense of touch. It was more of a felt presence. And she didn't move her arm away. If I wasn't wrong, she moved ever so slightly closer.

Then, I felt a small finger curl around mine. I hadn't worn any gloves, but my sleeves covered most of my hands. Only the tips of my fingers dangled out freely, and Rose had moved her left index finger and wrapped it around my right pinky. I looked at her. She looked at me.

My attempt at a smile came out as a feeble, awkward, self-conscious half-grin. I was thankful, though, that hers seemed to match mine. Then, in a sudden act of uncommon boldness, I paused and turned to her, grabbing both of her hands in mine.

Rose's eyes were at first fixed on the ground, her mouth contracting and expanding in a nervous, faltering smile. She looked up at me, and I caught the full force of her gaze. I leaned my face in towards her, watching if she'd match me. She leaned in and kissed me.

And time halted to a pinpoint moment, the taste of her dominating my every thought, my entire being. The kiss continued.

At some point we stopped holding hands and were instead wrapped in an embrace, her hands around my waist, mine around her back. Eventually, we pulled back, both of us grinning and then chuckling nervously.

"I, I've kind of been hoping for that for a long time," I admitted.

"Me, too."

We stood there awkwardly in silence because there's no smooth way to transition from a passionate kiss to whatever comes next, especially on a cold November at dusk.

"So..." I voiced awkwardly. We laughed, returning to ourselves. We were back. Not *back* back because that moment lingered between us, floated above us like an invisible Aphrodite, but we walked on. And we talked. And we clung to that time together.

"Rose," I said, after she'd just finished divulging the secrets of a senior prank she'd been involved in with—no surprise—Kenny as the ringleader.

"Yes?"

"You asked me earlier what was going on?"

"Yes?"

"The thing is, actually I was deciding whether or not I want to go home for Thanksgiving to see my parents."

I scrutinized Rose's reception of the news, still suspicious from that day's interactions, but I couldn't determine anything.

I knew the timing was bad, to wait until after this beautiful moment, after we kissed, to share that now, actually, I wanted to get away from her. Except I didn't want to get away from her at all, it was only a few days. So why had *I* felt the need to state it so ominously, if it was no big deal?

"It's just a few days," I reasoned. "I'd leave next Tuesday evening or Wednesday morning and be back by Sunday. I know it's no big deal, but people have been acting strange around me all the sudden, giving me these grand gestures trying to get me to stay. First it was Tom who seemed pretty pissed off at me until he suggested that I join him for Thanksgiving, and then Barb at The Book and Bean asked me to join her and her family. Pastor Amos stopped me. And then even Mrs. Copeland was about to invite me, I'm pretty sure."

I spit all this out really fast while Rose stood there.

"What do you think?" I asked.

"Well..." she began—did she pause extra long?—"that's normal, right? You're only gone for a few days to see your parents in St. Louis for Thanksgiving. It's not like you're circumnavigating the globe."

"Right?!" I said with relief.

"I think that you shouldn't worry too much about it. People here are maybe a little cautious towards newcomers. And maybe when they find someone they like, they can't understand that you wouldn't want to be here every single second for every little tradition."

"Hmmm..." I pondered aloud. "I guess that makes sense."

"But, yeah, uh, you should go," Rose said. And now that the words came out of her mouth, I realized that I was sad she *wasn't* giving me a hard time about going, that she wasn't inviting me to spend Thanksgiving with her, and the image of snuggling up beside each other watching *Christmas Vacation* flashed back in my mind.

"Well, at least *one* person in this town doesn't want me to stay," I said jokingly, trying to disguise my own sensitivity, but she dispelled that immediately.

"Hey," she grabbed my arm with both her hands, pulled me to herself, and smiled. "You should stay. With me."

That constricting in my chest returned. I longed for another kiss, to fall onto the ground together in a passionate embrace. But that moment had passed. She did, however, kiss me on the cheek and pulled us towards downtown.

"You don't have to beg," I teased her. She kept one arm looped around mine, and that's how we walked down Main Street. "Where are we going by the way?"

"You'll see."

We continued our promenade, and as far as I was concerned, Main Street could just stretch on to eternity and make this time last forever. Then another thought struck me as we passed the feed store. *Why are we going this way? Where is she taking me?*

I tried to hide my nervousness, but the stranger popped up in my mind. My eyesight transformed into guided missiles, projecting out in front of me, over the covered bridge to the train depot, bouncing along the same route I had taken to the edge of town, to a man wildly screaming *Fuck you!* while a gun waved past my head.

We stopped at the covered bridge.

"Wait right here," she said. She left me, and I dispelled air from my lungs in short, hitching breaths, calming myself.

Swiftly she had taken a small path, barely visible, that branched off to the right and wrapped around under the bridge. I had half a mind to follow, but I decided to obey her command. I needed a moment to compose myself anyway. She returned minutes later holding something in her hand.

"Where'd you go?" I asked.

"Nunna your beeswax," she replied with her nose upturned in mock defiance.

"What?" I gave a confused grin. She laughed.

"That's what I always told my friends when I was a kid. Speaking of which, I was a bit of a magpie growing up. I was always collecting random treasures, and I had a hiding spot just below the bridge there. Sometimes I still go there to look at them, and, I don't know, just to remember those times when I was a kid."

I was touched, and I was also curious about what treasures she might have, how she managed to keep them hidden for so long, and where. I guess my inner child was also alive, curious and jealous of hidden treasure, like being in the plot of a pirate novel. Rose approached me, though, grabbed my hand, and pressed something round and hard into it.

I looked down to see an oversized marble lying in my palm. On further examination, I noticed—with difficulty in the limited light—that the marble was clear save for some tiny object at the center.

"What's this?"

"It's called a sulfide marble. They used to be a popular novelty, a clear marble with an object inside, usually an animal or a mythological creature or the bust of someone famous."

"And which one is this?" I asked, squinting in the darkness.

"Which one is what?"

"Is it an animal, mythological figure, or a famous person?"

"Oh, it's an animal. Can you see it?"

I looked a little harder, and sure enough.

"A snake?"

"Yep, a snake."

"I hope this doesn't have any hidden meaning about how you think of me," I chided.

"It's just something I found a long time ago and had it in my hoard of odds and ends below the bridge. I was deciding between that, a key, or an old tin can of Spam."

"A can of Spam!" I laughed. "How did a can of Spam make it into your treasure?"

"Hey! I was like seven years old. Lay off me. The question you *should* be asking yourself is why Spam made it into the Final Three as an option for you."

"Okay, okay, that's true. The marble is better. So why *did* you give this to me?"

Rose grew somewhat serious for a moment.

"Because if you do go home for a few days, I wanted to give you something to remember me by."

She was silent for a moment and then burst into fits of laughter.

"What?" I said, grinning but not understanding the joke.

"I...I..." she was still laughing. "I had this image in my mind of this really cute gesture, but as soon as I said it, I realized how corny it sounded."

I chuckled too, but honestly, I was so enchanted by her that she could have given me that Spam can, and I would have gone along with it.

"Anyway, so there you go. And even if you don't end up going home, you can just put it in your apartment as a reminder of how cheesy I am. Who knows? Maybe it has magical properties and will keep the ghosts away," she teased but then assured me by snuggling into my chest. Of course, I forgave her though I continued beating myself up for ever mentioning the house's odd behavior. I slipped the marble into my pocket, very much glad at the token, cheesy or not.

"Anyway," I continued. "I think I want an exchange. I want to see what other treasures I'm missing out on. Take me to your hoard!"

"Never!"

CHAPTER THIRTEEN

I rolled over and looked at the clock.

1:43.

I groaned and turned to my back, staring up at the ceiling. About a week before, whatever strange thing that went bump in the night had made its nightly clamor at 2:00 instead of 3:00. Apparently, it didn't know how to adjust its disturbances for the end of daylight savings.

On the one hand, the regularity of the house's animation took a little of the edge off. On the other hand, the foreboding, the anticipation was considerably worse. Seventeen minutes to wait until... until what? What exactly happens at 2:00 every morning?

Fifteen minutes.

I thought of Rose. I thought of our kiss and warmed some.

After she had handed me the marble—now sitting on the dresser—she had invited me to grab a drink with some of the others.

Only Mike and Eleanor and a new girl, Tess, joined us. I got the sense that Tess was not as close with them as the others were with each other. For a brief moment I was afraid that's how they saw me, too, but I realized that of course that's how they saw me. I'd only been in Somewhere for a little over three months. Rose, though, had cast a smile at me from across the table, and I was satisfied nonetheless.

Twelve minutes.

Rose and I had actually walked into the bar holding hands. That got raised eyebrows from all three of the others who were already there cradling their dewy glasses. Eleanor beamed. Tess resumed a normal face. Mike seemed a little put off. We all had a good time, though; a few drinks, some greasy appetizers, and a card game Tess taught us, a variation of Spades called Seven Up, Seven Down. We called it quits after one game, though–Eleanor winning easily–and began saying our goodbyes. Everyone except Mike.

Hastily, Mike ordered another beer, assuming, I guess, that his commitment would convince others to stay for one more round. His plan backfired, however, as we left anyway. I shot a final glance over my shoulder. I don't know why, but I felt a small jig of satisfaction to see him hunched over his beer broodily as we left. He had been in a whiny mood the whole night.

I said goodbye to Tess and Eleanor–who shot me and Rose a mischievous smile–and then I was alone again with Rose. Part of me wanted to linger, to be with her longer, but sometimes you know when the moment is over, like a movie scene. This was the part when we smile sappily at each other, and then the camera follows us individually as we stumble to our destination in a cloud of ecstasy and dumb love. At least, I hoped she had the same wistful and stupid grin on her face as I had walking back to my place.

Seven minutes.

I had gotten in around 10:30, not too late, but I was surprised to see Mrs. Copeland still up when I stepped into the kitchen for a glass of water. She invited me to a game of bridge and asked me about Rose. I blushed.

Five minutes.

We played for almost an hour. When I came up to my room, I watched an episode of *Friends* while I got ready, and then fell asleep pretty quickly.

Four minutes.

I continued staring at the ceiling and glancing at my clock. I tried to close my eyes. Maybe I could fall back to sleep and ignore it. I laughed to myself. Knowing that wasn't possible.

Three minutes.

My gut constricted.

Two minutes.

One minute.

The loud noise below. I had stopped breathing. Bracing myself for whatever might come next. Sometimes there was nothing more.

There was a charge in the air, a pulse radiating along the walls. I could sense that. But I heard nothing else. No "tremors," no "leaky shower pipes."

Very slowly I turned to look at the wall, at Pieter Bruegel the Elder's painting, ready for the village to be gathered around a hanging woman.

I couldn't see it from where I was. I tried to stay in bed, but I had to check. Growing up, I often spooked myself out watching horror movies with friends, and then, before sleeping, I'd had to check all my closets, usually leaving the door open for good measure. That's how I felt checking the painting. I wouldn't be able to sleep without knowing.

I tiptoed closer and closer. My eyes landed on the scene.

Everything was normal. A group gathered around the inn. Mary on her way. Laborers mid-task, some trudging across the frozen lake. The large tree is empty.

I breathed deeply.

The clock read 2:06.

I returned to bed and was just about to lay down when my eyes caught the silvery moon spilling through the windows onto the floor. The light shifted, almost imperceptibly. I wouldn't have even noticed had my nerves not been dangling precariously on tenterhooks.

Someone was at my window.

I jerked my head around, scrambling out of bed.

Nothing.

Once again, I crept slowly, stopping at each window to peer out, first to the landing outside the door and then deeper into the inky blackness beyond.

Nothing.

My hand trembling, I unlocked the door and opened it. I was waiting for a cold hand to grip my ankle, a person hidden just below the window where I hadn't been able to see. But the landing was empty.

I walked out and looked down the stairs, once again into the dark surrounding the house. My pulse returned to normal, I considered going down to the kitchen to make some tea or hot chocolate or something, but I didn't want to be in the cold or the dark or—the real reason—outside of my room. On our deepest level, we're all just kids scared in the dark, huddled beneath the covers waiting for the monsters to pass.

I went inside, locked the door again, and climbed into bed.

2:11.

I closed my eyes, and was asleep in seconds without further incident, my own fright, a fast-acting barbiturate.

Several days passed. I realized that my paranoia about the Thanksgiving invitations had not been unfounded: I received half a dozen requests to join "Somewhervians" for Thanksgiving (Rose had shared with me the official moniker of the town's denizens). Even Mrs. Copeland finally asked me; she was having some other ladies over for an epic day of bridge.

"Oh, yeah? Are we playing in the kitchen?" I asked innocently. That seemed to trouble her.

"Um... of course not. I'll, uh, be cleaning up the living room finally. You'll actually get to see it for once," she said, forcing a grin.

Eleanor, Kenny, and David all asked me. David, investing more and more of his time towards his craft brewing, insisted that he had three new micro-batches of beer that he wanted me to try. Conspicuously–but not surprisingly–missing from the invitations was Mike. He had grown frostier and frostier towards me, so his silence came as no great shock. I *had* begun to wonder about Mattie, though. I hadn't seen her since that Halloween night.

Rose never asked me. At least, not again after my feigned (not-so-feigned) hurt at the park. But that didn't change how things were between us. I still saw her every day. We held hands. There were no kisses quite like the one at the park, but there were kisses. I melted every time I was with her, just a puddle.

The most random invitation, though, was a checkout guy at the grocery store named Stuart. In his defense, he was related by marriage to Kenny, so I'd already been invited to that gathering. Cue eye roll.

In the end, I decided to go home for Thanksgiving. I didn't know why I was making such a big deal about it. I guess because of the strange reaction of the town.

And Rose.

Still, I'd only be gone for a few days, and while Somewhere had grown on me—attached itself to me—I wanted to see my parents, needed to see them. I was worried about my mom, and even though I was grateful for the independence conferred upon me by my life in Somewhere, I couldn't bring myself to skip Thanksgiving. Not yet. Aside from my year abroad, I'd never spent a Thanksgiving or Christmas away from my family. I was sure there'd come a time–maybe next year–but I just wasn't ready yet.

So, I packed my seldom-used car and left. It was late afternoon the Tuesday before Thanksgiving Day, the sun already curling its fingers around the edges of the horizon and flooding the sky with its seeping orange glow. I wound my way through the streets of Somewhere, amazed that I was leaving. It'd only been a few months, but it felt longer. Not just in that colloquial sense, but it truly felt like time somehow moved slower.

As I meandered through Somewhere on my way out of town, people stopped whatever they were doing and simply stared. I recognized several of them: David, Tracy Whitaker, a lady I'd seen once at Mrs. Copeland's, that girl Tess. I waved at them, but only David waved back and only faintly. They all gaped at me peculiarly.

Finally, I pulled onto a longer, straighter stretch of road, the highway that would take me out of Somewhere. My speed steadily climbed as I maneuvered the stick from first to second, second to third, third to fourth. I was cruising at about 45 mph, my hand resting on the gear shaft getting ready to shift into fifth.

And then I just stopped. Abruptly.

My car didn't die, it didn't lurch terribly like manual cars will do when accidentally downshifting at high speeds, there was no squealing of tires from the brakes locking up. It just stopped.

One moment I was driving, the next moment my car was off. My foot was still pressed down on the accelerator, the gear still in fourth, the key turned in the ignition with all the lights on the dashboard on, but the engine wasn't running. The car started rolling backwards, so I stepped on the brake.

After a minute, unable to wrap my head around what might have caused the car to die in such a manner, I started it again and let it idle. Rather than bring the car back up to speed, I rolled forward in first gear, keeping my speed around 10 mph. I had gone maybe another hundred yards when my progress was again impeded. This time, rather than my car shutting down, it was as though I'd hit an invisible barrier, like one of those silly pranks when someone has stretched saran wrap across a door frame. This sensation was similar, but without the painful whiplash; I was just frozen.

The car was still running. After a moment, I realized that I wasn't completely stuck in place. Rather, I was moving maybe half an inch per second. That's all I can really remember of the experience, like swimming through mud. And suddenly I was confronted by the very strong suggestion that I should put the car in reverse, drive back to Mrs. Copeland's, and just enjoy Thanksgiving. Go see Rose. Take Tom up on that Turkey Bowl game offer.

At first, I looked around me as if an audible voice whispered to me these ideas. But I knew it was futile. I knew no one was there, that the thought I was grappling with was not from outside myself. Except it was. And it wasn't. The idea wasn't mine but it was. It originated from outside but had emanated from inside me, had gone out and come back in, the outside voice and inside voice uniting into one powerful enticement.

And why *not* drive back to Somewhere? There wasn't any strong reason to go home. *It's just Thanksgiving. It's better to wait until Christmas anyway.* But like my conversation with Tom, I was certain I would quite literally run into this same dilemma again.

I had images of my parents in my head, the sound of my mom's confused voice over the phone, and memories of past holidays.

Rose was in my head. The kiss. Holding her less than a few minutes ago. Maybe. I couldn't be sure of the time.

In the end, I can't say that I conquered the barrier. Whatever obstruction was there must have only been so thick, my indecision too long, just enough hesitancy somewhere inside me to prevent me from turning around. I had continued inching forward little by little, and at some point, I was released.

I moved forward freely once again, still in first gear, still creeping along at no more than 10 mph. But something felt different, so I increased my speed and pulled the gear shaft down into second. Nothing stopping me. Third gear, same. Fourth, fifth.

Fifty mph and an amalgam of relief and regret as I coasted further and further away from Somewhere, increasing my speed. 80 mph. Only then, my old Ford Aspire reminding me shudderingly, did I slow back down, easing back to a steady 65. I reached into my pocket and gripped the sulfide marble, the snake encaged in glass.

CHAPTER FOURTEEN

Around 7:00, I pulled up to my parents' house, stepping out of my car and into the beetle-black night. I was surprised to find that they hadn't left the porch light on for me. All my life they'd left that light on whenever they knew I was coming home. I'd talked to my mom just a week before and had left her a voicemail yesterday. But, I reasoned, this *was* the first time I was going to see them post-college. *Things have probably changed.*

I rang the doorbell and waited.

After a minute or two, I tried the doorknob to see if it was unlocked. I rang again.

"Who is it?" I heard, startled. Looking down, I realized that the doorbell was one of those new security systems with video and a speaker.

"Uh... it's Lee."

"Lee?"

There was no recognition in my mom's voice, and my heart slid into the cave of my stomach. I sighed, the corners of my eyes beginning to burn. My parents' door stood before me ominously like a hard fact, them on one side and me standing there stupidly. The door a period at the end of a sentence I already knew but didn't want to read, chose *not* to read by distracting myself in Somewhere: My mom was not okay, and I didn't know how I would be able to cope with that.

"Mom, it's your son," I said, trying to hold my shit together. "Can you put Dad... er... Charles on?"

"Charles!" I heard my mom yell on the other end. "I think there's someone pulling a pr—" The voice went silent. My mom must have realized she still had the button pressed down.

I continued to wait. My pained concern began giving way to frustration. *This is ridiculous*, I thought. *I'm stuck outside of my own goddamn house.*

"Can I help you?" my dad's voice came on.

"Dad, it's me. Can you see me? Is the video working?"

"The video works just fine," he responded in a steady voice. "What the hell do you want?"

"Dad, come on!" My tone was meant to communicate a *cut-the-crap*, but my reply was merely packaged in panic. I had never in my life heard Dad utter so much as *darn* or *heck*. Those were just replacement words for cursing. *Hell* might be at the very bottom of the list of cussing, but I don't even think my dad could form that word in his mind. What was going on?

"Boy, I am not your father, and if this is your version of some kind of sick prank, well just wait 'til the cops show up. I don't even have a son, you little prick."

Oh, God. Oh, God. Oh, God, was all I could think to myself. *Not Dad, too!*

"Dad! Come on, this isn't funny," I said, not even attempting to conceal my fear now. There was silence on the other end for a few moments. Then I heard footsteps in the house, and my dad opened the door. Apparently my mom had stayed behind.

As Dad opened the door, he appeared to be on the verge of saying something, but when he saw me, he fell silent. We stood, looking at each other. In my heart and mind, I was willing him to recognize me. *Please, Dad. Come on.*

"I... I...," he hesitated. "I don't *think* I've seen you before. You do look familiar, though."

I couldn't help myself. I collapsed on the porch in tears. I lost myself. I was playing at being a grown man, but I was just a kid, fresh out of college. I couldn't bear this cruel knife twist, my own damn parents not even recognizing me.

I'm not sure how long I stayed in that position, my cries embarrassingly loud. At some point, my dad awkwardly shushed me and brought me inside. He led me to my room which, the way he and my mom were acting, I half expected to be bare of my memory. It was all still there, though: the sports posters from high school, the meaningless trophies on the shelves, the books, the stain on the carpet from where I spilled Coke once, the tacky old baseball comforter that I could never bring myself to update.

It was all a bizarre nightmare, something I could have imagined in my dreams as a five-year-old. I was in my own bedroom with all my stuff in my parents' house, and they still acted like they didn't know me. It was completely illogical which made it all the more terrifying. I allowed my dad to lead me to the bed, and that's where I stayed.

I heard him and my mom talking somewhere outside my room, but it was muffled, so I didn't pay attention. Eventually, sheer exhaustion lulled me to sleep.

I woke up late the next morning. Multiple times in the night I had considered leaving my room, but I was too scared. I have this weird way of simply ignoring anything that makes me anxious. I know that I'll eventually need to confront it, but I'll put it off as long as I can. And if possible, it's best to tackle some problems in the morning, in the daylight. The night plays tricks with my mind.

So, when I finally woke up, I considered continuing my self-isolation, but I worked up my courage to leave my room. Also, I was hungry.

My room was in the hallway just off the kitchen, so when I opened the door, I could immediately peer in and see my mom sitting at the table with a bowl of cereal and reading something on her phone.

I ambled towards her timidly. She looked up and smiled.

"Hello," was her one-word greeting.

"Hi."

"Do you want some cereal?"

"Um, sure. Is Dad here?"

My mom's eyes narrowed for a moment, and she said with a constricted voice, "*Charles* is already at work."

I grabbed milk from the fridge and a bowl from the cabinet, uncertain of what was going through my mom's mind. Did she know it was me? She couldn't have; she was not acting like the person I knew. Normally she would have greeted me with a big hug and a million stories. She would have gotten up this morning and made me my favorite breakfast: fruit crepes with a side of bacon.

Out of the corner of my eyes, I noticed her staring at me, no doubt curious about why I seemed to have a perfect knowledge of the layout of their kitchen. I reached for the bowls in exactly the right cabinet. Two cabinets over, I reached for a glass. I retraced my steps back to the first cabinet and pulled the drawer out for the silverware. She tried to feign disregard, but I saw the wheels turning in her mind.

"Uh, do you mind if I make some coffee?" I asked.

"We don't have a coffee machine," she replied, with a look of triumph. *This is just a lying stranger after all*, she might have thought to herself.

"What about that old, red Mr. Coffee machine that was sitting over here?" I pointed. Her mischievous grin immediately vanished. She was visibly shaken.

"Oh, uh, that... we got rid of it about a month ago." Mom looked like she wanted to say more but instead averted her eyes back to her phone and fell silent. Clearly, I had rattled her. *Good*, I thought, *baby steps*.

I sat down at the table with my mom and ate my cereal, the din of crunching Rice Krispies—like some kind of construction site in my mouth—drowning out the awkwardness. I decided that I was in a better mood. Concerned about the reception I received from my parents? Yes. Staving off the growling dog of panic? Probably, yes. But recovering somewhat from my initial shock as well. Truth be told, I got a good night's sleep. I hadn't heard any movement in the house at 2:00 a.m., and had experienced no alarming dreams. In fact, Somewhere, for the moment, was only buzzing on the edges of my consciousness.

Whatever mental lapse was going on with my parents would need to be addressed. Today. Soon. I'd leave after getting ready and go visit Miriam, my mom's close friend who was like an aunt to me. Or more like a big sister even if she *was* mom's age.

In an hour I was out the door. I realized quickly that not having a cell phone was certainly inconvenient. I wanted to call Miriam, but I was nervous about using my parents' phone, not wanting to push the limits too much since I was, after all, still a stranger to them. In Somewhere, it just didn't have a major impact. For whatever reason, that hidden town on the edge of nowhere, Missouri (*Pun not intended,* I laughed to myself), hadn't really arrived to the 21st century. Everyone there, like Mrs. Copeland's house, had a landline. Everyone. I literally had not seen a single cell phone, and, besides a passing reflection here or there when I was using a landline, I hadn't really even thought about it.

Not important, I thought as I drove. "Strange though," I muttered. *How do you just not notice something like that*? I had personally made the decision to forgo the use of a cell phone, but how convenient that my spartan resolution should so seamlessly coincide with the town's own luddite disposition. And for a moment, I wondered how much I *had* made that commitment on my own or if, rather, the idea had been suggested to me. I couldn't remember. Anyway, I brushed aside the wandering footprints of thought and returned to the present, determined at least to pick up a cheap pay-as-you-go phone after visiting Miriam. She wouldn't mind my unannounced visit, though. Hell, she'd been doing that to us for years, conspicuously dropping by in the evenings when she knew she'd be invited to stay for dinner (or at least pick at the scraps of the leftovers if she'd arrived too late). She was many things but a culinary sensation was not one of them.

I pulled into Miriam's driveway: a small, quiet house located in a cul-de-sac in the back of a subdivision, butting up against the woods. Her lawn was a flood of leaves, and the trees were all bare. It looked like the perfect cozy home for the Thanksgiving season, though I reflected with some sadness that the holidays were always difficult for her.

Miriam was a young widow; her husband had died when I was like seven or eight, and they'd never had any kids. She had already been a good friend of my mom's, but after her husband's passing, she became like an adopted sister and, by extension, my aunt. I could tell her anything. Back in high school, I *had* told her things that I was too afraid to talk to my parents about. She was a bit of a loose cannon herself and had somewhat of a colorful past, so she was easy to open up to: a judgment-free listener but wise and often able to point me on the right path even when I wasn't willing to listen to my own folks. Miriam was the classic fun aunt even if we weren't related by birth. I was sometimes surprised that she and my much more conservative mother were so close, but I wasn't mad about it.

I rang the doorbell. I beamed and gave her an enthusiastic wave as she opened the door, standing there in an old Van Halen shirt, cut-off blue jean shorts, and barefoot—despite the cold. Her wild mop of hair was wiry and streaked with gray from old age.

"Miriam!"

"Yes?" she asked with a faltering voice. "Can I help you?"

Whatever quasi-balanced state of mind I'd managed to achieve that morning immediately plummeted down the silo of my body, scraping and bouncing along my insides as it fell. *Oh, God. Please no. Not again!*

This scene kept playing out like an old sitcom rerun. I could even hear a phantasmic laugh track echoing in my brain, like I was the butt of some hilarious joke.

I waited for her to open the door fully. Maybe she just didn't see me properly.

"Hey! It's me, Lee. I'm in town for Thanksgiving."

"Lee?" It wasn't a statement of recognition. It was a question.

"Geez, Miriam. It's me, Lee Thompson."

"Thompson. Thompson." She gurgled it around on her tongue like a mouthwash. "Like Susan Thompson?"

"Yes," I responded, exacerbated. "Her son." It took everything within me to maintain composure and not to curl up in a ball on the ground again.

"I know Susan. She's one of my best friends. But..." she glared at me, "she doesn't have any children. I don't know what kind of stunt you're trying to pull." Miriam started closing the door.

"Wait!" I shouted, desperate and unthinking. She opened the door, but her look of anger remained firmly fixed on her face. I decided to take a different approach, a mad scramble, a Hail Mary pass to save the game.

"Please, Miriam," I said, "just give me a second to prove I know you. Look, I... uh... I know your husband passed away many years ago." She only looked more pissed when I mentioned that. "I know that you're like sisters with my mom. You have two cats, Sunny D and Ferdinand. Uh... you like to paint but say you're not good. You like to sing and say you're not good, but you actually have an amazing voice. You would always sing me 'Blue Moon of Kentucky'" when I was little."

Miriam's expression morphed from anger to a half smile when I mentioned "Blue Moon of Kentucky" and then settled on confusion.

"That's a weird thing to sing to a kid," was all she said. But the door cracked open a bit more. Not literally. If anything, I'd spooked her and she had pulled her actual door a little more shut, but I saw this hesitation as an opening, if only I could wedge myself further in somehow.

"You... you have carpet in your bathroom," I continued, "and have said for years you want to get rid of it but never do. Your microwave is from like the 19th century; you have to wind up the dial and everything. You have a hole in the wall in your living room that *I* accidentally made when I was sliding across the hardwood in my socks, but you hid the hole with your sofa. You got high at a Tom Petty concert when you were in college."

"Okay, okay," she stopped me. "I don't know what the hell is going on, but maybe you should come inside." With a sigh, she swung her door open, and I stepped in. "By the way, I may have been in college for that concert, but I ditched finals and flew to–"

"To Germany," I interrupted. "Yeah, I know." Despite everything, I marveled at Miriam's life. "And you supposedly have the vest Tom Petty wore."

She raised an eyebrow. "Not *supposedly*. It's in the attic." She grinned as she ushered me inside to her living room and gestured to the couch.

"Coffee?"

"Yes, please."

Miriam busied herself in the kitchen for about five minutes, getting the coffee ready while I glanced around the living room. I was much more in control of myself now despite the revelation that Miriam, too, didn't recognize me. It was surreal, though, a feeling that was compounded by being in this place which was so familiar to me, almost as familiar as my parents' own place—*more*, perhaps, because my parents had only lived in their current home for about five years whereas some of my earliest memories were right there in Miriam's house. For fuck's sake! I had been at Miriam's maybe a week before I left for Somewhere!

She entered and handed me a mug.

"Just black, right?"

"Yep."

We both paused and stared at each other, eyes wide open.

"How'd you know?" I asked, hope rising inside me.

"I... I honestly don't know." She took a seat and stared in concentration at the floor, like she was trying to solve a math problem but just couldn't arrive at the answer.

"There's something in there," she resumed, with her hand resting on her forehead. "The more I think about you, the more I feel a fuzzy familiarity. I don't know how to put it. But you don't feel like a stranger to me. But when I concentrate, nothing's landing. I... I don't think it's old age." Her last statement was made questioningly, a momentary fear that had gripped her.

"No, there's nothing wrong with your memory," I replied confidently.

"How do you know?"

"Well, first, and I'm not a medical expert, but I believe that you could recall all the other events in your recent past without any problem."

"I think so."

"Let me ask you this: Describe for me what you remember when my parents came over to grill out here this past summer."

"They were here!" her eyes were wide again. I sat there silently nodding for her to continue.

"Um... well, let's see. They brought all the food practically. I had—"

"—all the booze. Yes, I'm familiar with the arrangement. My parents will not drink unless they're offered it." We both laughed. "What did you have for dessert?" I asked.

"German chocolate cake, actually."

"You seem surprised by that."

"Well, I know that your parents both love cheesecake which is what we almost always have. But someone—ugh!—someone I know loves German chocolate cake, but I can't think of who."

"Me, Miriam. *I* love German chocolate cake. Me and my parents came over for a small farewell gathering."

"I know!" she shouted, clearly frustrated.

"You do?"

"Well, yes and no." She settled down. "In my brain... I mean, I'm not stupid. Someone I know loves German chocolate cake. I can't think of who it is. It must be you. But there's no other recognition in my brain. I've gotta be losin' it!"

"You're not," I assured her. "Look, I'm just as in the dark as you are, but ever since I moved to Somewhere—"

"—where?"

"Somewhere. It's the name of a small town in northeast Missouri. I moved there in August. I got a job at an art gallery. I'll explain more. But first, what I was saying was that ever since I moved there, my parents started acting kind of strange whenever I'd call. I thought it was just my mom, but one of the main reasons I came back for Thanksgiving was because I thought she was losing her memory, like maybe I needed to take her to the doctor."

"Your mom's memory seems fine to me."

"Yeah, that's kind of the point. When I got home yesterday, not only did my mom not know who I was; my dad didn't either. It freaked me out, man!" I called Miriam *man* like she was a high school buddy, something I'd accidentally done a long time ago, but she'd thought it was so funny and given me such a hard time about it, that it kind of stuck. For a moment, I forgot that I was still a stranger to her.

"I didn't know what to think. I guess I thought perhaps maybe both my parents were suffering from some kind of memory issues or early onset Alzheimer's or dementia or whatever. I don't know, but I've been trying to explain it away or come to some sort of rational conclusion. I came over here because you're family, and I thought you could help clue me in on what's going on with them. But you *also* don't know me. That's not coincidence or collective dementia. It's collective amnesia where the only thing forgotten is me!"

Miriam didn't respond right away, but I felt optimistic.

"Okay," she finally said. "I think I believe you. All of it. I can feel your presence there in my mind somewhere, like a word on the tip of my tongue. But this is all so surreal for me. I want to help you if I can."

"Definitely."

"Well, I'm not sure exactly what I can do besides being a friend, and maybe this old computer up here..." she pointed to her head "will kick in, and I'll start remembering some things."

"Thanks," I murmured, wanting to cry from gratitude.

"So, do you have *any* guess as to why these things might be happening?"

I considered it. Until Miriam, I'd have said *no*. But again, this was simply too much coincidence. To be fair, even before Miriam there was too much coincidence—*both* parents suffering from memory failure at roughly the same time unrelated to any specific traumatic event? Possible, I guess, but highly unlikely. But then Miriam, too? Who was younger than my mom by almost ten years? Not possible.

"Okay," I said, and let the word drop out of my mouth like slow-dripping molasses as I continued processing. "I have zero idea as to how it relates or what the actual cause may be, but I can at least say that several funny things have happened while I was in Somewhere." Miriam had always been my confidant. And what I hesitated to say to others in Somewhere—apart from asking Mrs. Copeland about the strange animations of her house, and my fumbling conversation with Rose—I was suddenly comfortable sharing with Miriam, even a Miriam whose memory of me was compromised.

"Somewhere," she repeated, like she still couldn't believe there was such a place.

"Yes, Somewhere."

"Right. It's just such a weird name."

"I know. Anyway, I've been staying in a town called Somewhere. I noticed my mom's memory problems the first time I called her from there. I don't have a cell phone. I've been trying to do the whole 'disconnected' thing, but I called my folks about once a week or once every two weeks or..." I trailed off. Come to think of it, I wasn't calling my parents that frequently, especially lately.

"Lee?" Miriam said, interrupting my thoughts.

"Sorry. Yeah, so every time I talked to her it took a little bit for my mom to realize who was calling or who I was. And now that I think of it, I'm not sure she ever fully knew who she was talking to the last time I called. It was like...it was like how she talks to you when you ask her something during a Cardinals game." Miriam laughed. She knew that feeling.

"And your dad?"

"I always thought it was just my mom, but yeah, it may have been him too. I was probably just distracted by my mom."

"Would you be willing to tell me what funny things happened while you were in... Somewhere?"

"Yeah, maybe that's best," I exhaled. I gathered myself to begin, to perhaps unravel this knot though I hardly knew how or even if the thread of Somewhere was connected to this memory loss. If nothing else, I felt grateful for the opportunity simply to process out loud the events of the past several months.

"I arrived in Somewhere in mid-August," I started.

And stopped.

I couldn't remember.

CHAPTER FIFTEEN

I panicked. This was worse than the realization that my parents or Miriam didn't recognize me. I couldn't remember myself. Or at least three months of my life.

I paused and thought back to last summer, to college, to studying abroad, to my childhood. I breathed a small sigh of relief. Those memories were intact.

And there were pieces of Somewhere, but I saw them in my mind as if they were a movie trailer, brief flashes of scenes kind of building the gist of my stay there. It was so fragmented, though, that I couldn't firmly grasp onto any one thing in my mind. I certainly couldn't recall out loud a continuous narrative of the events to Miriam.

She looked at me, my eyes no doubt bugging out of my head.

"Lee, what's wrong?"

"I... I can't remember," I stammered.

"Can't remember what?"

"I can't remember what happened in Somewhere. Well, I can remember some fragmentary pieces, but it's, like, broken in my mind." *Or my mind is broken*, I shuddered.

"What? How?" Miriam looked at me, puzzled. Concerned. *Great*, I thought. *I had convinced her that she knew me, but just when I got her on my side, I'm suddenly here acting like a madman.*

"Okay, here's what we're gonna do," she said, standing up abruptly and with energy. She bounded off to the next room and came back a moment later with a notebook and pen. "Come with me."

I obeyed her, scrambling to my feet, and followed her upstairs to the guest room, a room I had spent many nights in.

The guest room faced out into the backyard. It was mostly just an island of orangish-brown leaves that had spread out around the one great oak tree, a wooden shed, and a small plot of furrowed ground where Miriam's garden lay empty for the upcoming winter. From this angle, I could see no other houses to my right or left, and beyond Miriam's backyard stretched the woods. I could see further than normal now that the trees were bare. There was the creek and the makeshift bridge I had built with my dad and John, her husband, just before he passed.

"So, what am I doing here?" I asked. "Is this where you stash my dead body and you record it in your notebook there?"

"You know, I'd feel very little remorse since I don't remember who you are," she responded with a malevolent smile.

"Alright, you're scaring me now. But for real?"

Miriam handed me the notebook and pen and pointed me to the campaign desk that sat near the window.

"Make yourself comfortable. You are going to write everything you can think of. I'm bringing you more coffee, and then I've gotta run some errands. I'll bring you back lunch." She paused, and her eyes lit up. "A Reuben from Mack's."

"Bingo!" I said. It was coming back for her at least, kind of, which was a small assurance.

When Miriam returned, I lay asleep on the bed with only a skeleton of ideas sketched into the notebook.

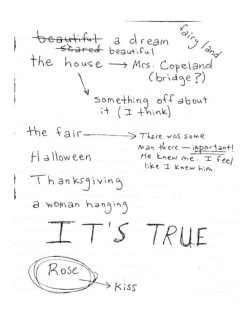

I, however, was oblivious to Miriam's return. I slept deeply and awoke to a dim room, dusk turning to night outside. I had slept through the entire day. Quickly I scrambled out of bed, embarrassed at having slept so long, but also concerned about my parents and if they were worried—even if they didn't remember that I was their son.

I grabbed the notebook and walked over to the door. But it was locked. I jiggled the handle but to no avail. I knocked loudly.

"Miriam!" I called. "Miriam! Uh...sorry, but I think I've accidentally locked myself in here somehow."

No reply. In fact, I couldn't hear a sound in the house besides my increased breathing. I walked around the room, unnerved. Part of me wanted to find something to break down the door, agitation turning my hands and fingers into crouching ocelots ready to strike. Fight or flight.

Get a hold of yourself, I thought. *The door's probably just jammed, and Miriam went out for some errands, she said. It would be stupid to break down the door and then try to explain that to her. I'll wait.*

I was facing the door with fading light filtering in from the window behind me, and my eye was drawn to a shadow on the wall moving back and forth incrementally, almost imperceptibly. Back and forth. Back and forth.

I didn't want to turn around. Somehow, I knew. I also knew, however, that I couldn't keep my back turned to it forever. I couldn't simply ignore it.

Tiptoeing to the window, a creak in one of the floorboards caused my whole body to tense up. I peered into the woods where a woman swayed over the ground, hung by the neck.

Her feet were bare, appearing just below the hem of a white dress, like a blanket that couldn't quite cover her whole body. She had black, wooly hair that was disheveled and poking about like an overgrown lawn, like she had once pulled it back but a chaotic chain of events had left her in this state of unkempt appearance.

The woman's dress was short-sleeved, presenting her arms like the drifting branches of a bare willow tree, not a vulgar thing but a delicate sadness, an eternal and final soft piano note at the tip of her finger.

Of course, most notably, what I'd failed to recognize about the woman whom I had already seen twice was that she was Black. She was not *eclipsed* in shadow, her skin *was* that soft, café au lait shadow.

Under normal circumstances, her blackness would be irrelevant, a footnote, mere ethnic trivia, but her presence suddenly revealed to me something I hadn't realized before: I had not seen a single non-white person in Somewhere. Not one. Except her.

I heard a click behind me and slowly spun around. The door had swung open. I glanced back over my shoulder at the hanging woman and then walked through the door.

Every light was turned off in the house, yet I didn't make an effort to turn them on. For some reason, I doubted that they'd turn on anyway.

I descended the stairs. Walked through the kitchen. Deftly managed my way around Miriam's place, a place I knew better than any in the world save the childhood home that my parents no longer lived in.

When I exited the house, the door to the back porch was open. I stepped onto the ground, leaves popping like mats of bubble wrap. "Enough to wake the dead," I said to myself, a wicked grin spreading across my face for reasons I could not name. Glancing at the hanging corpse, though, my smile disappeared as apprehension seized me, afraid she could hear me.

Dusk, I thought. I had heard somewhere that dusk was the true witching hour despite the legends that placed the diabolical time later in the night. Dusk, that strange amalgamation of day and night, the world between the worlds, the soft kiss between the natural and the supernatural, the brief window when devils are visible.

It was late in the dusk of evening when Tom Walker reached the old fort.

The line from Washington Irving's early American short story resurrected from the shallows of my mind–neatly buried since Mrs. Mercer's 10th grade English class–and now surprised me with its presence. The hair on my arms stood up.

For a while I only shuffled along, eyes fixed on the ground five feet in front of me. I wouldn't bring myself to look at the woman. Had I not sensed–rather than seen–my approach and slowed to a halt, I might have run into her dangling feet.

My eyes moved upward, my throat swallowing down whatever threatened to come up. This time, I stared into her face.

The woman's eyes were closed, but her mouth hung open. From the room's window in Miriam's house, she had emanated a sort of peacefulness, a gentle, swinging flower bent over and swirling over the surface of a pond's water. All this despite the crude circumstances.

But now. Now, when I truly set my gaze on the woman's face, I felt only revulsion at the grotesque image. Her face purpling, mouth agape, tongue bloated and limp, lolling out over her lips. Suddenly my own tongue felt heavy, and I was afraid I would choke on it. I would suffocate right here in Miriam's backyard.

I heard a faint, mumbling noise. A gurgle almost.

What had moments before been a phrase in my mind was now climbing through branches of this small woods, hissing at me serpent-like: "It was late in the dusk of the evening when Tom Walker reached the old fort."

I shrunk back, feeling assaulted by my own mind, naked, vulnerable, unsafe. All the while, this line from Irving's story continued to be repeated back to me.

Aghast, I realized the sound was not reverberating through the woods but rather was spilling out of the woman's mouth, trickling out like a noxious gas.

With horror, I watched the slightest of movements at the corner of her mouth, turning upwards into a faint grin, like she was playing a trick.

"It was late in the dusk of the evening...".

Then the voice stopped abruptly and everything was silent and still. Even the body stopped swaying and seemed to be tied to the earth by an invisible rope. The mouth was no longer smiling, not a breath of wind stirred.

A cold hand gripped my wrist from behind, and I screamed. But it was Rose.

"Rose?"

She looked straight at me, yet I could not discern her facial expression. At first, she said nothing, but then she finally spoke.

"It's true."

I awoke with a start, Miriam prodding me with a look of pale concern, like she'd seen a ghost. I sat up immediately like a spring trap being tripped, my head on a swivel, looking around, disoriented.

"Wh- what happened?" I asked.

"Lee, you were screaming. You scared me."

I began steadying my breathing. It was only a dream. My right hand hurt, though. I opened it up and saw the marble that Rose had given to me. I had been clutching it so tightly that it had imprinted itself deeply into my palm, and a bruise was starting to form. Surreptitiously, I slid the marble back into my pocket.

"Are you okay?" Miriam placed a hand on my shoulder hesitantly, probably wondering if that was an appropriate gesture towards someone she technically couldn't remember. To me, though, it was normal. She had comforted me all my life, from monsters under the bed to broken bones.

"Yeah, I think so. Sorry. Bad dream."

"That's okay. You wanna come down?"

"What time is it?" I asked, curious. It wasn't dusk; that was certain.

"A little after 1:00."

"Oh," I replied with some relief. "So, I wasn't sleeping that long."

"A couple of hours."

"Well, in the dream it was much later."

"Ready for some lunch?" Miriam asked. "It's probably cold now, though." I scooted off the bed, my stomach rumbling and the Reuben calling my name, but as soon as my feet hit the ground, I paused.

"What's the matter?" she asked, seeing my delay.

"I remember now."

"Yeah?"

"Yeah. Everything, I think. Umm... would it be okay if I ate up here?"

"Certainly," Miriam said with a smile, whisking herself away and returning a moment later with the sandwich. She let me be as I scarfed down the sandwich and wrote, remembering it all as if I were still in Somewhere.

I sat in Miriam's pickup with her as she drove. The notes had taken a few hours, but I was confident I had written down everything. Of course I spared some of the details, especially with Rose. Whatever little episode or dream had occurred back there seemed to open the door in my mind that had momentarily shut, and now it remained wide open.

I felt different somehow, like two minds had melded into one, or two doors were standing open in my mind when all my life I had been convinced there was only one. Maybe there were more than two even. While I was in Somewhere, life outside of Somewhere was a bit of a fog to me. Obviously, I could recall details—unlike whatever amnesia I had been experiencing earlier. As I sat in Miriam's guestroom writing, though, I got really *meta* and started reflecting on the memories I had had of this place when I was still living in Somewhere (reflecting on reflecting on here... *If I'm not careful*, I thought, *I am definitely going to go crazy... if it hasn't happened already*). But I remember, while being in Somewhere, that the details of my life outside of Somewhere were detached, like the biography of someone who wasn't me but who had maybe intersected with me for a time, had borrowed my skin-suit for a while.

Sitting in that truck, however, I felt completely tapped into both places—more lucid, full of more knowledge. I thought of the Bible story of the serpent in the garden, not just offering some delicious fruit but the opportunity to be like God, knowing good and evil.

To be honest, I was having trouble identifying what was good and what was evil or if those were even relevant terms, if *anything* was really evil or really good. I wasn't even sure if the things that happened in Somewhere were bad at all, neither could I distinguish between all that happened when I was awake and the things that took place while I was dreaming. Or were they a kind of vision?

My hand rested over my right pocket where I could feel the lump of the marble, faint, like the slightly raised ground of a freshly filled grave. It was a talisman, I thought, and when I touched it—especially when I put skin to metal—the connection to Rose and Somewhere was even stronger.

Miriam was driving me around town. It was an idea of hers. She wanted to see if there were others who recognized me, if it had only been her and my parents who couldn't. Maybe, she posited, the memory loss only affected the ones who were closest to me. She had called my mom to let her know that I was with her. "Who?" I could hear faintly on the other end of the phone. I rolled my eyes. "Oh, yes, that's right," she said, laughing. "I had nearly forgotten about our strange guest. Miriam, you wouldn't believe—"

"—Susan, I'm sorry to cut you off, but I gotta get going. Tell me later. I want to hear more."

"Yes, okay, but are you sure you should be spending time with him alone? He *is* a stranger, though he seems like a nice young man." Ouch.

"I'm sure," Miriam responded, and she glanced at me. "Actually, I *do* know him," she lied, "... er... distantly. I'll tell you about it another time. Tell Charles I said hi. Love you."

Well, she probably did at least know me a little more than when I first rang her doorbell earlier in the day. Plus, she had read my notes.

"Is this true?" she had asked, a bewildered expression on her face.

"It's true," I said, my own words startling me.

"And this Rose?" She raised one eyebrow quizzically. I blushed and averted my eyes. *I had left out the details, right?*

"Well," she said, putting down the notebook when she had finished, "if I thought you were a word on the tip of my tongue before, now I feel like I'm only missing the final letters, like I'm playing a game of hangman."

My eyes shot up to her.

"What?"

Funny choice of words, I thought, but "Nothing" is all I said.

"Okay," Miriam spoke as she pulled into a parking lot, "let's start here."

The church. If Miriam's place had been my second home growing up, this was easily my third. Sunday School, Awana, youth group. I was in church twice a week–or more–practically my entire life growing up.

We walked into the office. I smirked as Miriam hesitated. She was a regular for as long as I could remember. On the contact card that got handed out at the beginning of services, there was a place to mark such things as guest, member, and regular attender. She had once crossed out the *Regular* and scribbled in *irregular*. She thought it was funny, and that's how she described herself ever since. She often said that she was a non-church person who somehow ended up being at church for the past twenty years.

She was right, though. Miriam was not your cookie-cutter Christian. She just didn't fit the mold. That's not to say that people treated her poorly for it. But they never really embraced her John-the-Baptist-prophetic-desert-wanderer-antiestablishment-hippie-rock-n-roll-vibe. I think stepping into the church office made her nervous.

We made the rounds from office to office, cubicle to cubicle, visiting the secretary, associate pastors, volunteers, and eventually the senior pastor, Reverend Joe Miller, another one of my parents' close friends and the man who had baptized me when I was a kid. No one recognized me, though everyone was mildly bemused at Miriam's uncommon presence in the church offices.

Afterwards, we drove to my high school but forgot that it was closed the day before Thanksgiving. We moved on to the Applebee's where I had worked as a busboy my junior and senior years of high school, and as a waiter during most summer breaks in college, including the summer before moving to Somewhere. Miriam and I ordered a plate of buffalo wings and some drinks. We didn't chat much but instead spent the time observing how the workers would react to me. Despite knowing the bartender, two servers, and the assistant manager—and probably several cooks in the back—no one demonstrated the least amount of recognition.

It was weird; I felt like a stranger in my own town, like I had never existed. I had my memories. And I had Miriam who believed my memories. There was really nothing more I could do but hold on to those most basic truths while everything else felt like I was standing on vanishing clouds.

CHAPTER SIXTEEN

It happened midway through Thanksgiving dinner. I almost didn't notice. We were all sitting around the table: Mom, Dad, Miriam, and me. Miriam had confided earlier in the day that she had to do some convincing to allow me to stay, that my parents had shared with her they were planning on asking me to leave because they wanted to enjoy the holiday just as a family. However, Miriam invoked Christian charity and religious duty which apparently did the trick.

The table was full: turkey and gravy, mashed potatoes, green bean casserole, sweet potato casserole, a walnut and cranberry salad, hot dinner rolls. A pecan pie was also in the oven to be served with the quart of Ted Drewes vanilla custard my dad brought home, the only ice cream he'd eat.

On any other occasion and under any other circumstances, the feast before me would have me absolutely salivating. I would have been fasting since the day before in order to absolutely gorge myself. As it was, however, I quietly nibbled away at the food with very little appetite.

The table itself wasn't quiet, though, as my parents chatted away with Miriam. They had just changed topics and started discussing Miriam's trip to Sedona last summer with her sister's family.

"You know where I've always wanted to go?" my mom declared. "England. Ever since Lee's semester abroad there and especially those quaint little villages—what were they called, Lee?" She turned to me.

Without thinking I nearly responded, but then suddenly my eyes popped wide open. I glanced immediately at Miriam who had noticed it, too. Neither of us said anything, but our looks held plenty of meaning.

"Lee?" Mom was waiting for a response. Dad, too, was looking at me casually, waiting for my answer.

"Uh, well, are you talking about the Cotswolds?"

"That's it," she nodded, turning back to Miriam. "You wouldn't believe it. The pictures that Lee was showing us, and then I got on the computer to see for myself, and it looks just gorgeous. Apparently, the government won't let the villages be modernized in order to maintain the historical authenticity. Lee said it's a bit of a tourist trap, but Lord knows I don't care. Take my money, I say!"

Miriam laughed politely, but I knew she was shocked by what had just happened. *Wait, does that mean that she also remembers?*

"Hey, Miriam," I chimed in. "Do you remember when we went white water rafting like five years ago?"

"You mean when the instructor accidentally hit you in the head with his paddle, and you nearly fell out?"

That was enough. They were back. They were all back. And I would bet money that everyone else in the town knew me again, too. I nearly cried from joy. My parents, however, were clueless to the little parade of happiness going on inside of me and were simply left hanging.

"Was there any more to that question, son?" my dad asked, laughing at me.

"No," I smiled. "Just remembering. Sorry, that was kind of random."

"Well, *you're* a bit random," he teased, "but we love you anyway."

"Hey, Dad, wanna toss the football around in a bit."

"Sure! As long as Miriam promises not to eat all the Ted Drewes."

"Oh, please," she scoffed, "you know I got that shit in IV bags in my house. I take Ted Drewes intravenously." We all laughed. Only Miriam would curse around my parents and not care, and she's the only one who wouldn't receive disapproving looks from them either.

The rest of that day, I felt like I was part of the all-American family. Dad and I threw the football some before we went in and watched the end of the Cowboys-Lions game and ate pecan pie à la mode.

The next day I forced myself not to think of Somewhere. I felt relief at having my parents and Miriam back. I felt possessive. Miriam certainly knew the reason. My parents just teased me.

"We don't remember you being this excited about Thanksgiving," Dad said.

"I don't know. I've just missed you."

"Missed us? We've been here the whole time." I hesitated. I didn't know what he meant by that. What did they think about my absence the past three months? Did they know I was gone? I wasn't ready to ask. I just wanted to enjoy the time.

We went Black Friday shopping on Friday. Later we put up the Christmas tree and watched *National Lampoon's Christmas Vacation*, and Miriam, with a devilish smile, had even covertly added some marshmallow vodka to my hot chocolate.

Actually, I did think of Somewhere briefly. I actually jumped a little, startled, because for a moment, just when Cousin Eddie showed up to Clark's house with his rusted-out RV, I felt a body snuggle up beside me. When I turned to look, no one was there. I realized, though, that I had been fingering the marble in my pocket. I imagined movement, the snake perking up inside its prison.

On Saturday, we visited a Christmas tree lighting ceremony. We decorated the rest of the house and checked *Elf* and *A Christmas Story* off our annual list of Christmas movies.

Also, I picked up a cell phone. Rather, I took my old phone in to start a new plan. I still didn't really want it. I had learned to live less attached to a phone, though the initial stages took some adjustment. Nevertheless, I thought it might be best to have *some* way to stay more connected. I didn't let myself consider what that meant, however. Would I need it to keep in better touch with my parents when I went back to Somewhere? Would I even return?

We attended church together on Sunday, and I wasn't surprised to find that everyone greeted me as if they'd known me all my life, which they had. After the service, though, reality could no longer be staved off.

I was supposed to go back to work tomorrow.

I'd always been a responsible worker. Simply not showing up was so far outside of my character. Also, I had told Mrs. Copeland that I'd be back by Sunday.

And of course, most importantly, what about Rose? The marble sat in my pocket as both a heavy load and an inviting door. I resented the burden but couldn't be without it. Rose was everything, but Somewhere scared me. I wished I'd never been, but I wanted to be back there immediately. I felt weary, and at the same time, excited. My own place. My own Somewhere. Where magic and reality collided, even if it was filled with secrets and mystery. *Because* it was filled with secrets and mystery.

The feeling grew over Sunday dinner. I started to find myself daydreaming, longing for my lodging at Mrs. Copeland's, to cozy up in the oversized chair and read—I still hadn't finished *Pride and Prejudice*, I realized. Or I might pop in a DVD and watch *Friends* reruns on that tiny TV, an idea even more enticing to me than Netflix and Disney+ and every other streaming service here at my parents' house. The hanging woman, the stranger, the sounds in the night all diminished, or, rather, they mutated into puzzles instead of horrors. How much had I *actually* experienced outside of the norm, after all? Mostly Somewhere had just caused this unsettling string of dreams. And when I began to think of it, how much of what I'd witnessed in my waking moments weren't merely a heightened projection of imagination due to the dreams I'd been having, a sort of afterimage, a further manifestation in my waking moments of what had been playing in my mind while asleep?

What was I afraid of, really? A bit of the supernatural? I wasn't even ready to call it *supernatural*. An enigma was more like it. Even so, why *shouldn't* I be willing to live alongside unexplainable phenomena? At the dinner table I nearly laughed aloud, lost in my own thoughts. To live all these years praying to a supernatural force and then to be shocked to discover that supernatural forces may indeed exist! To long for a bit of magic and then be startled by its revelation! There was a sense of pride, a tug-of-war in my mind, about whether I would cower before strange events, before the possibility that what I secretly wished for, what–I now realized–I secretly knew all along, was, in fact, true.

It's true. It's true. It's true.

I thought about an artist who had always fascinated me during my studies, another British artist, Madge Gill. She was a mediumistic artist whose main body of work was created in the early 20th century after being possessed by a spirit guide. I wasn't exactly ready to begin cavorting with weird spirits, and I certainly shuddered at the thought of possession—I'd seen one too many horror movies for that—but Madge Gill's work had always left me with a sense of ripping the canvas between the material world and the immaterial, or maybe the *extra*-material.

But then there were my parents. And Miriam. I had lost them, *really* lost them, and had just won them back. Miriam looked up at me from her plate as though she could sense my inner machinations and smiled. I returned the smile and forced myself back into the conversation, to be with them.

"—that I shared a whole bottle of wine with my friend Trina in high school," I heard my mom say. "Let's just say we were a little more than slap-happy at that slumber party."

"Sue..." Dad chided. I rolled my eyes. Mom had told this story several times throughout the years. I think she liked the idea of keeping up with

Miriam's wild past. Her telling had evolved in correlation with my age. When I was younger and alcohol was strictly verboten and anathema in my house, my mom had first shared how she accidentally drank too much cough medicine one time when she got sick while staying at a friend's house. That was after Miriam had finished her own crazy account of a drunken camping trip with a group of hippies she'd met while backpacking in Colorado in the '80s. My dad's face grew five shades of red deeper until I thought his head might just pop, but he held his tongue because that was just after Miriam's husband had died. I heard him and my mom fighting later that night, something about how she was simply encouraging such reckless behavior with her cough medicine story and corrupting her own son.

But that was a long time ago. My mom had never stopped elaborating on that tale, especially as I got older and certainly when I could drink legally. Mom moved from cough syrup to a sip of wine to finishing the leftovers of a bottle of wine to consciously opening a bottle of wine and drinking it together with her high school friend. My dad had stopped scolding her and now just teased her a bit.

For the moment, all was well and good, but by Monday night, I was feeling shitty, wondering what Tom must be thinking after I missed my shift. I rolled over on my bed, grabbed my phone, and opened up Google Maps, considering the drive time and when I might head back.

One problem: Somewhere, Missouri didn't seem to exist.

The next morning, nearly a week after I'd left Somewhere, I headed to the library. Miriam, who worked at an organic food store—her husband had had a substantial life insurance policy, so she only worked because she enjoyed it—was able to switch shifts with someone and join me. Mom and Dad wouldn't be able to take off work and, frankly, I just wasn't able to confide in them yet the same way I did with Miriam.

"So, what do you want to know?" she asked me as we scooted our chairs up to a bank of computers, a stack of books about Missouri sitting in between us.

"Whatever I can find."

I started with a Google search: "Somewhere, Missouri." Or I should say *re-started*.

The night before, after finding no Google Map results for Somewhere (besides the names of a bunch of random businesses: It's Noon Somewhere, It's 5 O'clock Somewhere, Somewhere on a Beach Tanning), I tried every maps application I could think of: Apple Maps, Waze, Bing Maps. Even MapQuest is still around apparently. I thrashed around in the garage after that, searching through a dirty cabinet filled with old and equally dirty travel maps, relics of '90s family road trips. I found several maps of Missouri and scoured them minutely for evidence of Somewhere but to no avail. The truth is, I wasn't entirely sure where it was. After the exit near Columbia, my memory was foggy. Even so, I marked off a square area of the map and systematically scanned up and down, making sure to hit every tiny Ma and Pop country town along the way, from unincorporated communities like Middle Grove and Maud to slightly larger towns like Princeton and Unionville.

My methodical search reminded me of playing Indian ball at an abandoned sandlot growing up. Anytime one of us really got a hold of a pitch and dropped the ball in the woods or the overgrown field, however many of us were playing, we would spread out about five feet from each other and comb the area one small step at a time until the ball was invariably discovered. It didn't matter if it took fifteen minutes or two hours, finding the ball was as much of a game as what we had been playing before. Only once could I remember that we finally had to give up after four hours of searching over two different days. This search for Somewhere was feeling similar: a defeat, a lost ball.

So, there I was, with Miriam, starting over, this time at the library where I figured I might find additional helpful resources. The search results were mixed and pretty much nonsense. An Instagram account called Somewhere in Missouri. A five-year old song by the same name on some person's YouTube channel. A list of random shops and restaurants in Missouri that had *somewhere* in the name, like my search in Google Maps. For a split second I thought I had struck gold when I saw "somewhere missouri" listed as a place on Foursquare's city guide website, but it turned out to be the name of a travel company that looked like it never got off the ground.

"Any luck?" I inquired of my partner.

"Nada."

I smirked as I realized, glancing at Miriam, how easily she could pull off being a librarian. She wore a flannel shirt with her hair tied back in a bun and a pen stuck into the middle of it, and she had foregone her usual contact lenses for a pair of round, plastic-rimmed glasses that made her look very bookish, a far cry from the rock and roll vibe she gave off when wearing one of her many band t-shirts.

"What?" she demanded with a quizzical eye.

"Nothing. Are you sure you want to work at Green Earth? Cuz you could definitely pull off being a librarian." She rolled her eyes but smiled nonetheless.

We each turned back to our respective screens to continue searching, but I was feeling increasingly flustered. And bewildered.

"This doesn't make any sense," I muttered to myself.

"Yeah, I'm not finding anything. This is weird." Miriam sat up straight and turned to me. "Lee, I'm being serious. You're not fucking with me, right?"

I couldn't help glancing at the actual librarian who was standing at a desk nearby. After hearing Miriam's language, She gave us the stink eye, and I snickered. "Sorry!" Miriam whispered.

"You're ruining your chances of working here," I teased. She slapped my arm.

"Lee, I'm being serious, though. What's going on?"

"I don't know," I insisted. "Honestly."

"How does a place just *not* exist?"

"Believe me. I don't know. I mean, it is a small, rural community, and they seemed pretty private. It's like one of the most quaint places I've been, but I never really noticed any tourists or out-of-towners, even for the fair or the Halloween parade, which was always kind of weird. Is it possible that some small towns aren't on a Google map? Or can they opt out or something?"

"No! Well, at least, I don't think so. Okay," she sighed, "let's look at the map again." She rolled her chair closer to my computer. "But this time, let's just use the satellite imaging over the town even if it's not listed."

"See, that's why I bring you along," I replied encouragingly. But I wasn't optimistic. I still couldn't figure out how I'd arrived in Somewhere—all three times! And frustratingly, I couldn't even recall the path I had chosen when I left Somewhere a week before. All of my recollections were vague, just rolling background images out my car windows, a sleep machine of soothing rural November images rather than ocean sounds.

"I went north after Columbia," I muttered. "No. I mean, I didn't exit at Columbia, it was actually at this winery just past it, I remember." Tracing my route wasn't easy. I had to zoom in considerably onto I-70, and after being certain that I'd passed over the winery several times without finding it, I eventually had to use the Street View feature and slowly creep along I-70 west of Columbia. Thankfully, it was actually not far past: Rocheport.

But from there, I was lost. Like the night before, I simply could not remember the route I had taken to Somewhere, and looking at Google

Maps made me even more confused.

With eyes closed, I imagined the winery to my right as I exited the interstate. I drove through open land for a few miles and then through the heart of Rocheport, passing various bed and breakfasts, quaint shops, and restaurants. I continued on a state highway north of town and through more open land. This is where I really started concentrating. Like sometimes when I couldn't remember my online password and I had to literally put my fingers on a keyboard to activate muscle memory, I sat in the library chair trying to envision myself driving—seeing, *feeling* where I was going. From there, maybe I'd be able to better trace the direction on the map. But it was futile. Even if I traced out a semi-radius as far north as the Missouri-Iowa border and as far east and west as I could go and still sort of call it *northern Missouri*—because even the Somewhervians referred to themselves as living in northern Missouri—I just couldn't find the place on the map.

I flipped through the pages of the Missouri reference books I had set down beside me, again with no luck. Most indexes listed towns in alphabetical order with a conspicuous absence between Smithville and South West City. But even the one book I found that had divided the state by regions was no help. I thumbed through every single page in the "Northeast" section and found nothing. Then, the Northwest section to be safe. Still nothing.

"It doesn't exist," I whispered, staring dumbly at the computer screen with the last reference book sitting open in my lap.

"What did you say?" Miriam asked, sneaking up on me.

"I can't find it." I reached my hand into my pocket and felt the marble, my talisman, my connection to Rose, to Somewhere. Perhaps it would trigger something. And it did.

I edged my thumb along the marble's curvature, and I thought of my hand in Rose's, I thought of subtly caressing her hand, pulling my thumb up and down along that bone just above hers. I knew with certainty that

I wasn't going to find Somewhere on a map. Still…

"I wonder if it had a different name before," I stated.

"What?"

"I don't know, maybe Somewhere is like an adopted nickname that's been used so long that's just what everyone else calls it."

"Like, any one of these other towns in 'northern Missouri'—" Miriam made air quotes to acknowledge my vague parameters—"could be what you know as Somewhere." I hesitated for a moment but shook my head.

"No, I don't think so. I don't think we're going to find Somewhere on a map."

"What are you saying?" Miriam shifted her posture and gave me a teasing look. "Wait, Lee, did you join a cult? Is that what this is? This community has removed itself from modern society and followed the teachings of Sister Star, who is actually the new Jesus?"

I laughed. "You got me."

"Let me guess, red Kool-aid? Do they have a bunker there with a bunch of weapons? Actually," she said as she took a seat, "did you know—"

"—did you know…" I interrupted.

"Huh?"

"You start every epic tale of one of your wild escapades with, *actually, did you know*." She paused and tilted her head up in reflection.

"Hmm… I think you're right," she said and chuckled. "Anyway, as I was saying, did you know that I once stayed with a hippie commune for like six months."

"*Only* six months?"

"Hey, shut up now! I'm not *that* crazy." I just raised my eyebrows and said nothing, smiling.

"Why'd you leave?"

"They ran out of pot," she replied and winked.

A while later, Miriam and I left the library with little to show for our efforts besides establishing that Somewhere was not to be found on a map. I didn't know exactly what that meant. I knew it wasn't a cult commune, as Miriam suggested, but a place couldn't just exist and not exist simultaneously, right?

We went and grabbed some Imo's pizza for lunch. The classic St. Louis-style pizza distracted me for a few minutes: the square-cut, cracker-thin crust topped with sauce and Provel cheese, a unique blend of Swiss, cheddar, and provolone. And sausage. It was the only topping I allowed. *God, I missed this,* I thought while devouring nearly half of the extra-large that we ordered.

"I'd have thought you were crazy," Miriam said as we climbed back in the car, "if I hadn't personally experienced the dramatic change of not knowing you to knowing you. Something weird's going on, and it's tied to wherever it was that you were."

"But you believe me, though?"

"I do. I'm not entirely sure why I do, but I do." She hesitated before saying, "Hey, I was thinking that if you go back, maybe I could go with you. You know, like for support."

I was mid-bite, and my hand froze in the air. I flashed my eyes at her with an expression of suspicion and aggression. I don't know what seized me, but there was no way in hell I was bringing Miriam. "That's not happening," I responded in a chilling tone.

The look of hurt on Miriam's face snapped me out of whatever momentary lapse I had; I apologized sincerely. She chuckled and shrugged it off, and we left together on that awkward note. I don't know why I reacted that way, but her suggestion triggered a sudden backlash of possessiveness towards Somewhere. It may have been a mystery, but it was still mine. *I* had found a place that didn't even exist. *I* was meant to be there for whatever reason. I may have invited her into the secret, but I hadn't invited her into the place itself.

I dropped Miriam off at her house and headed back home. If I had known that I'd be leaving St. Louis a few hours later, perhaps I would have taken her for ice cream or something and tried to prove to her that we were okay. Instead, she would learn of my absence and probably wonder if it was her fault. Maybe, indirectly, it was.

CHAPTER SEVENTEEN

I took the Rocheport exit around 1:00 in the morning. Under other circumstances, I might have laughed at how familiar I'd become with this place simply through a computer screen, but I was too focused to find humor or irony in the situation. The marble was still in my pocket, now a warmth, a constant presence, a companion.

My car's headlights extended through the night, far-reaching arms pulling away the curtain of darkness so that I could navigate to where I knew I needed to be. I'd decided I wanted to be back in Somewhere. Mysteries and all. Unanswered questions that I wanted answers to.

And Rose.

And, honestly, everything about Somewhere. I wanted to be back in the art gallery—though I'd have some apologizing and maybe begging to do for failing to show up two days in a row. I wanted to see Maggie and Lenora again. I wanted to visit the Amendment 21 Brewery again. I wanted to sit down for a hand of bridge with Mrs. Copeland. And most importantly, besides Rose, I just wanted to be back in my cozy room again, to pick up my half-finished *Pride and Prejudice*, maybe watch some *Friends*. In my space. *Mine.*

I had tried to move on from my aggressive reaction to Miriam's request to join me in Somewhere, but I couldn't. *Who the hell does she think she is? That's the problem with people; you open the door a crack, and they want to take the door off its fucking hinges. God! In what world does she think it's okay to invite herself to this place that I found?!*

According to my thinking, I had discovered some unknown land, though, like Christopher Columbus discovering America, it was pure dumb luck that I had stumbled upon Somewhere. In fact, unlike Columbus, I hadn't even been searching for my destination. If anything, it found me.

It found me. It wanted me. *No. I'm being stupid. And I treated Miriam poorly, who may be my favorite person in the whole world. I have to fix that. I'll call her once I get to Somewhere. That'll be the first thing I do in the morning, even before I talk to Tom.*

In my mind, I continued that game of ping-pong, clearly recognizing the foolishness of my thoughts and the obvious incoherence of my selfish attitude towards Somewhere but then getting sucked right back into them anyway. Generally, I'd say that Miriam didn't cause me to leave. At least she didn't push me away. But sometimes, you don't know what you have until someone wants a piece of it, too. I couldn't get her suggestion out of my head even when I had returned home. It festered that afternoon and at dinnertime with my parents. I did have flashes of peace. In fact, my parents didn't realize how close they were to inadvertently causing me to abandon all notions of ever returning to Somewhere when they began discussing what they wanted to do that Christmas season. That's what I needed, not to renounce Somewhere but to replace it. I needed a new vision. And the power of my family's holiday plans, combined with the recent scare of losing them, was almost enough to bury Somewhere in my mind.

Almost.

I left Rocheport behind me and began winding through the countryside. *This is it,* I thought. *This is where I inexplicably find my way to Somewhere even though it's not on the map.* I was panicky, though. Before, I had found my way while unconscious of my actions, completely unaware of the strangeness of my arrival. Now, I was in my head. I knew that something enigmatic was supposed to happen.

It was like trying to get back into a dream. The first time you're there, you're just there. But when you wake up and long to be back, you find that you can't get in. And occasionally, in your trying, you accidentally do, in fact, fall back asleep and land right back there in the dream! But upon waking, you realize you have no idea how you achieved that and resign yourself to luck and maybe a little bit of magic.

I didn't want luck, though. I wanted to be there. And I was afraid something wasn't going to work. The last three times that I was on this road, I was in a state of peace and wonder—a hazy, pleasant fog. But I wasn't feeling that sensation this time. Instead, I was hyper-aware. Almost as though Somewhere knew I was watching and didn't want to be seen.

I continued driving, trying not to think but to feel. Whatever that meant. Very New Age, Jedi-ish crap. I felt like young Luke Skywalker in *A New Hope* trying to guide the missiles into the Death Star's main reactor with only his unaided vision. Only here I was trying to guide my car into a town that, according to every possible reference resource I could find online and in my local library, didn't even exist.

Was I supposed to turn there? I wondered. *Or here?* I stopped the car. I had no clue where I was. I checked the GPS on my phone though I didn't know what good that would do for me since I didn't actually know where Somewhere was located, only a vague general direction, and even *that* I was unsure about. According to GPS, I was exactly where I thought I'd be: in the middle of nowhere, about an hour north of Rocheport.

I put my car back in gear and crept along for about another forty-five minutes, making very little actual progress because at every turn and intersection, I was paralyzed by hesitation. The truth was, I didn't recognize a single road, including the road I was on. Instead, I was amazed how I ever arrived in Somewhere in the first place.

I turned around. I drove all the way back to Rocheport—beyond, actually. I got back on the interstate, going east towards home. I exited at Columbia and circled back onto the interstate going west. I wanted to approach the Rocheport exit with my mind reset. I breathed in deeply, exhaled, and tried imagining one of the times I'd arrived in Somewhere before. It'd been daytime, but I could now see the edges of the horizon growing lighter as dawn approached. Perhaps that would help me visualize. The enchantment of that drive to Somewhere, the magic lingering in the air, the fairy tale I was entering into.

I felt a mild thrill of hope as I entered Rocheport and drove through its middle and out the other side. (A few people were already out and walking their dogs in the early morning darkness.) I had let my mind drift, I had allowed myself to enter that state of peace and unfocused wonder, that daydream. *I think I'm doing it,* I told myself. *Wait, no. Shit! Don't think about it. Just let go.*

That's how I drove. This second try was certainly better, certainly in a different frame of consciousness, relaxed. But occasionally, thoughts would crowd in, analyzing my progress, and I'd have to stuff them back down and simply drive. I tuned out everything else. At one point, my car jolted over something in the road, which jarred me back to reality. I was afraid I'd hit something or someone in my forced unfocus. It had only been a large branch, though, and satisfied, I returned to whatever state of consciousness I'd been in before, willing myself to notice nothing but the vague contours of the road.

How long that went on, I didn't know. Eventually, I had to bring myself back out of that contrived dreamlike state and reassess the situation. It was early morning, the sun compelling daggers of shadows to lay on the ground slantwise around me. I stopped the car. I wasn't in Somewhere.

"Oh, shit!" I exclaimed, looking down at my phone right as it powered down. I hadn't had time to charge my phone before leaving my parents' house, but I didn't think it would be a problem since I hadn't anticipated driving in circles. A charger lay on the passenger seat, but my old Aspire certainly didn't have the adequate port to charge it. And to make matters worse, I glanced back at my dashboard to see the gas light on.

"How long has that been on?" I exclaimed, letting out a small yell of frustration. I moved to check my phone for the nearest gas station. Oh, right, it was dead. I released a string of expletives and mashed my head against the beeping steering wheel.

Deliberating internally, I wondered if it'd be better to shut off the car and conserve gas while I walked to a nearby house and asked directions to a gas station, or would it be better to just keep driving and hoping I found one (and stop for directions if I saw someone)? Once again, I wasn't exactly sure how far I was from Rocheport, but I figured I wasn't making it all the way back there on my diminishing supply of gas, yet I couldn't remember a single gas station after leaving Rocheport. I opted for the latter option, willing myself to believe that a gas station had to be nearby, certain that clutching my talisman would yield positive results.

It didn't.

Less than a minute later, my car sputtered to a stop. I let out a loud, exasperated *Fuck!* before sighing and settling into the reality of my predicament.

After waiting about forty-five minutes and hoping a car would drive by, I grew restless and decided to seek a house. Missouri country folk were generally welcoming, friendly, and willing to lend a hand whenever possible. Hell, I bet that the first place I found would probably have some reserve gas themselves.

I followed the road in the same direction I had been driving. It took me longer than I'd hoped, but I saw a long lane leading to a farmhouse after a while. I noticed one of those plastic Little Tikes slides on the front lawn and a host of other kids toys. *Geez*, I thought, *what would it be like to grow up this remotely as a kid?* Then another idea struck me: *What would it be like to live on the edge of Somewhere?* I shook my head, now convinced that Somewhere, somehow, was so tucked away that geographical proximity probably meant nothing. And there I was trying to find it, find Narnia practically, like a madman.

I sauntered along the lane in no hurry as I deliberated whether or not I should ring the doorbell so early in the morning. Farm families are different, I reasoned; they had probably been up since before dawn anyway, attending to various chores. My deliberations didn't end up mattering anyway because about fifty yards from the house, the front door opened, and a man walked out onto the wide veranda, staring at me.

I slowed my pace even more, hesitant. The guy's scrutiny never wavered from me; his eyebrows were knitted together, and his lips were pursed to create an overall visage of hostility and intimidation. *So much for the kind, Missouri country folk thing,* I thought. Instead, I was starting to get a *Hills Have Eyes* vibe and nearly chuckled at the irony of getting slaughtered in an event completely unrelated to my trying to return to Somewhere. Or was it related? My mind was all over the place.

"Can I help you?" the man said when I approached within earshot. Strange how the exact same words in the exact same order but with a markedly different tone are used to greet customers in a store, the customer who's always right. Because at that moment, the only thing that I felt the man wanted to help me with was burying a load of hot lead into my fleeing back.

"Um, yeah," I responded, swallowing the bile that was creeping up my throat and crossing my legs to keep from shitting myself. "My car broke down a mile or so back in that direction." I pointed. "And I was wondering if you might be able to tell me where the nearest gas station is?"

"Don't you damn city folk always have some slick new phone to get you places?" was all he said, his steely glare unchanging. I pulled out my phone.

"It's dead."

He continued staring at me, unflinching, silent. Finally, he spoke up again.

"Well, you must be kinda stupid." He laughed, not good-naturedly. I resented the remark, but I wasn't going to argue with him. I attempted a small grin as he descended the steps.

"Follow me."

To where he stores the bodies, I bet.

He walked around to the back of the house and entered a small workshop. Sure enough, he had about four 5-gallon gas cans. He grabbed one and handed it to me. The weight of the can immediately yanked my arm down, nearly pulling my shoulder out of its socket. That got the man going.

"Haha! There you go."

"Um, thanks." I set it down, messaging my shoulder. "You're good with me just taking it?"

"Well, bring it back."

"Yeah, yeah, of course," I responded.

"But I'm not too worried. If you *were* a dick and just took off, I'm out ten bucks, but I've gained one more reason to hate city folks."

"How do you know I'm from the city?"

The man gave me a condescending look like, Come on, isn't it obvious?

"Well, among other reasons, you don't live in a place like this and not know your neighbors, even if the closest ones are miles away. And besides, just look at yourself and look at me. Do we look the same?" He had a point. I was wearing a puffy, Patagonia coat, jeans with tapered legs, and a pair of TOMS loafers despite the cold. I owned boots, but I had left them in my apartment.

On the other hand, he wore a heavy canvas coat and pants—both slightly different tones of beige, Carhartt—and big, steel-toe boots caked in mud.

"Touché. Anyway, thanks again. I'll bring it back in about half an hour or so."

"No problem. No rush," he said, waving me off a little less menacingly than before. I began walking away but then turned back.

"Hey, have you heard of a town called Somewhere?"

"Sorry?"

"Is there a town nearby called Somewhere?"

"Somewhere? Are you shitting me?"

"No, no. I uh..." I didn't know how to respond. How do you explain to a tough-looking farmer dude who only minutes before looked like he might grab a shotgun and blow a hole through your chest that there's a town nearby that apparently doesn't exist and that you're trying to find it?

I couldn't discern the new look on the man's face. Meanness or utter aversion at what he perceived to be an absolute idiot standing in front of him.

"...never mind. A buddy of mine had told me there was a small town in these parts called Somewhere—yeah, I know, weird name—but anyway, I didn't believe him, and it sounds like you're confirming it."

The man shook his head.

"Just bring back the gas can," he said as he trudged back to his house. I'm pretty sure he murmured something like *fucking morons*, but I couldn't be sure.

"Nice one, Lee," I told myself as I hauled the heavy gas can with me, exhausted by the time I recognized the last bend. Finally, my car was just around the corner.

Only it wasn't.

"Fuck!" I was too tired to be more creative with my cursing.

I looked around. The landscape looked the same. But then, as I looked further ahead, I realized that I wasn't sure if it *was* the same. Everything sort of blended together where I was. Just a bunch of Missouri farmland and forest.

I shuffled on for about another fifteen minutes. *This can't be right,* I thought. I had lost nearly all capacity to use my arms, so I set the gas can down and decided to forge ahead a little further. I could come back for the gas can, but there was no point continuing on like that and draining away my last bit of energy.

Being free of my burden slightly assisted my mood, but I could not find my car and was growing angry and panicky.

"This can't be right," I said the same thing to myself again. I continued on much longer than I had planned but finally turned back. A while later, I knew that I'd passed the spot where the gas can should have been. *Some douchebag must've stopped and grabbed it,* I speculated. But it was just something to reassure me. There had been no side roads, and no vehicle had passed me in either direction. I figured I'd be back at the farmhouse any moment, and maybe I could just lean into the whole "stupid city guy" character and maybe ask the guy to drive me to my car with another container of gas. I'd offer to pay.

But the house wasn't coming into view. Once again, completely distrusting my bearings, I persisted until I was absolutely certain I'd surpassed the distance. More to stymie the fear growing within me, I laughed and said aloud, "I wish I had a smartwatch. I bet I've already walked my ten thousand steps."

I circled in place. In one direction, the road wound away through a grove of trees. In the other direction, the road extended onward to the horizon, probably miles. Bunches of trees freckled the landscape in that direction, but otherwise, it was just wide-open sky and Missouri countryside.

Nothing seemed familiar. I was tired and now hungry. Knowing nothing else to do, I removed myself from the side of the road and planted myself on a bed of brown leaves below a giant, bare oak tree.

CHAPTER EIGHTEEN

Night enveloped me.

I quickly scrambled to my feet, realizing that I had not only fallen asleep, I had slept the entire day away. In the distance opposite the road, I noticed a faint light. Thinking that in the daytime I would have noticed a building or car or whatever it was emitting that light, I was momentarily puzzled. Shrugging it off, though, I figured that the deep, country darkness surrounding me was making the distant light visible now when it had been unnoticed earlier. After glancing around me again, I began trudging in that direction over the dead grass, away from the road. I was baffled to soon realize that the light was coming from the farmer's house. *How'd I end up on a different road than before? Or is it the same road, just winding around in a way I hadn't paid attention to earlier?* My confusion gave way to relief, though, indicating the fearful state the darkness had left me in: I bet the guy was pissed at me for not returning his gas can, but what other option did I have?

After walking up the lane, I stood hesitatingly just below the porch, dimly illuminated by one naked bulb. I observed my surroundings, noting the absolute sense of isolation in the darkness. Everything was pitch black, no stars or moon. Turning, I set my foot on the first step, which let out more of a shriek than a creak. Startled by the noise, I quickly removed my foot. After pausing for a moment while my nerves recovered, I laughed quietly to myself and walked up the stairs and to the front door. I took a deep breath before knocking, having no idea what time it was. I braced myself for whatever wrath was in store and rapped my knuckles against the wooden door which pulled in a few inches at my touch.

I hesitated, not knowing what I should do. Sensing that I hadn't knocked loud enough to gain anyone's attention, I did so again but with more force, each time my knuckles chasing further the ever-widening doorway. There I waited for several minutes, knowing that it might take some time for someone to wake out of deep sleep, put on the proper clothes, and make their way to the front door. But I heard no movement inside. One more time, I knocked and waited. No response.

Having no other recourse besides turning back, I pushed the door the rest of the way in and stepped across the house's threshold. I didn't think that my surroundings could grow any darker than what I had just walked through, but I was essentially blind in the interior of the house. Fumblingly, I felt along the wall for a light switch but instead bumped into an entry table where my hand brushed over a flashlight. *I guess they're prepared.* I hesitated. *Prepared for what?*

Flipping on the flashlight's switch, a light beam penetrated the darkness, illuminating tiny dust motes. I scanned the walls and finally discovered the light switches, but nothing happened when I flipped them on. *Prepared for what?* echoed again in my head. *Why wouldn't their electricity work?*

"Figures," I said aloud but immediately regretted it, afraid of my own voice in the silence that sat imposingly around me, like a hall of wax monsters. I still wasn't sure if anyone was there and didn't want to catch anyone off guard or, worse yet, have the farmer sneak up on me with a loaded gun, thinking I was a burglar.

"Hello," I called out weakly, fearfully. "Hello," I said again with a louder voice. "It's Lee. The guy you helped earlier with the gas can."

Still no reply. I continued to sweep the flashlight back and forth around the house. On my left was an empty dining room, on my right was a staircase, and beyond that was an empty living room with a fireplace.

Straight ahead was a hallway with doors on both sides leading back to a kitchen area. I tiptoed towards the kitchen but halted when I heard noise above me. It was the lightest of thumps, but it was the first sound I had heard that wasn't my own. Pausing to listen, I noticed that the thumping continued at intermittent intervals, usually many seconds apart.

I stood in place for a while. The sound didn't cease, but I heard no other noises, no other movements. I knew the smart thing would be to simply tiptoe my way out of the house and away from the place altogether, but I didn't. By then, I was convinced the house was empty, and the allure of a roof over my head trumped my instinctive impulse to leave. Any number of common things could go bump in the night, and I wasn't in Somewhere, so I wasn't anticipating any unexplainable, supernatural phenomena. However, my nerves on edge, I had to specifically remind myself of that rationality to avoid paralysis.

I tried to climb the stairs quietly, but every step gave out groan after loud groan. Except for the small beam of light spilling from the flashlight, I wore the deep darkness around me like a coat. My stomach was uneasy as my back was turned to the first floor. I felt as though something, someone, was watching me. I felt the presence of the farmer somehow. Had I left the front door open?

I spun around, the beam of light slicing the wall and stopping at the front door, but it was closed. Still, small windows on either side looked like strange eyes.

I stepped onto the landing. To my right, a door stood slightly ajar. Down the hall to my left were several more doors. The noise was coming from there, a door on the very far end of the hall where I could finally see the faintest bit of light. The moon must have come out from behind its cloud cover.

"Hello," I said again, my voice now a comfort rather than a disturbance, as I inched my way to the far end of the landing. I was truly frightened then and thought of leaving, but it hit me that I was equally scared of the dark outside the farmer's house. I was trapped "between a rock and a hard place," as they say. I forced my feet, now lead weights, to continue.

As I grew closer, I noticed a shadow on the floor—created by the moon's luminescence—but the shadow was rhythmic, almost like a metronome, appearing and disappearing with the occasional thump that I had been hearing from below.

I stepped into the room and cried aloud in terror, falling backward. The hanging woman was swinging, her feet thudding against the wall under the window. Her skin was pale, a trick of the sickly moonlight because I knew she was a Black woman. Her head bowed, her hair an unkempt hive of tangles indicating what exactly? Some kind of struggle before *this* had happened to her? The woman's eyes were closed this time, which almost made my fear greater, like maybe she wasn't fully dead, like maybe the eyelids would raise and she would stare at me in accusation, like maybe I had something to do with all this.

As if reading my mind, I watched her head turn towards me while her eyes remained shut. Then her mouth opened. I sat transfixed on the floor in terror, my hands planted beside me, the flashlight lying to the side, unheeded and unnecessary in the moonlit room. With her mouth agape, the woman let out the most horrifying scream: deep, guttural, pained.

My reflexes kicked in, and I scrambled to my feet and sprinted down the hall. I nearly crashed past the staircase, but I managed to turn and descend. I was about halfway down when I slowed.

I noticed the fireplace lit below me. I could hear the crackling, see the lights dancing along the walls below, feel the warmth. I forgot about the woman above. I continued my descent calmly, and when I reached the bottom, I turned into the living room, not at all surprised to find Rose on the couch. She turned to me.

"Hi, Lee."

Absent-mindedly, I released the marble in my pocket. How long had I been holding on to it? I walked over to Rose and sat beside her, placing my arm around her as she cozied up into me, her head resting on my chest.

We stayed there like that for a while, gazing into the fire, mesmerized by the movement of the flames, the popping of the wood, the feeling of each other's bodies pressed into one another. Aside from her greeting, we had not said a word. I guess we didn't need to; we were perfectly content how we were.

After some time, however, Rose lifted her head up off of my chest and stared into my eyes. She leaned in closer; I could feel her breath on my lips, see the inhale and exhale of her chest, and we were suspended in that moment, my breath speeding up in anticipation, until finally she pressed her lips to mine.

Our bodies intertwined on the couch, kissing fiercely and sensitively, wholly present and wholly gone, the sweetness of her mouth, the softness of her body, the shape of her as my hands slipped up and down, as her hands dug into my back, unified into one, yet distinctly separate in our bodies and even, in some ways, standing apart from ourselves as spirits. With every ounce of my being I wanted Rose. We continued like that, our passion building. One of Rose's hands slipped under my shirt, fingers skimming slightly over the surface of my stomach and chest. I reached for the bottom hem of her shirt, beginning to tug ever so slightly upwards until—

"—Lee?"

I blinked. I looked at Rose. She was bundled up in a winter coat with a knit cap and a scarf. Her cheeks were touched with a blush of pink from the... *Cold?* I wondered to myself. I glanced around me. Where was the fireplace? And why was the couch so hard? Peering down, I realized that I wasn't even sitting on a couch; it was a bench. Around me snow was falling, and we weren't in the house; I was with Rose in a park off of Main Street. I was back in Somewhere.

"Wh-where...how..." I stammered.

"Ready?" was Rose's only response.

"For what?"

"What do you mean *for what*? We're meeting up with everyone for the Christkindlmarkt."

"The what?"

"The Christmas market," Rose said, rolling her eyes at me.

"Oh, alright, yeah. Hey, why are we here then?"

Rose blushed.

"Wait," I said, and my eyes widened as a rush of memory flooded over me. "You said you wanted to take a quick detour, then you said let's sit down here, and..." I looked above me. Hanging down from a bare branch was a golden string dangling a small bunch of mistletoe. I raised my eyebrow at Rose. "You're pretty mischievous, you know?"

"Hey, I didn't hear you complaining before—" she replied sardonically.

"I'm not complaining. Who's complaining?" With that, I leaned over and gave her what I assumed was *another* kiss though I couldn't be sure.

"Okay, let's go," I said, standing and pulling Rose up with me.

We walked the short distance to the outdoor market while a million thoughts jumbled around in my head. I remembered arriving in Somewhere but couldn't remember how. It had been a few weeks ago. Everyone had seemed surprised to see me; in fact, I had given Mrs. Copeland quite a shock when I entered the kitchen early the morning after I had arrived (I had gotten in late and had gone straight to my apartment). I was apologetic to Tom, and he seemed cool with me. I could recall little snippets of events over the previous weeks: working, being in The Book and Bean, visiting Maggie and Lenora again, spending time with Rose. I had also been over to the Whitakers' again, and the girls had told me all about their Thanksgiving and setting up the Christmas tree in their new Christmas pajamas.

All these memories, though, played in my head more like a movie, like I was watching them but had never experienced them. What felt more immediately real was trying to find Somewhere: getting lost, running out of gas, the farmhouse. I had fallen asleep under a tree after losing my car, the gas can, and the house, but I wasn't sure that what had followed— the hanging woman, Rose and the fireplace—wasn't a dream. Still, how could I explain the overlap of memories, of both being in Somewhere and not being in Somewhere at the same time.

And remembering both.

One thing I was absolutely certain of, though, was that I was now back in Somewhere. Curious, I felt down to my pocket; the marble was still there.

The Christmas market dazzled me. Despite the simmering mishmash of thoughts inside me, I was enchanted by the scene and quickly pushed everything else aside for the moment.

Shop windows were illuminated by strings of lights and elaborate displays; model trains, wreaths and holly, miniature trees, painted and frosted glass. On the sidewalks in front of the windows, dozens of booths were lined up with their various local wares: soaps, candles, honeys, jellies, bread, pastries, chocolate, toys, artwork (was I supposed to be working, I wondered), Christmas decor, cheeses, scarves, and so much more.

Glowing cozily, the street lamps hung over the townspeople as they milled about, laughing, playing, and buying. Christmas music sounded in the background but was frequently cut off as a band of carolers swept up and down the cobblestone street in joyful song. I felt like I was in a Dickens novel.

"Hey, it's Kenny," I laughed and pointed when I first saw the carolers.

Something felt incongruent about Kenny, who was kind of a clown, to be dressed up in Victorian apparel and singing alongside others who, to be honest, looked like the kind of people Kenny would make fun of. He seemed earnest, however, even if he still sought to be the center of attention with a few rhythms and bodily movements that didn't exactly match the group's.

"Yeah," Rose said, "he's been doing that for several years, and you know, somehow it suits him."

At that point, Kenny noticed us, and his face beamed. He waved but, in so doing, dropped both his battery-operated candle and his songbook. He quickly bent down to retrieve them while waddling to try and keep up with the departing group of carolers. Just then Mike, David, and Eleanor approached us. But no Mattie.

"Lee!" David shouted. I had to think back over the last two weeks, but the access to memories was stilted, like I had to manually flip through an old card index to determine if I had seen David since being back in Somewhere. I *had* gone out with Rose and others, but I couldn't recall David being there. No, now I was sure of it. This was my first time seeing David since before I left for Thanksgiving.

"Hi, David, great to see you. Hey, so I've been wondering, where's Mattie been?" I asked everyone.

Something clearly passed between all of them–even Rose–a strange ripple that I couldn't decipher. But I got no clear answer.

"She's gone," Mike stated, nonchalantly. *Uncaringly*, I thought.

"What do you mean gone?"

"I think she went on a trip or something," Rose jumped in.

"Yeah, she was talking about traveling, remember?" Mike seemed to snarl. At that point David interrupted.

"Anyway, she'll be back. But, I'm glad I ran into you," he said and then dashed off inexplicably. We all stood there frozen for a moment, wondering what had just happened. Unsurprisingly, he came back with beer: two large bombers and ten plastic cups. Of course, we had nowhere to sit or comfortably enjoy them, so he awkwardly set out all the cups on a bench and began pouring a sample of each beer for everyone.

"Hey, Rose," I heard Mike say, shuffling closer to her while we all stood around tasting the beer. Each time I hung out with Mike, his expression and demeanor seemed to grow a shade darker. I had noticed from the beginning that his attitude towards me wasn't exactly the most jovial, though when we were at the Halloween parade, he had been nice enough towards me. That seemed to change. Whenever we all hung out, I caught him frequently glancing over at Rose with a look of longing (which also made me self-conscious, wondering if I looked that pathetic), so I concluded that his coldness towards me was due to a sense of encroachment. But as Rose and I were basically an unofficial couple, he would have to get over it, I thought.

"Hello, Mike," she replied with what I interpreted to be an unenthusiastic smile. David and Eleanor were chatting beside me, and I had been engaged in that conversation but started tuning them out as I nosily tried to catch what Rose and Mike were saying to each other. Ashamedly, there was probably a hint of jealousy, fear, and possessiveness on my part towards Mike.

"I came by Somewhere Sweet the other day," I could hear him say.

"Yeah? I didn't see you."

"You weren't there."

"Oh, sorry about that. Were you looking for something in particular?"

"No, just, I was in the area and thought I'd say hi."

"In the area?" I saw Rose laugh good-naturedly. "I think in Somewhere, you're always in the area. It's a pretty small town." Mike seemed hurt by this jest but tried to cover it up by chuckling. I have to admit, I was enjoying their exchange, but Rose seemed ready to shift directions, and she got David's attention.

"Hey, David, where'd you get these beers, by the way?" David paused for a moment, clearly relishing the moment.

"Well, I went and grabbed them from Zoe's." Zoe's was the high-end food mart on Main Street—fine cheeses, salamis, olives, chutneys, wines, and so on. Apparently, they also sold craft beers. "But..." David continued, "look at the label." Rose picked up one of the large bottles.

"Suzie Q's Booze," she read with a puzzled look coming over her face. "Is...is this *yours*?"

"It is!" he answered excitedly. "I've finally started working on some of my own beers, and I convinced the owner at Zoe's to stock some. What do you think?" David's expression soured as he turned to Eleanor who had earlier declared that she only likes light beers and never touched the samples. "I already know *your* opinion."

"Sorry, David," she said. "But to make you feel better, *if* I liked this syrup stuff, I'm sure yours would be awesome."

"Not all craft beers are stouts," he replied, but he appeared to be appeased.

"Yeah, no, it's really good," Rose nodded when David had turned his attention back to her and then to the rest of us who all joined in nodding in agreement.

"But David," Rose queried, "did you name your beer company after your sister?"

"Yeah, so?"

"Man," Mike chimed in, "she's like twelve."

"And your point?"

"My point is that it's weird." David scowled at Mike, but then he looked around sheepishly to verify if everyone else felt the same way. We suddenly all collectively seemed preoccupied with the ground, the bench, the beers in our hands, anything but looking David in the eye.

"Fine," he declared. "I can work on the name."

"I will say, though," Mike offered, "if we must live through the curse of this annual Christmas market, I'd rather do so with beer in hand, so for that, I thank you."

"Ah, yes, our resident Scrooge," Eleanor answered, "whose only explanation of a jolly annual tradition is that it's a curse."

"Guys, stop saying *curse*," David said.

"Alright, Mr. Superstitious." Eleanor rolled her eyes, giggling.

We wandered up and down Main Street, enjoying mulled wine, candied nuts, cookies, popcorn, eggnog, and whatever other treats we came across. Browsing and buying various handcrafted items, I reveled in the atmosphere. For the others, this was a tradition they were accustomed to. For me, I approached the experience with fresh eyes, determined to soak up all the festive environment. I found myself at times breaking off from the rest of the group, just studying everything, like a kid who had discovered Christmas Town, the North Pole, and Santa's Village.

This was why I wanted to be in Somewhere. Despite the unaccountable mystery of arriving—getting lost, the phantom woman, my magical appearance next to Rose simultaneously hours *and* weeks ago—the magic of the place and my ever-increasing fondness for its people were a magnet. This conflation of wonder with a little bit of terror was weirdly alluring. Still, I think even then, traipsing around Main Street during the Christmas market, I had a sense in the back of my mind that time was short.

For nothing is secret, that shall not be made manifest; neither anything hid, that shall not be known and come abroad.

Where had I heard that? I remembered, again: projected in my brain like a movie that I'd seen but not experienced. Pastor Amos had preached from that passage the previous Sunday, when I was there and not there.

CHAPTER NINETEEN

2:00.

There was nothing subtle about my first night back in Somewhere (the first night back that I was directly conscious of anyway, not simply remembering as a sort of implanted memory). I woke with the impression of being watched, not so uncommon in and of itself. But the strength of that feeling was greater than before.

My eyes had blinked open when I heard movement on the landing outside the door to my studio. As I looked at the clock, I noticed the silver light of the moon awash on the floor, emanating from the windows behind me. There was a blip in that projected light, though, like someone passing by the window. For a moment I wondered if this was not just the spirit of being watched but actually the real thing. Was Mrs. Copeland outside my door for some reason?

At 2:00 in the morning? I wondered. *When the house goes apeshit each night?* I had a hard time imagining Mrs. Copeland outside in a nightgown in December looking in at me. And the thought of it gave me renewed chills despite having become somewhat accustomed to the goings on inside the house. I sat up in bed, determined to keep my breathing steady, and turned slowly.

Perhaps because of my absence from Somewhere, or perhaps because of a deliberateness that I hadn't experienced before, I wasn't prepared for what I saw.

A figure *was* outside on the landing. Startled, I fell out of bed and onto the cold floor. Air was moving like I had just opened a walk-in freezer, and on my hands and knees, I looked up. Breathing heavily and beginning to panic, I slowly crawled towards the window. I wanted to hide, I wanted to be anywhere else, but I also knew there was no use. If it was Mrs. Copeland, I was being silly, and I needed to just dispel whatever fear was there. If it wasn't her, well, it's not like it hadn't seen me.

Trembling, I inched forward, straining my eyes, trying to determine the features of a face or something, but it was indistinct. Just as I felt I might be able to make out who it was, the curtains of my window began to slide shut of their own volition until I was cut off from both the figure outside and any light. I was in total darkness.

I heard the creak of a door on its hinges, and while I hoped it might be the bathroom door, I knew it was the door to the connecting attic space. A renewed push of frosty air passed along the floor, and I knew its origins.

Wanting nothing to do with whatever was going on, I figured that I would just let it pass. It always did. So, I crawled back into bed, and like a little kid, I pulled the covers over my head, breathing rapidly, trying to calm myself down. That act of cowardice, however, seemed to anger whatever manifestation was disturbing the house.

The door to the attic space began banging violently against the door frame: open, close, open, close. A defiance welled up inside of me against the riot of noise, and I shot out of bed.

"What!" I yelled.

The door, which had just finished banging shut, then slowly creaked open. What I thought had been total darkness was not completely so; a faint light radiated from the attic space, and I heard whispers crawling along the walls like skittering spider legs.

"It's true, it's true, it's true, it's true, it's true, it's true."

Anticipating some vision of the stranger in the woods outside Somewhere, I shuffled across the wooden floorboards of my room and passed through the door. There was nothing there but attic: angled ceiling beams running above me with insulation, like cotton candy, stuffed between.

Another noise pulled my attention to the other end of the space, something I hadn't noticed before. I walked over, and there at my feet was a small contraption that I didn't immediately recognize, framed by panels of wood. Then I realized: it was the entrance to the rest of the house, and the contraption was a retractable ladder. Likely, on the other side of this door was a drawstring that could be pulled down, and this ladder would slide out to the floor below.

I heard the noise again. It was coming from inside the house. Mrs. Copeland—or someone, or something—was moving about the house below.

Which isn't a big deal, I had to remind myself even if I had stopped believing it.

I gazed back through the door behind me. I thought I could just make out my bed in the dark. I wanted to go back to sleep. I thought I might even turn on the lamp and read, just unwind a little, toss those unusual events from my mind. But I knew I couldn't. Something was behind all this, *all* of this, these strange happenings in Somewhere which had followed me even to St. Louis. And while part of me wanted to ignore it, the other part wanted answers. I was determined to be in Somewhere, and these frights, these animations, while unnerving, had, over time, managed not to deter me but to expand my mind to new realms of possibility. Somewhere wasn't merely an escape *from* the mundane, I was realizing; it was an opening door *to... to what exactly?* I wasn't sure.

Looking down at my feet, I was afraid that trying to descend from the attic would cause too great a disturbance, so I traced my steps back across the attic space and through my room. I slept in a t-shirt and pajama pants, so I slipped on my house shoes and a hoodie and slowly opened the handle to the door outside. I held my breath. I couldn't see anything on the landing anymore, but my nerves were still pulled taut. The icy air immediately struck my skin like a million little daggers, but I braced myself against the cold and closed the door behind me. Everywhere was now covered with a few inches of snow, a serene winter wonderland, which made my present circumstances that much more incongruent.

Normally I wouldn't notice, but as I stepped down the stairs, I was hyper-aware of every minor creak and groan, of every chomp of the rubber soles of my house shoes against the snowy covered wood steps. I felt completely vulnerable in the open dark—what might be watching me? The figure that had been outside my window was unaccounted for. Was it out here? Or, as I assumed, was it only a manifestation of my mind? That was no real assurance, though, as that meant it could manifest itself again at any moment, and I knew my nerves couldn't handle it. Once more, I thought of my bed; I could have easily changed courses right then and there and headed back up the stairs and to bed. This could all be over. I was sure the energy charging the house was gone, that I could get some sleep.

My eyes drifted away from the house to the distance, to the place, a few miles out, where I had first encountered the stranger. I imagined footsteps approaching, but the problem was, in my fragile state of mind, I couldn't be sure what was my imagination and what was real. *Is any of this real?* I took one more step down timidly, but the noise in the woods was growing louder. I bolted up the steps, arrived back at the landing, and reached for the handle, but I let out a groan when I realized it was locked.

I jiggled it furiously with my back turned to the trees behind me. Out of frustration, I banged the palm of my hand against the door, but when I looked up and through the window, my heart stopped. The hanging woman was there, swinging over my bed, the shafts of silvery light from the moon behind me penetrating the window and illuminating the lower half of her dress.

I yelped and left the landing. A moment later I was grasping the handle to the back entrance of the kitchen, trying to maintain composure. I fumbled with the handle out of both fear and cold but eventually turned it and pushed the door in. It hadn't been locked.

I closed the door behind me, locked it, and pulled together the curtains that covered the door's window. With my back against the door, I closed my eyes and let my breathing return to normal before leaning over to flip on the switch. I paused.

The door from the kitchen to the rest of the house was open, the threshold Mrs. Copeland explicitly told me never to cross.

I couldn't exactly see much through the doorway, but I was stunned that it was open at all. My hand still hung mid-air, ready to turn on the light, but I let my arm drop. Turning on the light, with the door open to the rest of the house, would cause a disturbance, I thought. I found myself tip-toeing mechanically to the open door.

There wasn't much to see as I thought, just a long hallway to the front of the house, a kaleidoscope of moonlight splintering irregularly through the stained glass transom above the entrance. I walked back to the kitchen and grabbed the flashlight that hung by a magnet from the refrigerator. Also, since I was finding it difficult to move about stealthily, I slipped my house shoes off and left them in the kitchen. Even in just my socks, though, I found that it didn't make a lot of difference. I'd take a few silent steps, and then a floorboard would squeak underneath me. In those moments, I'd pause and hold my breath, but for the time being, I heard no other movements.

On the left wall of the hallway, pictures were hung. I found two closed doors: one a linen closet and the other a small bathroom. On my right, however, an arched entryway opened into a kind of entertainment room. An old TV sat in one corner with a small sofa facing it; the console appeared to be fifty years old or more. A few sets of large shelves were on two different walls, filled mostly with various games. But in the middle of the room, surrounded by four chairs, was a square, wooden table with what appeared to be green felt running over most of the top of it—colors were hard to distinguish in the dim light. I noticed a deck of cards resting on one corner of the table.

"Bridge," I whispered quietly and smirked, shaking my head. Mrs. Copeland hadn't been lying about her bridge parties when she invited me to stay during Thanksgiving. Another arched entryway connected the entertainment room, so I quietly shuffled into the adjoining room, the front room which appeared to be an unused sitting area. Antique furniture was placed everywhere, and there appeared to be an over-abundance of trinkets and odds and ends: lace, doilies, decorative pillows, dolls, busts, an empty white bird cage, ornamental boxes, and gilt frames that contained several Dutch landscape paintings. An old but well-maintained set of Louis XV-style furniture lined two walls, and a marble coffee table rested on top of a white area rug. The whole room could have been a Victorian curiosity shop. I passed through another arched entryway to my left and was back to the hallway, now standing next to the front door.

I breathed normally now, insulated from the outside by the interior of the house, and the exoticness of being in a place where I'd never been allowed helped me feel distance between me and the haunting of my lodging a few floors above. However, just remembering the woman hanging over my bed sent a quiver through my body; I quickly turned my thoughts back to what lay in front of me. Opposite the Victorian room was open space, no wall or entryway. If I had entered the house from the front door, the Victorian room would be on my left, accessible through the arched entryway, and the hallway would run directly in front of me, leading to the kitchen, but the space directly to the right was open, with a staircase leading up to the second floor and running along the other side of the wall from the hallway. The rest of the room opened up and ran the same length of the hallway, practically to the other end of the house. It reminded me of Maggie's painting room and all the space she had there.

Like Maggie's house, Mrs. Copeland's also had a giant chandelier. Additionally, a large stone fireplace was visible about halfway along the outer wall. Under the chandelier sat a long table with eighteen chairs set up around it.

This could be used for a serious feast, I thought, but I also couldn't imagine Mrs. Copeland ever hosting a gathering that would warrant such a large eating area. Then again, it wasn't as if I'd lived in Somewhere very long. For all I knew, Mrs. Copeland, as isolated as she seemed to be normally, might be known for extravagant parties, or maybe she used to host them in the past when her husband...

I realized that I had never spoken to my landlady about her past. She was clearly a widow, but beyond that, I had no idea.

All these thoughts passed through my head rather quickly. I didn't pause long—only a few seconds to take everything in—but kept making my way across the room. I had circled around the table and was determining whether or not I wanted to ascend the stairs to the second floor. It seemed like a risky move, though, since that was where Mrs. Copeland must sleep. I was just taking a step back in that direction, though, when a gust of cold air swept across my feet.

I turned to face a door on the far wall where I felt the cold air emanating. It grew stronger and more concentrated as I approached the passageway. I opened the door and was certain that the temperature dropped at least fifteen degrees as I passed through the frame.

Here I decided to go ahead and turn on the light, figuring that by pulling the door shut behind me, I could risk it without catching the attention of Mrs. Copeland. A light flickered on above me, but it was dim. Only one of the three bulbs in the fixture worked.

I thought the room would be a storage space which, admittedly, it could be used for. But I was surprised to discover that this was clearly once part of a much larger kitchen, partitioned now by the installation of a wall. The floor didn't match what was in the current kitchen, which must have been updated more recently, but it was covered with tiles, and a few cabinets lined sections of the walls. Besides a little dinginess and dust accumulation, there was nothing else inside the room. Except for one more door. The cellar.

Cold air continued to emanate from under that door, and I was suddenly gripped by its presence like it was its own entity. Just like in Maggie and Lorena's house. Just like in the Whitakers' house. What was it about these cellar doors that had utterly captured my attention? I really couldn't answer, but I sensed there was something significant. I stood nervous, on edge from all that had already passed that night. But I *had* to know what was down there. I inhaled deeply and opened the door.

I yelled and fell to the kitchen floor before I could even take a step down, crab-walking backward and bumping into the cabinets behind me. Silhouetted through the cellar door frame was Mrs. Copeland. She had been only inches away from the other side of the door, waiting for who knows how long—I hadn't heard a sound as I entered the room.

She stepped out into the dim light, a wild anger on her face. She had never really intimidated me before, but I was terrified now.

And yet, something was different about her. As she towered over me, I saw her more alive, not just her energy, but her skin. She appeared more fleshier, though I knew that wasn't the best way to describe it. I didn't really have words, but there was something about her physical presence that seemed more material, more actual.

I waited in that position, in abject fright, for a while. Mrs. Copeland simply hovered over me, unspeaking but with absolute fury etched upon her face. I continued to wait, trembling. Finally, at the point that I thought maybe she would say nothing and I would need to plan my next move, she spoke.

Only it wasn't the voice I was accustomed to. The sound of her voice was grating, like she was utilizing vocal cords for the first time after years of disuse. Her words came out faltering and guttural.

"G-g-get ooouuuttt!" she managed to scream.

Now at my breaking point, I scrambled to my feet and sprinted out. I yelled as I banged into one of the chairs around the large table in the great room. I reached the entryway and was about to try and exit out the front door but thought better of it. If it was locked, my nerves would not allow my muscles to exercise the precision needed to unlock it. I knew the kitchen door was unlocked, so I sprinted down the hallway. As I passed through the kitchen, I shuddered, imagining Mrs. Copeland still there, just on the other side of the false wall. Reflexively, I grabbed my house shoes and aimed for the back door.

Then I was outside and into the cold December night, no longer concerned about what might be out there versus the strangely animated Mrs. Copeland.

CHAPTER TWENTY

"What the hell?" I heard as I groggily batted my eyes open. The voice sounded upset but then changed its tone.

"You've got to be kidding me," it chuckled. "I show you the private den, and you decide to move in." I stared into Pastor Amos's face from a somewhat compromising position. Not knowing where to go in the middle of the night, I walked to the Whitakers. In the snow. In my house shoes.

I had stood at their front door, at the point of knocking. I knew they'd probably be startled, but they'd quickly get over it. But I thought of the girls and how sometimes kids don't bounce back so quickly from being scared. So instead, I traipsed around back to the shed-*cum*-private den. I was afraid that it'd be locked, but it opened right up.

When I entered, I was severely tempted to keep the space heater on for the rest of the night, but knowing what a fire hazard they are, the last thing I wanted was to accidentally burn down Pastor Amos's sanctuary. Not to mention, his shrine to human knowledge was highly flammable. So instead, I turned on the space heater for about fifteen minutes just to warm myself up and thaw out my feet. I was legitimately concerned that I might end up with frostbite, but thankfully my feet and toes warmed up nicely and were functioning fine the next morning. Then, since the only covering I could find for warmth was a thin afghan on one of the chairs, I grabbed that, covered myself as best I could, and then rolled myself up in the rug on the ground. I knew it was absurd, but it was the best I could think of at the moment. And that's how Pastor Amos found me, a human-rug hotdog.

"What are you doing here?" he asked. "You know what, save it. Come inside; there's breakfast, and, you know, it's not a shed in winter." He shook his head, continuing to laugh to himself as he walked me back to the house.

When we got inside, I glanced at the clock. 9:47. I had slept pretty late, no doubt from the exhaustion of the night's events. It was just the two of us in the kitchen as Tracy and the girls were already gone.

My host turned on the stove and started frying some sausage links and eggs. That, combined with coffee and orange juice, revived me quickly, and the fear of the night before felt more like the distant memory of a bad dream. But of course, Pastor Amos was curious, so I couldn't exactly leave it behind me.

"So," he said once I had cleared my plate, "what's going on?" I struggled to know where to start or what to say.

"Umm..." I began and stopped. I had hoped words would follow, but none came. Pastor Amos didn't appear to be in a rush and just waited patiently for me to find my thoughts.

"Do you remember that conversation we had a while back? My weird dreams? And then, well...you sort of went into this whole thing about thin places and magic." He laughed.

"I do have a tendency to rabbit-trail at times. But yes, I remember. Go on."

"Well, the dreams have never gone away. Sometimes they're more intense; usually, they're pretty mild, and I've just sort of gotten used to them. They even follow me. I had them when I was back with my family in St. Louis."

"Humans *do* have a tendency to dream no matter where they are," he said, gently giving me a hard time.

"I know, but this is different. It feels different anyway."

"So, how did these dreams bring you here last night?"

"Well..." *Here it goes,* I thought. "I'm not sure they *are* always dreams. I think maybe they're real. Some of them, anyway."

Pastor Amos was no longer in a joking mood but stared at me intently, scrutinizingly. We sat in silence for a time which made me uncomfortable.

"You probably think I'm crazy, huh?" I asked.

"No. I certainly don't."

"Well, then. What do you think?"

"First of all, I think you didn't fully answer my question. What brought you here last night?"

"I...uh...I did something I wasn't supposed to. I was having one of my intense dreams or visions or whatever. I mean, it felt real. But I was in my room at Mrs. Copeland's, a small, converted studio space in the attic. I heard a noise in the house, the same noise I've heard for a long time, and I finally decided to check it out even though I've been strictly forbidden from entering the house other than by accessing the kitchen from the rear entrance.

"And I'm telling you, the whole time I was seeing things and almost went back to bed except... except..."

"Except what?" Pastor Amos interjected.

"Except that I had a vision of a dead woman hanging above my bed. I don't know if it was a dream or not, but there was no way I was going back to bed." *How can I go back to that bed now?* I wondered. "So, I went through the kitchen and into the rest of the house." I paused. Pastor Amos's voice dropped a little, all his attention focused on me and my story.

"What did you find?" he asked with a look of curiosity that surprised me. He certainly appeared to believe my story.

"Um... I looked through all the rooms. I mean, it's a pretty normal house. And then…" Instinctively, I glanced over at the cellar door that was in the far corner of the kitchen. I got that strange feeling in my stomach again. Something there. And the cold air again. I imagined Mrs. Copeland standing on the other side. I remembered the vibrancy that she emitted, clashing conspicuously with the garbled voice with which she had spoken to me.

Pastor Amos had glanced over at the cellar door as well, following my movement. He looked back at me. For a moment, everything in the room was suspended in absolute stillness and quiet, a spring set to release some immense reaction. I sprung. Not knowing what I was doing, I leaped from my seat, sprinted over to the door, and ripped it open.

There was nothing on the other side but steps descending into a cold, cement cellar, but I had little time to take it in. The door slammed in front of me, and though I thought I saw a look of fury flash across his face, Pastor Amos was immediately composed and spoke in a steady voice.

"Buddy, what do you think you're doing?" he said, placing a hand on my shoulder.

"I…I don't know. I'm sorry," I apologized. "I don't know what got into me. I just…uh…I guess I was reliving whatever happened last night. I'm sorry," I said again, looking into his face, trying to shake away my embarrassment.

"Look, I get it. You had a weird night. How about we take our coffees out to the den; since that seems to be a place you're already pretty comfortable with."

"So, why don't you start again?" he said as we sat down. "What did you find in the house?"

The hesitation returned to me, but I was determined to say it. I trusted this man, I needed to get this out in the open, and I needed answers. It was time to speak.

"I found the cellar door, opened it, and behind it, waiting, was Mrs.

Copeland." There was a pause. Pastor Amos, who had been leaning forward in attention, gently sank back into his high-backed chair.

"Do you mean to tell me," he started slowly, "that you found the owner of the house... in her house?" He smiled a bit condescendingly at me. I hated it.

"There's more to it than that!" I blurted out. "I can't explain it, but there was something horrible about her. She *seemed* more real somehow, but her voice was all strange, and why would she be in the cellar every night in the middle of the night?"

"How do you know she's in the cellar every night?"

"Well, I don't technically, but I hear the same movement through the house at exactly the same time every night. I swear I'm not making this up. Something happens in that house every night. I have seen things." I half-heartedly began sharing a few of the incidents, but sitting across from the calm man of God, with the clear light of day streaming into the windows, my account sounded hollow, even to me.

To my relief, Pastor Amos looked at me intently, through me even. He at least appeared to take me seriously. After a ponderous minute became sustained, awkward silence, however, I cleared my throat.

"You know," he said. "I'm thinking about our conversation the other day at The Book and Bean. You remember?" How could I forget? *It's true*, whispered in my mind.

"Sure."

"Well, I was just thinking about something Steinbeck once wrote. You ever read Steinbeck?"

"A little." That was somewhat true. I had read the Sparknotes summary of *Of Mice and Men*.

"Read more. Anyway, he wrote a book about traveling around America with his dog. And he ends up in this creepy old house somewhere in New England. And he's thinking to himself how his *unbelief*, not his belief, is what leaves him unprepared for the dark. My interpretation is this: If you believe in magic, you have magic to fight magic. But if you don't believe in magic, what will aid you when the monster you don't believe in shows up at your door?"

As I considered his words, he stood up and walked over to one of his shelves, pulling out a book with strips of paper sticking out weirdly, like the Frankenstein's-monster version of a book.

"Here we go," he declared, with his finger pointing to a page. My eyes barely had time to scan the section in question before he snapped the book shut. "Steinbeck. *Travels with Charley in Search of America.*"

"I'm still not sure that I'm tracking with you."

"It just means that it's natural to be afraid of the dark, even if there's nothing there, especially when there's nothing there, because we don't know what to do with it. It was easier when we thought every bump in the night was the devil. We'd just go exorcise it. Call down the angels of heaven. But in the modern age, we don't know how to fight darkness."

"So, what are you saying? That I'm not going to be able to fight the things of darkness in Mrs. Copeland's house unless I believe they're real. I *do* believe they're real. Or something. I don't know." I pressed my fingers into my eyes, trying to stave off the tension headache forming.

"Could be," Pastor Amos responded. "But what I was really getting at is that the *darkness* is filled with horrors. That sometimes we imagine things going bump in the night even when they don't. But that this is perfectly natural and can even cause more fear—"

"—Wait. Aren't you the one who was waxing eloquent the other day about how you're a true believer or something? And now you're telling me that I'm probably making it all up?."

"But conversely," he continued with a look of rebuke for interrupting, "Steinbeck observed that there are those who knew the things were there and were deadly, even if he didn't fall into that camp himself. So, I'm not telling you anything. I read you a passage from a book that I thought was interesting. *You* get to decide how much it does or does not apply to your situation. Steinbeck wasn't a sage, though he did make some keen observations. He didn't believe that anything of substance was there in the dark, but he was afraid. Maybe you do believe. Maybe in you, history has looped back in on itself, not modern man, but pre-modern man. The word *modern* anyway is misleading because *pre-modern* or *medieval* is treated pejoratively, as though only the modern man is enlightened.

"As you said, Lee, you know where I stand. But regarding Steinbeck's passage, you have to determine if there's anything there in the dark. I simply find it interesting, as Steinbeck noted, that we find all kinds of things in the dark. Maybe they're in our imagination, maybe they're not. And the other point I was getting at is that, *in the light of day*, we have to sit down and resolve what we believe."

I sat and pondered Pastor Amos's words. He was right. The truth of the matter was that, in the light of day, my experiences the night before *did* appear differently. Once again, I was tempted to blow off the seemingly supernatural events as some gross exaggeration of the mind. Certainly, something strange was happening in that house, something strange was affecting the timeline of my arrival and even the very existence of Somewhere, as I had discovered with Miriam. But Pastor Amos had a point; what was so wrong about Mrs. Copeland being in her own cellar in the middle of the night? A bit weird, perhaps, but not so out of the ordinary. Still, the night before was only one notch in the carving of my jack-o-lantern experience in Somewhere.

"But Lee," he added, "for whatever it's worth, we'd love for you to stay with us if it'd help."

"Thanks, but, um, maybe I should give things another shot first. Can I use your phone first?" I asked. "I think I'm going to call Mrs. Copeland. May I use your phone?"

I patched things up with Mrs. Copeland. I was glad that I called her. The image of her at the top of the cellar steps hung in my mind, and I'm not sure I had the courage to just pop back into the house and try and talk things out rationally.

Her voice sounded perturbed over the phone, certainly. She scolded me severely, reminding me of our agreement and the limits of my stay. I figured it best not to remind her that she *had* invited me to play bridge in the main part of the house over Thanksgiving.

Instead, apologizing profusely, I promised not to enter the other parts of the house again. Though I couldn't see her, I think she warmed up after that. Her voice grew softer, embarrassed even. She explained that she often did laundry in the middle of the night due to insomnia. I'm not sure if she thought I was a fool, though, because that hardly explained the precision or the uninterrupted frequency of her nightly descent—that had to be the noises I heard in the house—into the cellar at exactly 2:00. That hardly explained why she had been standing on the other side of the cellar door at the top of the stairs... in the dark. I didn't mention any of that, though. I resolved to make peace, tail between my legs. I needed a place to stay while I continued unraveling the tangled yarn of my experiences, plus I didn't want to continue sleeping on the hard floor of Pastor Amos's study in a rug cocoon (or to wear out their hospitality by inviting myself to stay with them). The thought crossed my mind that I wouldn't mind staying with Rose, but that, too, was out of the question.

Charlotte had arrived home with her mother after "feeling sick" (a girl had made fun of her at school), so after getting off the phone with Mrs. Copeland, I went to her room for "tea." At first, I tried ignoring the yawning dark throat of her closet, but as if my head were attached to an invisible wire, I found my gaze slowly being pulled in that direction. While Charlotte was distracted by setting up the party of stuffed animals, I scooted closer and closer until I could peek in and examine the drawing once again.

And it was there. Only it wasn't. There *was* a drawing sketched in black crayon, a dramatic departure from the colorful artwork hanging around the rest of the room. But it was not the hanging woman or even a woman at all. Instead, there was just the sketch of a tree, and there was a sun and a bird.

So, what had I seen before? Hadn't both Anna and Charlotte spoken of the woman? I felt like my mind was splitting, like mortar was being chipped away slowly, and bricks were loosening up, beginning to fall out of place, like if I tipped my head too far one way, a whole load would just slide right out, and I'd find myself to be the recipient of a one-way, straight-jacket ticket to Looneyville.

"Charlotte?" I began to inquire about the drawing.

"Uh huh?" She was adjusting the posture of a pink elephant and looked up at me. I hesitated.

"Umm... is the tea ready?"

Approaching The Book and Bean—a quick treat before work—and feeling a little calmer after patching things up with Mrs. Copeland, I was on the point of turning to my right to enter, but someone caught my eye. I had been spotted as well.

"Lee!"

I couldn't believe it. I had completely forgotten about him. It was the man from the fair, the guy who recognized me when I first arrived in Somewhere. And like before, almost immediately, two men quickly escorted him away, only briefly glancing in my direction. This time, though, I remembered who he was.

CHAPTER TWENTY-ONE

Jimmy.

That was his name. The guys at the fair had called him Carl, though they were probably just making something up on the spot because that man was definitely Jimmy. I couldn't remember his last name because I didn't know him that well, and I probably hadn't realized who he was the first time I saw him because he was now sporting a whiskery face and long hair as opposed to the clean-shaven, trimmed guy I remembered.

Jimmy was an older fellow counselor at a camp I had worked at during the summer after my second year of college, probably in his mid-thirties, kind of dorky, but really nice and very knowledgeable about the outdoors. Supposedly, he had started working there when he was in college but never finished his studies, opting instead to make a career out of working for the camp. He was tall but skinny and wiry, and the lasting memories I had of him were from our backpacking adventures.

Camp sessions lasted two weeks. Normally all the campers would bunk in small cabins, but halfway through their session, we'd take them on a three-day, two-night camping trip. Hike in eight miles, camp, spend the next day hiking to and from a waterfall and playing around, camp, and hike out. The kids, laden down with their gear, would be eager and excited for about the first two miles but then would struggle the remaining distance. Jimmy, on the other hand, was like a mountain goat crossed with a sherpa. He'd always carry the heaviest load and then inevitably, sneakily and without complaining, add a few items here and there from the packs of the kids who were struggling the most. But, it never prevented him from bounding up ahead of the group and onto any rocky out-cropping, hill, or elevated position. In the final mile, all the kids would be looking at their toes, concentrating on nothing else but willing the signals from their brain to their feet to keep moving. Meanwhile, Jimmy would be singing camp songs, telling jokes, and cheering everyone on. By the end of the summer, that hike was fairly easy for me, but I never had the enthusiasm or energy that Jimmy had. That's what I remembered of him.

So, I was completely taken aback when I finally realized who the man was. Jimmy was whisked away before I could react, but I recovered after a moment of shock and darted after him. I ran down the side street just by the art gallery, but when I spilled out onto the next street, he and the men who had taken him were gone. I stood there, stumped. *How the hell did they just disappear?*

But then I saw Jimmy's face from the backseat of a beat-up, forest green Jeep Grand Cherokee, straining to look at me with a stupid grin on his face. I wanted to run after, but something told me to act normal, so I ducked back into the side street for a moment and waited before popping out just as the vehicle was turning into a more residential area a block away. Wanting to act naturally, I maintained a quick walking pace but never broke out into a run. When I arrived at the spot where I saw the Jeep turn, I looked down the road just in time to see it making a left about a quarter of a mile away. There was no way I was keeping up with it any longer, so I slowed to a more leisurely stroll and made my way in that direction.

At approximately the place I thought the Jeep had turned—the grid of streets intersecting every fifty yards or so made it hard to tell exactly—I turned. I was banking on a lot of luck, hoping to see the Jeep parked in some driveway. Of course, given enough time, I could probably find it. Since the homes were so old, practically none of them had garages, so I'd see any vehicle parked outside. The issue would be that I didn't want to look suspicious. Clearly, I was not meant to come into contact with Jimmy since that was the second time he'd been taken as soon as we met, and I wanted to know why. I figured I could only zig-zag around the streets so much before it'd start looking odd.

Thankfully luck was on my side. I didn't see the Jeep along the first street I walked down, but doubling back on the next street over, I saw it idling in a driveway next to an equally decrepit-looking Ford Ranger, exhaust rising visibly out of the tailpipe in the frosty air. The house door swung open, so I dashed behind a large yew shrub.

The men who had taken Jimmy were now standing on the front stoop, chatting with an older lady I didn't recognize. I couldn't see Jimmy among them. After a minute or so, the men lumbered back to their vehicle and drove off. I stood there for a few minutes deciding my next move, but I eventually gave up and walked away, taking a mental note of the address. Based on the men's reactions, I doubted that I would get a warm reception from the old lady either, and if I ever wanted to speak with Jimmy, I would need to wait for a more opportune moment or at least sneak back when people's guards weren't up.

I had exhausted too much time following Jimmy, so I headed straight to the art gallery, but later that evening, I was meeting Rose at the bakery where she worked.

That night I told Rose everything. We sat together at the bakery after hours, just the two of us. It was the first time she had invited me to hang out with her there, though I had dropped by on a number of occasions before. Always happy to be with Rose, the excess emotion from the previous 24 hours produced an even greater demand to be with someone who brought me so much comfort. I felt desperate to find some kind of equilibrium. Being with Rose was like a salve, and as soon as I walked through the front door of Somewhere Sweet, I immediately felt a sense of calm.

Or at least a calm mixed with the heightened senses that always accompanied being in Rose's presence—the pull of my gut, the rush of blood to my face (and other parts), the awkward awareness of every movement of every limb on my body.

I walked in right as Rose was locking up, and she motioned me into the back.

"The inner sanctum?" I teased. "Are we mere mortals allowed back here?"

"Oh, that's right," she retorted. "I'll need to blindfold you first, take you for a spin around the block, and then lead you secretly to our destination."

"You mean, there?" I pointed.

"That's just what you think. This bakery is simply a front for our truly secret hideout."

"Okay, interesting."

"Alas," she sighed dramatically, "I guess you can just come to *the back*"—she gestured with air quotes—"for now."

I chuckled and followed her, followed every detail of her: hair tied back in graceful disregard–all the more striking–the brief glance back at me and the depth of her eyes, the deepness of a forest, the contours of her face, cheeks, lips. Lips. Lips. Rose lips. Rosy lips. Rose.

Being with Rose was a reverie.

I knew from before that the back of the shop must have ample space based on the limited area in the front of the store, but I was still impressed by the size of the operation when I actually beheld it for the first time. Two long, wood-top baking tables ran the length of the room, separated by a few feet. Shelves were lined with ingredients: flour, powdered sugar, baking powder, cocoa powder, baking chocolate, pots and pans, and so much more—the tools of the trade. Additionally, two large refrigerators, a commercial oven, and a commercial mixer were scattered around the room.

All this I took in quickly because my eyes were drawn to the far end of one of the bakery tables: a dinner set for two with candlelight, wine, and a sprig of holly. Speechless, I looked over at Rose who blushed.

"I thought it'd be nice to celebrate just the two of us," she said meekly. "It's—"

"—oh, I can't handle this anymore," a coarse voice interrupted. Startled, I glanced towards the back door where Rose's older coworker had been lingering without my notice. "You two lovebirds make me want to take your picture and barf at the same time. Have a good night."

"Good night, Myrtle," Rose responded as the door closed. I raised my eyebrows.

"Oh, Myrtle's great. But she can be a bit crusty at times." I shrugged, smiling.

Now, it was just the two of us.

At first, we just stood there, both of our faces reddening. I imagined this as a scene from a movie. The orchestra in the background is cued. I gallantly and confidently cross the room and embrace the beautiful girl. The camera pans out and fades, an implied happily ever after.

Of course, it didn't happen that way. First, I'm not a very gallant person. Second, this wasn't a movie, and there was no orchestra with us. Instead, I muttered, "This looks great," and *Rose* crossed the room to me. She grabbed one of my hands in both of hers, whispered, "Merry early Christmas," and kissed me. Softly. Like a secret. But her lips remained on mine, willing time to let us stay in that moment and defy its logic. I let her hands fall from mine and wrapped my arms around her, pulling her to me, our bodies pressed together. The moment, of course, couldn't last forever, and we eventually pulled apart, our faces rosy with both longing and satisfaction.

"Ahem," Rose cleared her throat in a gesture of transition. We needed to cool off.

"So," I laughed. "Dinner. What's on the menu?" Rose walked over to the oven and pulled out two porcelain dishes that she had been keeping warm: Chicken Cordon Bleu. That paired with a small salad, fresh croissants from the bakery, and Chardonnay made for a delicious meal.

The timidness and awkwardness soon wore off, and we were laughing and enjoying our meal together. *God,* I thought, *she's just so damn easy to talk to.* I felt alternatively special and undeserving of her attention. Secretly, I even relished Mike's jealousy. I had never been the one to elicit envy, but with Rose, I understood why. She was incredible, and I couldn't believe that she even wanted to spend time like this with me.

I thought back on that vision, though, my first day in Somewhere. The two of us together, older. Like we were fated to be together. *Fate. Is that all this is?* Fate felt unnatural, forced. Like I wouldn't be able to be with a girl like Rose—which was probably true—without this mechanistic intervention. Or maybe it's totally natural, and all life is just one big predetermined story manipulated by some master storyteller. *Kind of like God,* I realized. Or maybe not *all* of life is predetermined. Maybe just my pocket. Or just a small portion of my pocket in this life. There was something about Somewhere...

"Lee, are you okay?" Rose asked, pulling me back into the moment.

"Yeah, yeah, I'm fine. Sorry, my mind was wandering a bit."

"Do I bore you that much?" she teased.

"No, sorry. Well, yeah... I mean no..." I shook my head at Rose's puzzled grin. "I mean, you're not boring me, but truthfully, everything's not fine."

"What's wrong?" She looked alarmed. "Did I do something?" Again, I was mildly pleased by this concern, as though I could be the cause of any anxiety on her part, Rose who was so far out of my league. But I assured her.

"No, it's not you."

"It's me."

"Huh?"

"It's not you, it's me." She smirked. It took me a second to realize she was joking. I laughed.

"Right," I said. "Believe me, it's always me. It could never be you. You're too perfect." *You are laying it on pretty thick there*, a voice in my head told me. "It's just that..." I trailed off, not knowing exactly how to communicate. It was one thing to share with Pastor Amos. I saw him as more than just a mentor, but at the end of the day, you talk to your pastor differently than you talk to your girlfriend. Especially your extremely gorgeous girlfriend whom you're afraid could leave you any second for a more perfect Don Juan which the world is full of.

"It's just that weird things keep happening to me in Somewhere. Well, since I've been in Somewhere. Weird things were happening back in St. Louis over Thanksgiving week, too." Rose grew still. She seemed to be processing, but I couldn't read her.

"Like what?" she finally said.

So that's when I told her everything. I didn't retract or hold back like I had the first time I tried sharing a few details right before Thanksgiving. Of course, I left out some of the more intimate details of our heavy make-out session in front of the fire at the farmhouse, but otherwise, I pretty much spared nothing else–the odd events in Mrs. Copeland's house, the stranger in the woods, the hanging lady both in Somewhere and in St. Louis, the collective memory loss back home.

As I finished sharing everything, I heard the phone ring, a faded yellow wall phone. Its curling cord hung below and gave the impression that a giant, sickly rat was climbing up the wall. Part of me wishes I had ignored it, had gently pulled the phone off the receiver and then set it back down. Part of me wishes that I had remained ignorant. Maybe things would have been different in Somewhere, maybe the whole damn narrative would have played out differently, and everything might have been resolved naturally. I wonder if even the things that went bump in the night might have eventually stopped, or I might have truly learned to live with them. But that's not what happened.

"Who's calling?" I asked nosily. Should I blame Rose here, too? Not for everything else that she was involved in, the things I learned about later, but maybe I blame her most of all for this one simple thing: her inability to maintain composure, to keep a poker face, to continue this charade a little bit longer.

The ringing obviously jarred her. She tried lying, tried shaking it off, but the hand was played, cards on the table, her face said it all. Something wasn't right.

Rose looked into my eyes, her own eyes...going glassy? *Are you really crying right now, bitch?* I hated myself for thinking that way, but I was startled, frightened, hurt. Reacting in the moment, leaping spread-eagle to every wild, fanciful conclusion without even waiting to verify facts.

Even then, however, I had half a mind to go comfort her. Even then, my mind was spinning, wondering if there was a way to *unsee* all that, to laugh it off and pretend it was something else. To go back to normal. But I couldn't. So, I just looked at her, stunned.

"I'm so sorry," she cried. "It wasn't supposed to be this way. We were supposed to be together. I didn't know what to do." My head was spinning, not comprehending.

"What the fuck, Rose." It wasn't a question with a question mark. It was declarative, with a period. Omit the *what*. Just *the fuck, Rose!* I did mean for my statement to come out angrily, but it was more of a gasp, a plea, a whimper. "Who... who is calling?"

She said nothing.

I was dizzy, my vision going in and out of focus, too stupefied and confused. But I heard a car pull up out front which snapped me back to the moment. Out of instinct, I glanced at the wall as though I might have X-ray vision. I then looked back over at Rose, crying, before sprinting out the back door.

Wildly I ran, weaving in and out of backyards, down streets, taking side streets, doubling back again. Eventually, I found myself approaching the far western end of Main Street and hanging a sharp left towards the train tracks in the distance, retracing my steps from that weird Halloween night nearly two months prior.

Once I arrived at the train depot, I darted to the front, feeling shelter from the eyes of the town. I tried listening for pursuit which was difficult amidst my pounding heart and rapid breathing, but I soon settled down enough to realize no one was approaching. Cautiously, I made my way back along the sides of the train station to glimpse Somewhere, and I was struck by its commonness. If I didn't know better, I'd wonder if everything that had happened in the past fifteen minutes or so was just another strange vision.

I questioned what had happened. I questioned possible motives. *Am I overreacting? But she was crying. Why was she crying if innocent? And what did I hear? A car, right? That's why I ran. But did I ever see a car or even hear a car chasing me?* My chest heaved in and out, pulling oxygen into my lungs, my hands now resting on my knees and my body sticky with sweat. I had managed to grab my coat in the act of fleeing the bakery, but the cold was still gripping me, the sweat turning to streams and beads of icy pain.

What was I going to do, though? Everything had changed. Whoever had called Rose was looking for me. *I think.* Were there others? Could I even go back? What did they want with me? Maybe it was no big deal; maybe I was exaggerating the situation. The truth of the matter was that I hadn't let Rose explain. Could it have been something harmless?

My head swirled, tears beginning to well up. What my mind continued returning to was the most profound sense of betrayal I had ever experienced. It was too sudden. One moment I'm the luckiest guy in the world, the next, I feel like I've been cuckolded. Only I wasn't cheated on; I was backstabbed by this girl who I thought truly liked me. Even then, standing with a hand planted on the train depot's wall as I continued bent over, gulping air, even then I felt her lips on my lips, her body wrapped up in mine. I shuddered, though, trying to physically expel the longing.

Absent-mindedly, my hand reached down to my pocket where the marble was still resting. My instinct was to pull it out and chuck it, but I didn't. I couldn't. Not yet. I knew then, though, that I didn't want to be in Somewhere. Whatever I had told myself back in St. Louis, it was all about Rose. What other reason did I really have to be here?

In a fit of impulse, I decided I was done. I shoved aside the nagging in the back of my mind that maybe I had misinterpreted things, maybe I should get some clarity or, if my suspicions were confirmed, some closure. But I ignored those considerations, pivoted, and leaving everything behind me—everything back at Mrs. Copeland's—I walked away from Somewhere.

Once I arrived at the train depot, I darted to the front, feeling shelter from the eyes of the town. I tried listening for pursuit which was difficult amidst my pounding heart and rapid breathing, but I soon settled down enough to realize no one was approaching. Cautiously, I made my way back along the sides of the train station to glimpse Somewhere, and I was struck by its commonness. If I didn't know better, I'd wonder if everything that had happened in the past fifteen minutes or so was just another strange vision.

I crossed the train tracks. Small hills rose in front of me, and I started the ascent. What I was doing was probably stupid, but I didn't care. I'd find civilization soon enough. The first road I came across, I'd just follow it to the nearest town. I hesitated briefly, wondering if I should apply that same logic and follow the train tracks instead, but since they were already a good hundred yards behind me, I trudged on. *No turning this ship*, I thought.

The hills were not steep and probably shouldn't be called hills at all—"elevated ground," perhaps. When I crested the patch of elevated ground I had been climbing, I turned around. I thought of that Bible story of Lot's wife who looked back on the destruction of Sodom but was turned into a pillar of salt. Somewhere wasn't being destroyed by hell-fire—though in that moment of grief, I darkly wished it would be—and I wasn't being turned into a pillar of salt, but I began to relate to the story a little bit. I wondered if it might not be more symbolic, like anytime in life you refuse to look ahead and instead choose to look backward to something that no longer exists, you end up turning yourself into a pillar of salt. I felt that. That hesitation, that drawing back. I was being stupid, I needed to fix this thing, this understanding.

I inhaled deeply, however, and turned myself back around. I was determined to shake the dust off my feet from Somewhere, from Rose.

Once I arrived at the train depot, I darted to the front, feeling shelter from the eyes of the town. I tried listening for pursuit which was difficult amidst my pounding heart and rapid breathing, but I soon settled down enough to realize no one was approaching. Cautiously, I made my way back along the sides of the train station to glimpse Somewhere, and I was struck by its commonness. If I didn't know better, I'd wonder if everything that had happened in the past fifteen minutes or so was just another strange vision.

Wait.

Shit!

What?

I'd been there before, in that exact position, thinking those exact same thoughts. I calmed myself, trying to suppress the unsettling feeling rising within me.

Déjà vu. Could you call it that when it's more than a *sense* that you've experienced something before but rather an absolute certainty? I paused to think, scrunching my eyes shut and bowing my head into my hands. With a dawning fear, though, the truth revealed itself:

I was stuck in Somewhere.

Dumbfounded. Scared. A myriad of feelings. But most prominent: I was mystified. What had just happened? And could I somehow circum-navigate Somewhere's grip on me, this invisible wall? I thought back to my exit before Thanksgiving and the car straining through another invisible barrier.

An idea struck me.

I sprinted past the railroad tracks and back up the hill. At its peak, I didn't turn this time but continued running. I only slowed down as I reached what I figured to be the edge.

Edge. Edge of what, exactly?

Then I plunged ahead. Not a walk, not a trot, but I crashed full force into–through?–the edge of Somewhere.

And there I was, sitting once again in front of Rose.

"It's just that weird things keep happening to me in Somewhere," I said. "Well, since I've been in Somewhere. Weird things were happen-ing back in St. Louis over Thanksgiving week, too." Rose grew still. She seemed to be thinking, but I couldn't read her.

The phone rang. I walked over to it calmly, as if I had been expecting the call. I tut-tutted.

"No calls tonight," I said, smiling innocently. "Just our time together." I unplugged the phone from the cord and set it on a counter. I stared at Rose and didn't flinch at the perplexed, questioning look on her face.

"Weird things," she finally spoke. "Like what?"

I *almost* told Rose everything. But I paused and took in my surroundings. An almost imperceptible smile formed on my lips. I watched the movie reel in my mind, plowing into the invisible wall with all of my strength before waking up back here in Somewhere Sweet. Before the phone had rung and everything had changed.

I might have been stuck in Somewhere, sitting across from this girl that I was both in love with and wary of, but I at least felt a modicum of control. Along with absolute bewilderment.

CHAPTER TWENTY-TWO

Christmas was only six days away, so despite a war no one knew I was waging—a declaration that I had drafted in mind at some point before time and space folded in on themselves at the edge of town—I had called an immediate momentary truce in honor of the holiday. Something just didn't feel right about sleuthing around during a holiday that had always had so much significance for me growing up. Besides, I felt different, like when I would dream as a kid and, on rare occasions, *realize* I was in a dream. That has always given me a sense of mastery. What might have been a nightmare otherwise suddenly became a playground. Absolute free reign to go anyplace and, in my kid brain, defy any law of gravity–I really liked flying in those semi-conscious dreams. That's *sort of* how I felt in Somewhere at that moment, though certainly less secure. The delicately balanced control of a man who knows a secret that others don't know he knows. Unfortunately, as I'd come to learn, nightmares aren't as easy to regulate as one would hope.

At first, I laid low. Even *with* my secret, I didn't want to act foolishly. What happened at Somewhere Sweet had both woken me up and scared me in a way that was far different than the night terrors I'd experienced in Mrs. Copeland's house or the various visions I'd been having ever since I arrived in Somewhere. The whole lid had been blown off. I couldn't even trust Rose.

Suddenly, I began to feel watched by everyone, once welcoming, now souring towards the outsider. What's more, exchanges between Somewhervians began to appear stiff, awkward, scripted. *Scripted!* Yes, that was it. Exchanges felt scripted, like they were hired actors on a set. I had the sense that the whole town was in on something that I didn't know about, and it involved me. Like when you enter a room where everyone immediately quiets, and you know they've just been talking about you. That's the sense I began having everywhere I went. Oh, and all my feelings of paranoia and unease were not helped by the fact that I was stuck in Somewhere, literally incapable of breaking the barrier without being magically whisked away through space and time.

The perception began growing in my mind that Somewhere wasn't a place filled with people but that it was its own entity, its own power, its own force. I wasn't dealing with a place of aggregate parts but rather a unified *thing*. Such thoughts made me shudder and also drew a despondent sadness. What did that make Rose? Pastor Amos? Maggie? These people I thought that I cared about? I considered Jimmy as well, but he was different. I knew him from the outside world. But had he been fused into this colossal mass, the power behind–beneath–Somewhere? In that case, what might happen to me?

Warily, I had returned to my apartment which returned to a dull haunt, the 2:00 signal only bringing with it far-away creaks and groans. Mrs. Copeland was still making her middle-of-the-night journeys, her unbelievable insomniac hour for "doing laundry." During the day, I tried to avoid her as much as possible, but I couldn't avoid *all* contact.

I also tried avoiding Rose, but that was more difficult unless I was ready to blurt out that in an alternate timeline, she had narced on me. I didn't really have any grounds for ignoring her without seeming suspicious. So, I continued seeing her. And Mike, David, Eleanor, everyone.

I think I did alright, able to maintain a pretty normal demeanor. And in so doing, I easily slid back into the routine of my community. I held Rose's hand. And it was good. I laughed with friends. And it was good. I drank David's weird beer concoctions. And they were... not bad.

During that time of latency, I called my parents. Once again, I was without a cell phone, suspiciously misplacing it on my journey back to Somewhere, a convenient fact that caused me to wonder at this town's inexplicable involvement in my affairs. There was nothing I could do about it, though.

With a shock, I had realized weeks had passed since I'd talked to my parents, even though it only felt like a few days based on my inexplicable awakening next to Rose in the park. I didn't experience the same meltdown that I had when I visited over Thanksgiving break; I was braced for the truth this time. So, it came as no surprise when my mom didn't know who was calling, but I still felt the grief of loneliness. I called Miriam next. Though she was clearly processing on the other end of the phone, trying to puzzle out some idea that was just on the tip of her memory, she, too, ultimately could not remember who I was. With a sigh, I hung up the phone and returned to the people of Somewhere, trying to find comfort there. I had harbored a faint hope that Miriam would be the exception, that she would come and rescue me. But who was I kidding? If she showed up in Somewhere, this monster would probably eat her up too.

How easily humans long for equilibrium and happiness, I realized. The mind will go to great lengths to excuse and justify in order to eschew cognitive dissonance. Maybe that's part of the reason I hadn't run away from Somewhere screaming and hollering at the beginning of my stay. There was something attractive here. Alluring. Enchanting. So, I kept seeing Rose and our community of friends. I kept going to work. I visited Pastor Amos and his family again. I visited Maggie and Lenora. I knew I was living in this dream. I could feel the edges of it melting back, knowing I was about to wake up, but I was fighting to hold on to it even while I knew that *I* was the one who needed to bring it crashing down. It was a strange dream, though, sirenic in a way: both a nightmare and a fairyscape, the loveliest place I'd ever been.

It took little time for me to start questioning what really happened with Rose at the bakery. Another vision? A trick of the mind? No one ever picked up the phone. The car could have been anyone for one of a thousand different reasons. This whole thing was based on what? A face that Rose had made? Come to think of it, I had a hard time remembering exactly how she reacted to the phone call. And surely I didn't rebound off the edge of Somewhere, pushed back in time. A dream. Just a dream. That's all it could be.

After the mini snowfall on the night of my quasi-return to Somewhere, in typical Midwest fashion, the weather had warmed just enough to turn everything into soggy mush. The first *significant* snowfall blanketed Somewhere on the morning of Christmas Eve. "Figures," I said to myself, rubbing the sleep from my eyes beside the window. Just another way this Missouri fairyland held you under its spell. I couldn't remember how long it'd been since I had actually experienced snow on Christmas.

The art gallery closed on the 23rd and wouldn't re-open until after the new year, so I had a lot of time on my hands. I thought Tom might ask me again if I was leaving to go home, but he didn't. *Does he know I can't leave?*

I had plans to meet Rose for lunch even though we'd already celebrated together (and it had turned into a nightmare for me). This quick get-together felt like work, a formality, and that realization saddened me. She had actually invited me for the first time to meet her family and to spend Christmas with them, but I declined. I lied and said I was already spending Christmas with the Whitakers which I wasn't. Despite everything, I still wanted to be with Rose, but there was that shift—unbeknownst to her I assumed—created by her actions in an event that I had somehow erased... or re-written. Whatever. So, I sullenly resigned myself to the fact that not only would I be missing the first Christmas with my parents ever, but I'd more or less be celebrating alone.

Since I wasn't meeting Rose until lunch, that left me the entire morning, which was good because I was in a reflective mood. I started at The Book and Bean—coffee and a breakfast sandwich—where I read for a bit. I was only inching along through *Pride and Prejudice* at this point, not because I wasn't interested but because I found it hard to concentrate on reading for long periods of time. Within about ten minutes, I set the book down, stared out the window, and then decided to leave.

"Going so soon?" Barb called as I was reaching the door.

"Enjoying the snow," I offered with a smile before leaving.

Walking along Main Street, I once again got that feeling of journeying through a Dickens novel—minus the top hats—or at least one of those miniature ceramic villages. The windows of these old brick buildings were adorned with holiday decorations, and panes fogged around the edges as store owners tried to combat the frigid temperatures outside by blasting heat inside. Garlands hung around the windows or on lampposts or pretty much anywhere one might conceive of hanging them. People were hustling to and fro, finishing last-minute shopping lists. Bing Crosby's "White Christmas" was playing through a speaker. A storybook setting.

I walked over to a tobacco shop a few streets away that I had seen on occasion. Despite the *one* cigarette I smoked in London and the occasional and mostly failed attempts at properly smoking a pipe when I returned from abroad, I was certainly not a smoker. Miriam, though, had secretly introduced me to cigars early in the summer, and I found myself yearning for one. My pipe smoking had primarily been for pretentious purposes only during my final year of college, but I *did* discover that smoking offered a strange serenity when I was in a contemplative state.

My paranoia struck again in the shop. I felt like the bald man behind the counter was looking over his hooked nose suspiciously, but he said nothing when I brought two cigars to him, one for the moment and one for the next day, my Christmas feast. I felt a bit like a smoking virgin, though, when I had to also purchase a plastic cigar cutter and a lighter. *Just grab a grape Swisher Sweets next time, for Pete's sake.*

Outside, I cut off the cigar's cap and lit a match, carefully holding the cigar closely above the flame but not touching it, slowly rotating it to evenly heat the tip, just like Miriam had taught me. I brought the cigar to my lips, pulled the smoke into my mouth, held it there, and exhaled. Pleased.

That was how I walked around Somewhere. Having already visited The Book and Bean, I avoided Main Street, choosing instead to wind my way in and around the streets surrounding it. I had no particular aim for my rambling; I just needed the movement, the space to think and to be, and the snowy outdoors was as good a place as any. But I realized I was lying to myself when I turned down a recently familiar street. I soon stood looking at Jimmy's house. And unlike last time, there were no cars in the driveway.

For a moment I stayed put and did a quick 360 gaze around me to see if anyone was watching. From what I could tell, I appeared to be alone, so I dashed to the narrow gap between Jimmy's house and the one to its left. *What are you doing?* I asked myself, knowing whatever it was would be better *not* in broad daylight a few hours before meeting my girlfriend for lunch. Still, I felt like the opportunity presented itself, and I didn't want to miss it.

There was some privacy from the tall, rickety wooden fences surrounding the backyard, but I was still visible from the upper windows of surrounding houses. I peered through a window, getting a limited view of the house's interior and saw no movement, so I crept to a back door and tried it. Unlocked! I assumed there was probably not a major security threat in Somewhere, but I felt lucky nonetheless. My excitement was tempered, however, when I stepped inside and realized that I'd pretty much just passed the Rubicon. I was breaking and entering, and a whole trail of footprints outside had followed me.

I almost turned back right then and there, figuring that darkness and snowless streets were two more necessary ingredients for this half-baked plan to work, but I told myself that I'd already committed this far, so I might as well have a very brief look around.

The back door opened into a mudroom off the kitchen. There, I stood for at least a whole minute, listening for any movement. Having no idea about the residents, I was clueless as to whether an empty driveway equaled an empty house. I heard only silence, however, so I continued further into the house.

I couldn't help but remember what sneaking around had done for me last time, the image of Mrs. Copeland at the cellar door still haunting my mind. I didn't know exactly what I was looking for, just some sort of clues as to why Jimmy was here. Truth be told, he could have been from Somewhere all along, and I wouldn't know any better. I had gotten to know him pretty well one summer at camp, but that didn't mean that I *knew* him knew him. Nevertheless, the puzzling way he had been escorted away from me *twice* right at the point of our meeting was something I wanted to know more about.

After slipping my shoes off to avoid tracking snowmelt—and further evidence—around the house, I crept warily into the kitchen. I scanned the refrigerator, walls, shelves, anywhere I could for pictures of whoever lived there and, hopefully, Jimmy, but the place was pretty bare. *Maybe I should leave a business card to the art gallery. They could use it.*

I moved around the rest of the house, and as I did so, I noticed movement out of the corner of my eye, arresting my attention.

At first, I wasn't sure what movement I had seen. Nothing out of the ordinary was there. Then I saw it again: the slightest shifts of light visible underneath the space of a closed door. I heard the groaning of floorboards as whoever it was stood up and moved towards the door.

Oh, shit. Oh, shit. Oh, shit. Oh, shit.

I was on the balls of my feet, ready to sprint out the back door in my socks and just grab my boots on the way, but I heard a recognizable voice.

"Hello. Are you back already?" the voice called from behind the door. Definitely Jimmy. Still, I hesitated, wondering if I should commit. He did seem genuinely glad to see me before being forced into that Jeep, so I assumed I was in no danger of his raising any sort of alarm, but, perhaps a bit naively, I hadn't anticipated his presence. I went for it.

"Uh, hi, Jimmy. It's me, Lee."

"Lee!" his voice sounded authentically pleased. "Oh my God! Jimmy is so glad you're here and that you remembered his name!"

I was perplexed by the way Jimmy referred to himself in the third person, but I was right earlier in thinking that "Carl" was simply made up on the spot by the strongmen escorts. Wait, did I hear crying?

Sure enough, sobs were coming from the other side of the door.

"What's wrong, Jimmy? Can you come out?"

"No, Jimmy cannot come out, but he wants to. He is trapped in his room. Jimmy got in trouble, and Momma made him stay." I walked over to the door and tried the knob. Sure enough, locked from the outside.

I felt a weight in my pocket and remembered the sulfide marble. *Would that work?* I suddenly sensed that the marble was magic, a key that would somehow conjure the door open. I pulled it out, fumbling a little, and tried the door again, heart thumping, not only in anticipation of getting Jimmy out but also in the possibility of discovering something very useful. My excitement was short-lived, however. It was just a marble.

"Jimmy, I'm trying to figure out how to open the door. Do you have any idea where, uh, your Momma would keep the key?" I waited for a moment as he mulled it over.

"Jimmy is thinking on the wood around the door."

"The door frame?" I glanced up, and there it was, the shaft hanging over the edge of the door frame above the door. I rolled my eyes, feeling stupid for ignoring the most obvious hiding spot.

After unlocking and opening the door, I saw Jimmy standing there all sad-dog-eyed, and I briefly imagined Mrs. Copeland behind the cellar door. In this case, though, he looked more pathetic than terrifying.

The whiskery face that I had difficulty recognizing before had altered even further into a short, unkempt beard, and the way his long hair fell around his head in awkward angles made it look like he hadn't combed it in years. Still, it was clearly Jimmy, and I thought back to when I had first met him a few years before, imagining the bounding, energetic guy leaping from rock to rock.

"Hi, Jimmy," I said again.

"Hi, Lee. It is very nice to see you. Jimmy is glad that the bad men are not here to take him away this time. But where would they take him?" he smiled. "Jimmy is already in his room." He giggled, and I gave a perfunctory smile.

"Jimmy, do you know how long your, uh, Momma or anyone else is going to be gone?"

"Only Momma lives with Jimmy. He never knows how long she will be gone."

A little tricky, I thought. I needed to be ready to bolt at any moment, but running out the back door in broad daylight is not exactly a stealthy getaway. Still, I couldn't pass up this opportunity.

"Can we sit down in the living room?" I asked, motioning in that direction. Jimmy hesitated. "What's wrong?"

"Jimmy does not have permission to sit in the living room with Momma. Only eating in the kitchen, going to the bathroom, and his bedroom."

"Is Momma here?" That seemed to confuse Jimmy, but then he understood what I was asking. He slowly made his way over to the couch. He gave a look of trepidation mixed with wonder as he cautiously sat down, and he smiled.

"Wow," he said, looking at me, "it is even better than Jimmy imagined it." I went to take my seat in an overstuffed chair.

"No!"

I bounced up, ramrod straight, eyes wildly swiveling around, ready for trouble. Nothing appeared to be out of place.

"You cannot sit there," Jimmy said. "That is Momma's seat." Frustrated at the panic he had caused me, but having no other seats available to me in the living room, I plopped down on the floor.

I waited for him to maybe say something, but he appeared perfectly content to sit on the couch and simply observe his surroundings.

"So, Jimmy," I started, and he casually looked in my direction. "You, uh, you remember me from Black River Camp."

"Of course, Jimmy remembers Lee. Lee was his favorite."

"Yeah? Well, I really enjoyed hanging out with you too."

I paused, thinking he might go on. *Nope. Looks like it's just going to be me driving this conversation.*

"How did you end up in Somewhere?" I inquired. "Are you from here?"

"Oh, no," Jimmy laughed, putting his hand up in front of his mouth like I'd seen Miriam's nephew do when he was a little kid. "Jimmy is not from here. He got here just like you."

For a moment, I stopped to collect myself and gather my thoughts. The whole experience was unnerving as this was not the guy I had known. Clearly, it was his voice, his body, his *shell*. But something horrible had happened to him.

"And how was that?" I finally said. "How *did* you get here?" I found myself leaning closer, my heartbeat increasing its speed.

"By magic!"

I sighed. I didn't necessarily disagree with him, but his response wasn't very helpful.

"Can you be more specific? How did you first arrive? How did you find out about Somewhere before you came?"

"Oh, Jimmy did not know about Somewhere before he came. Jimmy was driving to pick up supplies for camp one day. He had to drive all the way up to Iowa, and it was just the perfect day. Jimmy had his windows down. He was on the highway, not going too fast, not going too slow, going just right. And then he just knew that he had to go in a different direction than what the map said. The drive got even better. Driving through the forest by the diamond ponds and the little colorful birds in the trees and all the butterflies and the way that the sun went through the branches like swords of light—"

"—and then what happened?" I interrupted. I wasn't trying to be rude, but I didn't know how much time I had before "Momma" got home. I kept popping up whenever I heard a car outside, but so far, all was clear. The irritation in my voice, though, may also have been triggered by how eerily similar Jimmy's account was to my own arrival in Somewhere.

"And then Jimmy was lost," he answered. "But not in a bad way. He got lost in a good way. He got lost here in Somewhere. For a long time, he didn't see any houses or buildings or farms or anything, but he wasn't scared, he just kept driving. And then finally he saw some houses, and then he saw the street with all the beautiful stores."

"And then?"

"And then he was here. Forever."

I forced myself to exhale, trying to process what Jimmy had just told me, but I couldn't make very much sense of it besides the similar euphoria leading up to my arrival.

"So, tell me about your time here," I said, checking outside again.

"Jimmy lives here now," he responded, smiling. "He loves it in Somewhere."

"But why are you locked in a room? Who is your Momma? She can't be your real mother."

And like the pulldown wall maps I'd had in every classroom growing up, a shadow fell slowly down over Jimmy's face, like he hadn't ever considered what I'd just told him. *What was wrong with him? This isn't Jimmy,* I repeated to myself.

"Jimmy was bad," he finally spoke, his face now devoid of any cheer, blank. "Jimmy said hi to you. He wasn't supposed to. He didn't know, but he knows that now. Still, he said hi to you again the other day. They don't like that."

"They don't like what? Who are they?"

"When a stranger speaks to a stranger. Jimmy knows better. He should be in his room. He should be in his room now." Jimmy made a move to get up, but I quickly crawled over to him and put my hand on his, trying to keep him seated, wanting to know more, but he sucked in his breath sharply as if I'd just hurt him. His face, turned towards his hand, slowly tilted upwards, his eyes meeting mine. He spoke, his voice changed.

"If you stay in Somewhere too long, you'll be like me too, Lee. At least until you become one of them. I'll be one of them soon. Then I won't have to stay in my room anymore." His easygoing face curled into an eerie grin, and he started cackling, a whole-body, shrieking laugh that shattered the glass of hanging silence that had encased us before. I imagined every neighbor, every person within a hundred-yard radius snapping their head towards this place, this house. I felt naked, exposed, as if the walls were not opaque walls of a house but rather a plexiglass cage in a zoo. I was suffocating, I would be trapped. I would be like Jimmy.

I jumped up and ran through the kitchen, sliding out the back door; my last fleeting glance at Jimmy was him falling onto the ground in wild laughter.

CHAPTER TWENTY-THREE

How the hell am I supposed to keep my shit together during lunch with Rose?
We sat down together politely at a little diner I'd never been to before, but despite whatever normalcy I thought I'd recaptured with her since the bakery incident, there was a canyon between us now.

She sat in front of me, but as clear as if I'd seen any ghost, vision, or apparition—and I'd seen plenty over the past few months—I gazed upon myself. But I wasn't exactly looking in a mirror. Instead, my head was split open right down the middle, gruesomely but cleanly, if that's possible. Like a skilled surgeon had taken a little medical buzzsaw apparatus and cut me just through the cranium from the forehead to the back of my skull. My hair stuck out at strange angles, matted with flecks of blood. My brain just sat there like the overused engine of an old car, steam rising above it.

I was confronted with this ridiculous image of Rose and did what I could to ignore it. One moment Rose would come back into focus, and the next moment head-injured-Lee would be there, like a radio setting bouncing between two different signals when you're on the border of both coverage areas. I wish I could recall whatever pleasantries Rose and I must have exchanged in that painful hour, but I can't. What I do remember was the end.

"I have to go," I said. To her. To Rose, not the harrowing phantasm of myself which had finally collapsed in on itself and allowed Rose to maintain her form in front of me. She was gazing awkwardly at the ground, like she knew we were in an uncomfortable situation, but also like she wanted to tell me something. She opened her mouth and brought her eyes up to meet mine but remained silent.

She knows. I don't know how I was certain, but I was. Somehow, whatever had happened that night, she wasn't fooled by my act of time-traveling.

I stood up and pushed the chair back.

"Bye, Rose. I...uh..." I trailed off, running my hand through my hair. Still distracted by that vision of myself, assuring myself that my scalp was, in fact, still intact. "I'll see you in a couple of days, huh?" She nodded but still didn't respond, not until I was halfway out the door.

"I love you," Rose called. I froze and turned to face her. There was this weight of sadness between us, like the distance wasn't a canyon but a space. I was the earth, and she was the moon.

I love you.

That's what I wanted to say. Instead, I gave a half smile and left, my heart descending into its own grave.

Back at the house, I was making coffee when Mrs. Copeland walked into the kitchen. It was one of the rare occasions I'd seen her in the past few days, and the awkwardness was now a neon curtain between us. Besides a brief hello, she made to leave quickly but then thought better of it and turned to me.

"So, how are things going?" she asked. A little taken aback by her small talk and nonchalance, I hesitated.

"Fine, fine. Good, actually," I lied.

"It's beautiful here at Christmas."

"Incredible," I agreed. "I've never seen anything like it."

"Yes, yes." She trailed off. I thought she'd leave, but she made another attempt at conversation.

"So, Lee, what are you doing for Christmas tomorrow?" I got the sense that this question wasn't casual or simply small talk.

"I'm going to the Whitakers." Another lie. Actually, the same lie I used with Rose. Double jeopardy or something, right? Mrs. Copeland seemed satisfied with that answer. *If she is trying to prevent my departure, like at Thanksgiving, maybe she hasn't gotten the memo that I can't leave this damn nightmare.*

"You've gotten pretty close with them, huh?"

"Yeah, I guess so. They've been really kind to me."

"That's nice, that's nice. Well, I'm going to be visiting my friend Leigh Anne. A bunch of us widower gals get together every Christmas."

"Bridge?"

"Of course." She almost chuckled, and the neon current fell down, even if only for a moment. I smiled. When she left, I realized the reality of my situation. I smiled more. The house would be mine the next day. And I had some more looking around to do.

I didn't sleep well that night. Besides the interaction with Jimmy that kept looping through my mind, the recurring image of Rose's sad face, and the unease I still felt back in my room, I kept thinking about the next day. In that sense, it really *did* feel like Christmas, being unable to sleep in anticipation of the next day. I reminisced about when I was a kid and had begged my parents to stay up all night with me to try and catch Santa Claus. They were hesitant but didn't know how to overcome my persistence. The next morning, after my severe disappointment with Santa's absence, they made up some long story about his needing to take care of Mrs. Claus that year. They even had a letter. But that was when I stopped believing.

As I lay in bed in a haunted house in a haunted town, trapped and potentially losing my mind, I considered my chats with Pastor Amos. By throwing off the myth of Santa Claus, I thought I was maturing. But Pastor Amos seemed to think that such an abandonment of the supernatural was a sign of ignorance rather than mature rationality. Thin places. Folk religion. The ghost of Samuel and the Witch of Endor.

"It's true."

I shot up and looked at the clock—2:00. It was difficult to identify the source of the voice, but it repeated itself over and over and over like miniature explosions, a room-wide domino fall of clinking whispers and pitches. In my mind or in reality, I couldn't be sure. I was losing certainty of all things, and I wondered if the distinction between what happens in the mind and what happens in objective reality–or what even is objective reality–was irrelevant anyway.

Slowly, I set my feet on the rug below my bed, wrapped in warm socks during that cold time of year. I perceived the sound to be coming from the opposite wall, which normally meant only one thing. I made my way first to the reading lamp and clicked it on, but the soft yellow light did not offer as much comfort as I would have hoped for.

I placed myself in front of Pieter Bruegel the Elder's painting. This time both the hanging woman and the stranger from the woods were there together, the stranger intonating his favorite incantation and waving a gun. I noticed the sound emanating from more than just the painting, however, and, half expecting to see the stranger over my shoulder, turned around cautiously, tensely lifting my shoulders up around my ears. But there was nothing there. Rather, I realized the noise was coming from the attic room on the other side of my own, but I wasn't in the mood to check it out or provoke the house more.

On the spot, I solidified my plans for the next day—or, rather, *that* day as it was a little after 2:00 am. The truce was over. War on Somewhere had begun. I just needed to wait a few hours for daylight. So, I crept back to bed and tried to ignore what I was hearing.

"It's true. It's true. It's true. It's true."

The voice continued that way, unceasing, until I was sure I would lose my mind. My room felt like an echo chamber, the words reverberating all around me rather than those two distinct points. Then the echo chamber was inside my mind. What had been a monotone repetition seemed to be rising in emotion and fervor until it was a shout. I felt that the house wasn't built with walls but with the bones of words, a fever pitch, and I wanted to claw into my brain and join the shouting madness or cut it out of me or simply die there on the floor of my mind.

And then it was over.

I lay there wet, covered in my own sweat, panting for air. Exhausted, I rolled to my side. I'm not sure if I waited five minutes or fifty, but eventually, sleep overtook me.

Merry Christmas.

I yawned and stretched myself awake, eventually sitting up on the edge of my bed. For a moment, warm hope undulated up and down throughout my body, the reflexive reaction to another Christmas morning, the elation brought on by an entire day ahead of gifts and festivities, movies and good food, and family. And on the rarest of occasions—maybe twice in my life—snow. Now three times. I could see it now out my window: deep, beautiful glistening snow. Forming fluffy mounds like fruit tucked inside a dish of whipped cream.

Then, I realized the truth of my circumstances. However, despite a brief moment of reflective sadness, I did discover a spark of joy nestled away inside me. It wasn't related to Rose or the holiday. Rather, it was the joy of knowing, of secrets being revealed. I was on a precipice finally ready to descend, or to fall in more likely. I was at the door, finally ready to open it. The brightness of the sun outside was a bonus, a cheerful invitation. Or a decoy. No matter.

I had no idea what that day would bring, but my body was electric with anticipation. I actually surprised myself, envisioning beforehand that the day would greet me with nervousness and fear. Instead, time slowed down and ushered me along merrily as I went about getting ready: showering, changing clothes, brushing my teeth, enjoying breakfast and coffee in the kitchen below.

I felt light, airy. Fairy. Changing. Changeling. Ha!

I felt silly and cried laughter into my hands, pausing to gather myself.

Somewhere itself was ushering me up a hill kindly, holding my hand on either side, ready to show me everything spread out below me. And I mean *everything*. Why had I been trying to force anything? What was I so concerned about? In time all things will be revealed.

But all things that are reproved are made manifest by the light: for whatsoever doth make manifest is light.

I had said goodbye to Mrs. Copeland as I entered the kitchen and heard the front door of the house close as she left. After finishing my breakfast, I cleaned up. I whistled while I worked. And laughed. I sat back down for more coffee but had hardly been seated when I stood back up again. And laughed. I made my way towards the back door. I had decided to go back up to my room and read. *Pride and Prejudice* really *is* a fantastic story. With my hand around the doorknob, I paused, remembering that I was going in the opposite direction I had been meaning to go earlier. Because I was going to go deeper into the house. Yes, Somewhere was taking me to the top of the hill to see.

But I brushed it aside, laughing.

"Time, time, I've got time," I hummed to an invented tune and opened the back door. On the stoop, I again hesitated, not with the desire to re-enter the kitchen, to do what I had set out to do, but instead, I wondered if I should actually go visit Rose after all. It felt like a good idea. Whatever else I needed to do could wait after all. Plus, I had my coat with me. Convenient. I was ready to go.

The marble was in my pocket, warming my leg. I felt it like a hand,

and as I turned and began walking towards Main Street and Rose's house beyond, the marble rolled up and down my thigh, a caress. It was reaching to touch me *there*, and I welcomed it. I welcomed Rose.

Blushing, I stopped, taking in my surroundings. I was about thirty yards down the sloping driveway in front of the house, no one in sight.

I turned, remembering I was going to read. Yes, read. I retraced my steps, inviting the marble to move in my pocket, inviting Rose's hand, but the dream was gone. *No matter*, I smiled.

On a whim, I looped all the way around the house rather than taking my normal route along the left side. Funny that I had never circumnavigated the perimeter of the house, one side wholly unfamiliar to me. But rather than a suggestion, I felt Somewhere more forcefully trying to spin me around.

No, that's not what we wanted, it seemed to say. Go to Rose or go to read, that's fine, but you need to go back around the other side of the house; you're familiar with *that* side of the house. That's what you're more comfortable with.

Not being able to properly interpret this abstract mental suggestion, however, I plowed ahead in consternation as if the problem were with myself and not some force outside of myself. I found my forward progress growing more difficult, like I was walking through a wall of tangled branches that kept trying to pull me back. My happiness was diminishing in correlation with my thwarted progress.

"I want to walk *here*," I spoke out loud to no one. A blast of cold reached me, not a winter breeze but a presence. Looking down to my left, I finally understood, and the enchantment of the morning simply turned off like a switch.

The cellar.

I understood then. I was not wanted there.

Why didn't you think of this before? Nearly every older house had these external cellar entrances, storm shelters essentially. A refuge in Tornado Alley.

Mrs. Copeland's cellar door was actually bricked over, but I was undeterred. I had discovered another entrance. Still, I found myself being influenced by the impulse to do anything else besides go into that cellar, an odd change of circumstance since, on multiple occasions before, both Mrs. Copeland's cellar and the cellars of other houses had drawn me in, not repelled me. The more I concentrated on this idea, the more I felt the contradiction swirling inside of me: both a desire to go below and an equally strong desire to run. Did the warring suggestions stem from the same paradoxical force, or were separate powers clashing invisibly inside of me and in the heart of Somewhere?

The idea occurred to me that I was a fish in a little glass bowl. Except the glass had grown opaque, and the sides were drawing closer, going to swallow me. If I wanted to leave Somewhere, I couldn't stay still.

I entered the kitchen again. Now, I felt the house was rejecting me like a bad blood transfusion. I didn't mix. I felt a stuffiness immediately, and I moved slowly as though wading through a scummy pond. I reached the door on the other side of the kitchen to the rest of the house and remembered that Mrs. Copeland had increased her security system. *Maybe...* I turned the knob, but this time it stuck in place, unyielding, uninviting, telling me to go away.

I barely hesitated, turning and wading back out of the house. I climbed the stairs to my apartment. My ability to proceed was slightly improved from what it was below, probably related to the distance from the source, I imagined. For a second, I gazed around my room, suddenly getting the impression that all the bumps in the night I'd experienced here were like parlor tricks in the antechamber. I was moving to the main room, the main event.

I proceeded across the room and opened the door to the unfinished portion of the attic, using an extra bit of force to pry open the door that had become stuck all of a sudden.

"It's true. It's true. It's true," The stranger said beside me, but I passed him by. My focus broke for a second when I saw Maggie beside me, unclothed like she was in the painting. This copy, however, leered at me in a way that Maggie never would, playfully, seductively. I knew it was only an apparition, a siren meant to entice me away from my odyssey. But I blushed nonetheless.

Finally, I stood over the door on the attic floor. Exerting a great amount of effort, I managed to pry it open, like lifting the storm drain cover off of a manhole. With a thud, I dropped to the floor below. I was on the second floor, a section of the house I had never visited before. I had half a mind to do some exploring before I continued on, but I shook off the thought. I could see that the hallway ran down and banked towards the front of the house, but I was standing right beside the stairs, so I began my descent. The sensation of wading through a pond of decomposing, stagnant water returned in full force, only now, with my descent, I felt more like I was voluntarily drowning myself, submerging myself in a lake of hell.

I traversed the great room where I was surprised by the light flooding in, the relative peace of a snowy day more disconcerting than if it had been stormy night lashing at the giant windows.

Am I making more of this than I should? It's a house. You're just walking to the cellar. Mrs. Copeland might be private, but at the end of the day, you're home alone on a bright, cheerful Christmas day, and you're simply spooking yourself, working yourself up to think there are monsters in the closet when, in fact, it's just a perfectly normal bedroom.

Still, I continued. If my feelings were merely an illusion, however, the door to the false kitchen was convincing. The knob turned, but the door remained shut.

"Open, son of a bitch!" I yelled, banging my fist on the wood. This sudden outburst of emotion betrayed the secret of my edginess, exhibiting how wired I was after all. My fear grew, noticing the manner in which my voice did *not* travel around the room as I would have anticipated. It was dulled, muffled, as though I were screaming into a pillow. Suffocating. But I banged again on the door with forearms and hands, and the door creaked slightly ajar.

Heart rate quickening, I crossed the final threshold to the cellar. This door gave no opposition, as though I was finally allowed to claim my spoils, though I wonder if instead the house merely maneuvered to a different strategy, giving in to my persistence and permitting me to lift the lid of existence and peer below the surface. To terrify me into submission, perhaps?

When my feet touched the concrete floor, I looked about the space. Upon first inspection, it appeared to be a perfectly normal cellar. At the bottom of the stairs, the concrete wall of the house's foundation was on my left, and a wall of shelves ran along my right with a space saved to reach the furnace. The furnace appeared to be in the middle of the cellar with storage shelves surrounding it, essentially creating a hallway of foundation on one side and storage walls on the other, wrapping around the entirety of the cellar. I advanced ahead to where the "hallway" turned to the right, walked the length of the house, and turned again, pausing now. I finally saw what I'd come to see, though I didn't yet know what it was I was looking at. Once more, I had to journey the length of the house, doubling back to the back wall where I'd started, though separated by the piles of storage and the shelves that cluttered the middle section. The only way out was curling back around the great *U* that the path formed around the edges of the cellar.

In the dimness of light—one small window on each concrete wall where it met the ceiling—I could see only a shadow before me in the shape of a rectangle: a coffin.

Even then, I made excuses in my mind. Was it so weird for an older person to own a coffin? I'd heard of that, people picking out their coffins before they died, wanting things done properly before they kicked the bucket. I guess I wasn't familiar with people then storing those coffins in their own houses; I figured the funeral home held onto it. But perhaps there was some sort of macabre practicality in Mrs. Copeland keeping it in her cellar.

I stood before the coffin, my breathing coming and going in short spurts, gasps. Just a box. A perfectly normal wooden box, somewhat rudimentary compared to some of the coffins I'd seen before. As if to assure myself of its entirely normal dimensions in a normal plane of existence, I ran my hands along the smooth top. It was solid. It existed. It was normal.

Feeling bile in the back of my throat, I wiggled the tips of my fingers into the crevice underneath the lid. *What the hell are you doing?* I screamed silently to myself.

I have to know. Invited. But by whom?

I forced my eyes closed as I lifted. Only when I'd opened it entirely did I open my eyes. Then I turned and vomited all over the dusty ground around my feet.

In the coffin lay Mrs. Copeland, unmoving. Arms by her side. But like the night I discovered her at the top of the steps, this corpse appeared more alive, more full of color, than the Mrs. Copeland I was accustomed to seeing.

How was this possible? I had heard her leave earlier. I mean, it was theoretically possible for her to have returned without my knowing and snuck down into the cellar, into this coffin. But this wasn't Mrs. Copeland. This corpse wasn't breathing.

I swear that what I did next wasn't me. It was the machinations of the house, perhaps. Was this why it had relented earlier, changing its mind, allowing me to pass through and bring me to this moment? I reached my hand in and, with the slightest of grazes, ran the tip of my finger along the skin of the corpse's arm.

Her eyes shot open, and she immediately sat up. In terror, I fell backward, only barely avoiding my own sickness from a minute before. As she made a garbled noise in her throat—just like the strange difficulty of speech she exhibited the other night, I bolted back the way I came, traversing the *U* of the makeshift cellar storage passageway.

I bounded up the steps, tore through the house, out the front door, and into the sparse cover of the snowy trees around the property. I would never enter Mrs. Copeland's house again.

CHAPTER TWENTY-FOUR

My one saving grace as I huddled under the cover of the trees was the coat I had brought down with me to breakfast. Shivering, I wondered what to do next, and where to go, and I was confused as hell from what I had just seen. I didn't have to wonder for long.

A far-off hum grew quickly into a roar. The noise peeled by me and came to a sliding halt: Mrs. Copeland stepped out of her car, the image of her demonic visage behind the wheel reminding me of that cartoon Cruella de Vil from *101 Dalmatians*. Though the tree cover wasn't thick, I had scooted back behind a full evergreen which allowed me to remain hidden from the sight of the house. Still, I felt the need to make myself smaller to avoid incurring the wrath of whatever version of Mrs. Copeland was before me.

She seemed to notice footprints headed into the trees, I nearly swallowed my tongue as she took two tremendous strides in my direction. However, she seemed to think better of it and instead bounded into the house, much more spry than I would have imagined someone her age. Not wanting to stick around and push my luck, I turned and ran. The property quickly sloped down at a steep angle until I was running, sliding, falling, standing, and running again all the way to the bottom. Part way into my descent, I heard a terrifying howl coming from the house, and I imagined that Mrs. Copeland had discovered my trespass. I didn't know how she could have learned so quickly of what I'd done except that she must have some telepathic connection to her other self.

Another self. My wild escape had not afforded me the time to contemplate the confirmation of what I'd learned. There were two Mindy Copelands: the normal one and the undead one, something straight out of a zombie horror movie.

Not knowing what to do but with adrenaline swimming laps through my body, I felt the need to move, so I began walking along a small lane that wound around below the hill where Mrs. Copeland's house was perched. I was moving in the direction of Main Street and the principal part of the town, Mrs. Copeland's above on the left and a valley leading out to the train tracks on the right. Suddenly, a car rounded the bend ahead and moved towards me. For a moment I thought it might be Mrs. Copeland, but a quick glance revealed a full car, a family of five, the kids in the back. I relaxed, remembering that it was Christmas after all.

I had to squeeze as close as I could to the side of the road to let the car pass. There wasn't a lot of room, what with the narrow road and a steep ascent up or descent down on either side. As the car passed, though, all five heads turned to me in unison, faces expressionless. It stopped almost immediately, and out of instinct, I ran.

I glanced over my shoulder momentarily to see the driver now standing in the road, watching me flee. He said nothing but got back in his car, presumably to follow after me. He'd have a bit of difficulty getting his car turned around on that narrow, snowy lane, though, which I knew would buy me a small amount of time.

When I rounded the bend, I saw the rest of Somewhere spread out in front of me. I had only a moment to take in the fact that the whole town seemed to be alive, abuzz with activity. It couldn't have been more than an hour earlier that I had been carelessly descending Mrs. Copeland's driveway and gazing out upon a sleepy town, no one in sight. Now cars were zig-zagging across streets, and people were milling about. I was too far away to fully discern the reason beyond the hustle and bustle of the holiday that contrasted so sharply with the quiet community I had witnessed only shortly before.

I was nervous; I felt it was portentous. The same panicky feeling I'd been having that everyone was watching me. But I could hear the car behind me trying to maneuver itself and turn around, so I acted quickly and left the road to my right, navigating another series of running, sliding, and falling as I descended even further. The slope ended not far from the back of someone's house where there was greater tree cover, and, importantly, it seemed to be where the residences ended. There was nothing behind me but trees and land. It was the direction of the stranger.

"It's true," I heard myself say, still without clearly understanding *what* was true. One thing I did know, however, was that truth was both more elusive and more full than I had otherwise considered. I felt that I had already aged years, decades, even. Who was I, puffed up by my little adventure to England a few years before when, all along, the world was not, in fact, wider but deeper? The enigmas of life were in this strange little village in rural Missouri, and I bet that there were hundreds of other little Somewheres dotted across the globe, and people were mysteriously falling down the rabbit hole while the rest of the world lived in ignorance. Or those who fell down rabbit holes and returned to tell their tale were scoffed at. Was I ever getting out of here? Would anyone believe me?

I thought of Pastor Amos, a self-proclaimed true believer. I wondered if I could go to him. But I had something on my mind, and I would see that out first. The problem, though, was that I needed to wait until nightfall.

I felt like a fugitive, but I thought, picking my way stealthily along the edge of Somewhere, I could just be a fool. Here I was, trying to remain undetected, figuring that everyone was on the lookout for me, but what did I know? Perhaps Mrs. Copeland was the only one distraught while everyone else was simply getting on with their Christmas celebrations. I couldn't shake the sensation that Somewhere was awake, that it knew my whereabouts–or at least that I was on the lam–although I did nothing in secret. I didn't have to sneak around too long before I found what I was looking for: a shed. Not a particular shed, just the first one that I could spot. I needed to get out of the cold while I waited for darkness. I was inspired, I guess, by Pastor Amos' own backyard retreat but was disappointed in my small hope that another Somewhervian might have a similar shed sanctuary.

At first, I couldn't bring myself to enter, afraid of being spotted by the property owners despite the distance from the house and ample tree coverage. The cold finally convinced me, though, so I darted inside. I rummaged around quietly, hoping against all odds to find blankets, but I had no such luck. The best I came up with was a plastic tarp which I wrapped around my body. It helped, but not much. I snoozed on and off, trying to pass the time by sleeping.

Dusk finally arrived, so I scrambled out and stealthily made my way to Laurel Hill Cemetery, hopped the fence from the back side––attempting to avoid the town's stares—and got to work. There were thousands of graves and little time before complete darkness. Methodically, I worked from the back and moved forward row by row, hunching down to view the names on the gravestones. For many of them, I had to brush aside snow, so it was a tedious process, and my back soon felt like that of an arthritic centenarian. But I persevered.

Rarely but occasionally, I came across a tombstone so old or so eroded or both that I couldn't make out what it said. I swallowed down the bit of panic I felt whenever that happened, wondering if I was wasting my time. Maybe what I was looking for was unintelligible, a faded piece of cement. But I carried on. I had no other plans besides possibly going to see Pastor Amos. Or I could keep trying to escape the border of the town, getting shot back through space and time until my head got so addled I'd be like Jimmy, some brain-fried lunatic locked up in someone's house.

That thought jolted me with renewed motivation, and I continued scouring the rows and rows of graves. I paused. It wasn't what I was searching for, but it caught my attention nonetheless.

Barbera Hamilton

1833-1886

Barbera. Barb from The Book and Bean? The inscription was simple, just a name and date with nothing else before it, as though the stone was waiting for an epitaph to be written or that there were no words to capture the thought. I quickened my pace but paid even closer attention to the names. Sure enough, there were others: Margaret DeJong, David Delany. I realized somewhat embarrassingly that, aside from Mike, David was the only person in my small circle of Somewhere friends whose last name I knew. Mike's dad worked on the largest farm, Schmidt Farms, so that was easy enough, and *David Delany* was marked somewhere on his beer label. So even though I had passed a Kenneth and an Eleanor, I couldn't be sure if these were the Kenny and Eleanor that I knew. I had actually passed two Kenneths—Kenneth Campbell and Kenneth Cook—which proved my uncertainty. But Maggie and David's tombstones, like Barb's, were empty of any epitaph.

Eventually, though, I found what I had set out to find in the beginning, the tombstone of Mindy Copeland, 1821-1886. Of course, all of the names that I knew were alongside several others with the same surnames. Families were buried in the same cemetery, living and dying here in rural Missouri. Though, according to Mrs. Copeland's tombstone, she surely couldn't have been born too late after the town's founding. Anything west of the Mississippi River, I always gave a general founding date of the early 1800s when I knew the Oregon Trail was in its heyday.

The truth is that probably any of those graves with names I recognized could have worked, but Mrs. Copeland's was the only one I was 100% certain of, the only one whose coffin I literally saw, touched, and—the thought still triggered my gag reflex—opened. Standing in the cemetery, a strange solitary figure—a little crazed now considering everything I had experienced—on Christmas under the cover of dusk, I was ready to put my theory to the final test.

"Shit!" I cried, suddenly realizing that I wasn't prepared for my task. Fishing a dead branch from beneath the snow, I poked it into the ground as a marker, climbed back over the cemetery fence, and sprinted back to the shed I'd hidden myself in earlier. I returned shortly after with a shovel.

I was a crazed, solitary figure, a painted silhouette whose colors were slowly bleeding into the surrounding canvas of night.

It was late in the dusk of evening when Tom Walker reached the old fort.

I was Victor Frankenstein scavenging the grave.

Who shall conceive the horrors of my evil toil, as I dabbled among the unhallowed damps of the grave... I collected bones from charnel houses; and disturbed, with profane fingers, the tremendous secrets of the human frame.

On my only two attempts to pierce the crust of the frosted earth with the shovel, I nearly broke my body. Defeated and sore, I hunched over the ground contemplating my options. Glancing sideways from my bent-over position, I noticed the tombstone next to Mrs. Copeland's, Vergil Copeland, who must have been her husband. Interestingly, though, his gravestone *had* an epitaph: *Till We Meet Again.* Simple. Normal. What one would expect on a gravestone. Also, I remembered that Mrs. Copeland had once told me that she had three sons. Though completely forgotten up until now, I wondered why I didn't see graves for them. Had Mrs. Copeland lied? Or might they have moved away–could that make a difference?

The answers to my questions didn't really matter, so once again, I began scanning the markers around me. Some of the tombstones had epitaphs, and some did not. Moving a bit beyond Mrs. Copeland's plot, I found another set of graves I recognized: the Whitakers.

For whatever reason, seeing the Whitakers' cemetery plots was the most jarring for me. Next to a series of first names I didn't recognize—previous generations probably—were Amos, Tracy, Anna, and Charlotte. Despite the winter air, my skin grew colder, a chill running up and down my body. I thought of the day—it was recent but felt like ages ago—talking to Pastor Amos in his kitchen and having that weird freak-out moment when I tried to sprint toward his cellar. And to think that whatever impulse I was following must have been correct. Their—even in my mind, I had difficulty forming the idea—their *coffins* were lying below us that whole time.

What's more, I realized with grief that strange pull had also compelled me while visiting Maggie and Lenora.

As I looked up from the Whitakers' tombstones, the ground felt like it was tilting underneath me. Tombstones marking empty graves–some of them. But not empty houses. The thought of all these houses spread out around Somewhere, and underneath them, in their bellies, were coffins with their corpses or whatever thing that was back at Mrs. Copeland's. The houses were crypts.

Dry bones. I thought of that passage in Ezekiel when God breathes life into the Valley of Bones. But this was the opposite. Instead of life-transforming dry bones, this town was like rot. Corpses were some sort of temporal token but of what? Of ghosts, phantasms trapped in this place? And here I was among them. Turning into one of them? Is that what was happening? Is that what had been happening to Jimmy, some poor soul who stumbled into this place of dolled-up decay and was now on the edge of madness, or had he already tipped over?

And Rose. What did that make Rose? I hadn't seen her name, but I was sure that, had I the time to scrape the snow off the rest of the grave-stones, I'd find the Weavers somewhere in here.

I was on the point of returning once again to the shed to look for anything that might help me thaw out the ground or something like a pick to better breach the concrete-like surface, determined that, if I were destined to enslavement in this mysterious hell, I would at least try to get some answers. I turned around, about to retrace my steps from my point of entry–the back fence–when, on the horizon behind the cemetery, I spotted a spire of smoke rising up into the clouds, barely visible in the final waning moments of light before complete nightfall.

Coming from anywhere else, I wouldn't have paid any attention. But I was struck by the oddity of its rising so far away from the rest of Some-where. The cemetery was the last landmark on this edge of Somewhere. Either something was burning or else another dwelling sat further still. I didn't think it was the former because the smoke did not appear to be rising from some great conflagration. Instead, it seemed to be the thin pillar of controlled chimney smoke.

Now, just a cornered rat in a shrinking box, I felt that I had no other option but to move forward, come what may. For the moment, I chose to put my grave desecration on hold and follow the beacon before me.

After hopping back over the cemetery's fence, I saw the sloping hill behind the cemetery, the gentle contours of the snowy terrain dotted with a dense grove of trees, and path I hadn't noticed before. As I entered the thick, evergreen forest, my vision was swallowed up by the dim light. I was now engulfed in the mystery–and magic–of the wood.

The closeness of the surrounding trees created a dry forest floor. In-stead of snow, I was crunching over a bed of pine needles. And despite the nightfall and the evergreen canopy blocking out any celestial light, I found that, as my eyes adjusted, I could faintly see the path and branches around me. It took very little time for me to realize another odd feature to this journey; based on my position in the cemetery, the smoke had appeared to be maybe a hundred yards away. But I walked and walked and walked. Ten minutes. Fifteen minutes. Thirty minutes. Not only that, I found myself turning, winding this way and that, doubling back from the direction I had previously come, then moving to my right, to my left, to my right again.

Before long, I was completely disoriented, completely in the grip of and at the mercy of the wood. What's more, I had a sense that I had made this trek before. Except that before I had been driving, the road winding through an idyllic Missouri fairyscape, and the final destination was Somewhere itself.

I had no way of knowing how long, but eventually, the tangle of trees opened up to a clearing. Directly in front of me was a cabin made of deep, dark wooden logs and a mossy roof. A stone chimney spit forth the smoke that had signaled to me before. I craned my neck and peered above me, a thousand dimples of light scrunching out of the contours of the night's face. I wondered if these were the same stars that I'd seen all my life outside this forest. Of course, they should have been, but here they seemed different somehow. More alive, more vibrant. Primordial even.

The woods encircled the cabin, an impenetrable wall. Here, in the clearing, snow was able to find its way to the ground, so at least there was a relationship here with the world outside. That and the energy that was connected to the same something that had animated Mrs. Copeland's house, that had followed me back to St. Louis, that connected everything in Somewhere. Before, I would have said that the energy of the house was leading me to what I found beneath, the secret of the coffin in the cellar. But it wasn't.

This was the anticipation, this was the source. In the house, it was something terrifying, something to be avoided or at least endured. Here, it was simply a fact, a presence.

I stepped forward. The sound of my shoe punching into the snow underneath was startling. I realized how loud the silence had been. Not for fear did I want to keep quiet; it was timidity, as though I were intruding. But I moved ahead.

At the cabin door, warmth greeted me from within. The door squeaked as I pushed, remembering too late that it was rude not to knock.

Pausing just across the threshold, I surveyed the cabin's interior: The three rows of bunk beds that took up the space to my left. A small table sat just on the edge of the first row of bunks, glowing with the light of several candles varying in size. The table was also covered by oddities: fruit, bread, old coins, dried flowers, and an open bottle of whiskey.

I'm not sure why I did it, but as soon as I saw that altar, I stepped to it, pulled the sulfide marble out of my pocket, and rested it among the other items. For a brief moment, I saw the ensconced snake wriggle before settling itself, almost–I had the idea–like it was cozying up at home. A pang shot through me, letting go of this connection to Rose, but I knew that this was where the object belonged.

Turning, I looked along the back wall: rows and rows of books displaying an impressive amount of human knowledge, and that, with the Persian rug on the floor, reminded me of Pastor Amos's shed-study. On another table, an old record player was spinning its vinyl disc, scratchy music ambling out of its old speakers, jazzy riffs of electric guitar sliding behind the soulful voice.

Well, my mom fell out of the juniper tree
On the back of a raven's wing
A silhouette over the path of a moonbeam
And the moon, she said,
Ain't no angel's ring
But come to me!
Curling her finger, come to me!
I followed that line to Hecate's bitter tooth

Boy!
And she set that fat book down
Upon my knee
This little spell 'l set you free
Boy!
I say, it'll set you free

A fire danced steadily in a stone fireplace in the corner of a cabin, light and shadow undulating in waves over *her*.

CHAPTER TWENTY-FIVE

It was peculiar seeing her this way, not dead, not hanging at the end of a rope, not haunting me. Normal. Except not *normal*, not in any mundane or boring sense. She clearly had the power.

I wasn't surprised, though. It was like hearing the answer to the riddle that I simply could not guess on my own, but upon hearing it, the answer was so obvious as to feel natural, anticlimactic even. Seeing her, however, was anything but anticlimactic. This was clearly a culmination. An arrival. The inner lair, as it were.

She sat in a simple rocking chair, pushing her body forward and pulling it back ever so slightly. Frayed slippers adorned her feet, stockings covering what little of her lower legs I could see from under her great faded dress. Despite her dingy and commonplace clothes, her fingers wore several silver and brass rings, all displaying strange symbols. Large earrings hung from her ears, and around her neck, where I had often seen a noose, was instead a necklace of rope stringing together what appeared to be several small leather satchels. Lastly, her long, gray-streaked dreadlocks were pulled back by a deep, crimson band of cloth.

The woman cradled a book in her lap and added to the surrounding books and a dim lamp on a small table beside her; it reminded me of story time with my parents when I was a child. That's almost how I felt with her, childlike.

But there was no mistaking the difference, the difference that made this woman before me stand out from my parents and, most sharply, from every single person I had seen in Somewhere. Her dark skin was the emblem of her African ancestry, dark like night, dark like mystery and the secrets that had been written in ink, filling in every pigment of her being.

"Hello, Lee," she greeted me. If my mouth weren't so dry, I'd have responded. It was the polite thing to do. But I couldn't, so I didn't. I stood there dumbly.

"It's good of you to visit me," the lady spoke, looking at me with penetrating, unwavering, steady, gray eyes. Out of reflex, I took a half-step backward.

"How do you know me?" I finally replied after, once again finding my voice difficult to operate. "Have we met?"

"We have *not* met in the sense that you mean, but I do know you. How about you have a seat?" She gestured to a very rudimentary stool nearby which I accepted. "I'm sorry that I could not be more accommodating, but that is the only other seat that I have. It was my brother's."

I glanced over at the bunks on the other side of the cabin, briefly wondering if there was anyone else here.

"No, no one else is here," she said, deciphering the meaning of my glance. "It's just you and me." The woman sat there across from me, her hands laid over the closed book in her lap, continuing to stare at me. In no visible hurry, she appeared calm, relaxed. I got the sense that time moves differently here, or at least felt different, enclosed in this forested cell.

I would not say that the woman was warm and inviting, but neither was she cold or threatening. She continued to wait, though, almost as if *I* had called this meeting.

"Am... am I supposed to be here?" I ventured. I wasn't even sure what to say.

"You *are* here," she replied. "Which means you are supposed to be here."

"How did I get here?"

"I assume that you took the path through the woods, no?"

"You know what I mean," I said and caught myself. I didn't mean to sound rude. "Excuse me. I just mean, surely you know that these woods... that this path..." I had no words. I was growing tongue-tied, my mind a jumble. "Those woods aren't normal, I don't think," I was finally able to spit out. "Do you have visitors very often?"

"First, say what you mean, and don't assume, though you are excused. But be precise. Words have power. Second, you're right, the woods are not normal, at least not in the way that you see things. Third, no, I do not get visitors here."

"Ever?"

"It has been a very long time."

"Why am I here?"

She raised an eyebrow. "I think I should be asking you the same thing. Why are you here?"

"I saw the smoke from your chimney, and I followed it here."

"Is there no smoke from other chimneys in that town?" She said *that* as if she lived somewhere distinct from the rest of Somewhere.

"Yes, there's smoke from other chimneys," I huffed and rolled my eyes, frustrated by this slow exchange.

"Then why did you come here? Or do you always barge into other people's houses when their fireplace is lit?" She said this with a wry smile.

"I was curious," I responded. "I didn't think there were any houses beyond Laurel Hill and especially not so isolated from the rest of Somewhere. So, I was surprised to see one, or the chimney smoke from one anyway."

The woman's eyes narrowed. "There's more than one secret beyond Laurel Hill," she stated as she leaned closer to me gravely.

"What do you mean?"

She leaned back into her chair, resuming her rocking.

"What do you know about... what do you call the town?"

"What? Somewhere?"

"Somewhere what?"

"No, the name of the town is Somewhere."

The woman raised an eyebrow at me. She snorted. "Apt."

"Is that not its name?"

"Oh, that's its name if that's what it wants to call itself. But when I lived there, it was called by another name."

"What was it called before?"

"Xenia it was called in my time. A funny name—"

"—funnier than Somewhere?"

She chuckled. "You got a point there. It's a funny name, though, because in Greek, it means hospitality."

"Why's that so funny?"

"Well, maybe ironic is a better word for it. Because there was nothing hospitable about that town."

"Somewhere has been a nice town for me until recently."

She glared at me.

"You don't understand," she asked. "Do you?" She let me marinate for a moment and think about what I'd said.

"I guess I do," I managed meekly when I realized what she was getting at.

"That's right," she continued. "For folks like you, Xenia *is* a nice town. Right out of a storybook, I presume. But one person's fairy tale can be another person's nightmare. It's all a matter of perspective."

"When was your time?" I asked, deflecting the direction of our conversation for a second. She had struck a nerve that I wasn't quite ready to address. This was an important moment, though. The woman was about to confirm or deny some of my suspicions. She seemed to understand that and didn't answer immediately. Instead, she gave me a serious look, like she was hesitant to divulge information with me. But she relented.

"You could say I left Xenia in 1886."

After visiting the cemetery and seeing the graves of people I knew—or I *thought* I knew—to be alive, I wasn't especially surprised by the woman's revelation. It still had a way of sucking the air out of me for a moment.

"Wh-what happened to Somewhere? To Xenia?" Again, she took a moment, scrutinizing me with those slate-gray eyes before responding.

"Child," she exhaled. "That's quite a story. You sure you wanna hear it?"

I thought of Rose and wondered where she fit into all of this. I wondered if I *did* want to know.

For nothing is secret, that shall not be made manifest; neither anything hid, that shall not be known and come abroad.

I sighed; it was time for the truth to travel abroad.

"Yes, I want to hear it," I said.

She began.

"My name is Marie Weston, and I was born in Xenia in 1842. My mother had arrived three months pregnant when her owners had decided to move here from Louisiana and start a new life in the fledgling Missouri town. Right before they left, however, they sold off much of their property: land and slaves, including my father.

"Some would say I was lucky, I guess, because my momma and me was house slaves working in the house of Master Delaney, and, in some ways, maybe they was right. I avoided the back-breaking labor of the tobacco and hemp fields. I slept in the house—a mattress in the corner of the kitchen with never enough blankets in the wintertime—while the others slept in bunks in cabins, *this* being one of 'em. This is where my cousins and uncles and aunts and friends slept. If it was cold in the house, it was a frozen hell here. Slave owners don't want no dead negroes; they lose money that way. But even that didn't prevent some of them from dying out here, including my cousin Freddie who died of pneumonia one winter when I was seven.

"I remember sneaking into the cabin after they said he'd passed. I wasn't supposed to, but of course, I disobeyed my momma on that one. His eyes was open and glossy, and I knew he was in the beyond, dancing in green fields that was his, nobody else's. But back on earth, in that cabin, he was stiff, iced over.

"But working in the house ain't no picnic either. In the fields, you're treated like an animal, you're in the open air like an animal, but it's all you know. In the house, you're expected to behave like a gentleman or a lady, but you're certainly *not* a gentleman or a lady, and the owners—even the nice ones—make sure you know that, make sure you know your place. In the house, you get a taste of it, a taste of how white folk live, your noses are rubbed in it like some bitch of a dog getting its nose rubbed into its own vomit. They make you think you should be thanking them, as if it's a privilege to be serving them in their elegant homes, built off the backs of your kinsman in the fields outside. As if somehow they'd built it all themselves, but those bastards couldn't last one day in the fields without a parasol or a whip or a glass of cold water under a shady tree.

"But you know what? For a long time, they had me deceived. They had me believing that I *was* special, that I was somehow better than everyone outside, even if my being there was just a win of the lottery, no different than being born with white skin.

"Well, when I was about eighteen, I fell in love with William. My momma had died a few years before, so as far as immediate family, it was just me by then. So, William was my miracle. He worked in the Schmidt fields not too far from the house where I lived. He was a fine man, courteous, caring, but also stubborn, and he didn't put up with too much goddamned foolishness. It got him into some trouble, but he was strong and worked hard, so they wasn't gonna do too much to him. Besides, getting new slaves meant going down South, and what with them boats to and from Africa being stopped as well, slaves wasn't as easy to come by, so I guess you could say that the "cattle" was treated with at least a little more respect. Well, "respect" sure ain't the right word. We was treated with a little more tolerance, you might say.

"Things was good with my William. I'm telling you, boy, that man was a man. In every way you can imagine. We'd 'a had thirty kids that first night of love-making if that was biologically possible. But, you know what? I couldn't get pregnant. We didn't know right away, but it didn't take long. We was still good, but I know that a wall was built up. Something unspoken. Something sick and festering.

"Not too long after, the Great Rebellion began. 'Course, we didn't know what to think of it here in Missouri, but the more and more we understood what the fightin' was really about, the more that the men was itching to join the cause. The masters was furious. They tried not to let on. I mean, Missouri was still part of the Union officially, but where we was, everything was just a burning pot waiting to boil over.

"Eventually, negroes was able to join the fight, and my William was one of them. Soldiers was granted freedom and a bit 'a money, but I guess with Lincoln ending up declaring all us free anyway, it didn't really matter. Still, I know my William woulda fought no matter what. He had that way about him. Plus, like I said, there was a wall between us. He tried to hide it. But I know he was suffering knowing he couldn't have no kids.

"What Xenia did to us—did to me—was a devilish nightmare, and I'm gonna tell you about it. But I will confess. I am no lwa either—a spirit or angel in my religion, in case you wondering. While my husband was out fighting, along with several other black men, I started attracting the attention of a certain white man, one of the handful of 'em who avoided conscription, probably bribed someone. And this one was one of the town leaders.

"At first, I denied his advances. He started coming around to my master's house more and more, and he would say things to me. White men never say anything to the help unless, well, they're looking for something more intimate. Mr. Delaney didn't like it, though. I heard them hollering at each other once. After that, that man stopped speaking to me...at least while others was around. But he still found me.

"Again, I put him off, but you know what? My William had been gone for a long time, and I told you, working in that house, I was made to feel special, to see myself as different. I enjoyed the man's attention. And eventually, I relented. To my absolute shame, a shame that has chained me down, I relented. I became that man's mistress. I felt loved, cared for. I thought that things would go even better for me. The town might hate me, but they'd have to respect me. The problem was he got real secretive. He made some kind of deal with Mr. Delaney because he always came to me at the house when nobody was around. I honestly don't think anybody knew about us. Which wasn't great for me. After a while, I had no shame, and I *wanted* people to know. It was worse that I was only an unknown mistress, that people saw him as a leader, and they didn't even know about us. I was ready to blow the whole thing wide open; I didn't care. But then the war was over, and I got word that William was coming home. Of course, I cut the affair off right then and there, but it didn't matter anyway.

"They say it was an accident, but who they fooling? The entire time that the men was gone, every one of them slave masters was moody and angry. "Ungrateful bastards," they'd say. "If it weren't for us, they'd be starving in some African village." Things like that. Never mind every single one 'a them was born right here on American soil. But they started saying that if those negroes want to leave us, they sure as hell ain't getting no protection or favor when they get back.

"I told you that we was valuable, but after the war, we was free. We lost all our value which was dangerous. So, about fifteen miles outside of Xenia, every one of them men—there was seven of them—died in a tragic accident, we was told. The men was traveling at night; they wanted to see us so bad. Then they lost they footing and fell down some gorge. Every last one of them. Forgot how to walk and died. The biggest load of bull ever. Of course, we never saw the bodies, and then they strictly forbade us to talk about our dead husbands.

"For over twenty years, I stayed in Xenia. I thought about leaving, but there just wasn't anything for me. I ain't stupid, but I didn't exactly know the world, and after grieving for my William, my situation wasn't terrible. The Delaneys was what they was, former slave owners. There is no excusing that. But they was alright with me. In the early days, they could have their spells of nastiness, but after the war, they was just shells. Plus, they had little kids that I watched grow up in those twenty or so years.

"There were no more "incidents" again like when our men got murdered after the war. I think the white men was a little spooked by what they had done. That's why no one ever talked about it. All the same, over the next thirty years, I watched every last Black person leave Xenia. The white folk wasn't violent to us anymore, but they sure wasn't friendly either. They was resentful. Resentful of our freedom. Resentful of losing their labor and, consequently, their fortunes. Though in the beginning, most all of us stayed, and the old masters wasn't paying us anything but room and board—basically the same we was making before—but it still wasn't the same for them, and it wasn't the same for us.

"I said my situation was alright. I mean that it was secure, and I didn't face any open hostility. I think they liked me. I was a "nice negro" I'd overhear. Now, I don't know if "nice" was correct, but I was penitent. Not towards them, mind you, but towards the memory of my dead William. I felt remorse for what I done, that I hadn't been faithful to him when he was out fighting. Fighting for our freedom. *My* freedom.

"Finally, though, about five years before I, uh, left Xenia for good, the affair started again. The truth is, I liked the man. He was different from the others in Xenia. I'm not saying he was an abolitionist or nothing. In that respect, he was really no better than anyone else. But I never felt that he saw me as below him. That our differences were differences of stations in life not in human value or dignity. That may seem messed up, that someone who sees you as equal under God should strive to make you equal in the eyes of society, but he always seemed to operate a little differently. A little abstractly. A little madly. And I liked that. He was a pastor, actually, but he didn't mind my own religious expressions. It was an open secret that I had brought African religion with me, though, of course, I was born here. And my mother was born in Louisiana. But *her* mother had brought it with her, and it had always stayed. Never in the open. The white men only wanted the Bible. It was a way to control us, to manipulate a holy thing and make a tool of oppression. They thought we was stupid, the way they'd use that text to keep us in chains. We wasn't stupid, but we laid low. The funny thing is that we *did* learn their scriptures, and we found the stories to support *us*. Crossing that Jordan River. That Jesus who had to be a dark-skinned man if he came from the part of the world that their Bible says. So, I respected the religion. Not our masters' version of it but the religion that belonged truly to the lowly ones. I respected it, but I kept my own.

"Like I said, the man I was sleeping with actually liked my stories. And he had his own. We'd lie naked together after making love—always in Mr. Delaney's house—and he'd tell me the craziest things, the craziest theories, about true religion. I imagine he's still telling those same stories to whoever'll listen. I never really understood him, but I liked the stories. That, of course, would jazz him up, and we'd make love again.

"But eventually, I got tired of him. I can't tell you the moment, but I got tired. At the beginning–well, the *second* beginning–I always felt like he was conquering me. In the end, I felt like I was conquering him. Like I had dried him out. He found out that I'd been sleeping with another man. And to tell you the truth, I didn't even like the other man. I was just bored. There wasn't no other black folk with me no more, I was just plain bored.

"I was actually on the point of leaving Xenia. I didn't think I ever would, but I had some cousins in Chicago, said it was a better place for me there, and I couldn't see no reason to say no. The night before I was gonna leave, *he* came by. And he was hollerin' mad.

"'You bitch!' he screamed at me, and boy, he was frothing at the mouth. And he reeked of alcohol. He was creating such a disturbance that Mr. Delaney come down—he had *never* come down before—but even Mr. Delaney was scared, so he just sent us outside. And that man kicked me and dragged me all the way to this spot where we's at right now.

"You think you're better than me," he's telling me. "You think you're some uppity bitch. Well, you're not. You're just a whore. The whore of Babylon. No, no, no. I take that back. The whore of Babylon is something. You're nothing."

"And he's telling me these things, but the whole time, between sentences, between words, he's slapping me, spitting on me, and in the end, that man raped me. Right there outside Delaney's house.

"I was scared of him. I was ashamed and broken, but that man wasn't finished. I saw murder in his eyes, and I was scared of him. But even then, I didn't want to give him the power, so even while his pants was down and he was still in me, I laid eyes on that gun holstered on his hip–he hadn't even bothered taking it off–so I grabbed it and blew a hole through my chest.

"That was 1886."

CHAPTER TWENTY-SIX

I sat stunned. Even after she had just finished telling me her story, I knew next to nothing about this mysterious woman. Nevertheless, I did feel as though I was seeing her, Marie Weston, more completely. She was beautiful and majestic, powerful and strong, terrible and righteous, scarred and noble. It took me a while to speak, but eventually, I found my voice again.

"The pastor, the man who..." I couldn't bring myself to say it. "The man who did those things to you, that was Pastor Amos, right?"

"It was." If she was surprised by my knowing his name, her expression didn't indicate it. For me, however, the weight of the truth nearly crushed me on the spot. All my memories were turning bicycle wheels, whirling in my head.

I couldn't help but imagine the man in the pulpit, quirky but affable. I couldn't help but imagine the jolly winks, the irreverent but lighthearted way he spoke. His earnestness when considering matters of spirituality. I couldn't help but imagine the way he doted on his daughters. A sadness gripped me, a deep melancholy because Pastor Amos, in a short period of time, had grown to occupy a large place in my heart, someone whom I had begun to view as a spiritual mentor. I felt caught up in a lie. Worse, I felt somewhat complicit in his own sins. And worst of all, I felt a self-centered shame, concerned more about my image than the actual pain inflicted on this woman.

I continued. What else was there to do?

"I have seen you before, many times..." I trailed off.

"Yes?"

"I have seen you, uh, hanging."

"Well, Amos was not about to let me have the final say. When he realized what I had done, he marched back to his own house and grabbed the rope, then to the Delaneys for a clean outfit of mine, and finally back to me to clean me up and change me. Oh yes, I bet he got his jollies once again, the bastard. Undressing me, seeing my naked body one more time." Marie must have seen my puzzled expression. "But that was nothing anymore. Just a shell. All that work, only to hang me."

"But...why?" I asked, not comprehending.

"He left me there and waited for someone to discover my body. He'd rather it look like a *proper* lynching than anything else."

"But surely everyone found out that you didn't die from hanging."

"Oh yes, of course, that couldn't remain a secret. I had a hole in my chest. But for him, it was symbolic more than anything. Lynchings always is. Punishment and symbol. Well, if he couldn't dole out the punishment, he sure as hell wasn't going to miss out on the symbol. That man–" she spat–"wanted to control my death just like he wanted to control my life. He couldn't handle me doing things my way."

"How do you know all this?" I asked. "You were dead."

"I still am, at least in the sense that I died. I assure you, I did not survive shooting a hole through my body *and* hanging at the end of the rope overnight."

"Right." I was silent, thinking.

"But how... how did this... how..." I was still so utterly bewildered and didn't even know where to begin framing a coherent question. Marie helped me.

"What happened to Xenia?" she offered, and I nodded. "You want to know how things are the way they are." She leaned in. "I bet you've seen some things."

I nodded again.

"How about this," she said, leaning towards me, "how about you start by telling me about Xenia."

So, I explained everything to her. Marie listened without saying a word, and when I had finished, she continued quietly for some time, but eventually, she spoke again.

"I don't understand it all either," she began. "I've been puzzling over it ever since I woke up in this place. But when I died, something big happened in Xenia. Amos might be a villain and a coward, but he is right about some things. There are forces and powers that transcend the comprehensible. I always believed in it as a theoretical, as an intellectual possibility, perhaps even a probability, but to say I was a true believer, well that's something else entirely."

True believer. Pastor Amos' words now made me sick.

"But even that don't sound accurate. It's not so much a belief for me but a manifestation." She paused emphatically. She seemed to grow in her chair and tower over me. "Because I'm it. I'm the real deal. What you've just described of Xenia, it's because of me."

I sat there with a confused expression on my face, not understanding and cowering before the energy emanating from Marie.

"I have always worn my gris-gris, lit my altars in secret, honored my ancestors, connected with the spirits in that way. I did my part to stay connected with Bondye. But I did nothing special before I died. I didn't place no curse or nothing on that well-deserving town, but when a person has been beaten down all their lives, I think Bondye listens. Or God, if you prefer. Or the universe. And at that moment, taking my life, I wasn't me, but I was a whole collection of me and they and I and she and him and all of us who have borne the weight of injustice. I was the universal sacrifice, the Christ, if you will, who turned the tables on the natural order of things, and so, what you call Somewhere, was born. So, yes, boy, it's me, and it ain't me, see what I'm sayin'? Either way, that is a town born under a curse. And I have been in this place ever since. I see into Xenia like a crystal ball though I only observe."

"What? You've been here the whole time? For over a hundred years?"

"Time is different here. You say a hundred years, but here time doesn't move like a line; it's just a stagnant thing. It's here resting with me. I don't feel it like you imagine a hundred years to be, like I would have imagined a hundred years to be before I died."

"So then, you're a ghost?"

"I guess it depends on where we are. Am I a ghost? Or an angel? Or some other thing? Are we even in your world? Are we in Xenia now? Is Xenia in Missouri anymore?" My mind was melting, trying to keep up with the perplexities of Marie's string of questions.

"I don't rightly know where I am," she continued, "so I don't rightly know who or what I am or even how I am. I am still Marie Weston, but what that means here in this place, I can't really tell you."

For a few moments, all was still again. But finally, I spoke because the weight of my experience in Somewhere still pressed into me.

"Ms. Weston, I have to tell you." She nodded, listening. "I thought Somewhere— Xenia—was wonderful when I first arrived. When I visited and when I first moved here, it attracted me in a way I have trouble explaining. I felt like all the old stories were becoming true, that I had somehow fallen into a fairy tale, that I had been searching my whole life for a magic which I finally found in my backyard, in Missouri, of all places. I have always been enchanted by castles and dragons and adventures. As I got older, I felt like those stories didn't belong to me. Alice in Wonderland; King Arthur, Merlin, and the Knights of the Round Table; Grimm's fairy tales; Aslan.

"The longing for those stories, for those worlds, was visceral, a deep, aching longing. I used to dream that I had found Narnia in the closets in my house, and when I would wake up from my dreams, I was left with profound sadness. A few years ago, I studied abroad in England for a few months, and that dormant desire was reawakened. Especially when I traveled outside of London, the old landscapes reminded me of those stories once again. The deep forests where fairies dwell, the small villages and green, rolling, pastoral hills, mountains where I might find some giants, ancient castles.

"When I came to Somewhere, I first felt a sense of fulfillment, of being abroad at home or being home abroad. I felt like I had entered the dream and never had to wake up. Even when strange and unsettling things were happening, I wanted to be part of the mystery, to know that I was living on *the other side* of whatever flimsy partition separated the natural and the supernatural, the real and the super-real.

"The first time I saw you, though, your image was jarring. And this is what I have to confess. Up until that point, I thought nothing of the fact that I hadn't seen a single person of color in Somewhere. Not that I was actively looking for some all-white paradise. I just was so oblivious that I hadn't even noticed. But when I saw you and then started looking around, I realized how odd it was. Even then..." I swallowed, paused. Looked at the ground shamefully. "Even then, however, I didn't pay much attention–enough attention. I chalked it up to the demographic reality of living in rural Missouri and, for the most part, put it out of my head. Of course, every time I saw you, I was reminded again.

"But the more I have considered, the more that the history of slavery and treatment towards African Americans—and I guess other people of color—has become a stain on our own stories, at least for the last four hundred years or so. To think that, running parallel to many of these fairy tales, people were being enslaved, treated less than human, and we just kept on writing our stories like nothing was the matter, either keeping African Americans on the margins or else writing them out entirely. So, the loss and the longing that I felt before becomes even stronger because it's no longer about the stories being unattainable; it's that they were never real in the first place. I thought I had dropped into a fairy tale, but this, too, turns out to be just one more farce. And not just a farce; a lie, a cover-up."

Marie rocked slightly, eyeing me with a stern expression. Then she spoke.

"Child, I want to care, or I want to *want* to care. And I *am* thankful for what you've said. I sense that it was genuine and that it does affect you deeply. But..." Marie rubbed her eyes, sighing, "I will confess to you as well. To be completely honest, I don't give a damn about your sad feelings. I don't give a damn because, for generations and generations, no one has given a fuck about me and my ancestors and our stories. And we had stories. We had beautiful stories. But now our stories have changed. They are about overcoming. About the dark night of oppression. They are sad beautiful. It is good, but it is terrible good. Not like the stories from before, the stories about my people before white men. You don't even care about my stories. I don't not like you, but I don't give a fuck about your stories, you see?"

I was taken aback by Marie's bluntness and then realized that I was not her friend. I don't think I was her enemy, but there was too much there between us to somehow hug and make up for four hundred years of oppression, even if I wasn't directly responsible for any of it. Despite the effect of the town's history on me, it still felt like exactly that, *history*. Marie, on the other hand, even rocking in peace, felt the immediate knowledge of what people had done to her and the people she was closest to. That history was alive in her, stuck in this place, a living secret. I still didn't understand all of the events of the past several months, why things happened in Somewhere the way they did, but I was gaining a much clearer sense.

"So, what's next?" I asked.

"They have my body, young man," Marie responded matter-of-factly. "You saw the graves in Laurel Hill. Every single person in Xenia should be dead by now, and they have the grave markers to show it, but they're empty. Like what you saw in Mrs. Copeland's house—I knew Mindy Copeland, by the way; I knew them all—just like what you saw in her house, every single person in that town is tethered to their unburied body. It's an ancient rite, primeval perhaps. That's what keeps the town alive even if it's not exactly on the normal plane of existence, which you've already seemed to figure out."

"So, every single person in Somewhere has their own body lying in a coffin in their cellar?" I asked. Appalled by the thought, I more or less already knew the answer. I just needed to hear it from her, to verify that this shit-show was indeed happening. Marie shrugged.

"Cellars do seem to be the preferred location. I would say that it keeps their most precious possession away from prying eyes though they are all in the same predicament. It's like an undergarments drawer. Everyone knows that everyone has one, but you're not going to display it in the front foyer. There is one other reason, though, that those bodies get hidden away."

"Yeah?"

"When people like you wander in."

"What do you mean?"

"I guess you could say that *life* is the lifeblood of this place. Xenia now depends on the living to sustain it. The town is hungry. It has to eat." Marie half-smiled, a cold look in her eyes.

"Is that what's happened to Jimmy?" She inclined her head slightly in confirmation. My stomach sank, envisioning myself in Jimmy's place, going mad as my mind unhinged itself from all rationality.

"But how did I get here if Somewhere doesn't exist in the normal sense?"

"Magic." Again, Marie had a deadpan look as she gave her one-word reply. As if her answer was the most natural in the world.

"Is there any way out?"

Eternity passed in the intermission between my question and Marie's response. I felt that she was the judge reading the verdict in my case. Would I leave a free man or be sentenced to imprisonment inside the belly of this phantasmal town?

"Yes."

I hadn't realized that I was holding my breath, but I let out a long exhale after her pronouncement.

"But it might not work."

"And if it doesn't? What happens?"

"Well, boy," she smiled wickedly; I felt uncomfortable. "In that case, you get to stay here."

"And lose my mind?"

"Yes. But you'd be with Rose." Marie cackled at that, and I sat there annoyed and a little embarrassed. I didn't know exactly what she had meant when she said earlier that she could see Somewhere like looking in a crystal ball, but I felt dirty, like I had been spied on.

"Okay," I said, ready for whatever plan she had for me. Knowing the alternative was madness and enslavement to Somewhere, I was suddenly quite bold. "What do I have to do?"

"You must bury my body."

"Do what?"

"Yes, you must bury my body. I may have caused this to happen to Xenia–even if I'm not entirely sure how–but all of this could go away, and we could all go through the celestial door beyond this purgatory when my body is buried in Laurel Hill cemetery. I think Amos knows this. This could have all been ended long ago, but perhaps he knows that the only place for him beyond Somewhere is the pits of hell. Or he thinks he can still torture me. Or both."

"You need me to save you?"

Suddenly I was blasted back by the ferocity of Marie's presence, the first time that she had stood up from her seat. She was terrible in her anger, and a vibrating energy emanated from her. Her eyes were diamonds of fury, and she stepped towards my retreating body. I bumped up against the wall and remained there, trembling.

"Do you think I need saving, boy?" she spat. "That I am some pitiful, helpless soul at the mercy of some little bully? Have you not been paying attention? Should I remind you that *I* created this, that *I* made this happen?"

"But...but you're stuck here," I stammered. "Right? Don't you want to leave?"

"Who's stuck? The only ones enslaved here anymore is them, forced to live out an eternal existence parallel to the world they once knew while never intersecting with it. All the while tethered unceremoniously to their undead bodies."

"But it looked so nice."

"Ha! Whitewashed tombs. Rotten bones underneath."

I thought of Rose again. Could Marie be wrong? Was it so absolute as all that? All bad? Was Rose complicit in Pastor Amos's sins?

"Don't you *want* to leave? Don't you *want* your body to be buried properly?"

"I want and don't want a lot of things," she said, cooling off a bit and sitting back down. "But I don't feel the connection to my body the same way they do to theirs. I already died, remember? I've been freed from all that. When I'm ready to leave this place, I can march right into that god-forsaken town myself and take care of goddamn business, you understand?"

"Then why don't you?" I asked, gathering myself, approaching nearer again and regaining my seat.

"Save *you*?" Marie looked at me somewhat contemptuously but placated nonetheless.

"Look, I've told you what you can do. If you're successful, I'm ready to leave this place. If you're not, you're not."

"You're just okay if I–if they–if I can't get out." Marie looked at me severely again.

"I'm not your mother. You asked me if there was a way out. I could have said no. Save yourself if you can. This conversation is over."

And it was.

Abruptly, I was standing alone in the snowy night, looking up a hill, the cemetery perched above me. And then I suddenly realized what Marie meant when she spoke of other secrets beyond the cemetery. They weren't ghosts, but I could see them, like I was watching an old film: dozens if not hundreds of Black bodies being buried there in unmarked graves, just beyond the gates of the cemetery proper, unworthy—in the eyes of the town—of a proper burial.

CHAPTER TWENTY-SEVEN

I spent another night in the shed from earlier, sleeping a few hours when the fatigue, too great to submit to the cold any longer, finally overcame me. The tarp was not enough to ward off the freezing temperatures. Miserable and shaking, I wrapped myself up as best as I could, longing for Marie's cabin and the warmth of her fire.

When I woke up a bit before daybreak, I was in a delirious state. Wracked with fever and chills, my throat screaming like someone had run a cheese grater down it, and my head pulsating with pain, I slowly started moving my limbs to bring life back into them. I groaned as my body rebelled against me for what I had made it withstand by camping out in the shed. I found that my mind had difficulty formulating clear thoughts; I was foggy, wandering mentally. Rose was in front of me, leaning over me, her face close to my face, her lips close to mine. She then sat up and started playing with the top button of her shirt. It was a side of Rose I hadn't seen before. She stared at me enticingly, moistening her lips with her tongue and biting them playfully as she unbuttoned the first button, then the second. I saw the lacy fringe of her satin bra, my body now fully charged in anticipation.

We're going to do this here? I thought at first with trepidation but then gave into the desire. My body burned more hotly, and it wasn't the fever. By chance, I glanced to my left where the shed door should have been, failing miserably in protecting me from the cold. It wasn't there, though. I sat up, momentarily distracted. I wasn't in the shed at all. I was in an unfinished basement. A cellar. A wave of panic crossed over Rose's eyes.

She looked over her shoulder, giving herself away. In the corner of the room was a coffin.

"No, no, no, no, no," I muttered aloud as I scrambled over to it. I knew, but I didn't want to know. I drew near and stood up. I wasn't really standing up at all, though, not raising myself up to look into a coffin; instead, I was climbing stairs to a front porch. I gasped and looked around.

I wasn't in a cellar after all. I was standing on Maggie and Lenora's wraparound porch. The door opened, and Maggie was there ushering me into her kitchen, to a plate of steaming food. I salivated. Lenora was already seated there at the table. But I was suddenly captured by a thought, and my head turned around the room, scanning. There it was, the door slightly ajar. I stood up and made my way there. I thought I could hear someone shouting, "Lee, no!"

Ignoring the plea, I pushed open the door and descended the steps. At the bottom, resting side by side on a large table, standing over the concrete floor, were two coffins. But I wasn't in the cellar. I was in the shed. And I wasn't staring at coffins, I was hovering dumbly over a group of garden tools.

That's when fear began clawing into my brain, and I wondered if it was the fever after all or was Jimmy's madness invading my own brain. Was I too late? Was I going to lose my family, Miriam, everything, forever?

I saw the dawn light outside the shed door and stepped outside, the blast of cold painful but momentarily piercing the fog of my mind. The early morning sun was a tropic of color, a reprieve from the melancholy that hung over me. I wasn't far from Laurel Hill and, through a mess of obstacles impeding my view, could just make out the bottom of the hill's slope on the north side of the cemetery. I was hoping to catch a glimpse of a dense forest, to see smoke rising above the horizon, to wind my way back through the forest and find Marie there again, locked in time. Perhaps if I asked kindly enough, she would let me stay there with her, a preferred alternative to losing my mind and being trapped in this hellish town forever.

It was time. Not because I was prepared but because there was nothing left for me to do, nothing else I *could* do, I thought. I heaved out a robust sigh of acceptance. I thought of Juliet when she was begging Friar Lawrence for some plan to escape her fate—marriage to Paris—and be reunited with Romeo. She was on the point of killing herself, so Friar Lawrence caved and offered a foolhardy plan with slim chances. But she was willing to go along with it because she was so earnest. I felt a little like that. Like I was about to die anyway—or become a mindless pawn in the machine of this cursed place—so whatever reckless plan I followed was just the attempt of a desperate man. Of course, Juliet died in the end, so I held out little hope.

I began my hike towards Pastor Amos' house, where I supposed Marie's body must be stored. She had never said so directly, but she had mentioned his name in connection with her body's current state, so he must be directly involved.

It was early enough and the day after Christmas, I assumed (it could have been weeks later for all I knew, *How long had I been in Marie's cabin?*), so besides some smoking chimneys, Somewhere truly felt like a ghost town, eerily motionless. That reality gave me a sense of foreboding, like a sleeping dragon that would rain down fire on me if I stepped too loudly. And crunching through the snow was no silent endeavor. Nonetheless, I managed to avoid contact with anyone.

Suddenly, I realized that I was neglecting an important detail in my plan.

I had to bury Marie's body.

Presumably, in Laurel Hill Cemetery. Which meant that, once again,

I had to figure out how to pierce the cement-like crust of the earth and dig out a grave. I huffed irritably as I reversed course and trudged back through the loud snow toward Laurel Hill, once again reminded of how impossible it all was.

This time, I arrived at the front, the side facing the town. I had nearly climbed the gated entrance once before when that annoying man interrupted me. I jumped over and quickly dashed deep into the labyrinth of tombstones.

I wasn't sure what I was looking for—just a patch of ground, I supposed—but I found myself being drawn deeper and deeper into the rows of the buried dead. Only I knew that many of the plots were empty. Hundreds of coffins were littered throughout the homes of this freak town, with freaky ghost people twice removed from their proper resting place.

However, as I walked, I sensed that I was descending, as though I moved towards the gaping mouth of some awful creature, about to be swallowed alive by Somewhere itself. I even imagined the ground pulsating at intervals like it was breathing a great dragon-like breath. For a moment, I strained my mind to remember if the back of the cemetery which I had entered earlier was built on a slope. But I knew it wasn't. The hill just beyond the back fence didn't begin its decline until outside of Laurel Hill. So whatever sensation I was experiencing was something unfamiliar and unnatural.

In addition to the feeling of walking downward, I considered how vast the cemetery was. I had been walking for a while, surely enough time to have traversed the graveyard at least a couple of times. For a moment, my attention was arrested by something in the sky on the horizon. Yes, at some incalculable distance beyond this impossibly proportioned cemetery was, again, a pillar of rising smoke.

Marie.

I would have sprinted towards it, abandoning my spot, abandoning my plan, resigning myself to a timeless prison in that purgatory, jazzy tunes billowing out of that anachronistic record player, an impassive comfort. Before I had taken off in that direction, however, I glanced back down at my feet. I had arrived.

I had arrived despite not knowing where I was headed. I wasn't standing at the throat of a monstrous creature, the perception I had a few moments before. There was an opening, though: Marie's grave, dug and ready.

In spite of everything, I smiled to myself, understanding Marie's hand in this. Although our meeting may have ended abruptly and not so cordially, she had sent me this boon. As if in response to my prediction, I looked up and noticed the wisp of chimney smoke from her cabin dissipate. I wished I could send up some signal of my own to show my gratitude, but I realized that the best gratitude I could show was to finish this thing.

"Or die trying," I muttered the cliche to myself as I wound my way back to the cemetery's entrance, finding that distance and time had returned to a normal measure.

Much sooner than I had hoped, I was standing on the edge of the Whitakers' property. I had still encountered no movement from the town, and there was none here at the Whitakers'. Could it be Marie's doing? My success seemed to be a matter of indifference to her, but perhaps she was willing to pull more levers in this machine than she had let on.

Calculating my next move, a wave of disbelief poured over me as I stood there, dreaming instead of waking up in my bed and planning to meet up with Rose or some other friends, or planning to come over to the Whitakers for dinner. Like none of this had ever happened. I realized, however, that there was essentially no point during my time in Somewhere that was really normal. I had simply normalized it in my mind. The truth was, from the beginning, I was met with inexplicable occurrences, one after another: from the visions of an older Rose to the groanings of Mrs. Copeland's house to my parents' mysterious amnesia, there had been nothing normal about Somewhere, and I had relished that. I had embraced that. And standing there, staring at the back of Pastor Amos's house, I realized that I still embraced the strangeness of it all, still preferred white hot mystery to the collective agnosticism of a society built around chores and routine, whose only true religion was occasional reverence and a bit of nostalgia. I only wished that I'd been more honest with myself about the problems in Somewhere, the Maries that have been sacrificed throughout history for the sake of convenience or power.

Scanning the house, I contemplated what to do next, and my eyes alighted on something: an outside cellar door. I breathed a minor sigh of relief. I had resigned myself to the fact that I might need to simply wait and watch until the Whitakers left their home (hoping Pastor Amos didn't visit the backyard and easily notice the conspicuous snow tracks I'd left). Remembering the cellar entrance outside of Mrs. Copeland's, I probably should have anticipated the same outside the Whitakers' house, but the simplicity of it slipped my mind. Now I could easily bypass detection with this direct ingress and egress, assuming the coffins were in the cellar, of course, and that the outside cellar access wasn't bricked over like at Mrs. Copeland's.

Looping around the back of the shed and tiptoeing my way to the side of the house while maintaining eye contact with the back sliding glass door, I soon arrived at the cellar door. No bricks and no lock! *They don't exactly have the problem of outside meddlers*, I thought, *besides the occasional visitor that they feed off of.* The thought made me gulp.

With a loud splintering sound that led me to believe this entrance hadn't been utilized anytime recently, I pulled the cellar doors open, hoping the disturbance hadn't been heard inside. More carefully, I pulled the doors closed over me in case anyone was to take a stroll outside. As I descended, my eyes adjusted to the dimness, aided by the bit of light filtering in through small, dirty windows.

Hesitantly, I shuffled slowly along the cellar floor, nerves ratcheted up to maximum sensitivity. However, here I didn't have to worry about navigating a labyrinth of shelves. Instead, in plain sight on the other side of the cellar, raised up on tables, were six coffins. No added suspense. Just fact.

I had the sudden urge to sprint back up the cellar steps, to breathe in the icy air, survey the snow and the trees and the world around me. Because I had the feeling that this was the end of the line. Whatever was going to happen was going to happen now. I once again pondered what might have been if I hadn't meddled, if I had tried to suppress the apprehensions that had bubbled up inside me. Of course, if what Marie had said was correct, I might have enjoyed myself only a little while longer before turning into a mindless zombie, à la Jimmy. As I approached the coffins, though, that's not the idea I clung to. I replayed the times with Rose, with David, Eleanor, Kenny, and everyone; the beauty of the town; the simple pleasures of working at the art gallery; the profound sense of being at once home and abroad, invited into a Missouri wonderland.

But I returned to the moment. I was on a path, *A one-way ticket to my own demise*, I thought.

"So, you figured it out, huh?"

The sound of Pastor Amos's voice didn't startle me. Despite my nervousness, when I actually heard his voice, I felt calm. Nothing would surprise me anymore. I turned slowly on the spot. I hadn't heard him descend the steps. I wasn't sure he had. I didn't know what kind of abilities or limitations he might have.

"You know," he said, passing by me and moving closer to the coffins, "I have to applaud you. In the entire history of Somewhere, ever since— well, I'm sure you've been told all about it from *her*—ever since then, no outsider has even come close to discovering the secret of this town. They didn't care to. They didn't have a mind for it. They weren't true believers."

He grinned at me, his words now a slap across my face.

"That's why I like you, Lee, why I liked you from the beginning." Pastor Amos had walked along the row of coffins, surveying each one as if he was tucking little children into bed. Well, at least two of them *were* little children. Sort of. But now he turned to face me. He leaned haphazardly against one of the coffins. From my angle, I couldn't see its contents, but I imagined that he leaned against his own. Or maybe Marie's. There were *six* coffins, after all.

Wait. Six? it suddenly hit me. *That math doesn't compute. Four Whitakers and Marie. Who's the other?*

"You know," he continued, "we don't determine who arrives from the outside. I guess that bitch told you how it works. How is she, by the way?" Pastor Amos paused, a smile screwed up into a snarl. "You're also the first person since Somewhere became Somewhere to ever see her. And I'm not just talking about the outsiders. No one in Somewhere has seen Marie."

Since you raped her, you mean, and caused her to kill herself and hung her dead, limp body?

"How do you know I saw anyone?" I responded.

"Because you're here," Pastor Amos grinned in response to my question, his smile plastered widely on his face like Alice's Cheshire cat, mad, shrewd, and reckless all at once. "I know you've seen her. She's never shown her face to anyone else, though." His smile faded, and he spat on the ground, a fierce look drifting into his eyes. I didn't point out that I didn't think Marie *could* show her face outside the confines of her own forested sanctuary.

"As I was saying," he continued, "we don't choose the outsiders we *devour*. We're not picky eaters." His sly smile had returned. "I am, of course, speaking figuratively, though as someone trapped between being dead and being alive, I wouldn't mind a bite of a more wild-type of steak, if you know what I mean. Spice things up in an otherwise drab eating experience."

"Is that what you want? You want this form of existence?"

Pastor Amos frowned.

"You disappoint me, Lee. I understand the precarious situation you find yourself in, but I thought you'd be impressed. I thought you considered yourself a true believer. I thought you'd understand that sacrifices are worth the price of admission for immortality."

"That's easy for you to say. You're not the one whose mind is getting eaten to feed a town's immortality." He looked at me sternly. And then laughed.

"You are not wrong, Lee. You are not wrong." His face grew more serious again, more earnest. "You remember our conversations. Thin places. The intersection between the spiritual realm and the world we see. Well, congratulations. You're walking in it. This town might be hungry, Lee, but it has helped me see. And it's flipped everything upside down, you understand? Light and dark. Black and white. Right and wrong. The whole damn paradigm is broken."

I wasn't exactly keeping up with what Pastor Amos said, but I just let him rattle on. What else could I do?

"We're taught that the monsters are bad. Kill the monster. Kill the dragon. But we're living in the belly of the beast right here. And somehow, in the vapor of its gastric juices, we've found real life."

I cringed at his choice of metaphors, but he didn't seem to notice. Or care.

"I may have misled you earlier," he continued, "if you assumed that I'd always walked on this line of truth. The fact is, before Somewhere, I was merely speculating, intrigued by the idea that our tight little orthodoxies can't even begin to comprehend the full scope of reality, an existence folded on top of our own, and, who knows, other realities on top of other realities on top of other realities." He practically cackled. "But no, I was no Faustus. I was too afraid to plumb the depths of pure knowledge, pure truth and discovery. I thought I would damn myself by being anything other than what I was, a humble pastor to his flock."

He must have sensed my objection and grinned cunningly.

"But it was my so-called sins that saved me. Not that you could really call it a sin. That whore came onto me." He spat. "No, it was, ironically–but revealingly–in my damnation that I found paradise, though not a disembodied paradise of purified bliss that we so desperately try to believe in. It comes with its prices."

He quieted, locking eyes with mine.

"You want to ask me something," he said.

"Yeah," I responded, hoping I didn't sound as unsure as I felt. I mustered up whatever courage I could find, determined to confront him. "How could you do it? How could you do what you did to Marie? And you're a pastor!"

Pastor Amos smiled at me patronizingly.

"You show your ignorance, Lee, to think that a man and his office are one. The man who is the pastor is not the same as the pastoral office itself. Sure, I made some mistakes; I'm not perfect. Besides, on this side of things, I see better how ridiculous of a construct morality is anyway. But a man has desires, son. You should know that. Unless you're some kind of girl."

"You're married. You have daughters," I insisted, ignoring his last comment.

"Look, maybe I'm not so proud of that part, okay." He appeared to be annoyed.

"And what were you preaching? You're a Baptist minister. Where's that in the Bible? Taking advantage of someone sexually."

"Are you deaf? I just told you, you little shit. What I say up there in the pulpit is not me talking; it's the Divine. Doesn't matter what I do, egregious as it may be. The office is anointed, and when I step up there, the office is speaking."

"If that's what helps you sleep at night," I responded, shrugging.

We were both now squared off against each other. His composure was gone, one small satisfaction in what I felt would probably be the end of me.

"You know what's the worst in all this?" I said, breaking the silence.

"What?"

"This whole time, I thought I had stumbled onto some kind of hidden paradise. Come to find out, you are just a bunch of racists stuck in time to pay for their sins."

I was carried away by my enthusiasm, but semi-consciously I still puzzled over where to categorize so many of the people of Somewhere, what box to put them in. What was Rose's culpability? David? Maggie? Barb? In that case, what was mine, born nearly a century and a half later? Most everyone from Somewhere seemed too nice to be capable of sustaining a nightmare institution like slavery, but was that only my perception because I was white? Had I been born with a different color of skin, would those same sweet, innocent people transform to little devils? Would Rose?

I considered how we all had a little bit of devil inside of us. I'd like to say *tucked away deep inside us*, but that's probably wishful thinking. Under the right circumstances, in the right cultural milieu, we'll damn near justify any sort of action. Shamefully, I realized that I probably wasn't as different from Pastor Amos as I'd like to admit.

"Young man," he spat, "you can bandy about whatever crude terms you want. Call me a racist, fine. But that's the problem with people like you. You try to put ideas in their simplest terms. You're too much of an infant to embrace the complexities of truth. I know that there is nothing different between me and Marie or any other negro for that matter. Not on the soul-substance level. And anyone who knows anything would say the same thing.

"I know," he continued when he saw me about to interrupt, "that you may have heard otherwise. And there are plenty of folks who truly *do* see themselves as superior simply based on something as arbitrary as skin color, but the institution of slavery was something more than that, richer, fuller. We have merely been fulfilling our stations in life as guardians and protectors. From the dawn of time, society has been stratified by the castes of the people, from the rulers to the aristocracy to the merchant class to the working poor and, finally, at the bottom, slaves. Those at the bottom need those at the top for subsistence. It will always be that way. Say what you will, but when those strata are erased, chaos ensues. Chaos is fine for a time, and history also cycles through periods of turbulence which is its own form of cleansing; it's a resetting. But equilibrium is found outside of the chaos. Look at the havoc that ensued when slavery was eliminated here. Huh? People need to know their places. They need to feel the security of fences.

"Look, I don't begrudge them Black folk and what they've made of themselves since President Lincoln went and made a mess of something he couldn't begin to comprehend. That's their prerogative. Things were different in my time, and that's *my* prerogative. Now, if someone at the lower order of things wants to climb, so be it. But that doesn't abolish the lower order. It's a zero-sum game. By climbing out of the lower classes, they're simply pushing someone else into it. Might not be in America. Might be in another country, for example. If America's become a melting pot today, so be it. But I guarantee you that there will be equilibrium. There *is* equilibrium. Chattel slavery might be over in the US, but that doesn't mean the social order is gone. It might just mean that the nation as a whole has risen to the top and is propped up by the lower classes globally. Blacks might not be slaves in America, but that doesn't mean there aren't slaves, the lowest rung on the ladder. We might not call it *slavery* anymore–sometimes we do–but that doesn't mean it's gone."

He finally paused, swallowing a deep breath of air. "And Lee," his tone softened. For a moment I imagined I had only been dreaming. Somewhere was back to normal. I had never found Marie, had never tried to escape. I was happy, and Pastor Amos and I were just chatting like we did before. Maybe we'd move out to the study, sip some whiskey. He stopped only a foot away from me, never breaking eye contact, and placed a hand on my shoulder. A gesture of warmth. Friendship. Even perceiving the deceit, I was tempted to unguard myself. "Lee," he said, "I'm done having this conversation."

Immediately, bombs exploded in my mind and all over my body. I closed my eyes out of shock, but when I opened them again, I noticed that two hands were grasped tightly onto each of my forearms as two versions of Pastor Amos grinned at me maliciously. My head spun around. The cellar had come alive. Or at least it had become crowded (*alive* and *dead* seemed to lose some of its meanings after my recent discoveries).

Sharp pains pulsated through my body—seemingly connected, somehow, to the chain connection of the twin Amoses—as I stood gritting my teeth. I noted four bodies sitting up in their coffins across the room, staring at me silently with a revulsive look of glee. I was particularly taken aback by little Charlotte with an unblinking half-grin as if she wanted to eat me alive.

"Daddy, are we going to do it to him, too?" I heard from behind me. Charlotte, Anna, and Tracy stood behind me, casually glancing back and forth between their doubles sitting up in their coffins and me.

"Do what to me?" I replied through clenched teeth. Pastor Amoses chuckled in sync. At this point, they seemed to be connected, one will, through the human chain that was my body.

"No, dear," they replied in unison, creating a terrifying amplification of their combined voices, an otherworldly, other-creaturely tone. "I understand you met Jimmy. On your own, *that's* what you would have become. Slowly joining us forever in Xenia." I noted his use of the town's original name. "That was the easy route, Lee. But you didn't want to take the easy path, did you?" And his eyes shifted to a coffin.

"Daddy?" This time Anna spoke up.

"Yes, sweetheart?"

"Can we watch?"

"Of course."

"Yay," Charlotte said in an excited voice that seemed natural for her age but was out of place in the context of what was happening. "Like the hanging lady."

"Yes, like the hanging lady," her father answered. As if on cue, I heard muffled screams coming from one of the coffins and then felt an immediate sense of relief as one of the Amoses released my arm and walked over to the animated wooden box.

"Shh..." He caressed the top of the coffin comfortingly, like he was placating a sick child rather than whatever was inside. "This doesn't concern you. Well," he paused, glancing at both versions of his family. "I guess it sort of does." They all snickered politely as if it was an old joke.

"It all concerns you, doesn't it?" he said, resting his hand now. "But you know what? Your curse backfired. Milton said it best. The mind is its own place, and, in itself can make a heaven out of hell or a hell of heaven. Blessings and curses. Good and evil. It's all just a bit of mirage. There's just pure reality, and we're living it, baby."

Pastor Amos ran his hand back over the top of the coffin, slowly, sensually, eyes closed as if he were remembering something.

"We are living it, baby," he spoke again slowly, breathing in some memory. Then his eyes flashed open, and his face contorted into a snarl.

"SO, FUCK YOUUUUUUU!" he screamed at the top of his lungs. I cringed, not so much by the action but from embarrassment at his behavior in front of his family, whatever deranged, psychopathic version of them was surrounding me.

Pastor Amos lumbered back over to me, grabbing my arm, once again re-engaging the human chain with his other self, pain newly boring into my body. They dragged me to an open coffin which was resting beside what I now knew to be Marie's closed prison. *Six coffins. All accounted for now.*

I made a lame effort to resist, limply kicking and trying to wrest my arms out of their grasp, but the pain was overwhelming, and my efforts were ineffective. Lifting me off the ground, they carried me towards the open coffin, my resistance now zero, just a dead weight, a useless sack of flour. Noises continued to emanate faintly from Marie's coffin, and for some reason, I gingerly stuck out my hand to touch it, to connect myself to the one person who might sympathize with me, with the end of me.

The brief contact I made triggered memories of my recent meeting with Marie in those strange woods, what felt like ages ago but was only a day before. I saw her face, light dancing to an unknown tune over her cheeks, the glow of nearby flames, the movement of her rocking chair. All this lit up in my brain.

My finger scraped across the surface of the coffin as the Amoses lugged me a few more feet and dropped me unceremoniously in my own coffin. In an act of finality and acceptance, I laid down of my own volition, at peace with whatever fate awaited me. The struggle was over.

The lights went out.

CHAPTER TWENTY-EIGHT

I naturally assumed the darkness resulted from Pastor Amos shutting the lid of the coffin over me. But after a few long moments, I realized that I never actually *heard* the coffin closing. I didn't have the claustrophobic sensation of low oxygen levels in a confined space. *Am I dead already*, I wondered. But unless my touching the bottom of the coffin instantaneously killed me, and unless death felt significantly different than I had imagined, I had my doubts.

In fact, right at that moment, I perceived a shuffling, some confused murmurs, and what I assumed to be the girls' voices across the room.

"Mommy, why did all the lights turn off?" a voice whined.

"Shh."

I pulled myself up to a sitting position, my body struck by a vertiginous wave of nausea as I tried to adjust to the absolute inky blackness. The moment hung heavy in the room. I knew, and I knew they knew, that something both unexpected and momentous was approaching. Besides the darkness, the only palpable sensation was confusion and nervousness. I probably should have been panicky myself, but I relished the simple fact that I knew this was unplanned.

A light struck up in one part of the room, but it was only a faint glow. Marie hung there unceremoniously at the end of a rope.

"The hanging lady," Charlotte gasped. Her mom hushed her again.

I strained to see the faces of the Whitakers, but the glow in the room was too indistinct. I could only vaguely make out the features of Marie herself, her head lolled to one side.

Without a word, warning, or even a sound, another Marie appeared, a carbon copy of the first but hanging in another part of the cellar. I heard a sharp intake of surprise from someone and a squeal, presumably from one of the girls. Both Maries hung limply, their only movement an almost imperceptible sway, as though a slight breeze were animating their lifeless bodies.

A third, fourth, fifth, and sixth Marie appeared; again, all like the previous. Finally, a noise shattered the silence, a metallic pop. I glanced over at the closed coffin next to me and noticed the clasp had been unlatched. The lid slowly pushed upward and then fell with a startling crash to the floor. I marveled at the strength required to accomplish that feat.

Expecting a Marie like the other coffin-copies of everyone else–somehow fuller, more alive even than their counterparts–I was instead met by a decomposing corpse sitting up next to me. I shuddered.

Marie's head swiveled; I would have screamed if my voice hadn't choked in my throat. Her skin was a grotesque patchwork of leather and bone, only hollow sockets met me where eyes should have been, and her hair was unnaturally long and wiry, the effect of death on her body. One characteristic remained the same as the other coffin bodies, though: she was unable to form words. Scratchy sounds rattled from her throat as her head continued to swivel around the room.

The room was now illuminated enough for me to make out a huddled group of the Whitakers in one corner. Bizarrely, duplicates of each family member stood beside them, but only one copy of each of the girls cowered in fear.

Manifestations of Marie continued to appear, hanging anew in some part of the cellar while the skeletal Marie's growl persisted, her neck a fulcrum for her rotating head, bony hands clutching the side of the coffin. This freak circus continued indefinitely–I don't know how long–until the room was filled entirely with the hanging figures of Marie.

Then the decomposing Marie next to me quieted. Stillness and silence were suspended, filling the space in anticipation. Without sound but with an action that felt like a thousand shrieking screams, every hanging Marie opened its eyes in unison.

Charlotte did scream but immediately stopped as light pierced the side of the cellar opposite me. A shaft of light grew and then was promptly gone. For a moment, I couldn't decide what it meant. But then I heard footsteps on the stairs and realized that someone was descending.

Marie Weston.

The woman I met in the private forest. She had come after all. Puzzled, I wondered at this revelation. Could she actually leave her fortress after all? Had she known that from the start and been deceiving me—or had I incorrectly presumed from our conversation that she didn't have the ability to move beyond the confines of her forest? Or might I have been some kind of mechanism that allowed her to re-enter Somewhere?

I quickly glanced over at Pastor Amos, one of the Pastor Amoses—I couldn't tell who was who—and one of them clearly appeared rattled. Marie came into view at the bottom of the stairs.

"What the hell are you doing here?" one of the Amoses stepped forward and asked; the other, robotically, hung back.

"What's the matter, Amos? Uncomfortable?" she only laughed as she glanced around the room, dozens of iterations of herself hanging wide-eyed and now fixing their gazes upon him.

"Where have you been?" Pastor Amos demanded.

"Oh, hiding out, you might say." Imperceptibly, Marie bounced her eyes in my direction and smiled.

"How's the family?" she continued, laughing again. Tracy stood there with a clenched jaw.

"Daddy, daddy? Who is that?" Charlotte asked, tugging at her father's pants. *The woman who was fucking your dad*, I heard in my mind, wondering if the thought was my own or if it was projected into all of our brains by Marie.

"I thought you were dead," Pastor Amos spoke slowly, agitated but clearly trying to maintain composure despite this surprising obstacle.

"Well, you're a dumbass." I stymied a chuckle, delighted by Marie's clear sway over Pastor Amos. I was mesmerized by her. She was a force.

"How the hell do you think all of this came to be? *Somewhere*? What a piece of shit mockery of a name. But it's fitting, isn't it? Xenia died with me all those years ago. And by the looks of things, you've just up and decided to run this thing by yourself. Well, I got news for you, Amos. You was never running the show. You was like the temporary manager. It's always been my show."

Provoked, Pastor Amos stepped towards her.

"Go to hell, you bitch!"

"Honey!" Tracy scolded, pulling her girls towards her. This only incited Marie's laughter even more, clearly enjoying herself.

"Oh, I'll be going soon enough," Marie said, "though I doubt you'll be too happy when I do. But I got some things to say to you.

"You're deluded. You're deluded by your theories of humanity and their stations. However enlightened you might feel by your knowledge about the world–oh yes, I remember our conversations. You were a strange pastor back then, and you seem to have only grown stranger in your ideas. It was some of those ideas that made me jump into bed with you. That and boredom, I guess. Although your presence in the sheets didn't really cure my boredom if you know what I mean." She winked at Tracy who drew back in disgust and pulled the girls to her. "You may feel enlightened," she continued, "and perhaps you are in some ways–but you got the whole idea of people wrong.

"The people on top always got their theories about balance and order, thinking they're god's titty giving milk to the nations. It's how they get away with everything. *That's* history for you! Centuries and millennia of despots and tyrants grinding the people into dust and having the balls to make them say thank you. People don't need strata and some fixed societal system; they need to be left alone. You say you're not a racist. Hell, I don't know! But you sure as hell was no friend to slaves. It's all greed. It's all power. Ripped out of the flesh of my people. Raised from the ground from the labor of my people. And when you're done, you just toss 'em aside like garbage, bury them in mass graves at the back of Laurel Hill. Or kill 'em and hang 'em up because you're too small of a man. You're too small of a man.

"But you've been heaping up curses, Amos Whitaker, for you and your family and your whole town. And the devil's finally come back for his due."

Tom, you're come for, rebounded in my memory, the words of the devil to Tom Walker.

"It's reckoning day... pastor."

I saw Pastor Amos flinch, which was appropriate for what happened next.

A look of mild confusion filled Pastor Amos's face. I sat there confused as well, but only for a moment. In the brief space of a second or two, I watched Pastor Amos' double step towards him, grab him by the arm, and then tilt its head towards his puzzled twin. I heard a shriek that quickly became garbled. Incredulously, I stared as the copy bit out the throat of Pastor Amos, blood spraying everywhere amidst the distorted sound of Pastor Amos's garbled groans.

I was horrified as the other copies did the same, the Whitakers' copies eating their counterparts alive. Chaotic confusion ensued as the whole room came alive. The hanging Marie's were all swaying as if by a tempestuous wind, a macabre backdrop to the bloody feast The true Marie was nowhere in sight. In the midst of this confusion, I tipped myself onto the ground and then staggered through the forest of hanging bodies, hands held tightly over my ears to block out the terrifying sounds of ripping flesh and snapping bones.

In the midst of that waking nightmare–or maybe I *was,* in fact, in hell–I found the bottom of the cellar stairs that led outside. I felt an unknown arm around me and allowed myself to be led up. In the wintry snow, I fell down gasping for breath, dizzy, my vision swirling like I was on a carnival tilt-a-whirl.

Hearing the cellar door bang closed and the sounds muted below, I slowly regained a presence of mind. Quickly, I scrambled to my feet and sprinted towards the front side of the Whitakers' house and into the street, attempting to create distance from what I'd just witnessed. Finally, I stopped and doubled over, breathing heavily. That's when I remembered the arms that pulled me up the stairs, and I looked about.

Walking towards me was Rose.

"Rose?" I muttered with what breath I could muster. "What are you doing here?"

"You have to go back," she answered, ignoring my question.

"Back home?" I asked, confused.

"Back inside. The Whitakers' cellar."

"What!"

"You want to end this, right? That's why you're here? Then you have to go back."

I just looked at her dumbly, unable to grasp what she was saying, so outlandish was the suggestion. After a few moments of stupefaction, however, I understood. The body. I was about to speak but stopped as a new sound hit my ears, faint at first but growing in volume.

Screaming.

The town had come awake. All around me I heard crashing, running, shouting, crying, wailing, and gnashing of teeth. The abruptness of its immediacy caught me off guard, as though a dormant radio had suddenly been switched on.

"Noooo!"

"Help me!"

I heard the frantic pleas all around me. I spun in circles on the spot, wide-eyed and mouth agape. Of course, most of the sounds were muffled, coming from inside the homes nearby, but some of it began spilling outside onto the lawns, out into the streets. Individuals being chased, hunted down, slaughtered by their own mirror images of themselves. As soon as they were detained by their copies, the copies began digging into their flesh, effortlessly sinking clawing fingers into them as if they were scooping soft sherbet out of a carton of ice cream.

White snow was tainted with spots of red, an explosion of color, a Jackson Pollock of grotesque patterns. Then I spotted Marie. She was winding her way between houses. Marie carried herself regally, fiercely. Queen of the damned, I thought. Without thinking more, however, I followed after her.

"Lee!" Rose yelled behind me, but I ignored her. Instead, I cashed in my diabolical carnival ticket for a hellish tour of this new underworld, a pandemonium. I didn't know if I was guided down into the descending circles of inferno by Dante's Virgil or by the devil herself.

We snaked our way through street after street, past house after house, watching on repeat the same scene over and over again with slight variations: shouting, shrieking chaos, a face and palms pressed up against the inside of a window before its twin seized it from behind, chomping or slicing or clawing, severing arteries, red liquid oozing or spraying or splattering in every imaginable design. I witnessed severed limbs, severed heads, piles of sinew and bones, and the constant gnawing of these zombie-like creatures.

I eventually worked up the nerve to approach Marie. Up to that point, I had been slinking along behind her at a distance of about twenty yards.

"Marie, what is happening to Somewhere, I mean, to Xenia?"

At first, she didn't respond. I wondered if she'd even heard me.

"The town is eating itself," she finally said, matter-of-factly.

"But why?"

Marie stopped and turned to me rigidly. Her face was chiseled with a stern expression, and her lips were pursed in a tight frown. Apparently, she didn't feel the need to answer that question. She turned back around and continued winding through the town, graphic scenes continuing to play around me.

Marie walked swiftly as if she was aiming for some final destination, but I got the sense that her only goal was to pass by as much of the town as she could. In any other circumstance and with any other outfit, I might think she was a power-walker getting in some brisk exercise. That was the absurd state I was in—imagining Marie in a tracksuit amidst a stadium of cannibalistic onlookers. In fact, watching Kenny and David explode like balloons of blood hardly registered as I passed by, though, at the moment, I guiltily felt a small sense of satisfaction seeing Mike meet his grisly end in such a graphic manner. Several questions rushed into my head, however, when, after all this time, I spotted Mattie. I let out a small groan, considering the affinity I had felt for her and my concern about not seeing her again. Now, to finally behold her, like this, at the end of everything, stirred in me a bitter sadness. I had hardly enough time to consider this, though, when her mirror-self pounced on her back, cupped her jaw in her hands, and with a tremendous lurch, ripped her head from her neck with a sickening tear. Even so, I had no time to dwell on it and instead continued hustling along, trying to keep up with Marie's dizzying pace.

It was not the first instance in which time itself was bending and twisting and folding and undulating in such a way that I couldn't make sense of how long that tour lasted. In some moments, following Marie just felt like a new state of existence, that life itself was simply one never-ending amusement park ride of macabre scenes: Marie's Madhouse of

Horrors. So, whether that lasted minutes, hours, days, or years, I couldn't determine, but when we finally ascended the hill that ran by the Whitakers' house, Rose was standing there waiting; she'd never moved. I did, however, notice her glancing about nervously, and I had to intentionally shove a rising thought deep down inside myself: Rose was operating on borrowed time.

"Satisfied?" she demanded as I approached. Her severe expression softened, though, as she grabbed my wrist and practically dragged me back to the side of the Whitakers' house, back to the cellar door. I glanced around, trying to spot Marie, but she was gone. Standing in front of the cellar door once again, I hesitated, stubbornly digging in my heels.

"I can't do it."

"We have to," she answered but then grabbed my hands.

"Look," she said tenderly.

This is not real. This is not real. This is not real. I desperately desired for all of this to disappear, for me to just be with Rose.

I opened my eyes, and there she stood, waiting now, allowing me this moment.

"You know..." I fumbled, "You know I saw a vision of the two of us together. Older. I thought we would be together forever." My words sounded sappy, but I was earnest; I knew she knew that. I watched her eyes squeeze together with tears. Memories of what had transpired between us still lingered in my mind, and the walls that I had constructed between me and her had nevertheless fallen down.

"It was just a dream, Lee," she whispered. "But I would have loved that dream." She gave a slight smile. "It's time, Lee."

We descended quickly with a sense of urgency. The hanging Maries were gone. All was just a mess of red, lumpy carnage. And eerily quiet.

We approached the coffins cautiously–I was a bit more timid than Rose–and saw all the coffins propped open, empty. Except one.

CHAPTER TWENTY-NINE

"We have to do this," Rose said as she slid her fingers under the lid of the one closed coffin and lifted it up.

There again was the skeletal, decomposing Marie, ugly and terrifying. I held my breath, expecting her to sit up again, to groan as her head twisted back and forth in an unsightly manner, but she continued to lay there unmoving.

"Lee, let's go!" Rose shouted, already digging her hands and arms under the corpse. I was repulsed, but I followed Rose's lead and helped lift Marie out of her resting place.

"Shouldn't we leave her in the coffin and carry the whole thing?" I asked, hesitating.

"Too heavy. This is the only way." I shrugged and continued to do as Rose said, too distracted to give it much more thought. Still, the idea of just dropping Marie's corpse into a pit didn't feel right.

We awkwardly held her, I grabbed onto her lower legs and Rose her upper torso, but I thought the delicate body was just going to snap, that limbs would rip from sockets or something. Perhaps it was another act of magic in this bizarre, deteriorating world that the body remained intact for its journey to the grave.

The buzzing outside continued, more of a ferocious bellow, as we resurfaced. I noticed movement around me. Someone had just stepped around from the front of the house and planted themselves about thirty yards from me. The face was stained bright red with blood.

Someone else stepped around the corner of the house, stopping near the first. Hearing rustling from my other side, I saw three more shuffle their way from the back of the house. All of these looked at me hungrily, the same bright red smeared across their faces, most heavily around their mouths.

"Take her," Rose said, trying to keep her voice steady.

"What?"

"Take her."

"But—"

"Lee, you have to go now before more of them show up. They're going to try and stop you." My eyes widened at the prospect of this impossible task. In my paralysis, others showed up. I remained steadfastly in place, now cradling Marie's shriveled body by myself. Conflicted by indecision or fear or both, I was rooted there, unmoving.

Then a scream rent the air. Other screams followed, and they didn't stop. I searched the faces of the crowd around me, but they seemed as dumbfounded as I was. I turned to Rose who only shrugged. I looked down at the body in my arms.

For a moment, I swore that I saw Marie's eyes open, the slightest suggestion of a smile curving up what remained of her lips, and I heard a voice in my mind.

"And he answered and said unto them, I tell you that, if these should hold their peace, the stones would immediately cry out."

I glanced down at the ground around me, still completely covered in snow. But there was a sense that the screams were emanating from below, out of the very earth which at that moment began trembling. The tremors, though, seemed to shake the torpor from those around me who began to approach. And that's when I finally took off.

I ran straight ahead, trying to avoid the encroaching mob, Marie's body awkwardly jostling in my arms. From the corner of my eye, I watched Rose sprint out ahead of me, crashing into some of those who had gotten closest, clearing a way for me the best she could.

Pure adrenaline pulsed through my veins, pushing me on with super-human energy. How else could I outpace a whole crowd of people while cradling a delicate corpse? But the ground continued to shake; the earth continued to cry out, one piercing shriek after another, almost debilitating in its incessant shrill.

I began to notice cracks in the ground, the earth pulling apart in places. It looked as though Somewhere would rip apart, the ground would swallow it up, eat it alive, just like the undead people had been doing to each other.

Picking my way through the deep snow as the ground trembled and shook was maddening. All I wanted was to arrive at the cemetery, but I was forced to slow down or else lose my footing, which I did on a number of occasions. Every time that occurred, I positioned my arms and body in a way as to protect Marie so that, by the end, my arms and shoulders were badly bruised and sore.

I somehow managed to outrun Somewhere's living dead. That is, until Laurel Hill cemetery emerged in front of me, blocked by a crowd even greater than the one that had gathered outside of the Whitakers' cellar door.

I stopped, panicky, unsure of what to do as the screams persisted, the earth convulsing, and a blockade of several dozen people–with blood-stained faces–impeded my progress. I glanced about me, hoping to see Rose trailing me, to see the other Marie marching about, Vergil in the throes of hell, but I had no such luck.

A hand grabbed my shoulder gently, and relief flooded my body, but as I turned, I tensed up again, terrified. I was expecting aid but instead was staring face to face with Mrs. Copeland, bright red smeared around her mouth like she'd just won a cherry pie-eating contest. Chunks of flesh–rather than cherries, however–plastered her face. She stood so close to me that I could practically smell the metallic-iron scent of the blood. Losing my footing, I fell into the snow, instinctively sacrificing my own body to try and soften the impact for Marie's.

I squirmed around on the ground, attempting to distance myself from Mrs. Copeland, pushing backward with my feet and legs, but my head soon bumped into the shins of another person hovering over me, several persons, actually. The crowd had advanced. I was surrounded.

"Aaaaaah!" I screamed in abject pain and looked in horror toward my feet. Mrs. Copeland, or whatever devilish creature in her form was at my feet, had just torn into the flesh around my shin, my own blood added to the canvas of her fiendish face, bubbling up out of the grotesque wound in my leg and pooling in the snow next to me.

I kicked out, knocking her back for a moment of relief while my leg felt like a thousand knives digging into the same spot. Hands grabbed at me from every side. I tensed, anticipating the next set of teeth to puncture my body and the pain that would follow. I almost welcomed the fact that I would surely pass out soon, and this would all be over. I hoped.

My vision dimmed. I stayed in that suspended state, body tense in anticipation, eyesight growing darker, losing consciousness. But I realized that no additional bites came.

Instead, I heard a commotion above me. The crowd was being dispersed.

"Jimmy!" I shouted, incredulous. I gained only a brief glimpse of his face as he ducked and tackled and pushed and shoved his way around the circle that had encompassed me. I knew, though, that I had very little time. I managed to prop myself up and get back on my feet, almost all pressure on my good leg as the other was just a pulsing stump of bloody meat. Stooping down, I gingerly pulled Marie back into my arms and began hobbling through the momentarily stunned group.

After I had traversed about twenty yards, I felt a hand wrap around my leg, but I turned in time to witness Jimmy stomp down on the arm with all his power; an audible *snap* was evidence of his successful effort. A broad smile plastered his face; he was having fun. But it was short-lived. The momentary distraction was his undoing as three sets of grasping arms pulled him down. I turned and quickened my pace as Jimmy's screams joined those that still flooded the air. I felt sick and did everything in my power to divert my attention away from the bile that was creeping up my throat. Even the seconds it might take for me to hurl could be the end of me, I figured.

In the end, I arrived at the cemetery gate, fiddling with the latch longer than I wanted.

It was up. The gate swung open. I was inside.

I hazarded a glance back, the scene as wild as ever, but inside the confines of the cemetery, I suddenly felt calm. I didn't expect them to follow me in. In fact, one person stood only a few yards from me on the other side of the gate, looking at me dumbly, head tilted to one side like some kind of confused puppy.

I turned and walked at a slower pace, picking my way between headstones and graves. Like before, I felt myself descending, my precious cargo resting in my arms.

I smiled despite the circumstances. I knew. I knew this was finally the end. I didn't know how *I* would end, but this was the end.

I didn't rush. I *couldn't* rush, my ravaged leg slowing my progress. Brief moments of panic seized me–the uncertainty of what *the end* meant for me–but the doubts were mere evaporating ghosts: shades of terror that were ultimately powerless and fleeting.

In my periphery, the gravestones grew, elongated, towered above me. Or maybe I shrank in their presence. Regardless, I meandered as though through a forest. The weight of Marie's corpse was as air to me, my deformed leg now forgotten. I briefly considered winding through the cemetery in a way that would extend this walk, but that was only a thought. Something to entertain. I knew I wouldn't act on it.

I remembered Rose. I thought of our walks. I was struck by the paradox of time, how little time had actually passed in Somewhere, but I felt old, a contentedness of age—I imagined—as one ready to take a long rest. And then I was there. In the heart of the cemetery, the hole opened up at my feet.

I laid Marie down, and in her sleeping face, I saw myself. I laid myself down.

EPILOGUE

I couldn't stop looking at the guy just a few booths down from me. Of course, he didn't recognize me–I had been invisible to him–but it was undeniable: I had met him late one night in the woods not long ago, terror on his face as he aimed a gun at me. A young man who had mysteriously slipped into Somewhere–presumably uninvited–as some drunken sod from one town over (*A real town*, I mused). And who managed to stumble back out none the wiser. Probably not remembering a thing.

I sipped a cup of scalding hot diner coffee. When I had stepped in, I planned on ordering only a coffee and getting back on the road quickly, but when I sat down, I was visited by such an appetite that I ordered the Super Grand breakfast: eggs, bacon, sausage, pancakes, and hashbrowns. I put it away quickly, but rather than pay my bill and leave, I allowed the waitress to keep topping off my mug.

"You lied to me," I say matter-of-factly. A quizzical look crosses Rose's face, though she doesn't rush to deny my accusation.

She doesn't respond. We sit on a ledge overlooking an unfamiliar valley. I know that it's Somewhere–Xenia–but I see nothing besides sloping, frozen wilderness. Maybe I perceive traces of a town that must have once existed long ago, but I can't be sure.

I can't be sure that Rose is here with me. Probably she is not.

"How much did you know?" I ask.

"Not too much," she begins but then falls silent. "Enough," she continued. "I was just a child when all the men died coming back from the war. We were told it was an accident, but of course everyone knew. The worst kept secret.

"They all left eventually. Slowly. All throughout my childhood. I wish I could say I was aware, but I think it was more convenient to pretend like they had never existed in our community. To lie to ourselves that Xenia had always been self-sufficient.

"Marie was the last one. She was different, but I guess in the end, she was the closest one to being part of our community. Not one of us per se but part of our community. It was awful what happened to her." Rose pauses. "I saw her that day," she says, almost in a whisper. "It was awful what happened to her," she repeats.

"Did you know that it was Pastor Amos who did that to Marie?"

Another silence.

"At first, no," she says, "I mean, officially, no one ever knew. But that's how things worked. If you ignore the suspicions, eventually, your mind will stabilize, and you'll learn to live in that suspension of truth. You don't agree with what's been done, but you don't say anything. If you leave just enough room for doubt in your mind, then you can justify your decision to continue going to his church. Besides, Pastor Amos was only one man who did something to one woman, but Xenia was filled with a town of men who did equally horrific things. They killed all those negro men, after all."

I fight back a sense of revulsion towards this girl who appears to me for a moment as a monster. But then I sigh, an infinite feeling of resignation.

"After she died," Rose continues, "we didn't understand at first what was going on. But people started getting sick. Within a day. And within a week, the whole town was dead." That grabs my attention.

"What!"

She nods.

"Yes, the whole town. All of us. Dead." Pause. "But then we weren't.

Like I had stepped out of my body. I remember it." Rose shudders. "I was standing over my body that was lying on the floor in my house. Where I had died, I guess. And my family was there; the same thing had happened to them. To everyone. Corpses strewn about Xenia and their duplicates standing around bewildered.

"There was nothing else to it. We constructed coffins for our bodies but never buried them."

"Why not?"

"We couldn't. We couldn't enter Laurel Hill." I nod, understanding a little more, only a little. Rose keeps talking, like she is confessing to me. Maybe confessing for the whole town. I am an inadequate confessor–unqualified to give absolution, don't want to–but I listen nonetheless.

"The first person wandered into Somewhere a few years later. We didn't know what to make of it. Some in the town wanted to get rid of her, but everyone felt a strange vitality with her arrival. So, one person became several, dozens over the years."

"Why didn't you stop it?"

"I..." Rose trails off. I wait for her to answer, but she is finally quiet.

"Why did you help me?"

"Not all of it was pretending," she says.

I remember that I am staring at nothing. There is no Somewhere, no Xenia. Only snow-laden trees in the middle of nowhere Missouri. I know—beyond any rational reason—that my car is resting under a pile of snow on an unmarked road.

I stand up and leave the place where I had been sitting. Glancing over my shoulder, I see Rose still there, staring out across that valley, unmoving. She had already been eaten by her duplicate. So this was what? Just an afterimage, I suppose, dissipating leftovers from the flashbomb madness that had been the recent demise of Somewhere. When I'm just about out of sight of her, I look back. She's gone.

Eventually, I dig my car out of the snow. I wind my way through wilderness on tiny, gravel country roads until I find a main road that takes me past a diner where I decide to stop for some coffee.

I pull up to the house at the end of the cul-de-sac. Miriam stands there, waiting for me on her front porch.

"Hey, stranger," she says with a slight grin. The *Hey, you* I mean to respond with sticks in my throat as I walk over and pull her into a hug, sobbing. I must have caught her by surprise because she drops something from her hand. Glancing down, I laugh a snotty, stuffy laugh before picking up the brown bag with Mack's printed on the side. A Reuben sandwich.

"Let's go inside and catch up. Then you can go see your parents. They've been asking about you."

Acknowledgements

I read an article in the New Yorker criticizing acknowledgment pages. They're unnecessary; readers don't care. I read another article on the website of a major publisher about the importance of acknowledgment pages and how they offer an additional glimpse into the author's life. So which is it?

Can you imagine an awards ceremony in which a recipient didn't acknowledge the community of support that precipitated the prize? Maybe it's not for the audience. Rather, we who create feel the burden of truth: art is not a solitary endeavor.

So, I share my sincere gratitude to Melissa and Brother Mockingbird for publishing this novel and the work that goes with it: countless hours spent reading and offering suggestions, coordinating cover art, formatting the book, and so much more. The owner of a small press wears many hats, and I'm certain Melissa does more behind the scenes to make our works come to life than any of us authors can understand.

Thanks to Nicole Langton and Jaida Temperly for your invaluable editing services.

Thanks to friends and family who have read my work over the years. Your feedback has helped me develop as a writer, and your encouragement (even if you were lying to me) has kept me "in the game." To my immediate family, especially my wife, just having the time and space to write has been an unmerited gift. I love you.

About the Author

Matthew Reed Williams was once hiking the West Highland Way in Scotland with a friend. To pass the time, his friend described a horror movie in great detail which spooked Matthew more than he would like to admit, especially since his first book is horror fiction. Often, though, scary stories are the best way to say what needs to be said.

Matthew grew up in the Midwest and has spent the majority of his adult life in Missouri where he works as a high school teacher and lives with his wife and kids.

www.ingramcontent.com/pod-product-compliance
Lightning Source LLC
LaVergne TN
LVHW020440060325
804842LV00009B/15